Allied Froth: Volume 2
The Castle

Steve Empson

HARVEY
BERRICK
PUBLISHING

First published in Great Britain in 2012

ISBN 9780957496118

Harvey Berrick Publishing

Cover design by Nicky Stott

Steve Empson

For Mum, Dad & Sis

CONTENTS

Acknowledgments

Part 3
The Man They Couldn't Gag

Curriculum Vitae

Name: Dexter Kitehawk
Address: Rathaven Mansions, Old Street
Date of Birth: Currently in dispute
Occupation: Unable to disclose without contravening the Official Secrets Act
Previous Career Details in Reverse Chronological Order: June 1965: Motorway Snack Bar Attendant
Hobbies: Dressing up in jazzy clothes and hobnobbing with people in tracksuits, er…
Qualifications: Englishman
Ambitions:

CHAPTER 28
HOW I SMASHED UP THE *QE2* SINGLE-HANDED
AND GOT PUT ADRIFT IN A LIFE-RAFT

"Monsieur Kitehawk," she said, taking the palm of my right hand in hers and leaning across the table at me, "Or shall I call you *Doctor* ...?"

"No, no," I said, "That's *Dexter*. Not *Doctor* ..."

She gazed into my eyes.

"No matter," she said. "Doxtor – *Dixter* – I can see by the way your lifeline goes off at a *tun-gent* that you *hwill* be going on a *hlorngue* journey ..."

"Another one?" I said, flabbergasted. "I haven't finished *this* one yet ..."

"*Keep quiet and look into my eyes ...* I can see you are the *artistic* type ..."

"Well," I drivelled on, "I have been *told* this before ..."

"And I see *something else* ..." she said mysteriously.

"Go on ..."

"I see you are *possessed* ..."

"Possessed?" I said, intrigued. "By the spirit of an *artist*, you mean?"

"No," she said, as she lost interest and turned her attention elsewhere. "By an *idiot* ..."

"I beg your *pardon* ...?"

But it was too late.

She'd already pushed her plate containing the remains of a turkey-leg aside (she'd been picking at it like a wizened old buzzard herself) and left the Dining Hall.

I'd had the great misfortune to be placed opposite an old hag called Madame Sosostris, *clairvoyante et fortune-teller*, at the first sitting for dinner on board the *QE2* bound for Southampton.

Taking advantage of the first-night 'informal dress' rule, I'd turned up in a shirt that had been jazzing twelve-to-the-dozen in a dockside tourist shop and a pair of my favourite herringbone slacks with the 24-inch flared leg. Sunglasses completed my attire, whilst keeping me suitably incognito.

I'd been lucky enough *both* to have been one of the first passengers on board *and* to have procured a cabin next to the gangway, and so I was able to pass the first few hours scrutinising the traffic to see whether anybody was following me.

And to make sure I'd finally got shot of Bonehead.

Don't get me *wrong* ...

I felt plenty of remorse at handing him over to the cuckoo-men.

It's just that I saved it all up till after we sailed.

He'd have to be a Houdini to get out of that one, and Houdini he *wasn't.*

The porthole had been a very handy spy-hole indeed ...

All kinds of hoy palloy had marched aboard laden with expensive luggage, amongst whom were enough highly suspicious individuals to fill a couple of lifeboats, though I couldn't actually identify anybody.

It might have helped if I'd taken my shades off. Being special World War Two blackout glasses, I couldn't see a thing through them, but I couldn't afford to be recognised *myself.* I was too close to arriving back on English soil to risk ruining things with an indiscreet gesture or a careless remark. All I needed was for some pursuing black hat to catch me gawking at them as they came up the ramp, and the game would have been as good as over.

Eventually, after having decided that the percentage return on my surveillance efforts was diminishing on a scale roughly equivalent to the decreasing number of late stragglers for the voyage, I'd set off in search of the Purser's office with Dirk's binoculars slung round my neck.

There, I spent a moment or two arguing the toss about the benefits of offshore immunity for traitors to the Crown, by which I was referring to *him* – the Purser – specifically, and thieves masquerading as the merchant officer class generally, before deciding to swallow the exchange rate and trade in all the President's over-inflated dollars for some real money. Albeit for a lesser quantity than I deserved.

Nevertheless, the effect of this transaction on my mood had been both instantaneous and extraordinary ...

Possessing a pocketful of pound notes and assorted coins of the realm (after so long without) was a morale-booster of that unique kind which only ever surfaces on nearing home after a long time away.

Like, for example, the first sighting through a train window of a red bus on the outskirts of London, as you hurtle back from holiday. *Or the first sighting of the white cliffs of Dover, I suppose, if you're a lost seagull.*

But moods are a *fickle* emotion ...

Wandering around and finding all the *QE2*'s bars shut had produced an exact effect of the *reverse* kind.

Like, for example, the first sighting of a bloke in a kilt as you wake up in Berwick on Tweed six hours after getting on the *Flying Scotsman* in mistake for the 5.10 rush hour special to Cuffley.

And it was while I stood there pondering my limited options for a drink, that I heard the sound of glass clinking and made the mistake of wandering into the Dining Hall.

Here it was, that I found myself parked at the helm of a *Marie Celeste* survivors' reunion and rueing the oversight which excluded me from a seat at the Captain's table. Madame Sosostris had immediately introduced herself to me as the "Wisest Woman in Europe", though I naturally took *that* with a pinch of salt.

"Is that so ...?" I said, thinking, *but we're not in Europe ...*

"Yes," said her travelling companion, a seedy-looking American man with thinning brilliantined hair, "And she has a *wicked* pack of cards ..."

So saying, he reclined back in his seat with an arcane furrow across his brow.

"If you're the wisest woman in Europe," I said to her, "Tell me who won the FA Cup final in 1872 ..."

She ignored me.

I thought as much.

It was around about then that she told me I was going on a long journey and, after the old bat vanished, I ordered some table wine, swilled some round my gob, spat it back in the ice bucket and legged it.

By this time the ship was in motion and I hit the nearest bar to find the place jammed packed and buried behind seven rows of dollar-waving Americans ...

"What's going on here?" I said to somebody standing on tiptoe up the back. "They giving it away?"

"*Giving* it away ...?" he laughed. "At seventeen dollars-ninety for a *Grasshopper*, you must be kiddin' ..."

"*Grasshopper?*" I said. "What *is* this, a bar or a zoo?"

I wandered around the vacant tables until I found a half-empty glass of lager.

I was tempted to *drink* it, initially.

But *then* I changed my mind ...

"Let me through!" I shouted, with the glass at arms-length and my nose pegged. "Some bloke's just *pissed* in this ...!"

Reaping the benefit of an instant parting of the waves, I strolled right through to the counter, ordered a beer and told the barman to put it on my slate.

"Name and cabin number?" he enquired.

"I'm afraid I'm not at liberty to disclose ..." I went to say ... *when I was struck by a moment of inspiration.* "... Grasshopper," I said. "The Reverend E. H. Cabin F26, but you can call me *Reg*. Thank you, my man ..."

I took my drink and went to find somewhere quieter to swallow it.

The Reading Room seemed like the obvious choice, and so I soireed in and occupied an armchair positioned by a window onto the sea.

"Would Sir care to see the newspapers?" asked a steward.

"Very decent ..."

"English or American ...?"

English or *American?*

"Do I *look* like an American?" I questioned him.

"*Newspapers*," he reiterated. "English or American *newspapers?*"

"*English*, of course," I said. "Don't you love your country or something ...?"

"Anything in *particular*, Sir?"

"Why," I said, "The *Daily Mirror*, of course ..."

As I watched him shuffle off, it occurred to me that I hadn't seen a newspaper since I was in Ecuador almost a year earlier. At that time, Mark Black was the newest icon amongst the burn-outs of the square mile, Professor Baudivin was missing presumed dead, and there were ritual murders taking place every other day on the streets of the capital.

As I watched him shuffle back again, I became quite excited at the prospect of catching up on what had been happening in the meantime. In particular, I was curious as to whether anything to do with the Allied Froth Corporation had surfaced in print.

"I'm afraid we don't have the *Daily Mirror*," he said, "But we do have the *Sunday Sport*. Would Sir like me to fetch it?"

"If you must ..."

Sunday Sport? What was *that?*

Well, it looked like the country had got itself into a right old mess in my absence ...

London buses on the moon, aliens with six heads living in suburbia etc. I'd never heard anything *like* it ...

"Oi! Pelvis!" I yelled. *I got up and took the rag with me.* "You got a ship-to-shore phone?"

He indicated to me that this was the case and gave some vague directions, hoping (probably) that I'd take a wrong turning and fall into the Atlantic.

In the absence of being able to find any number for the editor, however, I dialled one of the numbers from an advert instead ...

Well, it said, 'Strict Sally wishes to hear from *you* ...' and so I naturally assumed she was the complaints department.

I took down a selected transcript of the conversation, but after about an hour and half I hung up in disgust.

But, as I went to jot down a note of the number for future reference, I realised with some surprise that it was identical to my *office* number in London ...

Corkscrews had told me that it was a special code number beginning with 0898 – a code common to all MI5 departments and others engaged in top secret work – instead of the *usual* London prefix.

I dialled it again.

This time it was engaged.

So I paced up and down with the paper in my hand, trying to work out the security implications.

And it was while I was doing *that*, that my attention was distracted by a light flickering off and on through the nearest window ...

Far out on the dark night ocean.

A *green* light ...

No question it was the same light I'd seen from Mark Black's jetty:

Daisy the Docker.

A long way from the docks ...

None the wiser for braving the night air, I chanced to lean over the rail for an estimate of the diving distance in the event of a forced exit, and discovered that somebody in one of the cabins down below was sending back an answering light (yellow).

The two lights were having a conversation in morse code, winking off and on in the darkness like two old flames fluttering their eyelids at each other.

I took out my notebook and pen and began recording the messages going to and fro:

First of all, the *green* light said this:

Good Evening QE2. We hope you will enjoy your shipment of fresh vegetables. The market for blow-football tables has improved, yes?

Then the *yellow* light said this:

The doughnuts were very nice. Come to tea again sometime. The rules of cricket are very confusing.

What did it all mean?

It was clearly rubbish.

Primarily, because I was making it up as I went along.

I never *did* learn morse code.

But there *was something* fishy going on ...

Darting belowdecks, I hunted out the source cabin and found the door ajar...

The signal light had been switched off and the cabin abandoned, but there was no question in my mind that the Captain ought to be told what was going on under his very nose.

So I raced up to the top deck, stepped over the red cordon and ascended the narrow stairway to the bridge ...

"Dexter Kitehawk," I said, bursting in and waving my bus pass around. "MI5. Captain, I have reason to believe that there is a Nazi spy on board this vessel, and I must insist on your cooperation in helping me to locate and restrain him ..."

"Get this man off the bridge ..." I heard the Captain whisper to one of his officers standing close by.

"Organised tours will be advertised in due course, Sir," said the officer, as he walked over to meet me. "But in the meantime ..."

"I realise you may not have been informed *officially* of my presence on this vessel," I said, strolling round him, "But you will obviously have seen a green light flashing out at sea in this past half-hour and wondered what it was. *Well*, what you may *not* have seen is another light flashing messages back to it from the *QE2*. One of the passengers or – *more likely* – one of your *crew*, is a spy ..."

"Let me see that ID card," said the Captain impatiently.

I shoved it back in my pocket. "No. We haven't time," I said. "Just get on the radio to Scotland Yard and tell them to have an escort waiting at Southampton. In the meantime, I will need to check that your facilities for holding this man will be secure and I would appreciate the loan of a couple of your staff to help apprehend him ..."

"Perhaps we should radio Southampton General and have the men-in-white-coats waiting at the dockside instead ...?" said the officer behind me, *exhibiting a rather smarmy laugh as he did so.*

"Where is this green light, then?" said the Captain.

"It's over *there* ..." I went to say, pointing at what had suddenly become pitch black ocean in the manner of a gothic heroine unable to demonstrate to her persecutors that which is demonstrably true in all other circumstances.

There was not a light on view anywhere.

Green or otherwise.

"I see ..." he mumbled. "Have this man put under guard immediately ...!"

"'Ere!" I yelled, backing up towards the exit ... "You *can't* do that ...!"

"*Can't* I?" he roared. "Well then, put him to work scrubbing the decks ... *AT THE* DOUBLE!!!"

As I scarpered down the stairway, I heard the pair of them burst out laughing behind me...

"You'll be *sorry!*" I yelled back from a safe distance. "Remember the *Titanic!* The Captain laughed when they told him it was *cold* out on deck! Ignore my warning at your peril ...!"

Following this, I wandered from one bar to another, getting steadily more drunk as I did so, until I got tired of bar-hopping and decided to buy a lampstand-sized bottle of *Grant's Finest* from a branch of *Harrods* situated on the Dolphin Deck.

The snooty sales assistant, in a hurry to shut up shop and bop the rest of the night away in the disco, lifted one up onto the counter as though I'd just asked her to donate her suntan to charity.

"I'm afraid we only take dollars here," she said, as I pulled out a handful of tuppenny bits.

"I beg your pardon?" I slurred.

"We only take *American* currency ..."

"But I thought this was *Harrods?*"

"It is ..."

I stared at her.

"Put it on my slate," I said.

"*Name?*"

"Reg Grasshopper ..."

"*Cabin?*"

"A3509 ..."

She reached for something under the counter which looked like a list of cashcard fraudsters, and proceeded to scan it up and down.

"I'm afraid your *name* doesn't appear on the passenger list," she said. "Nor is there a *cabin* of that number. Now, why would *that* be ...?"

"That is because I'm an undercover MI5 agent ..."

"Well, Mr *Grasshopper* – or whatever your name is – that's where this *bottle's* going. *Back under cover.* And that's where *I'm* going too. *Under the covers.*

6

Goodnight ..."

So saying, she lifted it back off the counter and put it away again.

"I think this is absolutely outrageous!" I yelled. "A *British* ship ... under a *British* flag ... with an *old* and *respected British* store like *Harrods*, only taking *Yank* dosh! You wouldn't get *this* on the *Canberra* ..."

"All complaints to Cunard, Sir. I'm only the sales assistant ..."

"I shall phone Lord Inchcape!" I yelled, continuing to harangue her as she ushered me out.

"Wrong company," she said.

"I shall phone him anyway!"

She turned the key in the lock. "*Do* that," she said.

"I shall be back ...!" I yelled.

"Don't fall overboard ..."

Later that evening, I got talking about the incident to a couple of English piss artists from Romford called Malcolm and Gabriella, who were returning from a weekend's holiday in New York, courtesy of *Blind Date*. Malcolm was actually the cameraman, but he'd swapped his camera for Gabriella on the flight over on *Concorde* and nobody had seen her lucky partner since ...

We all agreed that action should be taken over this scandal and, as soon as it was quiet and dark on the Dolphin Deck, we carried a couple of deck tables inside ... and hurled them through the plate glass windows.

Shocked by the dramatic eruption of alarms, we grabbed the bottle of Grants and legged it ...

On one of the murky lower decks we took refuge in a store room and sat huddled together, knocking back the scotch and listening to members of the crew rushing about outside as though the ship was under attack by the *Luftwaffe*.

Malcolm and Gabriella were so drunk that they decided to abandon ship.

And take *me* with them ...

Before I could raise a word of protest, they'd clocked me over the head, pushed me in the dumb waiter and carried me out on deck through one of the deserted dining rooms.

Then they'd inflated a life-raft, lowered it over the side, and ... *chucked me overboard.*

Then they'd apparently sobered up, thought better of it and retired below to their cabin, forgetting all about me in the process ...

I woke with a start as I hit the water, lunging about in the terrifying blackness and catching hold of the raft more by luck than judgement ...

"Help! *Help!*" I yelled, watching the enormous lit-up hull of the *QE2* floating past. "Man overboard ...!"

Just as I drifted past the stern of the ship and away into the dark night beyond, I saw a *hand* wave goodbye ...

"Cheerio, Doctor Kitehawk ..." she called. "Nice meeting you. I told you that you would be going on a *hlorngue* journey ...!"

"CAN'T YOU GET *HELP*, YOU OLD BAT?!!!" I screamed.

"Dear me no!" she shouted. "It wouldn't do to interfere with fate ..."

But then she seemed to *pause* as she went to turn away from the rail, as though she'd had second thoughts.

Thank Christ for that, I thought.

"And *by* the *way*, Doctor Kitehawk," she shouted. "*1872*: Old Etonians beat Royal Engineers 2-1 at Kennington Oval ..."

CHAPTER 29
SKETCHES OF THE NORTH ATLANTIC,
ARCTIC LAPLAND, RUSSIA & SCANDINAVIA

My name is Dexter Kitehawk. I am a professional Englishman. I eat spaghetti with a knife and fork, and, if any misfortunate little horrors should knock on my door on Halloween, I treat them to a little trick I learned with an open window and a bucket of water. Which is why, perhaps, every November 1st I find a huge pile of dogcrap on my doormat. But I'll get even with those bastards one day ...

I am a member of Her Majesty's Secret Service by trade. More than this I cannot divulge for fear of putting my fellow countrymen at risk. Over the past year or more I have been engaged in what seemed at times to be a one-man struggle against the greatest threat mankind has ever faced, though it does not yet know it. In case of my demise, I begin to set down what I have learned, so that others may one day find it and use it against the forces of evil.

It must be about December 16th ...

Flotsam and Jetsam

Here, I broke off from my internal castaway message and chucked it all into the sea in a theoretical bottle, because it occurred to me that the *QE2* was no further away than it had been ten minutes earlier. It seemed the engines had stopped, and the floating mass of lights was at a standstill on the night ocean.

If this was due to somebody alerting the Captain to my situation, I considered the launch of a rescue attempt unlikely at worst, doomed to failure at best. The sea may have been unusually calm and the night crystal clear, but it was as cold as hell frozen over, and I had neither the means of propulsion, nor the means of signalling anybody. I also had no experience yet of how fickle an Atlantic night could be, but – even without a deterioration in conditions – I was already wet through, and a death by exposure was still the most likely possibility...

There it was again ... the green light, twinkling off and on, in the opposite direction to the apparently becalmed *QE2*. Dirk's waterlogged binoculars offered no elaboration as to its source, but they did give me an interesting perspective on the liner ...

A lifeboat with a crew of three was being lowered into the water, although something told me that it wasn't a rescue party. *They looked more like a trio of convicts breaking out of jail ... or a trio of saboteurs*, perhaps, leaving the ship disabled like a sitting duck.

As if to underline my unease, traces of mist were beginning to obscure the departing launch, along with the slumbering Queen *and* the green light behind me.

On lowering the binoculars, I found myself being enveloped by a thick sea fog ...

I might just possibly have been waiting in the loneliest spot on the planet as I sat there shivering the freezing minutes away, listening hopefully for the approach of a boat whose occupants had seemed ominously unsuited to vindicate its designated purpose, wherever they were going.

I *could* hear it, though, somewhere out there at visibility zero, its motor becoming increasingly audible until ...

Suddenly, in a clearing in the mist, less than fifty yards away, it passed by right in front of me with its contingent of dark shapes huddled at the stern like Wynken, Blinken and Nod...

"Ahoy there!" I called out, but to no avail.

The shifting hands of vapour clasped together as quickly as they'd parted, and the curtain closed up again around them.

If they *heard* me, they didn't respond.

And that left me waiting reluctantly for an invitation to the frostbite ball, while my carriage to somewhere considerably warmer receded tantalisingly out of reach forever ...

Even the *Devil* doesn't want to know you on a night like this.

Or *does* he ...?

Moments later, the sound of the motor *stopped* receding and died abruptly, to be replaced by a series of *creaking* and *clanking* noises ...

"Oi!" I persisted.

Oi ...!

That has to be an echo, I thought.

"Can't somebody *help* me ...?"

Help me help me ...?

Clank

Clank ...

... Grind ... Squeak ...

Silence.

"HELLO THERE!"

HELLO THERE HELLO THERE HELLO THERE HELLO THERE

Bump!

"*Eh* ...?"

Spinning about on my axis, I found I'd collided with an irresistible grey wall sheering up dead into the blank night ...

"Stone *me* ...!"

I kicked out with both shoes and sent the raft bobbing back in the opposite direction, until the breathtaking face of a vertical ice cliff had vanished back into the mist ... only to find myself drifting in silence between frozen shafts of Atlantic razored at extraordinary angles above the water line, like the columns of a chemical temple, or the vegetation of a graveyard at sea ...

"Hello ...?"

Hello Hello hello hello

WHOOSH ...!

Whatever it was that had just passed underneath my inflatable, it created huge furrowed waves on either side and almost toppled me overboard ...

I watched in astonishment as it hurtled away through the water like a motorised shark.

Some moron had just fired a *torpedo* at me ... through an *ice* field!

Laugh?

I almost *pissed* myself as I swung round to hurl a mouthful of mortified invective over my shoulder ... only to be struck on the back of the head by a copy of *The Corporate Handbook* flying through the air!

Then dozens of volumes shooting out of the fog from all directions — some complete, some not — all disintegrating as they hit the water, pages scattering across the tops of the waves ...

Suddenly, the sea spat up an enormous waterspout and all kinds of debris rained down around me, littering the water with planks, bricks, bottles, tables and chairs, and the body of a man floated past on a raft made from a London pub sign ... *and now a rattling of chains and a squealing of pigs and an echo of falling towers, as a roaring wind sweeps across the water, displacing the fog to whip up the waves, so that in a matter of moments the whole scene has become a storm in a bottle ...*

Clank, Clank, Grind, Squeak ...

With a dull murmur of engines, a loathsome mass of luminescent green spreads across the water ... just before a *second* object rocked the raft.

Only *this* time, it really *did* knock me overboard.

It was a *periscope* ...

A monstrous mechanical black whale rose up from beneath and lifted me right out of the water, with my hands clinging on to its slimy metallic hull and my face bathed in ghostly green light from the raised signal beacon overhead.

The sound of the hatch cover grinding open sent me scuttling towards the base of the tower, where I lay draped in the shadows like a washed-up squid, playing dead *a la method*, wondering what to do for the best.

Up above me, a dark figure scanned the fog with binoculars and spoke in hushed tones to somebody out of view.

Several uneasy moments passed before they disappeared back where they'd come from and closed the hatch behind them.

Clank !

I allowed myself the luxury of a sigh of relief.

But it was a luxury I could ill-afford ...

With a *start*, I realised that I was going to be left to a watery grave the minute the sub dived:

The life-raft was nowhere in sight ...

I scurried up the ladder and started banging on the lid ...

"Let me in ...!"

No response.

Nothing.

Come on, come on, I cursed, *switch your bleeding hearing aids on ...*

I stuck my hooter in front of the periscope and made a funny face, yelling for all I was worth:

"Let me in, *can't* you ...?!!!"

Nothing.

Nobody watching.

Nobody at home.

"Let me *in*, I *tell* you!"

Becoming more panic-stricken by the minute, I grabbed the hatch-wheel, wrenched it anti-clockwise ... and *opened* it up with surprising ease.

Cor dear, what a stink, I thought, as I peered down into the gloom:

"Anybody home ...?"

Apparently not.

Well ...

Stink or otherwise, I was unable to afford the luxury of choice, and so I got ready to climb down to an operations deck apparently devoid of crew.

Deserted.

Perhaps they were all off having a cup of tea?

Careful to ensure the hatch was closed firmly behind me, I began the descent as quietly as I could.

I was *in* luck.

I could get in and *hide* ...

Bo Tau

I might just as well have parachuted in playing a barrel-organ.

My delicate footfalls had only just brought me to the last rung of the ladder, when somebody shoved a *gun* between my shoulder blades ...

I turned round, slowly, to find a welcoming committee made up of what appeared to be the cast from an old war film ...

A couple of them were in German navy uniforms, the rest in donkey jackets and striped jerseys. About a dozen altogether. Give or take. All armed, and all lined up like the winning entry in a malicious glare competition ...

A few more seconds and I'd probably look like a tea strainer on legs.

I was dripping all over the deck – a mixture of sweat and seawater ...

"*Ah ...!*" I said in an exaggeratedly friendly manner, holding out my mitt to shake hands. "What a night for a swim! *Reggie Grasshopper, comedian.* Just a courtesy call. And to whom do I have the honour ...?"

The bearded leader of this gang of ruffians – who I took to be the Captain – gestured for somebody to frisk me ...

"Oi!" I protested, as one of the extras tried to shove his hands inside my coat. "You *can't* do that! What kind of hospitality do you call this?"

"Be silent!" commanded the Captain.

"This is the last time I'm coming all the way out *here* to entertain the troops..."

"A comedian you *may* be, an entertainer you *might* be ... *funny* you are not," he replied drily.

"Now look," I said, "I've always been willing to take each German as I find him. Some may accuse you all of invading the beaches, spitting on the buses, gobbing off the Eiffel Tower etc etc *par encore*. But *not* Reggie Grasshopper. *Oh no.* I've always been prepared to accept the possibility that there are a few decent apples in a predominantly rotten barrel, and I'd like to give you all the chance to prove me right. What's on the menu tonight? Cor, I'm as hungry as hell and I could murder a tin of frankfurters ..."

The second officer slapped me round the face with one of his leather gloves ...

"Shut up!" he hissed.

"I will give you just five seconds to tell me who you are and what you are doing here," said the Captain bluntly. "And then I shall execute you ..."

"I was laying telephone lines," I said.

"What ...?" he said, dropping his aim slightly.

"I was laying telephone lines – *for the Queen of England.* You know, on the bottom of the Atlantic. Your sub came along and ensnared my equipment in its propeller. Frankly, Her Majesty will not be amused when she finds she can't dial her favourite seafood takeaway in New Hampshire at Xmas Day cheap rates. Her husband *is*, after all, a *countryman* of yours ..."

While they all looked at each other, I wondered feverishly whether they'd bought my story.

"Put him in irons," said the Captain. "We'll deal with him later. *Schnell!*"

Phew! *That* was a relief ... but *not* for long.

Just as I was being led away, somebody stepped out in front of me:

"Herr *Kitehawk!*"

"Eh ...?"

"You are *looking* well! So *good* to see you again! We have had to wait so *long* to renew our acquaintance! Perhaps now we will be able to get to *know* each other more ... *intimately.* So *good* of you to *drop in* ..."

My heart sank like a stone to the bottom of a pond.

"Who's *she?*" I said to my captors. "The local *nutcase* round here?"

"Kitehawk? *Kitehawk?*" hissed the Captain. "Are you telling me this is *him...?*"

"Oh," said Fräulein Dorf, with an air of smugness, "This is *him* alright, no question ..."

"Do you mean to tell me that I have committed a criminal act of *war* on account of this idiot ...?"

"Now *look* here ..." I tried to say.

"...when all the time he was sitting on top of us ... *literally*? Do you realise I have just fired a missile at the world's most famous civilian ship ... the world's most famous *passenger* liner?"

"Don't worry," I said. "You missed ..."

Here, he broke off to demand a status report from his periscope crew.

Quite frankly, I found it a bit incredible that they should have attempted to sink the *QE2* just to kill *me*.

"Visibility poor, Herr Kapitan, but she is still afloat. Do you want the second missile fired?"

"Of course not, you fool!" he shouted.

"Oh, *go* on," I said. "As a *personal* favour to me. Aim it at *Harrods* ..."

"Anyway, Botau," she said, "You have only *yourself* to blame. I told you to put me ashore again and I would take care of him *quietly* ..."

"This elaborate form of execution was ordered precisely because you failed in New Orleans, Fräulein Dorf. Is this not the case? And, because the Corporation had to be *sure* ..."

"About that second missile," I said. "Fire it anyway. The Captain of the *QE2* – his name's *Churchill* ..."

"Well," continued Dorf (the pair of them completely ignoring me), "Now *you* have failed also. Perhaps he is not the fool everybody believes him to be ..."

"Well, I *have* been *told* this ..." I drivelled.

"Now it is *my* turn again. I demand you hand him over to me for interrogation. He shall not escape this time. As Gestapo officer I outrank Naval personnel ..."

"Not *here*, you don't," he said. "At sea, a Captain has sole command over all those on board his vessel ..."

"Good for you, mate ..." I said. *I was beginning to get a right crick in my neck looking backwards and forwards from one to the other.*

"Then I *relieve* you of your command ..." she said.

"You do not have the authority ..." he replied.

"I *have* the authority," she insisted.

I looked at Botau with imploring, puppydog eyes, in an attempt to gain his sympathy and persuade him to hold out for jurisdiction over me.

The *alternative* was unthinkable.

"And on what grounds do you relieve me?" he said.

"Incompetence," she said.

"*Incompetence* ...?"

"Incompetence ... and *drunkenness* ..."

"'*Ere*," I said, "You're not going to let her get *away* with that, are you?"

"As a matter of fact ... I am *not*," he said.

Thank Christ for that, I thought.

"First Officer Staedtler!" he suddenly yelled.

"*Ja, Herr Kapitan?*"

"Take the prisoner, Kitehawk, and ..." (*Here, he paused for thought, while the First Officer grabbed my arm*)

"*Ja, Herr Kapitan ...?*"

"And fire him out of torpedo tube number one ..."

I let out an involuntary raspberry – in *shock*, more than anything else.

"*Jawohl, Herr Kapitan !*" he yelled.

"You have no imagination, Botau," said Fräulein Dorf. "And you are wasting a perfect opportunity to interrogate this man. I demand you hand him over to *me* !"

Staedtler hesitated ...

"*Kapitan ...?*"

"Dispose of the prisoner," said Botau. "At once. That is an order!"

Once again, Staedtler attempted to drag me away ...

"I'm *warning* you, *Herr* Kapitan ..." she said.

"We have no need to interrogate him. We know what damage he has done and, if we execute him now, he will do no more. I have not the time to waste on him. I have shipments to deliver and we have tarried too long in these waters ..."

"Then I demand you summon Mark Black to rule on this ..."

"While I respect Mark Black's rank within the Corporation, he is nevertheless a civilian and carries no weight on this vessel ..."

Finally, Clara Dorf hissed something at him in German and Botau raised his hand to halt First Officer Staedtler:

"*Alright*. Have it *your* way. But I don't want to hear or see this fool again. So whatever you do, *do it quietly*. First Officer, hand the prisoner over ..."

"*Ja, Herr Kapitan ...*"

"No, no," I said. "I'm quite happy to inspect the torpedo tubes ..."

I shuddered at the thought of what lay in store, as two strong-arm men carted me off with Clara Dorf leading the way.

My teeth went on edge just *thinking* about that dentistry equipment.

"You're wasting your time," I said. "I'm on the national health these days..."

Before reaching the place of torture, we encountered Mark Black standing in the aisle, nonchalantly regarding us as we passed by ...

"Mark!" I yelled. "Me old mate! *You're* an Englishman, aren't you? Help me out of this sticky mess, for *God's* sake ...!"

"Sorry, old boy," he said, "But there's nothing I can do ..."

Tales of an Arabian Knight

In a dingy, secluded cabin, lit by a dim electric bulb, I found myself once again tied up and at the mercy of Ms Dorf ...

I *say* cabin, but it wasn't much bigger than a broom cupboard.

And I was sitting in the corner with my hands fastened round my back, occupying a good thirty percent of it ...

I gathered the sub had dived, and that we were on our way from the vicinity of the liner.

"Where are we going?" I enquired.

"I shall ask the questions," she replied, choosing to come and sit cross-legged on the floor in front of me.

"No, *go* on," I said, "Just fill me in on a few things. It can't possibly matter now, can it? I can't escape from here. I'm curious. Where are you headed?"

She was silent for a moment, looking at the floor.

"I do not *know* where we are going," she said, almost despondently. "Botau is an idiot. I am a reluctant passenger on board this vessel ..."

"*You and me both,*" I mumbled. "How did you escape from New Orleans?"

"With Shavers. By steamboat ..."

"*So* !" I said. "You *were* on there, after all ..."

She chose not to elaborate.

"How did you get off the steamboat?"

"Over the side. Botau picked me up. And I have been sailing up and down the American coastline ever since, waiting for a chance to seize you again ..."

"You mean this submarine sailed up the Mississippi?"

"*U-Boat.* It is a *U-Boat* ..."

"Pardon?"

"*U-Boat.* Do you not speak English? *U-Boat* ..."

"But how did you keep track of me from a U-Boat?"

"It was not *easy.* Shavers was supposed to *deal* with you and keep me informed by radio. We did not *hear* from him again until several weeks afterwards. By that time, the man was a babbling *idiot* and had allowed you and your friends to cause very much damage, including making public the file on every senior American financier of the Corporation – a feat for which I *personally* congratulate you. The *long-term* effects of this are still to be assessed. The last *message* we received led us to believe he had traced your whereabouts in New York and that he intended to finish the task. We never *heard* from him again. If it had not been for one of our contacts picking you up – quite by chance – on Long *Island,* and giving you a lift to the *harbour,* you might well have *evaded* us again. Anyway, that is *enough* questions. Shavers will not be conducting any more business for the Corporation for a while. Shavers has been grounded ..."

"*Grounded?*" I laughed. "That's *one* way of putting it ..."

"What do you mean? Have I used the wrong word? *Demoted*, then, to an ordinary member. Off the *active* list. His contract has been suspended. He has had his rank removed ..."

"Shavers is dead," I said.

She looked up at me in surprise.

"*Dead?* You have *killed* him? Is this *possible* ...?"

"No," I said. "I didn't kill him. The *Mafia* killed him. The *Mob*. He's stone dead ..."

She didn't say anything for a while, staring at me in an odd sort of way, trying to scrutinise my face to see whether I was lying.

"I did not *know* he was involved with organised crime," she said at length. "He was more of an *idiot* than I thought ..."

"*He* wasn't involved. I was. The Mafia killed him by mistake. They thought he was *me* ..."

She started laughing ...

"You? *You* were involved with the *Mafia?*"

"Well, by mistake, yes. *And* a few other villains. There's quite a long queue of people waiting to see me. So, in a way, you're quite lucky to have *jumped* it ..."

"Perhaps I have *under*-estimated you, *Herr* Kitehawk. I must *think* on this a while. But you must not get *too* comfortable. I shall be back later ..."

So saying, she got up, switched off the light, walked out and locked the door behind her.

I *still* didn't know where we were headed, or just what exactly it was that Botau was up to. But, as I dozed off in the dark, I was just glad I still had all my *teeth* intact ...

When I woke up some hours later, the dim bulb was back on, and – *with a start* – I realised Fräulein Dorf had returned ...

Like before, she was sitting cross-legged in front of me, staring at the floor with that unnerving demeanour of endless patience.

"I was not very *interested* before in what you'd found out," she began. "But I have changed my mind ..."

"So ...?"

"So, you will begin to tell me *everything* you know ..."

"Aren't you going to torture me first?"

She raised her head.

"If you wish," she said, all matter-of-fact. "Now or later. It is of no consequence ..."

"I *don't* wish ..."

"Then *tell* me ..."

"*I see*," I said. "So I tell you what I know and then, when you've *heard* it all, you torture me to death *anyway*, is that it?"

"In an *eggshell*, yes ..."

"Then I'll tell you nothing. My lips are sealed ..."

"Oh," she continued nonchalantly, "I can *unseal* them at any time. I may *not* have my dentistry equipment with me, but I have a *cattle prod*, some *cooking oil*, my *darning-set*, my *pet wasp* ..."

"Alright, *alright* ...!" I squealed. "What do you want to know ...?"

Once again she lowered her head.

And her *voice.*

"*Tell* me about Mark Black. What have you found out about *him* ...?"

"You must know more than I do," I said. "He's a stockbroker and a big wheel inside the Corporation. I met him through his brother, Laurel, in Dubai. He made his money shipping lager and he manufactures it all over the world on behalf of AF International. He's got a house on Long Island, and he's in love with a girl called Daisy. What more can I tell you?"

"You haven't told me anything yet," she said, rummaging around in her pockets.

I noticed that her tastes hadn't got any cheaper – she was still wearing all that expensive jewellery.

"Oh yes," I said, stalling for time, "And he's the founder of the Mark Black Institute ..."

She sneered at the floor.

"And he knows the secret of *el-dust* ..."

"Perhaps you take me for a *fool?*" she said, suddenly glancing up.

I gathered she'd *found* what she was looking for, because she had a set of pocket nail-clippers in her hand, and she was sitting there testing them, twitchily.

She wasn't planning on clipping her *nails*, though – I guessed *that* much.

She was looking at my *strides* ...

"You should have been a manicurist," I offered.

"Yes," she said, as she sliced off a piece of trouser-leg. "I can perform a *manicure* very *well*. I also perform a *circumcision* very *badly* ..."

So much for *flattery.*

I started to sweat ...

"Such a *peculiar* custom," she said. "Don't you think ...?"

"Don't worry," I said. "I couldn't afford your prices ..."

Despite being terrified, I couldn't take my eyes off the nail clippers.

They were studded with *diamonds* ...

"*Something* you might like to know," I said, "Pertains to a fortune in Nazi treasure from the last war ..."

She *stopped* clipping then.

Just south of my *flies.*

I could feel the cold steel resting on my exposed leg ...

"Well?" she said. "*Go* on ..."

I held my breath.

"Why do you want to know about Mark Black ...?"

"I ask the *questions*. Tell me about the *treasure*. I'll *know* if you're making it up ..."

"The equivalent of ten million American dollars in gold and jewels ..."

She gestured for me to continue.

"Well, Mark Black has it in his possession – his *personal* possession ..."

"Ten *million* dollars? How do you *know* this? I have not *heard* this before. *Whose* treasure is it? How do you *know* this?"

"A man called Bertolt told me ..."

"Bertolt? Bertolt *Rimmer* ...?"

"*Yes* ..." I said hesitantly, not quite sure what her change of tone represented.

All of a sudden, she got a grip on my vulnerable zone ...

"Speak!"

"*Yes* ! *Yes* !" I squeaked, like an operatic mouse. "*Bertolt Rimmer* !"

As she relaxed, I could see a pair of cash registers whirling around in her eyes.

Appealing to her greed seemed to have won me a breathing space.

"I must *think* on this," she said. "But I shall be back ..."

But she *didn't* come back for what seemed like a month. With the exception of some grizzled old sea-dog in a striped jersey who came in twice a day to leave a tray of bread and water, the only sense impressions I had during this period were the odd sonar blip penetrating the sound of the engines on at full pelt.

Then, just as I was dozing off one day – or *night* – the door suddenly burst open dramatically, and in she marched ...

The manicure equipment came straight out again ...

"I find you have been *lying* to me. I have radioed my contacts in the *Corporation* and they have informed me that there is *no* lost fortune in Nazi treasure. You will have to do better than *this* if you wish to prolong your agony..."

"No, no, *wait* ...!" I squealed. "... There's *more* ... Mark Black – he *does* have this treasure, and it's hidden underwater in one of his swimming pools ... *after all*, you must be suspicious of him yourself, or you wouldn't have been asking *me* about him. How do you think he financed the redevelopment of London's Docklands ...?"

"*Bitte* ...?" she said, dropping her clippers in astonishment.

"Oh," I said, "You didn't *know* that? Mark Black's been lining his own pockets for years at the expense of the Corporation. He's currently among the world's ten richest men ..."

"*Himmel* ..."

"The Arabs are all in his pocket as well – OPEC, all that lot ..."

"*Arabs* ...?" she mumbled, not really listening now.

"And did you know he was on the shortlist for this year's Pullitzer Prize? Word is, he's written a novel designed to blow the cover on the Corporation for good. So you see," I said, "He's actually a *traitor* ... as well as being a tea-leaf, of course ..."

She stumbled up and backed out of the door with a shocked expression on her face.

Silly cow, I thought.

"I must think on this," she said in her usual way. "But I shall return ..."

"*Yeah*," I mumbled under my breath. "But don't take *too* long. I might not *be* here ..."

Rueing the fact that this type of exploit always looked easier on the telly, I dragged the nail clippers towards me with my *feet*. Then I leaned forward until I had half my body weight in blood draining into my temples, and picked them up by my *teeth*.

Finally, after dropping them to my side, I grasped them with my right hand and worked feverishly for some hours until I managed to fray the ropes and pull them apart, so that – for the first time since coming on board – I was a *free* man...

Full Fathom Five

A free man ... *in a locked broom cupboard*, that is.

Here we go again, I thought, as I wrenched off the grille covering the submarine's network of ventilation shafts:

I poked my snout around a bit first, and then I climbed in.

At least, I *say* climbed in.

Squeezed in with considerable difficulty would be a more accurate description.

There wasn't enough room to swing a cockroach.

In *fact*, it was such a tight fit that there was no possibility of turning back, or of replacing the hatch cover behind me.

Not only *that*, but I had no idea where I was going, or what I was going to do when I got there. My chances of *escaping* from the sub seemed highly remote.

There *was one* thing to be grateful for, though.

Viz. There was no possibility whatsoever of bumping into *Dirk* out on a midnight stroll.

That bloke wouldn't be turning up in places where he wasn't wanted for a long time.

Well ...

He might not have been in there, but I reckon his *laundry* was. There was an almighty pen and ink trapped in that shaft, and the further I went, the worse it got.

So bad, if you *don't* mind, that I decided to go back where I'd come from ...

Facing forwards but crawling *backwards*, I turned left and right so many times that, after a while, I didn't know *where* I was.

So I went *forwards* again ... *and suddenly crashed right into the source of the stink* ...

Sticking out of a side-shaft, devoid of any trousers that I could detect, was ... an enormous great *arse* !

Coughing and spluttering, I scuttled backwards again, trying to catch my breath ...
"Hey, Bud ...?" came a voice.
"You talking to *me*?" I yelled back into the murk.
"Well, I sure as hell ain't talkin' to Adolf Hitler ... or *am* I?"
"You are *talking* to an *Englishman*, mate ..."
"*Englishman*? Hey! No *kiddin'*? All I've run into for *months* round here is Krauts. The whole tub's full of 'em. Ain't seen an American for even longer. But an *Englishman. You'll* do *fine* ..."
"For *what*?"
"Well, I've got myself into a tricky little situation down here, and I'm gonna need your help to get me out of it. *Say,*" he went on," Don't I *know* you from someplace ...?"
I backed up a bit further ...
"I don't think so ..."
"Always *did* get on well with the English. Except *one*. Some guy I had in the back of my cab once. Ended up owing me a whole stack of fare and a lot more besides. In a way, he's responsible for me bein' down here now ..."
I suddenly realised who he was.
It was the farting cab-driver from New Orleans ...

And this meant *big* trouble.
Not just for *me*, but for everybody on the sub.
Did they *know* he was on board?
"*See,*" he carried on, "I was lookin' for a bidet, when ..."
"What?"
"I was lookin' for a bidet ..."
"Bidet?"
"Yeah. *Bidet.* I got this *gas* problem, see ..."
"No kidding ..."
"Yeah, and so I thought I'd come down to the john and siphon some off, only I don't let nothing go unless I got the means to clean m'self up afterwards..."
The penny dropped. "Oh !" I said. "You mean a *bum-washer ...*"
"How's that?"
"Well, where I come from, we call 'em bum-washers, mate. Personally, I wouldn't have one in the house, but then I'm an Englishman ..."
"Come again?"
"Well, they're a constant reminder of something us Englishpersons would rather not admit to having to do ..."
"Yeah, well ..."
"Anyway," I said, "I must be off now, so ..."

"Hey!" he yelled. "Ain't y'gonna help us out of here?"

"Did you ever *find* that bidet you were looking for?"

"Nah, I never did. That's why I crawled in here. To *look* for it. And that's when I got stuck ..."

"Do you mean to tell *me*," I said, "That you've still got all that *gas* building up inside you?"

"I sure as hell have, and that's where it's gonna stay until I find some proper washing facilities ..."

The man was a human time-bomb !

I started crawling backwards fast ...

"How did you get out of Lake Pontchartrain?" I yelled back down the shaft.

"They brought me up in a diving suit. *Only it filled up with gas*. When I reached the surface, some guy tried to take it off too fast and a spark from the zip ignited the whole thing. Next thing I know, I'm at the bottom of the Mississippi and this sub comes along. I just hitched a lift ..."

About ten minutes later, I found myself peering in at floor level on the Captain's cabin, with my nose pressed up behind his ventilation grille:

There was an almighty *row* going on in there between Botau and Fräulein Dorf ...

I was in a dilemma, really. Should I alert them to the danger, or should I sweat it out and wait for an opportunity to escape this death-trap somehow?

I decided to sweat it out. One look at Clara Dorf's eyes told me she wouldn't let me escape for a *third* time ...

"Fräulein Dorf," Botau was saying, "We are almost in Stockholm harbour. My men are scouring the ship for him now and I can assure you they will find him by the time we arrive. When they do, I shall execute him *forthwith*. I order you to go to your cabin, and I relieve you of all jurisdiction over the prisoner ..."

"Botau, you are a *drunk*. Kitehawk is *mine*. He will die *slowly* at my hands and his remains will be washed ashore in little pieces all along the coast of Sweden..."

"Leave my cabin *immediately* !"

"And what of *Mark Black*? That man is a *traitor* and still roams this vessel at will. I order you to *restrict* his movements until I have had more time to gain information ..."

"*Enough* ! *Go* ...!" he suddenly commanded, banging his fist down on the desk so hard that he upset several stacks of books and papers placed precariously all along its edges.

One sheet in particular floated over towards the ventilation grille on the minor draught which entered as the Fräulein stormed out the door ...

She'd *gone* though, nevertheless.

And so I began the long wait for Botau to *follow* her, but this was obviously something he had no intention of doing ...

Instead, he began painstakingly to pick up each of the pieces of paper from the floor and balance them all back in neat little piles on the edges and corners of the desk, spending an age pushing them as close as he could to the point where they just might topple off with a slight movement.

Then, when he'd finished, he sat down and pulled out a large bottle of whisky from the desk drawer, looking like a man relaxing after finishing a creative masterpiece.

To pass the time, I tried to scan the rogue document nestling just beyond the vent:

It *looked* like a shipping order. For thousands of gallons of *Allied Froth* to be delivered to assorted smugglers' coves all across the south coast of England.

What I *failed* to notice, however, was that Botau's gaze had settled on the grille:

The moment I *did* notice it, I saw a troubled expression come over his face...

Whether this was because he'd seen *me*, or the *sheet of paper*, or because he'd clocked the *smell*, was difficult to tell. The gas was building up something chronic in that shaft, no mistake, and when he eventually wandered over to investigate, I backed off quick.

To my horror, he began to unscrew the plate ...

All of a sudden, he whipped it off and plunged his hand inside, just missing my face by a couple of inches ...

So I crawled back a bit *further*.

The trouble was, I couldn't crawl back *fast* enough to get out of the way of the unpredictable movements of his outstretched rummaging arm, and his hand suddenly lighted on my nose.

As it began to feel around my features, I sensed a *sneeze* coming on ...

KERBLAAM ... !!!

I came out of that open grille like the human torpedo the Captain had earlier tried to turn me into ...

... taking *him* with me as I went ... *DOK!*

His head cushioned my landing as I slid to an abrupt halt against the far wall of the cabin, leaving him flattened beneath me like a rumpled carpet roll.

But the *real* damage was elsewhere ...

The cab driver must have shot out of *his* end of the shaft with such velocity, that he went straight through the Gents like a bullet and straight on into the control area, where his over-inflated body wrecked vital equipment and clattered the navigation crew to the deck like a row of milk bottles.

It was no comfort that we were in Stockholm harbour.

Because we were *sinking* straight to the *bottom* of it ...

I'd been in some *situations* in my time, but *this* took the prize:

Plunging to the bottom of the drink in a damaged U-Boat, with the Captain lying spark-out underneath me and sleeping like a baby.

Where *was* everybody ...?

The increasing pressure was already starting to force the bolts from the walls ... and *that* wasn't the *only* bolt it forced ...

I suddenly got an attack of depth-madness ...

"Let me out of here, you swines!" I yelled, clambering to my feet and climbing out over the mountains of bodies piled up in the corridors of a sub which had taken on the look of a ghastly underwater tomb ...

When I reached the navigation area ... *well*, what a sight!

There was wreckage everywhere.

And *there*, lying in the *middle* of it ... was the *cabbie*.

Snoring and burping like a buzz-saw engine.

The *smell* was horrendous.

Worse *still*, he was *alive* ...

And that meant only *one* thing.

The explosion was just a *starter*.

The *real* blast was yet to come.

It would only take a spark ...

All of a sudden, I heard movement behind me and swung round to find Botau stumbling in and rubbing his head.

He looked like he was trying to work out what day of the week it was ...

[NB. Months afterwards, I heard on the news that the Swedes were convinced they'd had a *Russian* sub trapped in the harbour. A Russian *nuclear* sub. This was apparently confirmed by what happened *next* ...]

Botau, with eyes bleary from concussion, surveyed the scene, absent-mindedly took a cigar and a cigarette lighter from his inside pocket and mumbled something in German ...

"Don't do *that*, you idiot ...!" I yelled.

But it was too late ...

The Santa Claus Chase

The sub blasted right out of the water like an *SS20* and took off into the air...

Ten minutes later, it skidded to a halt on the white beaches of Lapland and I stumbled out dazed onto the frozen tundra.

I didn't know it at the *time*, but it was Xmas Eve ...

Thinking I was probably only seconds away from being spectacularly refrigerated, I made for the only haven in sight – a little wooden cabin situated about a hundred yards inland from the frozen sea.

On I went, forcing one foot ahead of the other, refusing to be distracted from the intense concentration required to reach my goal, until something other than the vagaries of the climate interfered with the whole determined process ...

Something made me stop to listen:

A *strange* sound.

Like somebody *singing* ...

Shielding my eyes from the driving snow, I gazed out across the icy wastes to find a character dressed in red approaching the cabin on a sleigh drawn by reindeers ...

As soon as he arrived, he gathered up a large sack from the boot, went inside and slammed the door shut.

I stood there scratching my bonce.

I really have gone off my rocker this time, I thought ...

I trudged the last few yards and peered in through the frosted-up windows:

There he was, sitting on a fur rug and knocking back a jug of something ...

In the absence of any audible reply to a rap on the door, I pushed it open and marched in.

"Come in!" he said in a cheery voice. "Come in and have a drink!"

I pulled up a rug.

"You having a party?" I said.

"I live too far out for parties. People always say they'll come, but they never turn up. *Bastards ...*"

Charming language for Father Xmas, I thought.

"You wanna charge 'em a deposit, mate," I said. "A fiver, say, payable in advance. If they don't turn up, *they* lose the fiver and *you're* a fiver richer ..."

"You may have a point there," he said. "But tonight's the one night of the year when a party is out of the question. I've got a long session ahead, and a lot of very important deliveries to make ..."

The hut was *enormous.*

Bigger on the inside than the outside.

And full of oversize pillow-cases.

A real *Santa's* Grotto ...

"What have you got in the sacks?" I asked. "Presents?"

"Presents," he murmured. "*For all the children of the world ...*"

Gratefully accepting his offer of the jug, I upended it with only minor ceremonial.

So he really exists, I thought, *this Father Christmas ...*

"You really *exist*, then ...?" I said.

"Of course," he said. "Don't you believe in Santa Claus?"

"I do now," I said. (*I was beginning to nod off ...*) "I do now ..."

He suddenly leapt up and coshed me over the head with a wrench !

"Mug ..." he mumbled.

By the time I'd transcended the land of miniature planets and heavenly orbs – *maybe an hour later* – he'd gone, although he must have been in some considerable hurry because the sod had left some of his *sacks* behind ...

Nursing my bump as I went, I crawled over to the nearest one and emptied about a hundred bottles of *Allied Froth* all over the floor, surprising myself into such a lengthy hypnotic trance that I only snapped out of it when I caught the faint strains of some familiar melody coming from beyond the window:

Rudolf The Red-Nose Reindeer ...

The door almost came off its hinges as I clattered out after him, just in time to see him disappear on his sled.

"What *now* ...?" I cursed to myself.

After dithering there in the cold for a good deal longer than common sense and badly shredded trousers ought to have allowed me to, I finally made my way round to the back of the hut and climbed into a snowmobile which I found parked rather fortuitously in his garage ...

I chased him for miles and miles – all through the night – heading south into Sweden, until I finally hit a passable road and pinched a car, and all the time he was just up ahead, apparently flying at about *three feet* off the ground ...

All of a sudden, an elk stepped out in front of me and I crashed straight into it.

The *car* was a write-off.

The *elk* just gave me a mean look and sloped off ...

I must have covered an awful lot of ground, though. If the signs on the roadside were anything to go by, I'd arrived back in the outskirts of Stockholm, and somebody was revving up a light aircraft in a nearby field ...

Slipping and sliding all over the place, I half-ran, half-skated my way across the snow, gave a cursory nod to the begoggled pilot and, dispensing with all other formalities, dived headfirst into the rear passenger seat.

"Follow that Sledge ...!" I shouted.

Once in the upper atmosphere, I could see Santa flying around in the distance, weaving across the airlanes like a drunk in a trolley bus ...

All of which was completely lost on my chauffeur, who took off in the *opposite* direction.

"Oi!" I yelled. "Where are you going?"

"Moscow," he said.

"Why?"

"Solo peace mission ..."

"Are we at war?"

"*No* ..."

"What about *Santa* Claus?"

"He doesn't exist," he said drolly. "Didn't your *mother* tell you that ...?"

A Brush With The Rusks

"Matthews," he said, half turning round and holding out his hand in greeting. "*Rusty* Matthews. Welcome aboard. And who might *you* be?"

"Hadn't you better keep your hands on the controls, mate?" I said.

"Don't worry," he said. "I can fly this thing blindfold. It practically flies itself ..."

"Does your insurance company know about you?"

"I'm uninsurable. Too many crashes ..."

What was it I'd said about never setting foot on a plane again ...?

"Kitehawk," I said. "*Dexter* Kitehawk ..."

"I take it you're an Englishman, then?"

"Can't you tell?"

"Join the club, matey ..."

So saying, he rotated his bonce 360 degrees to display a fully-grown set of wing-whiskers, the latter of which were starched in staggered steps to match his cardboard airman's scarf ...

But I *refused* to be distracted. "You do *realise*," I said, "That while we sit here congratulating ourselves on our mutual exclusivity, a particularly nasty criminal dressed as Father Xmas is flying in the opposite direction loaded with sacks of *Allied Froth*, which he is aiming to deliver down the chimneys of little children all over the world ...?"

"A criminal? What *kind* of criminal?"

"One of many. One of a worldwide network of Nazis ..."

"*Nazis?* He's a *German*, then?"

"Well, put it *this* way, mate," I said, "He ain't one of *our* lot ..."

"Sorry old boy, but I can't help you. *Now*, if he was a *Russian*, it might be different. But I'm afraid Jerry just doesn't fit into the picture right now. Perhaps later ..."

"Later may be *too* late ..." I said despondently.

I did *try* to look on the bright side. I *had*, after all, left a tubful of Krauts immobilised on the beaches of Arctic Lapland.

But this had to be set against the fact that I was now heading out over the open sea, with the lights of Stockholm, Benfleet and London all receding behind me into the night ...

"*What* line of business did you say you were in, old boy?" he asked.

"Oh," I said, "I'm on a charity march. The idea is to see how close I can get to the capital of Sweden without actually *arriving* there, and how many times I can do it in one night. I've had two near-misses so far ..."

"Who's sponsoring you?"

"The Government ..."

"And who does the money go to?"

"The Mark Black Institute ..." (*I threw that one in just to test his reaction, but it proved negative*).

"Never heard of it ..."

"No," I said. "*And neither has anybody else ...*"

"Anyway," he said, "Looks like I may have to add to your disappointment, because when I'm finished in Moscow I shall be coming straight back to Stockholm and landing in town ..."

"Yes," I said, "And just what exactly are you planning to *do* in Moscow, if you don't mind me asking? Some kind of publicity stunt, is it?"

"Hardly," he said. "I'm going to buzz the Kremlin a couple of times, drop some leaflets and then get the hell out again ..."

It suddenly struck me that he was serious ...

"You *do realise*," I said, "That the minute you invade Soviet air space they'll shoot us down and ask questions later ...?"

"Not a bit of it, old boy ..."

"Hoping to catch them napping on Xmas morning, are you?"

"That's about the strength of it, yes ..."

"Don't you know they're all *atheists* out there?!" I screamed at him. "They don't celebrate Xmas! This is just another *working* day to them! They'll probably be extra vigilant today, just in case ...!"

"Won't matter old chap. This plane won't show up on any radar system yet invented ..."

"Oh yes?" I said. "And why's that?"

"It's made of balsa wood ..."

At that precise moment, my left foot plunged straight through the floor ...

"Yes," he went on, "I meant to warn you to be careful back there and not move about too much. The passenger seat's just for show, really. The plane wasn't built to take two people ..."

"Well, that suits me *just* fine, because you can put me down the first opportunity we get. What's that up ahead?"

"The coast of Finland, I think ..."

"*Think*? THINK!" I screamed at him. "Don't you *know* ...?"

"Helsinki to the north ... or south ..."

"Well," I said, "You can put *me* down in the nearest field ..."

"Couldn't do that, old boy ..."

"And why's *that*, may I ask?"

"It'll use up too much fuel. I've only got just enough for the round trip as it is. I haven't worked out yet the effect of carrying an extra passenger. We may land just short of the runway when we get back to Stockholm – on a preliminary estimate – but you can take it from me, that if I have to land *and* take off again, I won't make it back at all ..."

"Well, that's no concern of mine, is it?" I said, as my other foot went crashing through the chassis and left me dangling half-in and half-out, host to an icy jet-stream ripping straight up both trouser-legs. *It was only by hanging on to the back of Rusty's seat, that I managed to stop myself falling out altogether ...*

I tried to argue with him but it was useless. *He pointed out that if he tried to land with me in that position, I'd get my legs chopped off.* I told him not to worry about it though, because they'd both have probably *dropped* off by then. My right leg *definitely* had frostbite. *My left leg had inflated like a balloon and was apparently flying under its own steam ...*

"You haven't got anything to drink, have you Rusty?" I yelled.

"*Xmas* drink?"

"Whatever ..."

"Brandy do you?"

"*BRANDY* ?!!" I screamed. "Are you trying to make me *ill* ...?!!"

"It's all there is, I'm afraid. You'll like the way *I* mix it ..."

As I clung there in a world of my own, listening to the sound of glass clinking, I had no idea that he'd taken his hands off the controls ...

... until something crashed up onto the soles of my feet and propelled me straight through the roof of the plane!

In one swift move I'd gone from dangling half through the floor like an unorthodox undercarriage, to hanging stuck through the overhead canopy like a human Christmas decoration. The idiot had flown too low over the Urals ...

"What are you doing up *there*, old boy?" he said, as he went to hand me a glass.

"I just *miscalculated* a little," I said. "Only, when you flew too close to that last mountain peak, I thought I'd *use* it to jump back into the cabin ..."

He retracted the drink. "Hang on," he said, "Have you got a lighter on you, or matches ...?"

"In my pocket. Be my guest ..."

My pocket was now on a level with his nose.

"And what exactly do you *want* with that lighter," I queried. "Or shouldn't I ask ...?"

"Well," he said, "A glass of brandy isn't the *same* this time of year unless you set it alight, is it?"

"No ..." I said, not really listening. *I was too busy trying to blow warm air up to my eyelashes.*

"What was it you were saying about mountain peaks earlier on?" he said, as he reached up to hand me the drink for a second time.

"I was just remarking how clever you were back there to fly so close to that last one and let me use it as a *step* up. And *by* the *way*," I continued, "If you're still *interested*, there's *another* one coming – *straight ahead* ..."

"Aaaaaaaaargh ...!" he yelled.

I managed to grab the glass from his hand just as he dived back behind the controls ... rather stupidly forgetting that the brandy was *alight*.

"*AAAAAAAAAAAAARGH* ...!"

Screaming out in agony, I accidentally tipped it all down Rusty's neck ...

"AAAAAAAAAAAAAAAAAAARGH ...!!!"

What began as a timely swerve by the pilot to avoid the oncoming peak, developed into a loop-the-loop as he went berserk trying to pull his airman's jacket off ...

Half-way through these acrobatics, his head and shoulders burst through the roof alongside mine, giving me just enough time to ask him what he thought he was playing at before he once again vanished below, disappearing so fast that it was as though he'd been yanked downwards by a giant pair of elastic underpants attached to a gravity boomerang on the South Pole ...

For some while afterwards we appeared to be flying along upside-down, with all kinds of strange groaning noises coming from the cockpit above me.
If I hadn't been wedged in quite as tightly as I was, I'd have fallen out.
But it wasn't my lucky day ...

Just as the groans began to subside and Rusty got hold of himself long enough to right the plane, I smelled something *burning*.
The brandy had set the *wings* on fire ...

We must have had the *luck* of the devil though.
Or the nuts and bolts of an embryonic phoenix, because the flames had no sooner taken hold when I spotted evidence of a city up ahead, and the familiar minarets of the Kremlin nestling under a steely grey dawn sky ...
"MOSCOW AHOY!" I yelled.
"Yes, old boy," he said. "Come down a moment and give me a hand with these leaflets, will you ...?"
"*LEAFLETS?*" I screamed. "Fuck the leaflets! I order you to *ditch* this plane immediately! Can't you see this crate is burning up?"
"Yes, and they told me *Airfix* glue wasn't inflammable ..."
Airfix?
I tried to imagine one of those little tubes sticking all this lot together and two grown men trying to fly to Russia on the result.
"You didn't *really* use a tube of *Airfix*, did you?" I asked. *I could already feel the heat getting dangerously close to both trouser-legs.*
"Tube?" he said. "*No.* I ordered six *lorryloads* straight from the factory ..."
"I don't suppose you thought to pack a fire extinguisher?"
"Too late now ..." (*he handed me a stack of papers printed in Russian*) "... Chuck these overboard, will you? And prepare for a crash-landing ..."

Against my better judgment, I slung them all out in a great arc and proceeded to watch them fluttering and flapping and smouldering like cinders in the breeze as they sailed down over Red Square, the plane itself following hot on their heels ahead of a great trail of thick black smoke pouring back into the sky behind us ...
If anybody *was* awake, we must have looked like the vengeful Tisiphone swooping in on fiery wings to incinerate the usurpers of the old imperial palace...

But I'll say *one* thing.
Rusty brought that plane down like a veteran ...
Using the fading lights of an enormous road bridge as runway markers, he glided in with the engine switched off to prevent an explosion, leapt out and freed me from my imprisonment without a moment to spare ...
We both backed off and stood there watching it burn up.

"*Here*," he said, handing me some more leaflets. "Take these ..."

"Why?"

"We've got visitors ..."

A car was approaching from the western end of the bridge ...

"Not *me*, mate, " I said. (*I handed them back to him*)

"Why?" he said, puzzled.

"I'm leaving ..."

I pointed at the oncoming vehicle and gave it a wave.

"Do you recognise those people, then? Do you actually *know* people here in Moscow?"

"No. But *they'll* help me out ..."

I stuck my hand out to flag it down.

"Why?"

"Look for yourself, Rusty, old chap. It's got a *GB* sticker on it. That's as good as a Union Jack to an Englishman this far from home ..."

The car screeched to a halt.

"I'm afraid you're wrong," he said. "It should say *KGB*. The *K*'s fallen off, that's all. You've just flagged down the Russian Secret Police ..."

"Yeah," I yelled, as I legged it over the side, "Don't make me laugh ...!"

"So long old boy ..." he called ... *and with the Igors and Borises leaping out of the car, that was the last time I ever saw Rusty Matthews.*

As for *me*, I found myself hanging by my hands from the underside of one of the engineering wonders of the Soviet world, with only a couple of hundred feet of freezing dawn air obstructing my escape to the concrete below.

The KGB must have presumed me dead and perished, as I swung there alone, getting weaker and weaker ...

Or *so* I thought.

Just as I was about to let go forever that lonely bridge, I heard the voice of an *angel* call me from above ...

Moscow Nights

"You have *nine* lives, Dex ..." she said, as she reached out her hand.

All three tons of it.

She'd put on a lot of weight since I last saw her in Brazzaville. Her KGB jacket was flapping in the icy Xmas morning wind, and her action caused the sleeve to ride up, revealing a whole spaghetti-cabled network of muscles rippling in her forearm ...

We were at *some* altitude.

"Is that *you*, Tash ...?" I asked hesitantly.

Right at that moment, I think I'd rather have taken a chance on Clara Dorf, with whom I had a relationship totally uncluttered by matters of unavenged jealousy and unrequited lust. There was no personal animosity in the Fräulein's case: she'd have rescued me, if only to save me for a more long drawn-out execution. *I was convinced Natasha only wanted my hand so that she could drop me into the void herself, and so have the satisfaction of a revenge she must long have desired.*

On the *other* hand, I was going to drop anyway ...

"The last I heard," I said wearily, "You were selling eggplants in Stockholm..."

"No you didn't, Dex, that's just your sense of humour. Give me your hand..."

In an instant, she'd whipped me over onto the criss-crossed stanchion she'd been leaning out from and pressed me to her bosom.

She *reeked* of after shave.

All of which sensory assault counted for nothing as she slung me across her shoulder and began the descent below, during which I had a timely blackout ...

When I woke up, I found myself bound back-to-front in a straightjacket, inside a 6 x 4 padded cell with nothing but a spyhole and a serving hatch in the door.

The funny thing was, the first thought that occurred to me, was that it was just like my old dentist's waiting room in Crowndale Road ...

Hearing a key jangle in the lock, I looked up to find Natasha marching in with two plain-clothes KGB strong-arm men in tow.

One of them looked like my former dentist.

In fact, they *both* did.

In fact, they both *were* my former dentist, which just goes to show you never can tell. All these years I thought there was just *one* of him, and that he was a Nazi.

"Tash, *Tash* ..." I wailed, "How could you *do* this to me? After all we *went* through together ...? Old cobbers and muckers don't go around doing this sort of thing to each other ..."

While my former dentists looked like they were trying to work out where to stick the pliars, she stared at me with a pair of merciless eyes.

"Come *on*, Tash," I whined. "Ain't we still shipmates ...?"

"Just my little joke, Dex ..." she said. "Release him ..."

This proved a little difficult for two craftsmen who were clearly sorry to have seen the last of the sledgehammer and hacksaw era, setting about trying to undo my joke tuxedo in a way which suggested they hadn't yet come to terms with such paraphernalia of modern dentistry.

"You see," she went on, "We have rather a surplus of these things," (*she meant straightjackets*) "Now that *Glasnost* and *Perestroika* have arrived. Mentally-deranged political opponents have become a thing of the past ..."

"Yeah ..." I said, as the two ruffians finally succeeded in dragging the offending article from my limbs. "Pity you can't say the same for mentally-deranged cakehole-surgeons ..."

She slapped me on the shoulder with a laugh ...

"Your humour, Dex!"

I sailed backwards through a chipboard wall and came to rest amongst some rubbish bins in the corridor outside.

I tried to stay conscious, but I must have been losing heart ...

And, as I sank into the inky blackness all over again, I couldn't work out what was worse:

Natasha as foe;

Or Natasha as *friend*.

"Now, look at all *this*," she said, with a grand sweep of her hand.

All I could see, as I regained consciousness, was a gigantic array of flashing, coloured lights.

First of all, I thought they were imaginary, but then I realised they were part of an enormous computer bank covering three walls.

It looked like the bridge of the *USS Enterprise.*

Or something like that.

"Reminds me of the scoreboard at Wimbledon," I said, scanning for the fourth wall.

"*Ah*," she said, beginning to drift off into a reverie, "*Wimbledon* ... I reached the quarter-finals in my last year there ..."

"You obviously use the wrong dentists, Tash ..."

"Went out to a Czech *babooshka*. Not surprising, is it? They feed those girls on a diet of gouda cheese, chimpanzee blood, mashed leotard and steroids. And then they all become Americans ..."

"Ain't it the case ..."

"Now, to *business*," she said, suddenly turning serious again. "I know you still *love* me, of course ..."

"Of *course* ..."

"But I realised long ago that your work is more important to you than romance. You should have given me a chance, Dex. That *Alexis* is no good for you. I vatch *Dynasty*. Did you know that Joan Collins came to Russia in 1953 for cosmetic surgery?"

Funnily enough, I didn't.

"Yes," she went on, "The only scientists competent for this kind of work at the time were Soviet scientists ..."

"Goes without sayink," I said, lurching into the vernacular.

"Don't take the piss, Dex," she snapped. "Or I shall end your *ability* to piss for *good* ..."

I gulped.

"Anyway, *Dex*, darlink. I have been trackink your world progress. You have done well. But you still have much to do ..."

"How did you escape from Zaire?" I interjected.

"You *know* that, Dex ..."

"Yes, but I heard on the grapevine that you were disgraced with the KGB and were expelled from Russia accordingly ..."

"I *was*, Dex, I *was*. It was a sorry episode of my life. But you fail to take into account the change in administration here in Moscov. On return from Zaire I was exiled to Oslo, where I had to earn a living in a common street market, selling bootlegged Russian cassettes. But, when Gorbachev came to power, all the KGB old guard were swept aside in a great purge and I was summoned to take over the hunt for Nazi war criminals ...”

“*And* ...?” I said.

“And,” she said, “I have gained some information along the way that is only of peripheral interest to my superiors, but which I think will be of great value to *you* ...”

“Go on ...”

“Vell,” she said, “You see these lights ...?”

I could hardly fail to miss them, covering three walls as they did.

“Vell, they represent our agents in the field ...”

“Yes ...?”

“Yes,” she confirmed. “And *this* one ...” (*here she pointed to a particularly bright red light on the electronic map*) “... will be able to hand you the information himself ...”

It was sparkling above Stockholm ...

“*Now* you’re *talking*. Does he know what’s in the *el-dust* file?”

“Our scientists have analysed every single product of AF International and found nothing that is not perfectly accountable to known science. No, he cannot tell you anything about *el-dust* ...”

“Never mind,” I said. “Who is he?”

“He lives near the harbour, and I vill give you his address before you leave...”

“Well,” I said, rising on my pins, “I’ll be off, then ...”

She restrained me with her tennis grip ...

“Not so *fast*, Dex ...”

“No ...?” I said, innocently.

“*No*. You look hungry. You could do with a meal. *Fatten you up a little.* How about dinner?”

“Er ...”

“Do you like Chinese?”

“Er ... I don’t like any sort of foreigners really ...”

Bursting into hysterical laughter, she suddenly crashed me across the spine with a forearm smash and followed it up with such a vicious backhand volley into my solar plexus that it left me winded, speechless, and vertically catatonic.

“Your *humour*, Dex ... it just *kills* me ...”

(It’ll fucking kill *me* one day and all)

“Fine ...” I wheezed. “*Chinese is fine* ...”

“Where to, then?”

“Oh, I don’t mind,” I croaked. “Any *public* place will do me ...”

She folded her arms in a matronly manner. “You have a choice,” she said. “My place or ... *my* place ...”

“I thought you’d never ask ...”

I choose not to dwell on what occurred in Natasha's apartment overlooking Gorky Park that night.

And the *following* night.

And the night after *that* etc.

Suffice to say she had her revenge.

On the fourth morning, she gave me a sealed envelope and a new passport, and put me on a train to Stockholm.

A train, a boat, *and* a train, actually ...

Once in Stockholm, I hit the nearest bar, only to find that they wouldn't let me in unless I handed over my coat as collateral.

"Get out of my fucking way!" I yelled. "I'm an Englishman!"

But they wouldn't *have* any of it.

So I looked for an off-licence.

That was no good either.

They only open on a Friday evening between the hours of 6.30 and 6.35, and the queues stretch all the way back to Harwich.

So, after hunting out the nearest dark spot, I opened Tasha's envelope, memorised the address printed therein and made my way to it through the freezing streets on foot.

When I got no answer from the bell, I rattled the knocker with one hand and battered on the wood with the other.

All of a sudden, the *door* opened ...

London Took The Disco

"*Baz*, me old mate!" I yelled, backing off at the speed of lightning ... "Fancy meeting *you* up this way ..."

But I wasn't quick enough.

His *hand* shot out and caught me round the *throat* ...

The trouble was, I hadn't ever bargained on him being *mobile* again, but *mobile* he was. His reflexes were as sharp as a knife and the expression on his face was saying, *how do you like the new slimline Baz* ...?

I couldn't believe it was possible for somebody to have lost so much weight in the time since I'd last seen him in China.

He must have been on a crash-course diet.

ie. A diet to stop him crashing through the earth from one part of the planet to the other ...

Without relaxing his grip, his psychotic, menacing stare began to soften and he started to smile ...

"Where you *been*, Coathook? I've been looking all over ..."

My mouth moved but nothing came out.

"Come *inside*," he said. "I've *got* something for you ..."

"Yes," his partner was saying, "When Baz came back from his trip, he'd put on a lot of weight. But I expect you've heard all this stuff on the World Service about food contamination from *salmonella, listeria,* etc. Well, Baz drew up a list of all the remaining foods he could safely eat and found it only consisted of peanuts and vitamin B capsules – and, well, peanuts are very expensive in Sweden ..."

"Yeah," I said, "That explains how Baz lost *weight*, but how did he get out of jail in Zaire?"

"I think I'd better let *him* explain that one ..."

"You know, Coathook," he was saying, "If you hadn't been in such a hurry to get in that balloon, I could have saved you a whole lot of time and effort in the hunt for Adolf Flite ..."

"How was *I* to know?" I said, sitting there and admiring the decor of this rather plush flat in the up-market end of Stockholm.

"Well, what did you think we were all *doing* there in the jungle? Collecting seaweed?"

I *wanted* to say, "Well, as a *vegetarian*, Baz, it wouldn't be so unlikely ..." *but I kept shtoom.*

"See," he was saying, "You're pretty new to this game, Dexter. *Dexter –* CAN I *CALL* YOU *DEXTER* ...?"

"Erm ..."

"Some of us have been at this game for years. CAN I *SAY* THAT OVER THE *AIR* ...?"

"*Eh* ...?"

"Every single one of those people on board that boat had a vested interest in tracking down Adolf Flite ..."

"For example?"

"For example ..."

"'Ere, *Baz* me old mate," I interrupted. "Before you begin, I couldn't trouble you for a drop of *Froth*, could I ...?"

"Wouldn't have it in the house, Dexter. Use your loaf ..."

"Of course not, of course ..." I said, disappointed. "Got anything else alcoholic?"

He turned to his partner. "Get the Anti-Freeze for him ..."

"Very decent," I said.

"I used it all on the car, Baz. Sorry ..."

"Well," he went on, "He's not having my *gin* ..."

She wandered out of the room.

"Where *was* I ...?" said Baz.

"*Here*, try one of *these*," she said, slinging a can of beer in from the kitchen.

"Cheers ..." I said.

"Well ...?"

"Well *what?*"

"Where *was* I?"

"Oh, er ... you were going to tell me about the passengers on the boat ..."

"Not *just* the *passengers* ! *CREW* as well ..."

"Eh ...? *What?* Even the *CAPTAIN* ? Old Pegleg ...?"

All of a sudden, he got up, dragged me off the chair and started to walk me to the door...

"Anyway, Dexter," he said, picking up a large envelope from a small table underneath the hatstand, "All you need to know is in this package – dates, times, contacts, ID's and so forth. I'm handing it all to you because I'm *OUT OF THE GAME NOW!* I've built up quite a respectable herb-smuggling racket here in Stockholm and I can't afford to get involved. I've got too much trouble on my hands with a consignment of *BOTULISM*-CONTAMINATED *PARSLEY* I brought over from Harwich in the petrol tank last week. Where will it all end ...?"

"But ..."

"Don't worry," he said. (*He handed me a second, smaller envelope*). "There's a ticket back to England in here and a few bob for a drink on the ferry. You'll probably get an OBE for this ..."

"*But* ..."

"I'll have the rest of *that* back, as well ..." he said, as he lunged at my half-finished can of beer and pushed me through the door.

"Erm ..."

"Never mind," he added. "It's only three percent alcohol ..."

So saying, he slammed the door shut on me.

I sicked up on the staircase and crunched off into the snow.

With no conception of time or distance in Sweden, it came as quite a shock to discover that the bus journey from Stockholm to Gothenburg took *seven* hours.

I'd already gotten a little tired – after just *one-and-a-half* hours – *of a ventilator gushing icy cold air straight into my face from a distance of three inches, and so I went to see the driver to lodge a complaint ...*

Half-way up the aisle, I fell headfirst down a steep flight of steps and could only watch helpless as my hat was sucked straight down the pan of the in-bus toilet and blasted out in shreds over a hundred square-mile radius of frozen Swedish countryside.

And I knew that if I didn't get my *nose* off the foot-flush, the *rest* of my clothes would follow my hat ...

"This is outrageous!" I squawked. "Can't somebody *help* me ...?"

"*Kalle Anka* ! *Kalle Anka* !" yelled a gang of Swedes, all laughing as they hoisted me up feet first and carted me back to my seat.

When the commotion had died down, the tallest of this mob leered round from the seat behind and introduced himself to me as *Gustav*. "You must be *English*," he said.

"Actually," I said, "I'm from Mission Control, French Guiana, and I was just getting a bit homesick. *Ariadne N'Kite'onk* ..."

"*Peter*," said another extremely tall bloke, who'd stacked himself up behind Gustav like the second tier of an unstable wedding cake. "We *like* England. We go *every* year ..."

"Oh, why's that, then?" I enquired, harmlessly.

"Best country in the world to get pissed in ..."

And on that note, I borrowed his hat, lowered it down over my eyes, and went to sleep.

When I woke up, we were still crawling along the road in the middle of nowhere, and I was cruelly disappointed to learn that I'd slept straight through the only stop-over in the entire journey, thus missing my one chance for a civilised piss in the process. *The fact that it took in a restaurant on the picturesque shores of a great inland lake was neither here-nor-there to a man with a bladder like an over-inflated zeppelin.* Whatsmore, I'd missed my one chance for a civilised *smoke*, and I was getting a bit tired of legging it out the door at each pick-up point for a quick tenth of a cigarette along with all the other poor sods with a smoking habit only to have to keep legging it back *inside* again ten seconds later. *Especially* as the driver drove off without me at one point and I only managed to get back on board because I could *run* faster than he could drive.

When I did finally hit the Departure Lounge in Gothenburg, my troubles were *far* from over. *Baz*, the cheapskate, had booked me onto an off-peak young person's student ticket, and I had quite a job convincing the staff I was *all* of seventeen years old ...

"What are you studying, then?" the cow said.

"As a matter of fact," I said, "I'm studying virology at Coppett's Wood Isolation Hospital and I have here in this envelope a tube of Deadly Anthrax (*strain* 'B'). The last time I dropped one of these on the floor I wiped out half of Europe, only I don't suppose you heard about it because it was hushed up by the EC Health Commission. Any other questions?"

At which point she demanded the full fare and threatened to call the police.

"Hanging's too good for you lot," I said, rummaging around the second envelope for some spare *krone* and wondering what kind of a dent it was going to make in my bar-time on the ferry.

She took my money and counted it out meticulously.

"Yes," she said, "And the *Luftwaffe* were too good to *you* in the last war ..."

I was just about to tell her that she'd know all *about* the *Luftwaffe* of course, because Sweden was Germany's *aircraft carrier* at the time, and how do I know *that?* Because my Uncle Grolly was knocked unconscious by a stray bolt from a Junkers bomber that fell on his garden during the Battle of Britain and when the doctors removed it from his brain it said *Made in Upsaala* on it but don't worry because he felt a lot better afterwards – that kind of stuff – when I heard an almighty *commotion* going on behind me ...

I glanced round just in time to see a ten-ton Swedish Mohican in a 53-hole Dr Martens body-suit being dragged away under duress by the Port Authorities. The slogan *Queen Christina League* was emblazoned across his T-shirt, and he'd apparently gone berserk because he'd heard there were foreigners in town.

Phew, I thought, *that's the one thing nobody can accuse me of being.*

(A *foreigner*, that is)

"THAT'S RIGHT!" I yelled. "LOCK HIM UP AND THROW AWAY THE KEY!"

I visibly jumped when he almost broke free, and I didn't like the look he gave me as they carted him away ...

"Well," I said, turning back to the woman in the ticket window, "There's far too much xenophobia around for my liking. It's about time somebody did something about it ..."

When I reached my cabin – a four-berth affair – I found myself in the company of two male Caucasians of dubious status and a spare berth.

I *say* cabin, but it was actually a partitioned corridor.

The security arrangements weren't too good either:

One tiny locker each, and mine wasn't big enough to stash the envelope in.

So I decided to be temporarily anti-social and let my two travelling companions hit the bar on their own, while I hit my bunk with the intention of reading some of what Baz had given me.

"Okay," said the first. (*He'd already introduced himself to me as Roger, a ballet student from Ashby-de-la-Zouche, or some other place in France*). "We'll see you in the disco later, then ...?"

"Disco?" I said. "You couldn't keep me away from it ..."

"Chow," said the other (whose name was Ludo, *apparently*).

"Yeah," I mumbled. "*Arrivaderci* ..."

Somewhere amongst all this lot, I thought, *must be the identity and whereabouts of Adolf Flite ...*

In view of the sheer amount of paperwork, I decided to start at the very beginning with a clutch of documents headed *Profiles*. They consisted, it seemed, of Baz's impressions of various characters connected with the case, people he'd met on his travels etc, and I quote selectively from them:

> **Black, Laurel**: Interpol Officer. *Interest in the case:* Other than brother to Mark Black, interest unknown. Claims to be a vegetarian. That's a laugh! He doesn't even eat fish.

> **Black, Mark**: Stockbroker. *Interest in the case:* Personal riches. *Background:* Eton; Cambridge; Institute of Directors; High-ranking official, AF International; Chairman LDRC; Chairman, British MUFON Network; Founder, Mark Black Institute; Founder, *Lagerland* Theme Resort; Honorary Arab. Charming bloke. Sold his grandmother into white slavery, made a mint gambling on the Stock Exchange, and then bought her back for a profit. Currently has her modelling for a hard porn outfit.

"Tell me something I *don't* know!" I said aloud.

Leithard, Martin: Head, UK Operations. Founder,
Waffen Excess Club, London. Famous womaniser. Owes me
a fiver for damages to my London residence. *UK Address:*
Rooms above the *Mannequin Arms*, Camden Town.

"This is *more* like it ..." I murmured ... when I became distracted by the
sound of somebody *throwing up* in the next cabin ...

It was only *then* that I noticed that the partition didn't reach all the way
either to the floor *or* the ceiling, and that the sounds of groaning and vomiting
were coming from *all* sides ...

"Can't you shut up!" I yelled out. "Where do you think you *are*, Trafalgar
Square? Can't you wait till you get *home* to do that ...?"

A further chorus of misery signalled a premature end to my concentration, an almighty
wail forcing me to duck out of the way as somebody's lunch came flying through the gap
between the partition and the next deck up ...

"WHAT *ARE* YOU ALL?!!!" I screamed. "FIRST-TIME *COUNCIL*
TENANTS ...?!!!"

I charged out of the cabin, envelope in hand, and went up to the top deck ...

But then I had to *descend* a floor, because *that's* where the *bar* was.

"They wouldn't do that in their own homes," I said to some old Swede in
the lift.

"They are dirty men! *Dirty* men!" he shouted, smiling at me benignly.

"*That's* right!" I yelled.

"*Hooliganana* ...!"

"What ...?"

Grabbing a sick bag with abysmal timing, he suddenly threw up all over my Hush
Puppies ...

"I suppose you think that's *funny*, do you?!" I shouted at him.

He shrugged his shoulders.

"They are dirty men! *Dirty* men! They do not wash their hands!"

"WHERE'S THE DISCO?" I screamed at him.

He smiled again, as if to say he didn't know.

"*Gertch'* you old git ..." I growled.

As soon as the doors opened, I marched out in a rage, kicking as much of the vomit off
my shoes as I could in the process.

About half of it all landed down the back of some madam in a fur evening
gown ...

When she turned round, I pointed at the lift.

The old Swede was still standing there with the sick bag in his hand,
smiling.

"Disco! Disco!" he beamed, indicating a door in front of me.

"*GET* HIM!" I yelled. "HE'S THE MAIDSTONE HAT-KILLER ...!!!"

Suddenly, a whole posse of her travelling companions sprung towards the lift as though they'd just got wind Jack the Ripper was in there ...

Fortunately for the Swede, the doors closed before anybody could reach him.

He was still shouting "Disco! Disco!" at me just before he disappeared ...

Sauntering into the bar, I found it virtually empty except for a chronically awful band at the far end who were playing a version of *Bicycle Built For Two* in Swedish, where the name 'Daisy' is transposed into 'Isabella' but where the rest of the words are in English because the band are really from Romford and can't speak Swedish and it's a Danish boat anyway, and all this at about half-a-decibel lower than subliminal volume.

As if to emphasise the shift in perspectives, I'd no sooner crossed the threshold when an insight into the general medical state of half the ship startled me into a dead stop. *The ferry had taken such an almighty plunge into a trough that I almost left my stomach on the sea bed before I'd had time to adjust to the poor quality of light...*

In fact, I *did* leave my stomach on the sea bed, and in its place I got a bag of freshly-caught of squid ...

I wobbled up to the counter, ordered a pint of Danish lager – *well*, any old port in a storm – and collapsed into a chair by the nearest table:

Kitehawk, Dexter: Professional idiot. *Interest in the case:* Nobody knows. Claims to be an MI5 agent, but case yet to be proven. Archetypal forerunner of the lager lout. Senile to boot.

"Why," I yelled, "This is preposterous!"

I stomped back off into the corridor and grabbed some old bloke round the neck ...

"Tell me where the *disco* is or you're a *dead* man ...!"

Consistent with expectations, I found a crowd of people three-deep at the bar, all waving notes around and all desperate for a drink.

But *none* were as desperate as *me* ...

I had to dig deep into my repertoire to get round this one:

"Gangway! Gangway! Get out of my fucking way ...!" I yelled, jumping up onto the backs of those in the third row. "I'm a professional stuntman ...!"

In this manner I managed to instigate a minor dispersal, but there were still two more rows of reckless currency-shifters to negotiate.

And occupying part of that row were *Ludo, Roger, Gustav and Peter* ...

"Having trouble getting a drink, boys ...?" I said. "*Right*. Follow *me*. Prepare to turn yourselves into a human battering-ram! *Ready*? One, two, *three*

..."

Once I'd barged my way through, I ordered several drinks on Ludo's account and took up my favourite bar-leaning position, where I continued to try to read more of the scandalous lies Baz had written about me.

I didn't take much notice at the time, but my four companions had joined me in propping up the counter as though I were some sort of Messiah of bar-room etiquette ...

Near Miss

"I'M AN ENGLISHMAN!" I suddenly yelled out about two hours later, for no apparent reason.

The barman – a Dane, I should think – gave me the same kind of meaningless smile the old Swede had given me in the lift.

I'd already begun to feel a bit lonesome, and when I stumbled across entries for Jane and Fiona in the files, I decided to hunt down some female company ...

In *retrospect*, ordering the DJ to play *La Bamba*, and then – *carrying my full litre glass of lager with me* – proceeding to scare half the women from the dance floor, was probably a strategy best consigned to the deep, but it did give the red-blooded an opportunity to take up a prominent position and indicate their mettle by advertising their hearts on their sleeves.

Well, *her* heart on *her* sleeve, actually ...

Stuck for choices, I went and accosted some lone Norwegian doxy who, the general exodus having apparently escaped her attention, was sitting nonchalantly at a nearby table and looking in the wrong direction.

"How-do-you-do," I said. "I'm conducting a dental survey for the Oslo area and ..."

At this precise moment, I noticed – out of the corner of my eye – a hand lifting my glass from the table ...

When I looked round, I found two shifty-looking criminals from somewhere like Essex standing there.

So I grabbed back hold of my drink ...

"Oi!" I said. "What do you think *you're* doing ...?"

We then spent the next few seconds tugging at the glass like olympic qualifiers for an exhibition tournament in jug-wrestling ... until he relaxed his grip.

"Oh," he said. "We thought you were a Swede ..."

"*Well?*" I said. "*So?*"

He finally let go.

"*Only,*" he said, "If you'd have been *a Swede,* we'd have had your drink ..."

"If I'd have been a *Swede,*" I said, "You *wouldn't* ..."

Fucking incredible, I thought, as I watched them slink off.

In broad daylight as well ...

"So," I said, turning back to Miss Norway ... *only to find that she'd vanished.*

By the time I'd returned to the bar, Gustav was unloading the spoils from a food-foraging expedition and lining up a banana, a tomato and a loaf of bread on the counter:

Quick as a flash, Peter pulled a serated carving knife out of his trousers and diced everything up into sandwich-sized pieces before I could blink an eyelid ...

"TO THE ENGLISH!" he yelled.

I had half-a-mind to query this exclamation, when the barman suddenly accosted me ...

"It's nothing to do with me, guv ..." I said.

"*You – Englishman?*"

"Yes?"

"There is a man round the other side of the bar wants to see you – he wants to meet *all* Englishmen ..."

"He must want to buy me a drink," I said, recklessly. "I'm on my way ..."

As I strolled round there, I dipped back into the files ...

Flite, Adolf:

"*This* is it ..." I murmured ... *when a pair of hands suddenly grabbed hold of my lunchbox and lifted me ten foot in the air ...!*

"English?" he queried of me.

I gulped.

It was the *Mohican* ...

"*Kalle-Anka! Kalle-Anka!*" I yelled (*pointing at the two drinks-thiefs from Dagenham*). "*Hooliganana ...!*"

He didn't hang about ...

By the time I'd hit the floor, he'd marched right over to where they were skulking, picked them both up by their jackets and hurled them through a window.

... as a *result* of which, one of them crashed his head on a fire alarm, and suddenly the entire boat was in chaos ...

Five minutes after that, some clown gave the order to abandon ship.

The next thing I remember is waking up in hospital in Holland.

I had, of course, lost all the evidence in the process.

I'd spent two whole years chasing Adolf Flite all over the planet, and instead of returning home a hero, I was coming back with medical escorts, a ruined man.

The *mistake* they made was to put me on a *plane* ...

Somewhere on the outskirts of London we almost collided with an airship ...

And who did I think I saw at the controls?

Laurel Black, that's who.

"Did you see that ...?" I said, turning to my neighbour.
"Never did," he said.
"No," I said. "Neither did I ..."
And do you know the only thing of importance I learned from my round-the-world trip?
It was the meaning of the phrases *Hooliganana* and *Kalle-Anka*.
The *first* one was obvious:
English football lager louts.
The second?
Swedish for *Donald Duck.*

CHAPTER 30
OMENS & PORTENTS

I woke up the following morning in a rowing boat moored to the Thames embankment.

Somewhere near Blackfriars Bridge.

The first thing that occurred to me was that I hadn't felt this bad since I swallowed a bottle of *Clearasil* in 1973 after some idiot told me it was good for a hangover.

Whether it *was* or not I couldn't say.

Because I then went on to immerse my head in a bowl of ice-cold milk on instructions from the same source (who'd sold it to me as a little-known Flemish remedy) and spent the next fortnight shuffling with a limp and speaking like Little Jimmy Osmond.

When I queried the validity of this procedure, I was told it only worked with *pasteurised* milk.

I could have sworn he'd said the milk had to go *past your eyes* at the time, but suffice to say I never tried this method again.

These days I immerse my head in a bowl of *Froth* and draw the blackout curtains.

A Question of Ethics

As I lay there bobbing up and down with the boat, I tried to piece together the events of the previous day.

I remember buying Tower Bridge from an American tourist.

And I remember riding up and down on the Docklands Light Railway and screaming, "Oh my Gawd, where's the *driver* of this crate ...!?"

But, before any of *this* happened, I can clearly remember arriving at the London City Airport and discovering that the only safe landing I'd made in my long global journey just happened to be at the world's only terminal operating without air traffic control.

I'd expected a big fuss on arrival for survivors of the Danish ferry disaster, but all I got was one reporter from the *East London Gazette* and a nurse in a blue uniform.

She was the size of a cumulo-nimbus and just as threatening.

She must have been a *private* nurse – they don't pay state nurses enough to eat like *that*.

"Where's the heroes welcome?" I'd said to the hack.

"No idea mate," he said. "I'm down here to cover a publicity stunt by the LDRC Chairman, Mark Black. He's arriving in the Royal Albert Dock at three o'clock ... by *submarine* ..."

I leapt off my immobile stretcher ...

"Get out the way ...!" I yelled to all and sundry ... *but the nurse had me bundled into an ambulance before I could make a dive for the check-out.*

They must have sedated me after that, because I woke up that evening in a private hospital room with a solitary bunch of red roses on the bedside locker, complete with greetings tag:

Dexter Kitehawk – You are not alone

"Well, that's a puzzler ..." I mumbled to myself, as I screwed it up and ransacked the locker for my clothes.

I'd only got as far as separating the waistband of my herringbone strides, when the door suddenly burst open behind me ...

"I'll give *you* puzzler, Mr Kitehawk!" bellowed a voice.

I tried to turn round with one leg half-on and one leg half-off ...

"Ah, nurse," I said, hopping around the floor like a kangaroo with a sore paw, "Help me on with this trouser-leg, will you ...?"

"Get back into bed at once!"

Suddenly, she dived at my midriff and rugby-tackled me to the floor – no mean feat for a woman of *her* size – *and the pair of us crashed onto the tiles, sending the medicine trolley into the far wall and causing me to howl out loud like a victim of aria abuse ...*

She'd made a *mistake*, really, because I'd landed on my bad arm, and the resultant spasm was filled with the kind of superhuman strength that only comes with great fear or great pain – in *this* case, *both* – and I automatically leapt up and hurled her against the bedside locker as though she weighed nothing more than a sack of feathers.

An apple fell out of the fruit bowl and knocked her out cold.

It was a Granny Smith's.

"Well," I said, bending down to inspect her name-tag, "Staff-Nurse *Ursula Major*, you may be a *Great-Bear* of a woman, but ..." (*here I laughed at my own joke*) "... You are no match for Her Majesty's *brightest star* at MI5 ...!"

I knotted some sheets together and legged it out the window.

I needn't have bothered.

I was on the ground floor.

Of *what*, though was a mystery.

The place was surrounded by a barbed-wire fence ...

Nurse Ursula's ID provided me with the means to get out past the sleepy guard, but an oxygen tank would have been a more useful aid to survival in the half-derelict, half-futuristic Docklands nightmare waiting for me beyond the front gate, all of which might have been superimposed on the Moon.

And I can tell you which hospital I *hadn't* been in.

Newham General.

Clinical Insanity Research Unit

A Division of the Mark Black Institute

"So *that's* his game, is it?" I cursed, hoofing it down a road skirting the edge of the world.

It was hardly ethical, was it, banging up in a nuthouse a man as sane as you or I?

Outraged to the point of vandalism, I went to kick an an old tin can on the kerb and withdrew my foot at the last moment:

It was an aerosol of spray-paint ...

After scanning hither and thither for witnesses, and satisfying myself that I was suitably unobserved, I picked it up and wrote in big letters on an adjacent wall:

DR MARK BLACK – GET FUCKED!

Then I decided to look for a pub ...

What happened between then and the following morning is not entirely clear, though it didn't take a mastermind to work it out. AF International must have had every outlet in Docklands sewn up for its product, and I *know* because I investigated *every single one* of those pubs and bars in my efforts to leave the area.

Who the *boat* belonged to, I couldn't say, but a pained glance over the side told me its name:

The Hun's Helmet

What a pretty little name.

The effort of looking caused me to collapse back in shock, though I realised that if I spent too long in the reclining mode a policeman was either going to come along and arrest me, or the increasingly hot spring morning sun would fry me to a frazzle.

I made an attempt to stand up, and I did it several times with the boat wobbling about all over the place, before I actually managed to get a hand to the embankment and climb up onto dry land.

I *say* dry land, but it actually took me another five minutes before I stopped skidding around on the damp mossy stone long enough to haul myself over onto the pavement.

I knew *exactly* what I wanted to do next.

I *wanted* to go straight to my office.

But nothing is ever as easy as it should be ...

My first problem seemed to be a lack of stomach for the fight.
The fight to get on a tube in the rush hour, that is ...
I had to let several trains go by packed to the doors like boxes of chocolate bunny rabbits before I was able to conjure up some of that old determination that had got me all the way round the world and back in one piece:

"Right!" I yelled, startling several of the other waiting early-morning commuters as another train rolled in. "I want this conducted like a military operation! *Ready?* After *three.* One, *two ...*"
I got ejected bodily by transport police and thrown into the street ...

So I decided to catch a *bus* instead.

What a Performance

There I was, just hogging the upstairs back seat of a driver-only vehicle, minding my own business and timing the average wait at each bus stop with a stopwatch (*the average was 15 minutes 55 seconds*), when some unidentified stranger began haranguing me:

"Late for work ...?" he called out.
"Who wants to know?" I shouted down the aisle.
"It's *me*," he said. "Don't you remember ...?"
I started to nod ... then I said "No."
Transport certainly hadn't improved in my absence.
"See that crane up there ...?" he said. (*He was trying to open a window*).
"Don't do that!" I yelled. "We'll all be sucked out ..."
"Somebody tried to jump off it yesterday – tried to commit suicide ..."
"Fascinating ..."
"Nobody knows who it was, though ..."
"I know who it was," I said, glaring at all the buses, bumper-to-bumper, nose to tail.
"Oh?" he said. "Who?"
"Chairman of London Transport ..."
All of a sudden, an inspector appeared out of nowhere, demanded to see my credentials, told me my ticket was two years out-of-date and gave me an appointment to see the magistrates at Bow Street.
Following this, I sat there rueing how that bus pass had got me all the way round the world without anybody questioning its validity, and how the one place I couldn't use it was on a London Transport bus.
I got off and walked.

Cracking the Whip

"Good-day Madam!" I said, as I breezed into what I thought was the bookshop beneath my office. *I walked smack into a row of shelves containing pornographic videos, catapulted myself backwards through the plate-glass window and landed on my arse in the kerb ...*

So *stunned* was I, that I didn't know what had happened for a minute. All I could see were two burly Greeks marching out after me with their shirtsleeves rolled up revealing anchor tatoos on their muscles ...

I lurched up and pulled my gun out. "Right!" I yelled.

They started edging backwards, not quite sure if *me* or *it* were genuine ...

"Come on," I added for emphasis, "One-two, one-two, *hup-two-three-four* ...!"

One of them was a bit slow turning back into the shop, so I prodded him in the neck:

"*Move* !" I hissed. "I'm a desperate man ...!"

I marched them up the rear staircase and straight into my erstwhile office, where I let out an involuntary raspberry ...

Etude en Bleu

Somebody was filming a video *in there!*

A woman dressed as a schoolgirl was draped over my desk, while a middle-aged gent was standing over her and wielding a cane ...

"Erm ..."

Sensing my hesitation, the two Greeks suddenly swung round to confront me ...

"Vice Squad!" I shouted, and pulled out my bus pass.

(The gent looked a bit sheepish, it's true, but the woman merely straightened up and folded her arms in a kind of bored, throwaway manner as though I'd just identified myself as a snoop from the *Boots* photographic department ...)

Something told me it wasn't a very high budget production. The camera was either operating itself, or the cameraman had legged it just prior to my arrival, via the same back exit I'd trailblazed *myself* two years earlier ...

Six of the Best

As for the *Greeks*, well ...

They were beginning to look singularly more unimpressed as each second rolled by.

So I launched into action and prodded the gent in the chest. "What's your connection with Iran?" I said. "I want names, numbers and addresses ..."

I decided to let him think about that while I opened my desk drawer and removed the only two items in it – an empty can of beer and a bottle of Greek wine.

The empty *can* was mine.

I had no idea who the bottle belonged to.

I paused for thought.

Well, I was in the right office, but it clearly wasn't *my* office any more.

In fact, its link with national security was now in doubt.

Or perhaps it wasn't ...

"Hey man, what *is* this?" said Greek #1. "I pay my dues ..."

"Now look here ..." the gent was trying to say.

I prodded him again. "I hope you're still working on those addresses," I said. "And, as for *you* ..." (*turning to Greek #1*), "I want to know what you're doing in my office ..."

"*Your* office ...?" he protested. "*Hey*, we lease this place fair and square from the lady who owns it ..."

"Is *that* so?" I said.

Greek #2 edged forward ...

"Yeah, that's *so* ..." he said.

I raised my gun (and my *voice*) ...

"Stand where you are!" I shouted. "And *you*," (*turning to #1*) "Go get me a black sack ..."

He went off and fetched it like a complete idiot.

He could have escaped ...

"*You*," I said, pointing at the leading lady.

"Who, *me*?" she said.

"*That's* right – *you*," I said. "Go and frisk *him* ..." (*pointing at her co-star*) "And get his ID for me ..."

She pulled out a wallet containing a Ministry of Defence security pass.

"Who's your boss?" I growled at him.

"I can't tell you *that* ..." he started to whinge.

"Right," I said, "You can either tell me *now*, or we can all go down the station and you can tell me there. It's up to you ..."

"The *police* station ...?" he said, horrified.

"*Certainly* the police station. Unless you'd like me to conduct this investigation in the middle of Charing Cross *Railway* Station – and *don't think I wouldn't* ..."

"Okay, *okay* ..."

"I'll make it easy for you," I said. "Down at Special Branch, we've had your boss under scrutiny for some time now, and I already *know* his name. So you don't have to incriminate yourself *or* him. Just tell me whether he wears a hat with corkscrews dangling from the rim ..."

"Why, of course he does, old boy ..."

"You're not taking the piss by any chance, are you?"

"Scouts honour. Room 345 ..."

"I thought you said you were Vice Squad?" said the actress/schoolgirl.

"Never trust a copper," I said. "Right, *you* ..." (*shoving the black sack at Greek #1*)

"Who, *me*?" he said.

"Yeah, *you*," I said. "I want you to go round this room and fill it up with videos. About half-a-dozen'll do ..."

"Why?"

"Evidence ..."

Two minutes later, I snatched the sack off him and legged it.

The Turn of the Corkscrew

That afternoon, without once needing to show my stolen security pass, I walked straight into the MOD at Holborn, marched up the main staircase and barged my way into Room 345, where I found him sitting behind a large desk with his head down in a pile of papers ...

"Ah," he said, without looking up, "Come in old boy. I've been expecting you. What can I do for you?"

"You can give me two years' wages for a start!" I screamed at him.

He carried on writing.

"Sorry, old boy," he said, "But I'm a bit short on the readies right now. Anything else I can do?"

"I'll give *you* short on the readies ..."

I slung the sack to the floor and went striding across the carpet ...

"Better lay low for a while," he suddenly said (*preventing serious injury to himself by handing me a typewritten sheet of paper*). "Consider yourself off the case. You're a hot potato. I'll get back to you. Thanks for all your efforts ..."

I didn't notice it at the time, but while I was reading what he'd given me, he got up, grabbed the sack and climbed out the window.

I didn't *notice* it, because I was too engrossed in what was written on the sheet.

It was the latest list of people to be condemned to death by the Ayatollah. And *my* name was at the top of the list ...

"You gutless chiseller ...!" I shouted after him.

I watched sullenly as his hat disappeared behind a chimney pot.

"You wanna be careful them paralysed hands don't slip off your cheque book and *bounce* you off the roof ...!"

And Other Tales of Horror

Twenty minutes later, I found myself in the same drinking den where I'd first met Fiona two years earlier and started whining like a hyena into my *Froth* ... *until I remembered the postcard she'd sent Ray and how I ought to look up a Miss West at Scotland Yard ...*

I walked in and stated my case to the Desk sergeant.

"Piss off you little sod, or I'll lock you up for the night ..."

I went all the way back to the Knacker's Yard and started whining like a hyena again...

"You still drink in here, do you ...?" came a voice.

Red-eyed and bleary, I made an initial attempt to look up, but I had too much trouble putting him into focus, and so I looked down again.

"Your face is familiar," I said, glumly. "But I don't recognise your shoes ..."

"Yeah. *You* know *me*. I'm in the *oil* business ..."

I looked up again.

"We're going on a pub crawl tonight and we wondered whether you wanted to come along?"

"Where?"

"Don't know. But we plan to finish up on the Thames ..."

"That's a coincidence," I said.

"Oh?"

"That's where I'm *living* at the moment ..."

"What, on the Thames?"

"No. Not *on* it. *In* it ..."

The following morning I woke up in a panic to find myself floating past Tower Bridge in the *Hun's Helmet* ...

"Aaaaaaaaaaarrrgh ...!"

By the time I'd clambered fore and aft and exhausted all possiblities of survival which didn't involve getting wet, the Pool of London was receding behind me, and I was drifting away downriver at such an increasing velocity that I overtook a train of empty barges all floating in the same direction and a working sand dredger straining its engines to keep pace with the outgoing tide ...

What can you do without oars?

It's a sorry thing to own up to, but I really didn't have the faintest idea how to stop myself. Generations of seafarers must have been turning in their tea chests as I draped my arms and legs over the side and kicked out randomly at the water to try to steer the boat clear of the fast lane ...

Two minutes later, I was lying flat out exhausted in an inch of bilge and staring up out of the boat at a derelict warehouse fronting the south side of the river, all over the blackened face of which was an astonishing graffiti message in white paint:

DEXTER KITEHAWK – THE MAN THEY COULDN'T GAG!

"*Strewth* ...!" I wheezed.

BLAAAAARE !!!

All of a sudden, I was sent spinning around in circles as the hapless helmet came within three nautical inches of being scythed in two by the *Vera*

Lynn, a Thames pleasure cruiser full of Kraut tourists on their way back from invading choice scenes of riverside development rising from the rubble scattered by their previous generation, and almost sunk in the propwash ...

"*Piss* off!!!" I yelled, like Barnacle Bill Bonehead himself, rattling my fist at something I could only see clearly once in each revolution of the compass.

But it was a lucky break, really.

Because *there* I was, still hastily rearranging my plans for the day to accommodate lunch in Belgium, when I spun close enough to the bank (north side) to sling out a rope and moor myself to the *Prospect of Wapping* pub.

I couldn't find any signs of life when I stepped up onto the landing stage-cum-terrace, so I checked to make sure my line was secure, got back on board and took the opportunity of another doze, setting my internal alarm for first bell as I did so.

As soon as I'd navigated the necessary passage of time, I strolled in through the back exit, ordered a pint and came back out onto the terrace.

About five minutes later, some irate barman sporting a bow-tie demanded to know in an antipodean accent if I'd finished my drink and told me to clear off because my boat was upsetting the customers and spoiling the view.

"Is *that* so?" I said.

"That's *so*," he said.

I hurled my glass through his rear window, casually went to step back into the boat, caught my right foot on the far rowlock ... and fell head-first into the river.

SPLASH!

"Pity Judge Jeffries doesn't still hold his *Bloody Assize* here!" he shouted at me, as I swam off with my *Hun's Helmet* in tow.

"As a matter of fact," I yelled back, "He was my *Grandad*. It was probably *him* who transported *your* lot out there in the first place! Why come back for more...?"

"Get on to Wapping police station ..." I heard him shout to another barman who'd surfaced to inspect the damage.

"Don't forget to hide your swag-bag first!" I yelled, just before I swallowed a mouthful of chemical waste. "Fucking convicts ..."

I never did hear from Wapping police station, and I was already in such a mood of dark depression that it would have been all the same to me if I had.

At Limehouse, I moored myself to a newly-constructed Thames walkway and went to sleep again, with my soaking-wet clothes steaming in the midday sun...

Enter the Bleeding Orchestra

I woke up paralysed from the neck down, rueing my lot with some conviction.

The Man They Couldn't Gag?

That was a laugh.

Two years work down the drain, the world's deadliest criminal still on the loose, and not a *cent* left.

No pay.

No nothing.

I didn't even have the *videos* to pass the cold winter evenings.

Not only *that*, but things were about to take a turn for the decidedly worse as a voice of doom suddenly boomed out from above:

"It's ...

An Ill Wind

That blows *nobody* any good ..."

Deep Throat

I opened my eyes to find an old tramp peering down into the boat at me.

"Why," I said, "Who's farted?"

I could have sworn I'd seen him somewhere before.

"There's an ill wind blowing right up my trouser-leg as a matter of fact," I said ... just as a great icy blast tore up my strides and nearly blew my *nifter* off ...

What happened to the spring sunshine?

"You don't dress for the weather," he said.

"Can't you piss off?" I said.

But he wouldn't *have* any of it.

I was a captive audience.

And it wasn't long before the roles were reversed and I was rattling out my life story in glorious technicolour and giving away all the secrets on the case.

What could it matter now?

"I've been all around the world," I droned, "Australia, America, Russia, China. I've even been to Torremolinos, but *I* couldn't find him ..."

"Adolf Flite," he mumbled. "*Him* ..." (I wasn't taking any notice). "Did you ever think to look in Germany?"

I stared out into space, downriver.

"I *never* did ..."

Suddenly I wasn't paralysed any more ...

I leapt up, not knowing whether to *kiss* him or *mug* him.

"'Ere," I said on the way by, "You couldn't spare us a few bob for a cup of tea, could you?"

He shrugged his shoulders.

"It's *you* ought to give *me* money," he said.

"Get fucked," I mumbled.

The word *Germany* was written in neon lights in my brain ...

"You'll be sorry ..." he called after me. "*You'll be sorry* ..."

Dance of the Mannequins

"TAXI!" I yelled, as I hit the Commercial Road.

"Yes, mate? Where to?"

I got in the back.

"My flat," I said.

"Don't bother telling me where it is ..."

"Nob Hill ..."

"Oh yeah?"

"Yeah," I said. "*Old* Street to you ..."

"And which direction would *Sir* like me to approach it from? North, south, east or west?"

"Cut the lip or you won't get a tip ..."

"Right you are, then ..."

And so saying, he tore off into the lunchtime traffic at about three miles an hour.

"Actually," I said, "You can approach it via an off-licence, if it *is* all the same to you ..."

There was a pause.

"Celebrating?" he asked.

"You *could* say that ..."

"Won the pools?"

"Better than that," I affirmed.

"Fallen in love?"

"Better *still*," I said. "I've found out where Adolf Flite is ..."

"Really?" he said.

There was another pause.

"Who's Adolf Flite?" he suddenly piped up.

I tapped the side of my nose.

"Never you mind," I said.

"Go on," he persisted, "Who is he? Long lost uncle?"

"Long lost *uncle*?" I laughed. "I should think he *ain't*. He's only just about the world's most notorious *criminal* ..."

"Yeah, *go* on," he said. "He can't be *that* notorious. *I've* never heard of him..."

"You *will*. Mark my words ..."

"I've heard of an Adolf *Hawksmoor*. He built that church over there – St Ann's. *He* was a notorious criminal ..."

"Fancy ..." I said, wandering off.

"Do you read much literature?"

"Lager?"

"*Not* lager. Literature ..."

"Can't you go any faster?"

"This is the A13. You must not be from around here ..."

"I'm a Londoner, mate. Born and bred ..."

"Yeah, but you're not an *Eastender*, are you?"

"So?"

"Shakespeare – *he* was from the East End ..."

"What?"

"Born in *Stratford*, wasn't he ..."

"Can't you take a short cut?"

"Matter of urgency, is it?"

"You *could* say that ..."

He suddenly shot off up a side street, and for the next few minutes I had quite a job hanging on to my hat ...

Eventually, he pulled over by an off-licence in Hackney.

"Won't be a tick ..." I said, as I breezed across to inspect the window display.

Trouble was, I didn't have any money.

So I went and borrowed some off the cab driver.

He must have thought he was helping out in some great matter of law and order.

Which, in a way, he was.

"Where's your beer?" I said to the proprietor.

"We don't stock much really," he had the nerve to say. "Don't get much call for it. Not in *here*, anyway ..."

I let out an involuntary raspberry and started laughing ...

"No *beer*?" I said. "What do you mean?"

"This is a *Wine* Shop. Plenty of vintage wines. Not much *beer*, though ..."

I wandered outside and looked up at his sign.

Then I wandered back in again.

"When I say *beer*," I said, "What I *actually* mean, of course, is *lager* ..."

"*Lager* you say?"

"Lager," I affirmed, hopefully.

"No, I don't believe ..." he hesitated, "... No ... I – *wait there*!"

While he was out the back, I took the opportunity to lean over the counter, ring up his till, and half-inch a roll of notes and a pocketful of small change lying therein.

Five minutes later, following all kinds of clanking and groaning noises, he reappeared, puffing and wheezing, and pushing an upright trolley.

And *on* that trolley was ... a party-size can of *Allied Froth*!

About *seven* litres-worth ...

"Is that heavy?" I asked, hardly being able to conceal my delight.

"It's made of gun-metal ..."

"I know," I said. "Outrageous, isn't it ...?"

"If you can lift it," he said, "You can have it on the house ..."

"Why," I said, "That's pretty decent of you. Perhaps I ought to lighten it a bit first. Got a can opener?"

"You won't need one. It's got a ring-pull – but don't open it in here. The man who delivered it gave very specific instructions on that point ..."

"Oh?" I said. "And who was that?"

"Travelling salesman of some sort. Here you are, he left a calling-card ..."

Martin Von Leithard
Allied Froth Promotions
Mannequin Arms, Chalk Farm

"Now, that's a stroke of luck," I said. "Can I keep the card as well?"

"Be my guest ..."

"You couldn't give us a hand out to my cab with this thing, could you?"

"You don't *want* much for your money, do you ...?" he said sarcastically, but he grabbed hold of the trolley all the same.

He must have been glad to see the back of it.

"Thanks," I said, as he helped me heft it onto the rear seat.

"Don't mention it ..."

"And here's two-bob for your trouble ..." I said.

He looked at it twice, mind you.

And then he got ready to push the empty trolley back into the shop.

"Thanks for nothing ..." he mumbled.

"Yeah," I said, as we drove off. "Buy yourself a crate of *Hirondelle*. It's *your* money, anyway ..."

I got out the roll of notes.

"Here," I said to the driver, "Here's fifty quid in advance ..."

"You found some money, then?" he enquired.

"Yeah," I said. "They had a cash machine in there ..."

"*Where*? In the *off-licence*?"

"That's right ..."

"Robot banking," he said, philosophically. "It's springing up all over the place ..."

"It was in *there*," I said.

"It'll take over the world one day ..."

"Listen," I said, "I ain't got time to discuss robot banking systems. Ferry me to Chalk Farm instead ..."

"You changing your order?"

"Mannequin Arms ..."

"I know it," he said. "Underneath the railway arches, painted completely black on the outside ..."

"What's it like on the inside?"

"Same. And it's full of waxworks and stuffed dummies ..."

"Staff or customers?"

I didn't have much luck with that can of *Allied Froth*.

I couldn't get the ring-pull off for love nor money.

Not that this was any cause for a lurch to the suicidal, mind you.

Since we were heading for a pub, there was no reason why my suddenly overbooked schedule couldn't be juggled to accommodate a little mixing of business with pleasure when I got there.

Except that by the *time* we got there it was *closed* ...

I stepped out of the cab and tried to peer in the windows.

But *they* were all painted black as well.

"In case you're shocked by my next actions," I said, "Remember I'm on police work ..."

So saying, I waited for a train to pass overhead, looked up and down the street, pulled out my gun and shot the lock off the front entrance ...

The first thing I noted as I breezed in was that the bar was full of *Allied Froth* pumps, and so I siphoned myself off a pint and marched up the back staircase.

When I reached the manager's office, I raised my gun, kicked the door down and burst in ...

Von Leithard was sitting behind his desk, smiling, in his Nazi cap.

"You," I said, pulling up a chair, "Are *nicked* ..."

I spent the next thirty minutes reading him his rights before I realised I was talking to a waxwork.

I've been had, I thought ...

After rifling his desk and finding only circumstantial evidence of his existence, I finished my pint and went to storm off again, forgetting how potent the poison was ...

By the time I reached the landing, my right and left legs had turned respectively to jelly and lead, and I fell head-first down the staircase.

I climbed in through the cab window.

"Any luck?" asked the cabbie.

"Depends which way you look at it ..."

"Any requests?"

"Yeah," I said. "You keep a wrench handy in this crate?"

"In the tool-box ..."

"Do us a favour," I said. "Go get it for us ..."

Once he'd delivered the said wrench into my hands, he got back in the cab and turned the engine over while I went to work on the party-seven.

"Where to, then?" he asked.

"Know any safecrackers?"

"No. You having trouble back there?"

"Old Street," I said. "ASAP ..."

He drove off.

"So," he said at length, "Are you going to tell me about Adolf Flite then ... or not?"

"Well," I said, "There's this *plot*, see, and ... oh, never mind ..."

"Why don't you try *heating* it ...?"

"What does that do?" I queried.

"Well," he said, "It sometimes works with bottle-tops and jars you can't unscrew. Run them under the hot tap. The metal expands, or contracts, or something like that ..."

"I could give it a try ..."

I pulled out my lighter and sat there waving the flame underneath it all the way from Camden Town to City Road.

"Any joy back there ...?"

"What ...?"

We'd got caught in a traffic tailback and were crawling along at tortoise-speed past a queue of people on the pavement, all standing outside the most monstrously ugly building I'd ever seen ...

"Well," he droned on, "If you won't tell me *who* he is, why don't you tell me *where* he is? You said you'd *found* him ..."

"Germany ..." I mumbled absent-mindedly.

"*Germany*? Whereabouts in Germany?"

The Barbican Theatre.

We were crawling along outside the *Barbican* Theatre.

I swear I could hear those screeching violins right out on the street ...

"Did you hear what I said?" he asked, partially craning his neck round at me.

"What was that?"

"Whereabouts in *Germany* is Adolf Flite?"

Whereabouts?

With my heart sinking like a stone, I realised I didn't know.

No idea.

No idea at all.

"Why," I said, "How *big* is Germany?"

"Big *enough* ..."

"*OW* !!!" I yelled, as the cumulative heat caused me to drop the blunderbus...

"You alright?"

"PULL OVER ...!"

Summoning up the colossal effort of will needed to lug the can of *Froth* with me, I got out of the cab, bumped it down onto the pavement, turned it on its side, casually rolled it along to the front of the queue ... *and stood it back upright.*

Then I ripped the ring pull off and sauntered a few paces away to a safe distance ...

A little plastic hand popped out holding a toy gun.

The finger pulled on the trigger, and a white flag sprung from the end of the barrel.

There was a message printed on the flag:

Bang!

"What a let-down ..." I mumbled.
I sauntered back to the puzzled queue, rolled it into the foyer and took my leave ...

I hadn't gone more than a few paces, when somebody rolled it back out onto the *pavement* again ... *and it came to rest at my feet.*

The ensuing explosion was roughly equivalent to 30,000 tons of TNT and blew windows out seventeen miles away.
On my way up past the NatWest Tower I passed the farting cab driver from New Orleans on his way down, but the Barbican was still standing ...

CHAPTER 31
CASTING THE RUNES

I felt several pairs of eyes watching me from behind spyholes as I passed down the dimly-lit corridor towards my luxury bachelor apartment at Old Street...

Two years.

I had that strange sensation that all wanderers have after returning from a long voyage.

Home.

It seemed shrunken in size to me – small and unfamiliar – like a distant memory.

I hardly knew my own front door, with its green paint beginning to peel around the edges.

"Where am I ...?" I mumbled, as a piece of Thames sewage slid out of my hat and dripped down my face.

I was in the wrong block.

I had a *yellow* door ...

Damning all council architects and their taste for sterile duplication as I went, I zipped round to the adjacent building and hunted down the equivalent mirror image No. 13.

Once located, I hesitated before inserting my key, wondering whether I should test it for booby traps.

Then I thought, *fuck it.*

The neighbours weren't *that* clever.

In *any* case, I was too curious to know what a backlog of about fourteen hundred unopened postal deliveries would look like to stand there poncing around on the doorstep.

As for the *postman*, well ...

He must have been some sort of Einstein himself.

Who the fuck he'd been delivering *my* mail to was a mystery, because I burst through the door and immediately got floored by an avalanche of *seven* letters.

No lorryload of Polish beer from that chain letter I'd answered two years' earlier, nor anything else for that matter.

Three were clearly bills, and I tore them up without opening them.

The other four I tossed aside in my rush to get to the fridge ...

A damp patch on the floor signalled that those bastards at the Electricity Board had cut me off and defrosted me, which meant I had no lights either, and no power to cook by.

Not that I had any *food*, mind you ...

There was nothing *in* it except a half-drunk two-years'-old bottle of milk.

By the looks of things, the other half had long since broken out and gone off to attack the milkman.

The freezer compartment was just as disappointing. All I could find was a solitary bag of frozen peas, and although they might not have been *frozen* any more, they might well have come in handy as shotgun pellets they were so stale.

One look in the bathroom told me that I wouldn't be going *hungry* though: *Sprouting up in the bath was one of the best potato crops I'd ever seen ...*

It was probably around late afternoon by the time I'd completed my tour of the indoor trenches, though it was always difficult to be certain of the time of day in a first floor flat whose windows all looked out onto an enclosed central courtyard more-or-less permanently shunned by the light. Mornings would break and evenings would set in that courtyard, like the subtle changes from one shade to another on a municipal decorator's colour-card, rarely uplifting the soul, but occasionally the soles of the feet as the casual traveller quickened his pace and hurried through on his way to places of more cheerful aspect.

Cor dear, I thought. *I'd forgotten how dark this place was. It's like fucking perpetual night out there ...*

The *bedroom* was even worse. The grease on the window-pane was so thick, that if there hadn't been a funny face carved into the condensation I'd have needed an oxy-acetylene torch just to cut my way through to find it.

If I'd had any food, I could have probably cooked breakfast on it.

Such were the home comforts that greeted the returning hero, and persuaded him of no reason to break his recently acquired habit of giving each successive passing location the benefit of a quick forty winks.

To *which* end, he pulled back the sheets, brushed off the mummified dandruff and sunk down onto the bed.

Sunk being the operative word.

And *drowned*.

Alive ...

I woke up with a start moments later, under the terrible delusion that I'd just witnessed Dirk give a Royal Command Performance at the Barbican for the Queen Mother ...

I was strapped to a seat in the front row, unable to move, while a group of grating violins accompanied him on a medley of terrace anthems from Highbury football ground.

The climax came when he left the piano to sing an unaccompanied serenade to Her

Royal Highness through a microphone positioned at the front of the stage.

There was only one line to this song:

Viz. "I was an organ grinder's monkey down the Old Kent Road, down the Old Kent Road, down the Old Kent Road ..." (etc), and he kept yodelling it louder and louder while the Queen Mum sat there rubbing her hands with a rapt expression on her face, and then all of a sudden he stopped, looked straight at me and announced that he wanted a volunteer from the audience to accompany him on the high notes ...

I lay there mopping my brow in relief and listening to the pulse racing in my ears.

But there *was* somebody *singing*, though ...

I roused myself and peeked out through the curtains:

Long shadows were drawing across the courtyard, and *there* – in the midst of the lengthening gloom – was the figure of Mrs Bagpope-Brindisi, my downstairs neighbour, hanging up her washing and mouthing the foulest, most raucous rendition of *You'll Never Walk Alone* I'd ever heard ...

I couldn't quite wrench the window open as fast as I would have liked.

So I put my fist through it.

Cor, it did narf hurt ...

Ten minutes later, after I'd managed to wrap a towel round the wounds, I stuck my head through the hole in the glass:

She was still at it.

"Oi! *You* down there!" I yelled. "Can't you *shut up*? There's people trying to *sleep* up here!"

Since she didn't appear to have heard me, I went and got the bag of stale peas and chucked a few at her.

She held out her hand as if to test for rain.

So I dropped the lot on her ...

When she got up off the deck, she looked round to see what was going on:

"*Oo*," she said, adjusting her bifocals, "Is that *you*? Have you *returned*? Have you *come back* ...?"

"DID YOU *HEAR* ME?" I screamed at her.

"You *know* I'm a bit hard of hearing. You're like a *bad penny*, you are ..."

"WELL, SHUT THAT FUCKING *ROW* UP, DO *YOU* HEAR? OR I'LL COME DOWN THERE AND LAY ONE ON YOU!!!"

"I *said* to my Harry," she droned on, "It'll be a sorry day when *he* returns – you mark my words ..."

"Get fucked, you old bat ..."

"What did *you* say?"

"I *said*," I yelled, "I'M SURPRISED THE COUNCIL HAVEN'T COME ROUND AND CARTED YOU *OFF*, YOU OLD BAT ...!"

"Pardon?"

"CLEAN YOUR BLEET'N' *EARS* OUT, I SAID!!!"

"You want *reporting*, you do," she said, as she took in her last string vest and wandered out of earshot.

"Stupid old cow!" I cursed.

As I stumbled back into the darkening room, I stubbed my toe on an old piece of cheese, fell arse over head onto the floor and lay there cursing the Electricity Board for cutting me off and badmouthing anybody else I could think of ... before hearing her start up all over again in the downstairs flat with a medley of East End blitz-spirit dirges.

Banging up and down on the floor didn't help, especially as I had shards of glass from the broken window embedded in it (– embedded in my fist, that is –) so I crawled out into the kitchen in search of some candles which I suspected lay hidden under the sink, the illumination of my immediate environment being the obvious priority.

The *first* one I tried to light must have been damp, because it flared up and seemed to go out again.

"What *is* it with this place ...?" I mumbled.

In the end, I chucked it back into the box where I'd got it, lugged the box out into the front room and started rummaging around for another one.

SWOOOOOOSH ...!

All of a sudden, a great yellow flash lit up the windows and a volley of rifle fire peppered the room ...

RAT-TAT-TAT-TAT-*TAT-TAT-TAT* ... PING!
I dived for cover thinking the Corporation were across the courtyard ...

Then, amid an explosion of green and red starbursts, showers of sparks, bangs, crackles and a great flood of *deja vu* going all the way back to my days of maritime service in the Chinese merchant marine, came a volley of a *different* kind.

This time in the direction of my front door ...

When I found Mrs Bagpope-Brindisi standing there, arms folded for combat, something told me she hadn't come up to admire my impromptu pyrotechnic display.

"Yes?" I enquired politely.

"*Look,*" she said, "It's about the racket you're making ..."

"Oh yes?" I said. "And what racket is *that*, may I ask?"

Just at that moment a molten fireball from a roman candle shot past my ear and singed her right sidebald ...

"Eeeeeek ...!"

Slapping her hand to her cheek, she rubbed the powder burn across her nose and started flapping up and down and squawking like a turkey ...

"What are you *doing* in there?!!!" she was screaming. "Are you *mad* ...?!!!"

"What I do in the privacy of my own home is certainly no business of *yours* !" I yelled at her indignantly, whilst leaning an arm on the door frame and trying to adopt a complacent mien in the face of the increasing heat blasting up the back of my shirt.

"You'll burn us all in our beds!!!" she continued hysterically, alternately clucking and wheezing like a mongoose.

"Don't be so *ridiculous*, madam," I said. "I've always considered these apartments a little dingy for my taste and there is no harm in my wishing to brighten things up a little ..."

"With *fireworks?*!!!" she screeched.

"*Certainly*, with fireworks, though I'm currently toying with the idea of sticking some gelignite into my light fittings and waiting for the LEB to re-connect me. It's about time Old Street was put back on the map, don't you agree...?"

"I shall phone the police!"

"I *am* the police, madam. Or did you not know?"

"You should be locked up ... *in a mental home* !"

"Come, madam," I said, with a grand gesture of my arm, "Join me inside for a candlelit barbecue ..."

She started backing off ...

"I'm going to tell my *Harry* when he comes in ..."

With the corridor acting as the main outlet for the thick, black smoke furling up behind me, it wasn't clear at that point whether Mrs Bagpope-Brindisi had vanished in it, or gone back downstairs.

But *gone* she appeared to have done.

"That's right ...!" I started to yell after her ... *when I suddenly realised my clothes had caught light* !

In a mad, panicked frenzy, I leapt out into the hall, tore my shirt and herringbone strides off and turned round to find the flat ablaze and rapidly going out of control ...

"FIRE! FIRE!" I yelled, jumping up and down frantically, "HELP! HELP...!!!"

I ran every which way, banging on knockers and ringing on bells, but if any of the other residents were at home, they certainly weren't letting on.

They're not fucking silly, I thought.

What happened to good neighbourliness?

Or all hands to the pumps?

Gone the same way as those little lice-infested terraced houses of fond collective memory, probably, along with the people who lived in them, if the overwhelming response to my cry for assistance was anything to go by.

And this left me with little choice but to grab a sand bucket and unwind the fire hose, temporarily oblivious to the fact that the corridor was turning into such a choking black funnel of smoke, that the location of my front door was about to become a complete mystery.

I stood the bucket down with a clank.

Then I lifted the nozzle of the hose up to my face:

All of a sudden, a jet carrying about eight gallons of foam shot out the end and blew me backwards thirty feet along the carpet ...

In the process, I dropped the nozzle and kicked the bucket over.

By the time I'd got to my feet, the hose was jerking away down the corridor all by itself and spitting like a cartoon cobra ...

For a moment, I was too astonished to move ... *until the transitory appearance of my front door in the eye of the firestorm sent me racing after the serpent, fighting my way through the smoke and foam like a West German street rioter ...*

"Aaaaa*aaaaaieee* ...!" I yelled, as I seized its venomous throat in a rattlesnake-tamer's hold and dived headfirst into the inferno ...

The *blaze* was out within seconds.

The rest of my *windows* followed suit as I went berserk trying to let air in.

I think it must have escaped my attention that it was starting to rain.

Because the *first* thing I did after I'd staggered back outside was to climb up onto a radiator and smash the skylight ...

I stepped down to survey the scene in the hall:

There was a thick, black coating of soot everywhere, certainly, and a foul smell of gunpowder and burnt carpets.

What the *neighbours* would make of it when they got home from work, I dreaded to think.

I had no idea of the extent of the damage *inside* my flat because, without any light, I couldn't see shite.

As I stepped backwards, I accidentally entangled my foot in the handle of the overturned fire bucket and went hopping and clanking around the floor like a frog in a money box ...

Kerjangle ... *KLANG* ! Kerjangle ... *KLANG* ! Kerjangle ...

"Aaaaaaaaaaaargh ..."

All of a sudden, I tripped forwards into the door opposite my own, nutted it square on the centre panel and cracked the wood down the middle.

DOK! ... *before tumbling over into a heap on the carpet.*

"You *charmless* plank of shit ...!"

I got up in such a temper, that I swung my foot at the offending door and broke it clean in two ...

CRUNCH!

Then I watched it fall inwards ...

CRASH !!!

Good job the *owner* wasn't at home.

Whoever he was.

"Now, *that's* a stroke of luck ..." I said out loud to myself.

There I was, just about to launch a kick designed to put the first fire bucket into outer space, when I saw gleaming up at me from the pile of dislodged sand, a half bottle of whisky

...

In the back of my mind, I had a vague memory of burying it well over two years earlier, though I must admit, the neighbours being what they were – *ie. a bunch of crooks* – I was surprised nobody had found it and polished it off.

I unscrewed the top and took a slug.

"Hm ..." I murmured, "A drop of ginger wouldn't go amiss ..."

I did stand there for a few seconds considering the ethical implications of what I was about to do, but, after deciding that it was all in the public interest, I kicked aside the remaining fragments of my neighbour's door, strolled in and raided his fridge, coming away with a litre bottle of coke, a handful of ice cubes and a suitably large glass from his kitchen cupboard.

Firefighting was thirsty work.

Not least in the necessity to make some sort of assessment of the post-conflagratory damage, for which purposes I wandered back out into the hall.

"Well," I said to myself, "It'll take a long time to clear *this* mess up ..."

They'd have to get the council decorators in at the very least.

The rain had been steadily pouring in through the skylight ever since I'd smashed it, and a nasty wind was beginning to howl down the corridor and whip up the soot, conditions which seemed as natural as anything as I concluded my internal report. There didn't seem to be much else I could do – at least, not until the technical boys came in – and so I poured myself a generous scotch-and-coke-on-the-rocks and stood there waiting for something to happen.

I must have been in a kind of a trance when, some time later, a piece of half-burnt paper fluttered out of my door and floated past my nose ...

I tried to remember whether I was insured, or whether I had anything worth insuring.

Almost in slow motion, something registered, and I tried to think what it was.

Carrying my drink with me, I wandered in the direction the wind was blowing ...

All of a sudden, it flew up in front of me like a Druidic greetings card and flapped away down the hall ...

Glass in hand, I chased it all the way out onto the staircase, where the sudden eruption of a scream stopped me dead in my tracks ...

"EEEEEEEEEEEEEK!"

Standing in front of me was Mrs Bagpope-Brindisi, looking fit to drop with fright.

"Out of my *way*, Madam!" I bellowed at her. "If I don't catch hold of that death sentence behind you, then we shall all perish at midnight ...!"

She fainted.

CLUNK!

Silly old bat, I thought. *What's the matter with her ...?*

I took the utmost care as I stepped over her prone body, mainly because I didn't want to create any sudden draughts which might dispel the delicate document from its place of temporary rest, nestling on the carpet, just beyond her overworked brain.

As soon as I'd accomplished this manoeuvre, I snatched at the errant piece of litter and gave it the third degree.

It was an *envelope.*

Or rather, a *piece* of one.

The piece containing the *postmark.*

A *recent* one, at that.

And, more importantly, a *stamp.*

From *out* of which gawked the considerably ugly boat-race of the German Chancellor ...

Somewhere inside the burnt-out ruin of my flat was a communication from the Fatherland.

Or what was *left* of it.

The *communication,* that is – not the Fatherland, which I understood still to be standing despite the efforts of the RAF to box its ears.

I certainly didn't *know* anybody in that country, and so it *had* to be connected with the case.

This was the only reasonable conclusion I could come to.

And so, bemoaning myself for not having scrutinised my mail more closely when I arrived earlier in the day, I hurried back to search for the remainder of the letter ...

As I *did* so, I caught sight of my reflection in the propped-open glass doors leading back to the corridor, and realised why she'd fainted.

I nearly fainted as well.

I'd forgotten I'd torn most of my clothes off.

All I had on was one argyll sock and a pair of Bermuda shorts ...

Off I went, crawling around on all fours as I ransacked my flat by matchlight, turfing out all kinds of rubbish into the corridor until I finally emerged with three letters in my hand.

They were all undamaged, and *none* of them was from Germany.

Once again, I was tempted to sling them, but – wary of compounding my folly – I poured myself another drink, moved away from the rain streaming in through the skylight and proceeded to examine them:

I had a feeling I'd seen the *first* one before ...

It turned out to be a note from a firm of solicitors acting for my Uncle Grolly.

Apparently, he'd cut me out of his will at the last minute and left all his cash to his pet goldfish.

He *was,* at present (*according to the letter*), in Parkhurst Prison medical wing and wasn't expected to last the week out.

Since it was dated over two years earlier, I assumed he was already dead.

All of which was of very little interest to me, as I couldn't ever remember having had an Uncle Grolly.

The *second* letter was a reminder notice that I was long overdue for my six-monthly dental inspection ...

My dentist always was a bit of a comedian.

I *mean*, what kind of people become dentists?

You don't just *drift* into it, do you?

The job centre don't just suddenly say, 'There's a vacancy in the local dental practice – report for interview at nine o'clock sharp ...'

Well, *do* they ...?

The *third* letter was a disappointment as well. Made up of bits cut out of old newspapers and magazines, it came complete with a London postmark:

DEXTER KITEHAWK
YOU ARE BEING WATCHED

I looked about me.

Since I couldn't *see* anybody watching me, I assumed the correspondent had his facts wrong and tossed it aside.

But where was that *German* letter?

I couldn't find a single fragment of it until I went to take another slug of whisky-and-coke and, as I raised my head, saw it pinned to the ceiling by an extinct firework rocket ...

It was covered in gunpowder stains, but – albeit minus a portion of the envelope – still appeared to be intact.

I therefore ripped it open in a fevered frenzy ...

Inside were a couple of travel tickets and a small printed invitation card:

Dear Occupant

You have been selected entirely at random by our central computer in Cologne to attend the unveiling of the latest product in our Allied Froth range.

Accommodation will be provided at the picturesque Schloss Froth, which overlooks Lahnstein-am-Rhein.

There, as an exclusive guest of the Flite family, you are invited to the First Annual Lager Barons Ball, during which the Grand Tasting will take place.

Entrance is by fancy dress only. Two tickets for the Orient Express have been provided for you (and a companion of your choice) to ensure your comfort en route.

Herr Flite, Chief Executive, A F International

I read it, but I didn't *believe* it.

I started laughing:

It was so *simple*.

An *invite* to the Schloss Froth?

I could have stayed at home for the previous two years and waited for Adolf Flite's address to drop through my letter-box.

And *then* I started *crying:*

I could probably have got it two years earlier from Directory Enquiries ...

What was he planning to unveil? What was in the 'latest product'? What would happen to those who tasted it? Who would be there? And ... *when* was it?

In the sudden dread that that I'd already missed it, I scanned the invitation for dates and found that I had a spare day to organise things – it was for the coming weekend, and my first priority was clearly going to be to get suitably togged up ...

As I drained my glass, I reflected on an upturn in fortune that was so long overdue it almost qualified as an international scandal.

There was little doubting the size of the win was worth the wait, though.

Just think, I said to myself, *how lucky I've been out of all the millions of people round the world to have been chosen at random to attend the crime of the century.*

What were the odds on *this* happening?

And it was *fancy dress* !

Nobody would *recognise* me ...

"I'M RUNNING A BIT LOW ON SCOTCH!" I yelled out at the top of my voice ... *in rectification of which dilemma, I wandered off to raid my neighbour's flat for a second time.*

This time to see whether he had any *alcohol* stashed in it ...

"Strewth!" I yelled. "Fancy keeping your dirty clothes in the fridge!"

Of course, I realised soon enough that I'd homed-in on his tumble-drier by mistake, and so I left the open bottle of coke inside it, closed the door and switched it on.

Well, I owed him a good turn ...

As for the *fridge*, well ...

Disappointment at finding it as impoverished of food and drink as my own gave me cause for a more lengthy inspection than had earlier been the case.

Though it was far from *empty*.

I hadn't noticed it *first* time round, but every single shelf was packed with *film* cartridges.

Except for the fruit compartment.

Not that there was any *fruit* in it, mind you.

But there *were* a couple of bottles of *Froth* ...

Thinking he must be some kind of camera buff, I helped myself to his armchair and tried to remember who he was.

Two years ago the place was unoccupied, as I recalled.

For a bloke with an expensive electronics habit, I mused, *he doesn't buy very resilient furniture ...*

This revelation came to me as I noted the contrast between – *on the one hand* – the array of cameras, tripods and recording equipment surrounding me – *and on the other* – a nasty gash in the surface of his teak coffee table, courtesy of the bottle top I'd just levered off on it.

I got up and gave it a kick to see if it would collapse.

In the absence of any evidence to confirm this, I smashed the now-empty bottle of scotch against one of its legs ...

"*Blimey* ..." (I scooted out of the way of the buckling heap ...)

All four legs did the splits and the table-top crashed flat on the floor in the middle of them as though the whole thing had been run over by a cartoon steamroller.

I kicked it round the room a bit, wondering whether I had time to get onto a French polishers from the *Yellow Pages* and have the thing restored before he got home from work ... *but on deciding that I didn't, I went and drew a funny moustache onto a portrait of Mussolini hanging on the wall instead.*

Then I sat down again.

And it was *while* I was sitting there that I noticed a cable sellotaped to the carpet ...

In *one* direction it was linked to a load of video equipment in a corner of the room.

In the *other* it trailed round the door frame and out into the corridor.

So I decided to *follow* it ... *outside* ... over the ceiling ... *and down the opposite wall* ... where it disappeared straight through a hole into my flat!

"Why," I shouted, "This is preposterous ...!"

I lit the blunderbus and wandered back into my apartment to discover that every room had a video camera and a boom microphone mounted on the wall ...

Closed circuit TV!

Fucking peeping Tom, I thought ...

I went back and smashed the rest of his flat up, including every piece of electronic surveillance equipment therein.

Then I returned to smash all the cameras and mikes in my *own* flat.

Then I went back out into the hall (*where it was still pissing buckets through the skylight*), smashed the top off the second bottle of *Froth* and started lurching and staggering around – *still half-undressed* – and singing the 1981 Tottenham Hotspur FA Cup Final single as performed on *Top of the Pops*.

And it was in *this* state that Mrs Bagpope-Brindisi found me for the umpteenth time that evening.

Only *this* time she *didn't* faint.

This time she was accompanied by her husband.
Harry Bagpope-Brindisi.
A 22-ton docker from Tilbury ...

CHAPTER 32
ONE MINUTE TO MIDNIGHT

But he was a nice bloke.

He only chinned me once or twice.

And suspended me from the skylight by my Bermudas.

And then he called the police to save me further damage.

What a toff.

"You, Sir," I called out to him as the Filth carted me away, "Are a gent. May I ever have the opportunity to do so, I shall shake your hand ..."

"Get in the van!" yelled the Sergeant, giving me a hefty kick to my rear end.

All of a sudden, Harry Bagpope-Brindisi broke away from his restrainers and took a wild but fruitless lunge at me ...

"Let me at him ...!" he shouted.

Isn't it funny the things you notice?

While Mrs Bagpope-Brindisi stood back behind the commotion and snivelled into a handkerchief, I saw for the first time that she had a birthmark on her left neck.

In the shape of a Dr Marten boot.

The six-hole steel-toecap 'Work Boot'

A nasty little number, camouflaged by its apparent dinkiness.

So-called because it was good for working people over with ...

"'Ere Harry!" I yelled, just before the doors of the meat wagon were slammed shut on me. "I heard some good *news* on the radio today! They've just abolished the dock labour scheme ...!"

I imagine he had a screaming fit at that one, but I wasn't there to see it.

The next thing I remember is waking up that evening in a police cell with a thumping head, a cauliflower lip and a mother and father of a hangover ...

Job Lot

Internal panic struck me as I lay there staring at the four grey walls.

How would I get to the Castle Froth now?

Chances were, I was going to be banged up for the rest of my natural.

73

It looked like my one opportunity had gone, and *with* it – did it but know it – civilisation's one chance of survival.

I had to get *out* of there.

But *how?*

I leapt up off the bench ...

"LET ME OUT OF HERE ...!" I screamed.

I rattled the door and nutted the bars on the hatch ...

"LET ME *OUT* OF HERE, I *TELL* YOU!!!"

"Shut up or I'll come down there and give you a good kicking!" yelled a voice from upstairs.

I sat down again.

But then I got *up* again ... *and sat down again.*

Sooner or later, I started to go over the events of the day and tried to assess what lessons I'd learned.

One.

Never tangle with a docker's wife.

Two.

Never tangle with a docker ...

I shifted about uneasily on the bench.

Primarily, because I hadn't had a decent crap for well over two years and had developed the most atrocious case of piles known to medical science.

In *fact*, I hadn't had any kind of emission at *all* for nearly six weeks.

Not a sausage.

Not a dickie bird.

Fuck Adolf Flite ...

My first priority on getting out would be to buy a couple of pounds of *Granny Smiths* and use them as biological detonators ...

My *second* priority?

Warn the Environmental Health Department of what was in the wind ...

Well ...

The old signal lights might have been stuck on red, but *something* was sure as hell coming down the southbound tunnel ...

Why now?

And why *here?*

Of all the places to get a result, the current surroundings were better suited to bricking things up than letting bricks go.

Hang on, I thought, *what's this I've spotted ...?*

Well, well, well ...

An *en suite* bucket.

As private as you like, hidden away in full view, right there in the middle of the cell.

Demure, forlorn ... an exquisite enamel ... er ... *chipped* enamel ... er ...

stainless? ... steel ... er ... rusty ... ugly tin can of a bucket.

Or something like that.

I peeked in to see whether the tide was in or out.

Hm.

Out, apparently.

Although ...

I thought I detected a slight *odor* ... (late-night kebab, possibly?) ... and the mere hint of a sheen ... (or was it a stain?) ... round the rim.

I paced up and down in a bow-legged circle.

Decisions, decisions.

Not that it wouldn't have been for the want of *trying*, mind you, but I couldn't hold on till they let me out of prison.

Well, *could* I?

In any event, I could feel the beginnings of a chain reaction rumbling along the old radiators, heralding the onset of a meltdown ...

Casting modesty adrift, I therefore descended on the dubious receptacle, parked the truck and waited.

Before long, I was heaving and ho-ing like a Norse opera singer.

I'd had one poking out for the last week, but I could never quite get hold of it.

This, however, was redundant thinking as I gripped the sides of the bucket in fevered anticipation and got ready to drop a real clanger ...

Hello, I thought.

The rumbling had *stopped.*

Temporarily.

It was stuck half-way.

Half-*out* and half-*in*.

I crouched there sweating.

On the EC scale of sizes it was *well* bigger than a carrot.

In *fact*, by the feel of things, it was close to registering somewhere between a tree-trunk and *Apollo 5*.

I think I began to understand what it was like to give birth.

To a hippo.

Even if I could have *shifted* it, I think I would have *preferred* to shift it back where it *came* from. *I was already in some considerable pain.*

And that was *before* the contractions started again ...

"Oh my *Gawd* ...!" I screamed.

Not only was it *big*, but it was coming out *sideways* to boot ...

It was a breached birth!

"Quick!" I yelled. "Get me a doctor! I want a *Caesarian* ...!"

BANG!

Suddenly, an almighty bomb blew the bucket to bits underneath me, letting out a stink

fit to gas half of China and enough blood to paint three of the four walls crimson ...
"AAAAAAAAAAAAAAARGH ...!"
I leapt up and down trying to fan the flames out from my tormented rear end ...

"Crikey ...!"
When I looked for the offending article amidst the ruins of the bucket, all I found was an hole in the floor.
"Strewth ..."
It must have been going at such speed, and with such an explosive force behind it, that it drilled its way right through the concrete and straight into the Earth!
It was probably just about to surface in Nutwood.
And by the looks of the trace deposits round the rim of the hole, I'd say that the means of propulsion was a little-known four-star brand composed of Zairean prison dishes fermented for two years in a cocktail of tequila and rocket fuel.
The *rice* had now broken out two years after I did, and I was going to have to break out all over again. This time from an *English* gaol ...
There ought to have been some arse-upwards moral that I could have taken to heart in planning my escape – something about trying to squeeze toothpaste back into the tube – *but I couldn't see it.*
It was *disgraceful,* really. *One of Her Majesty's agents locked up in a common police cell.*
What I *really* needed was for somebody to pick up the phone, pull rank and get me released on the grounds of national security, enabling me to breeze out past the front desk blowing raspberries at the Duty Sergeant as I went, but Corkscrews already had a poor track record in that department.
For the time being I was stuck.
No mistake.
And the air in the cell was dangerously volatile ...

I managed to avoid suffocation (just) by tying the Argyll sock round my hooter and using it as a breathing filter, but the mob upstairs were obviously not so resourceful:
By the sounds of outrage coming from that direction I gathered the stink had already penetrated the first landing ...

Here he comes, I thought.
Mr Duty Sergeant.
Clomping down the stairs in his jackboots ... squeak clack ... squeak clack ... (sound of goose-step on floorboard) ... squeak clack ... squeak clack ... Squeak Clack ...
ZING!
He slid back the observation hatch and poked his beady eye in:
Then he start gagging ...

ZUNK! *... and slammed it shut again.*
Then he stomped back off up the corridor.

"*Phew*," I muttered. "*That's* a relief ..."

Hold up!
What's this?
He's coming *back* again ...

Fuck me, I thought, *he's going to open the cell door ... jingle jangle ...* GRUNCH!

This time, he was sporting a *surgical* mask:
"Right!" he shouted. "*You*, sonny, are in *trouble*. What's been going on in here?"

I tried to say, "I take it, then, Sergeant, that you are unfamiliar with *Disaster Survival Syndrome* (DSS), and the psychologically-damaging effects of *Ferry Trauma*..." but, distorted by my ventilation apparatus, it came out sounding like Schnozzle Durante's swan song.

"Are you taking the piss?" he said.
I shrugged my shoulders.
What more could I tell him?
He wandered over to examine the broken slops bucket.
He didn't *like* what he saw ...
Turning to face me, he flexed his braces, twiddled his Blücher moustache and rolled up his sleeve ...

"I suppose plea-bargaining is out of the question?" I said, but this just made things worse. It came out as "A fwee-fwa-fwa, a fwee-fwee-fwee, argy-bargy ..."

Thus provoked, he began to march towards me brandishing a great knotted spud potato of a fist ...

In the Nick of Time

"H'Guvner! Hart Here!"
This timely intervention came as another member of the Filf fraternity poked his head in the door, and — notwithstanding the large clothes peg obstructing his conk — requested a private word outside with the Sergeant.

Or so I interpreted his words.

The *Sergeant*, in turn, fixed me straight in the eye, told me it was merely a "... stay of execution ..." and confirmed that he'd be back for me "... *right away*..."

So saying, he planted his King Edward back in his pocket, went outside and closed the door behind him, looking like a disappointed dentist in a power cut.

Stay of execution?
Did that mean he was going to *hang* me?

To my relief, following a short interlude in which the pair of them stood there whispering in the corridor, I heard both pairs of feet disappear up the staircase ...

Talking of Power Cuts

Five minutes later, all the lights flickered and went out.
It did briefly cross my mind that somebody upstairs might have been testing out a faulty electric chair and had blown all the fuses.
Well, you *hear* these sort of stories, don't you?

Man Hangs Himself in Police Cell

Take my *word* for it.
It's hard enough trying to *shit* in a police cell.
Never *mind* hang yourself.
Unless the difficulty of attempting the *first* procedure leads to an accident of the *second.*
Which I suppose is always possible, given the noted logistics.

Man Accidentally Sits on 'Old Sparky' in Paddington Nick

Officers today wired up a prisoner's commode to the mains as a practical joke went wrong ...

Police Clear-Up Rate Comes Under Scrutiny by National Audit Office Following Complaint by Widows and Orphans Association

Comparisons Made with Chile and Argentina

Or the tabloid version:

Mass Murder Under the Blue Lamp

Cops yesterday denied involvement in the disappearance of a missing LSE Boffin after a garotte was found in a British Transport Policeman's pocket. A spokesman for the Brighton Belle ...

... said it was business as usual, as commuters tucked into a three-piece suite comprising neck-of-stiff, jacket potatoes and leak soup.
Or such were the imaginary headlines with which I chilled myself as I stood there shivering in the dark, waiting for the Sergeant to come back and execute me.
I *mean,* who knows what goes on under the noses of the very public the boys in blue are supposed to protect? Who can say what dreadful deeds are perpetrated in *our* name behind the facade of law and order?
I *mean,* how comes I was the *only* prisoner in this dump?
Perhaps I was the only one *left* ...?

But Not For Long

Eh ...?

Killer Enters Police Cell in Dead of Night ...

For it was *while* I was standing there shivering in the dark, that a key turned silently in the lock, the door creaked ever so slightly on its hinges, and ... *a freezing draught blew in from the corridor.*

A Tide in the Affairs of Men

For a split second, I thought I saw the hand that held the key – like a *detached* hand – *before it disappeared back into the darkness outside, gesturing for me to follow as it went ...*

"Do I *look* fucking silly ...?" I called out hesitantly.
No response.
Doodley-squit.
Zilch.
"Well, *do* I ...?"

If I'd waited any longer I could have probably floated out of there on my own ocean I was that scared.

Because, despite being soaked from the thighs down, there was *one* thing I couldn't deny:
The door was open and a chance for freedom beckoned ...

I stuck my neck out into the corridor and looked both ways:
"Any *murderers* out here ...?"
Left.
Right.
Left *again.*
Right again.
Perceiving nobody out there – *murderers or otherwise* – *I decided the hallway was deserted.*
And so I *bleeding* well scarpered ... up the stairs ... *and on towards the reception area* ... where I paused by the double-doors.
But only long enough to take a deep breath.
After which I pushed them open a crack with my foot ...

Shit.

The Sergeant was sitting behind the desk ...

Wait a minute, though, I thought.
Is he *asleep?*
Perhaps he'd been gassed ...

I couldn't believe my luck.
The man had fallen asleep on duty!
Or *had* he?
He *looked* asleep, but he was sitting bolt upright ...
The desk telephone was off the hook, the handset lying loosely in his right palm as though he'd just received news so shocking that he hadn't been able to replace it on the receiver.
Perhaps his dear old *mum* had just topped herself?
Or perhaps the *Spiritualist* Association had just rung up and cancelled his membership?
Either way, I needed to test the water in some delicate way which wouldn't intrude on his grief.
And so, as a mark of respect, I untied the sock from my nose ... *chucked it across the room and ducked back behind the door.*

I waited a few decent moments, and then – after straining my ears unsuccessfully for evidence of an audible reaction – I peered in:
There it was.
Sitting where it had landed.
On the desk, right under his nose.
And since he hadn't moved, I took it he was in the land of nod ...

I breezed over, grabbed his notebook and pen, and left a message for him:

NO PRISON WAS EVER BUILT COULD HOLD ME, COPPER!
signed, D Kitehawk (The Human Elastic Band)
P.S. Do something about that smell downstairs – it ain't civilised!

In a final piece of daring, I tacked the note to the sock, pinned it all to his chest and stood back admiring my handiwork.
The Human Elastic Band.
But what did it mean?
And *then* I yelled out in fright and jumped back a step ...

"Oh my *Gawd* ...!" I cringed.
I started chewing my fingers ...
His *eyes* were *open* ...!

I soon realised he wasn't *looking* at me, though.
He hadn't even *noticed* me.

Waving my hand up and down in front of his nose failed to elicit a blink.
Not a flicker.
He was staring into space like a man hypnotised, frozen in time ...

All through this, I'd been aware of a repetitive voice coming from the displaced handset, presumably instructing the Sergeant to replace it forthwith, and for some unknown reason I chanced to take it out of his hand and put it to my ear:
"*At the Third Stroke, the Time sponsored by Allied Froth will be Eleven, Fifty-Nine, precisely ... beep! beep! beep! ... At the Third Stroke, the Time sponsored by Allied Froth will be Eleven, Fifty-Nine, precisely ... beep! beep! beep! ...*"

Fear of a different kind gripped me ...
Unable to fathom what was going on, I took one look around me ... *and made a dash for it ...*

A doorway just round the first corner served as my initial pit stop, where I hid myself as best I could, shuffling from one foot to another and intermittently peering out for sign of the old Bill like a fruitcake in a trolley shop.
A passing hearse served to persuade me that time was on the move again, though I must have been stationed there for a good five minutes more, desperately trying to catch my breath, before I understood what kind of an *establishment* I was taking *refuge* outside ...

Sitting in the window on a rug of artificial grass was a giant alabaster headstone:

D. Kitehawk
R.I.P.

In a state of shock, I staggered back onto the street and looked up at the name above the shop:

DARC
Undertakers

It was only when the queue from a late-night bus-stop all screamed and disappeared at my approach, that I realised I was still inappropriately dressed for polite society, and that if I didn't do something about it pretty quick I was going to become a self-fulfilling prophecy and freeze to death in the pose of Lucretia Borgia's chef just after he was told to swallow his professional pride.
To *begin* with, I didn't even know where I was.
I could have been *anywhere* ...

More screaming – well, *this* time, howls of *derision* from a passing coachload of women returning from a hen-night – convinced me of the need to take fast evasive action, and in an attempt to gain myself a breathing space, I jumped over a wall and landed in a railway marshalling yard, somewhere in West London.

Locating an old goods truck full of sand, I climbed on board and fell asleep.

CHAPTER 33
THE MAIDSTONE HAT KILLER

I woke up the following dawn inside a cement mixer on a building site in Rochester, Kent.

Laugh?

The look of *horror* on my face was almost set in concrete.

Of course, I didn't *know* it was Rochester at the time, and I'm not sure I twigged I was inside a cement mixer until I'd climbed out and found my black box flight recorder.

I could see my goods truck, coupled to a lot of others high on a viaduct above me. The sides of the trucks were all flapped down and the trucks were all tipped sideways.

Looking at the situation, I was surprised the *fall* hadn't killed me.

How I'd got into the cement mixer from the mountain of soaking wet sand beneath the viaduct was a mystery, and I could only assume that some early morning navvy had come along and shovelled me up without noticing.

Not that I could *see* any navvies – or anybody else for that matter – but I was bound to encounter *somebody* on the way to the site gates ...

I was *damp* as well as cold, and I *still* wasn't dressed for the Henley Regatta.

By the looks of things, they were putting up some kind of supermarket complex.

It was ugly – but not *that* ugly.

Bang on cue, some burly character suddenly leapt out of the guard hut ...

"Stop right there!" he shouted. "Who are *you?* Where have you been? You're not allowed on this site – where's your pass?"

"Don't worry," I said, gesturing towards the half-finished structure with one hand, and picking a demolition safety helmet out of a wheelbarrow with the other. "I'm the *Architect.* And all this will have to come down again ..."

So saying, I placed the helmet on my head, left him looking dumbfounded and strolled out into the street.

And it was in in this fashion that I followed the road running beside the railway in the hope that it would eventually lead me to a station, *ie. decked out very nicely in Bermuda shorts and crash helmet ...*

At the first sight of a copper, I darted down a sidestreet and jumped into a dustbin, being careful to replace the lid on top of me.

It was a successful piece of evasion, but once again I dallied too long and fell asleep.

I woke up just as the bin was being emptied into a refuse lorry ...

In retrospect, I suppose I was more than lucky that it wasn't the kind that had a *crusher* in the back, though this particular sprinkling of fortune's dust of dreams counted for very little as I came to rest amongst a ripe bed of choice Kentish garbage ...

I was still floundering around and trying to gain my footing when we reached the next port-of-call, a performance which added vital seconds to the escape process and allowed several tons of rancid fish to be dropped on top of me before I managed to scramble out and land amongst a stack of cardboard boxes on the fringe of an early morning street market in the process of being set up.

I didn't *know* it at the time, but I'd acquired another accessory in the *clothing* department:

Hanging down out of the back of my hard hat was a dead kipper, and it was only long after I'd left Rochester that I realised the accompanying smell wasn't inherent to the town ...

"'Ere!" I called out to some bloke selling duffle-coats. "How much do you want for one of *them?*"

"50p each, or £1.50 for three ..."

"That's cheap ..."

"Yeah," he said. "Old stock. Trying to shift 'em before the summer ..."

"Go on ..."

"How many do you want?"

"None. I ain't got any money ..."

"I'll tell you what," he said. "I'll give you one *gratis* ..."

"Why?"

"Because it'll give me a lot of pleasure just to see how you're going to streamline it in with the rest of your wardrobe – the *hat* particularly ..."

"That's no problem ..."

I squeezed my arms into the sleeves and pulled the hood up over the helmet.

"Do you know," he said, "You *remind* me of somebody ..."

"Oh?" I said, trying to inspect myself in his full-length mirror. "Who's that, then?"

"Eddy," he replied.

"Not *Duane* Eddy, surely?"

"No," he said. "*Prince* Eddie. *Royalty.* You related?"

"Yeah," I said. "Only round the wrist, though ..."

"It don't *show*, honest. You look a *treat* now. The last time I saw anybody dressed like that they were crawling out the back of Liberal Party Headquarters the night Idi Amin nationalised Uganda ..."

"Yeah," I said, "Do you just have *one* scriptwriter, or have you got a whole consortium of staff on the payroll?"

"No, I told you, Eddie sends down all my lines direct from the Gaiety Theatre. Andrew Lloyd Webber likes to try 'em out on the man-in-the-street before he puts them on the West End stage. I'll tell him he's on to a winner with this one, shall I ...?"

"I take it I get those *other* two coats for the same price then?"

"Be my guest," he said. "I'm going off for a cup of tea. I've never known business this slow ..."

"Very decent," I said. "You were wrong about the *hat* clashing, but I'll tell you where my real problem is ..."

"Go on," he said, lingering.

"*Lower down ...*"

"Can't help you there ..." he said, and walked off.

Which was a pity.

It was a good coat, but it was only quarter-length.

And it was for ages 5-7.

So it only came down to just below my ribs.

But it was a start, and everything had to be considered as potential for the fancy dress party.

Which is why, out of a deference to respectability, I lost no time in tying the other two coats safely round my waist and going for a wander amongst the shoppers ...

There were quite a few traders out by this time – selling clothes, mainly – though an assortment of other goods were scattered about in isolated pockets of the market.

One of the first of the stalls I passed was selling records, and I found myself strangely drawn to it by the atrocious racket coming out of the loudspeakers positioned thereon ...

"You got a *licence* for all this?" I said.

"What's *your* problem, mate?" said the stallholder.

"*This* one top of the pops, is it?"

"It happens to be *numero uno* – number *one* to you – right at this very moment. How many do you want?"

"What is it?"

"It's a cover version of *Atlantis* – all the proceeds go to the victims and relatives ..."

"Of what?" I enquired casually.

"Of the Danish Ferry Disaster. Where *you* been ...?"

"*Oh* no," I cursed. "Not *another* disaster record ..."

"That's right," he said. "And how many have *you* bought?"

"Wouldn't have it in the house, mate. I think all the proceeds should go to the victims of *disaster records*. Every time there's a major tragedy, they wheel out some was-been for an orgy of self-gratification and free publicity at *my* expense..."

"What's a *was-been?*" he interjected.

"A *has*-been who *never was* ..."

"It all sounds like sour grapes to me. Are you a failed musician or something?"

"As a matter of fact," I said, "I was personally commissioned to record a cover version of Tennessee Ernie Ford's *Sixteen Tons* only last year ..."

"Oh yeah?" he said. "And what was *that* in aid of?"

"Victims of the Deptford Dogshit Disaster. Any more questions?"

"Did *well*, did it?"

"Patchy response, really," I said. "It did well in Catford but caused outrage in Barking – you know, pretty much as you'd expect, really ..."

"Look," he said, "If you think you're so high-and-mighty, why don't you do something *yourself* to help? Something *different*. Something *constructive* ..."

"I *am*," I said. "I'm holding a sponsored record collection. I'm knocking on every door in the country and asking people to donate their old charity records – you know, *Band Aid, Live Aid, Ferry Aid, This*-Aid, *That*-Aid – I've even donated my own very highly-prized 1981 Tottenham Hotspur Cup Final single featuring Ossie Ardiles ..."

"Oh yeah?" he said. "And *then* what?"

"I'm going to tip 'em all on a big bonfire and burn the lot ..."

"And how does that help victims of the Danish Ferry Disaster?"

"Well, it helps *me* !" I screamed at him.

"So?" he said.

"Well, I was *on* that ferry, *wasn't* I!"

"Yeah – *what*," he said, "Just get back this *morning*, did ya?"

He looked me up and down.

"You should have taken your crash helmet off," he concluded. "You could have swum here a lot faster *without* it ..."

Ennobled by this heartwarming little encounter, I wandered off and sold the spare duffle coats to some kindly old dear who was pushing two kids around in a pram.

She looked a bit hard up, so I only charged her ten quid each.

"You don't wanna come and work on *my* stall, do ya?" said the bloke who gave me the coats in the first place. "I've never seen selling like that before ..."

The first thing I did with the proceeds was to buy a pair of shades.

Then I went potty ...

The *sun* was up, the *crowds* were out, and I smelled ...

Bargain Fever

Bargains !

Either the bush telegraph was working overtime, or someone must have seen me coming.

In less than five minutes I'd acquired a gigantic beach towel awash with images of Hawaii for £6, and a bag of fresh cherries for £2.50.

Why?

All I know is they were a *bargain*.

I *detest* cherries at the best of times.

Which is *why*, if you'd been passing through the market that day, you'd have seen some bloke in a micro duffle hood standing there by the bent shower equipment, intermittently wincing and sobbing and squelching as he dribbled cherry juice all down his bermuda shorts.

In the end, good sense got the better of me, and I started chucking the rest at the few passers by who were silly enough to stray within range ... until *one* of those passers-by turned round and *glared* at me:

"I thought I'd seen the *last* of you, Coathook ..."

"*Christ* ..." (I accidentally blew a spray of half-chewed cherry bits all over my own face in surprise ...)

"*Fancy* bumping into *you* down here, Baz!"

I dropped the empty bag behind me as nonchalantly as I could, dredged up a big gorgonzola grin and got ready to leg it ...

"What's the juice from your end?" he suddenly demanded to know.

"Oh, er ... *juice?*"

"*Juice*, yeah. *You* know, *juice* ..."

"Well, I lost that *file* you gave me. You couldn't fill me in on a few details, could you?"

"I haven't got time now," he snapped. "I'm here on business ..."

Me too, I thought.

Fucking *police* business ...

With nothing better to do, I followed after him, and when he took down a pair of jazzy shorts from a stall selling swimming trunks, I absent-mindedly did the same.

"Do you want both of these in the same bag?" asked the woman running the stall.

I watched him pull out a roll of banknotes ...

"Yeah," he said. "It's alright. We're friends ..."

"*Business?*" I said. "You're here for herbs, then, I take it?"

"*Herbs?*" he said. "I'm *not* talking *herbs*. I'm talking *bargains*. B-A-R-G-A-I-N-S. And, more particularly, *mirrors* ..."

"Of course ..."

"Now," he said, "What I want you to *do*, is buy up every cheap mirror you see and meet me back at the car park in one hour. Any questions?"

"Yeah," I said, "That's no problem, Baz, except I'm not exactly strapped for cash right at the moment ..."

"Here, take this ..." (*he peeled off a couple of fifties from his wad*) "... and, if there's any change, buy yourself an ice cream ..."

"You are a *complete* gentleman," I said. "A *gentleman's* gentleman ..."

So saying, I watched him disappear into the crowd, drawn by a pool of reflected light near to a stall selling antiques.

I didn't know why Baz *wanted* mirrors but, not to be outdone, I decided to *invest* in a few for myself ...

I bought up every mirror I could find – large ones, small ones, shaving mirrors, compact mirrors, bathroom mirrors, full-length mirrors *etc.* I *even* bought some mirror tiles and a *Daily Mirror*, but then I found I had no arms left to carry any other bargains, so I threw them all into the nearest ditch and went back to the serious business of togging myself up, about eighty quid better off than when I arrived by dustcart.

First of all I purchased a Union Jack kipper tie.

It was *handsome*.

But it needed something to *offset* it.

So I procured an antique Nazi helmet ...

Ideal for a spot of gardening, playing tennis or threatening the neighbours.

And, since my summer range was in need of a new injection of blood, I invested in a genuine suedette car coat for £2.50 (ideal beachware), a chef's hat for £24.99 *(just the job now that Milwall were in the First Division)* and a pair of black desert boots for a fiver (they didn't *fit* me, but they looked the *business*).

A pair of tartan boxer shorts completed my spree, designed to cut a fine figure in the master bedroom at the Schloss Froth ...

Later on I spotted my benefactor rifling through a huge secondhand clothes stall run by a man known locally as the 'Colonel.'

As I tried to turn round and go back the other way, a telescopic arm suddenly reached out and grabbed me round the neck ...

"Where's my *mirrors*, Coakhook?" he said, without looking up or letting go.

"Erm ..."

"Anyway," he said, "I haven't got time for that now. Get a load of these *bargains* ..."

The stall was one enormous mountain of old togs, and I didn't know quite what item to grab first ...

"Look at this *cheesecloth* shirt," he said. "I offered him a quid for it but he only wanted 50p ..."

I was too busy inspecting a pair of bottle-green corduroy trousers to take much notice of what Baz had bought, but just as I was puzzling over whether it was worth buying a size 48 waist and trying to get Mrs Bagpope to take them in for me, I was thrown off the scent ...

"No, no," said Baz. "It's no good you looking at anything *here*. The Colonel's just sold the entire lot to me for 95p and given me a suitcase to take it all away in. He even tried to throw in his lorry for two quid, but I'd never get it in the car boot ..."

"I got a few good bargains," I told him, trying my best not be overshadowed by his business nous.

"Oh yeah?" he said. "Like *what?*"

"Like this kipper tie ..."

"How much was *that*, then?"

"Only three pence," I said, proudly.

"*Three pence?*" he said. "That's cheap ..."

"*Ain't* it," I confirmed.

"But it's no *good*, though ..."

"Oh? And why's that?" I asked.

"Because it's *too* cheap. I don't consider it a bargain unless it costs me an arm and a leg. Which is why, Coathook, I'm bequeathing the entire lot to you and going off to shift some cash ..."

"*Just a minute ...*"

As he walked off, I noticed a copy of *The Corporate Handbook* sticking out of his back pocket ...

"Where do you *want* this lot?" yelled the Colonel.

"I'll take 'em with me ..." I said.

In order to *do* that, I had to do something with the armfuls of bargains I'd *already* accumulated, and so – for want of a *better* strategy – I wrapped the beach towel round my middle, put the swimming trunks on over my bermudas, swung the kipper round my neck, swapped the hard hat for the Nazi helmet and the duffle for the car coat.

Then I tried to gather up the jumble of clothes in front of me ...

The overcoats were easy – at least *three* of them disappeared under a nearby hedgerow, carried by their native population of wildlife, but a surplus line of luminous Kent County Council safety vests turned out to involve an *entirely* more problematic skill altogether ...

There I was, struggling to pull the last one over my head, when I interrupted my breathing processes for just long enough to keel over and pass out.

When I regained consciousness, I found the Colonel had loaded up the rest of the clothes in the lorry, left the car keys sitting on my lap and disappeared.

I stood up shakily to find a crowd of people all staring at me:

"Wossa matter with you lot?" I said. "Am I dressed funny or something?"

All of a sudden, somebody let out a piercing screech ...

"*THERE* HE IS!" she cried. "THE M2 HAT-MURDERER! CHOP HIS BOLLOCKS OFF ...!"

"*Madam ...*" I went to say ... *but was deterred from further intercourse when I saw how ugly the crowd looked ...*

Shuffling backwards like a Italian infantryman, I retreated to the truck, leapt on board and slammed the door shut after me.

As a result of which, both the wing mirrors fell off.

I *tell* you, I don't know what that mammoth van *ran* on, but an enormous chimney on the cab roof suggested something predating the golden age of dinosaurs.

Some sort of *fossil* fuel, maybe.

Like *amber*.

Or *peat*.

The *dashboard* was a bit of a puzzle, as well.

Like, for example, *where* was it?

Never mind, I thought. *Brakes ... gears (all twenty-eight of 'em) ... yep, the rest of it seems to be here.*

So *here* goes ... *and, with a volley of fists banging on the windows, I started her up, swerved out of the car park, hit a milk float, scattered six more vehicles in the wake of my non-existent HGV licence, tried to do an illegal U-turn, followed my own momentum round in a complete circle, jackknifed across all four lanes of an inner city arterial road and went careering off up the central reservation doing a handstand on the steering wheel ...*

My obvious priority was to get back to the flat – what was *left* of it – and to retrieve the invites and the train tickets.

But I didn't have much time.

So, it's all a bit of a mystery why I chose to cross via the Dartford Tunnel and make the same mistake two days running by getting caught up in a tailback at Limehouse ...

I got so bored during the course of this farce, that I offered a lift to a hitch hiker who overtook me on foot, walking unimpeded down the fast lane ...

"I don't know where you're *going*," I said, "But I'm turning off down the Highway to avoid the traffic ..."

"That's fine by me," he said. "Do you know why they *call* it the Highway?"

"No idea," I said. "Anything to do with highway robbery?"

"Sort of ..." he said, before giving me a potted history of the notorious Ratcliffe Highway where so many grisly murders had taken place in days gone by.

These days, it was probably notorious for *other* reasons, because by the time we *got* there it was cordoned off.

"That's a shame," he said. "Never mind, Whitechapel's nearby. The history's just as colourful. The Great Plague's buried just a few feet beneath the pavements. On a good day you can actually smell it ..."

"*Whitechapel* ..." I mused. "One-time haunt of Jack the Ripper ..."

"Still *is*," he said. "He runs that Wimpey Bar over there ..."

Following this charming little interlude, he proceeded to extract an envelope from his rucksack and surreptitiously scrutinise a photograph contained therein, casting me an odd glance sideways as he did so.

If I hadn't been concentrating so hard on avoiding the bumper of the fire engine in front of me, I might have queried what he was *up* to, but, as it was, he put the envelope away again soon enough and began to relax.

"I wonder why the Highway's closed?" he said. "Maybe there's been another murder, in-keeping with its tradition ..."

"No," I said. "A lorry shed its load. I just heard a message on the radio ..."

"Oh," he said.

He sounded disappointed.

So I tried to think how I could *cheer* him up.

"It's alright," I said.

"Oh ...?"

"It was a lorryload of *murderers* ..."

CHAPTER 34
THE NEIGHBOUR FROM HELL

"*Where* did you say you were going?"

"Victoria Coach Station ..."

"Coach?" I said. "You can have this truck when I've done with it, if you like ..."

"Thanks anyway," he said. "But it would defeat my purpose ..."

"Which *is* ...?"

"I'm planning to hitch round the world ..."

"Don't bother," I said. "I've been there ..."

"Oh?" he said.

"I just got back. It's overrated ..."

"You must have missed quite a bit. Civil unrest, poll tax riots, water meters..."

"*Water* meters?" I queried.

"Government's introducing them. Provinces first, London next ..."

"It won't catch on in London," I said confidently.

"Oh?"

"Well, most Tory voters travel to work on public transport just like the rest of us, and I happen to think that when they find themselves banged up in the rush-hour tube on a hot day with a trainload of plebs who haven't been able to afford to wash for six months, there'll be quite a *stink* ..."

"Mm ..."

"As for *riots*, I'm planning to hijack a Poll-Tax Shirkers Detector Van ..."

"*And* ...?"

"I'm going to drive it down Whitehall, crash it through the security gates and ram it straight up the Prime Minister's arse at 100mph with the horn on full blast playing *Boogie Woogie Bugle Boy of Company B*. That sort of protest gets noticed in high places. So don't *worry* about it. You don't *have* to flee the country ..."

"No," he went on, "I'm not. It's a sort of holiday, really, but I'm planning to work as I go. A self-financing expedition. Grape-picking, you know, that kind of thing ..."

"Yeah, I know. Condom testing, bank robbing, muck-raking generally.

Try Bolivia. They've got all the best jobs out there ..."

"You sound like a cynic," he said. "I was thinking of kicking off with France, anyway. What did you make of it?"

"Fucking banana republic ..."

"*What?*" he said, casting me one of his sideways glances.

"As far as I know, anyway. I've never been there. Where is it?"

"First stop over the Channel ..."

"*What* Channel?" I enquired.

"The *English* Channel. The one they're building a tunnel under ..."

"Building a *tunnel?*" I said. "*Who's* building a tunnel?"

"The French are," he said. "How long have you been away?"

"The *French?!!!*" I screamed at him in outrage. "Do you mean to tell me that foreigners are tunneling under the English Channel? You must be mistaken ..."

"No," he said. "No mistake ..."

I went into such a shattering mood of despondency that I drove the wrong way round the Aldgate Ring Road five times and nearly killed a nun on a pushbike coming in the opposite direction ...

In my rear view mirror I saw her swerve and wobble to the side of the road ... *where she toppled off, leapt up, hitched up her skirts, pulled a gun out of her garter belt and fired a shot at the truck ...*

I tore off towards Houndsditch.

Spotting a telephone box at the junction of Bishopsgate and Liverpool Street, I pulled over and dialled Directory Enquiries.

"Get me the War Office!" I screamed down the receiver.

Click ... click ... click ... click ... click ... "Can I help you?"

"I'd like to report an invasion," I said.

"Thank you," she said. "I'll just transfer you to somebody else ..."

Click ... click ... click ... click ... click ... "Yes?" came a familiar voice, although I couldn't initially place it.

"I thought you might like to know," I said, "That the French are tunnelling under the English Channel ..."

"Oh yes I *know*," he said, enthusiastically. "But it's alright. *We're* tunnelling under the Channel *ourselves* and we're going to meet them halfway ..."

"Is that supposed to be funny?" I said.

"Oh no," he said. "Not a bit of it, old boy ..."

"Is that *you*, Corkscrews ...?" I went to say, when ... *to my horror, I saw a representative of the City of London Plods questioning my passenger through the open truck window ...*

He was about sixty foot tall, brandishing a radio on a long white lead and a trucheon in a long white hand.

Not only *that*, but he had something looking like a fireman's hat on his head.

My *first* thought was to clear off and leave my travelling companion to it, but I had to think twice about losing all my fancy dress equipment – time was getting short.

As I dropped the handset, I saw the PC gesture for the ignition keys and go for his radio...

"HELP! *HELP* ...!" (*I lurched across the pavement with my arms across my chest as though I had some terrible injury* ...) "Somebody's just been *shooting* at me! There's a nun on a pushbike down the road and she's gawn berserk with a *scatter* gun ...!!!"

To my relief, the PC's eyes lit up and he tore off down the road fingering his truncheon and talking into his radio as he went ...

"That was a close shave," I said. "I thought we were done for there ..."

"He was just admiring your truck," he said. "Apparently, it's an antique. He was actually trying to *buy* it off me. Wanted to know if I'd take thirty grand and a couple of tickets to the policemen's benevolent ball ..."

After I stopped crying, I pulled myself together and drove off like a crazy man.

"So, anyway," I said, "You were telling me about your holiday plans ..."

"Well," he said, "As I say, it's a working holiday, really – in more senses than one. I'll be working to finance myself, but I'll also be following up a case. All the leads point to places overseas, and I shan't return until I've cracked it ..."

"*Case?*" I queried. "Are you are a Nazi hunter?"

"No," he said, surprised. "What makes you say that? I'm an Inquiry Agent. Missing persons, matrimonial squabbles – *that* kind of thing. Name's Trevor ..."

"No, no," I said, "It's Kitehawk. Dexter Kitehawk ..."

"No, no," he said, "That's *my* name ..."

"What?" I said. "*Kitehawk*? That's a coincidence ..."

"No, *no*," he said, "*Your* name's Kitehawk. *My* name's Trevor ..."

"Inquiry Agent? Now there's a stroke of luck ..."

"Oh?" he said. "Why's *that*, then?"

"Are you in any particular *hurry* to get to Victoria Coach Station?"

"Depends," he said. "Why?"

"I might be able to put a bit of work your way. It just so happens I need a hand with a couple of jobs. It shouldn't take long ..."

"How much are you paying?"

"Well," I said, "I can't afford to give you any cash, but how do you fancy going to a party?"

"*Party?*" he said. "What *sort* of party?"

"Germany. On the *Orient Express*. All expenses paid ..."

"What's the catch?"

"No catch," I said. "I've got two free tickets and a lot of short notice. As I say, if you help me out, then the spare ticket's yours ..."

"What *are* these jobs," he said, gesturing at the back of the truck. "Pick up? Delivery?"

"Sort of," I said. "A bit of both, actually. Plus some possible assistance when we get to the party ..."

"Okay," he said. "Suits me. It's a deal. What line of business are you in?"

"Who me?" I said. "Oh, emergency services ..."

"Really?" he said. "Fire? Police? Ambulance?"

"Yeah ..."

"Which? All of them ...?"

"Yeah," I said. "*No*, actually," I veered, "Local Authority UXD Department..."

"UXD department? Don't you mean UXB – as in '*Danger* UXB'?"

"Danger?" I said. "Oh, it's *dangerous*, alright ..."

"Oh?"

"It's the Unexploded Dogshit Division ..."

"So," he said, "What do you want me to do?"

"Well," I said, "It's not grape picking – well, not *exactly*, anyway – but it's good, honest work ..."

"When do we start?"

"Right now ..."

I swerved over to the kerb in Clerkenwell and leapt out of the cab.

Without wasting any time, I grabbed a shovel from the side of the road and went round the back of the truck to get the Colonel's suitcase.

"Okay," I said, "I want you to go up and down every street in the neighbourhood until you've collected every lump of dogshit you can find and filled up this case ..."

"*What?!!!*" he snapped.

"Yeah," I said, "It doesn't matter what colour or texture, but preferably it should hum a fair bit. Skip the dehydrated flyblown stuff. It don't work as well as the fresh stuff for the purpose I've got in mind ..."

"What about you?"

"Oh, don't worry about me. I've got all the paperwork to do for this shipment ..."

So saying, I handed over the equipment and got back into the driver's seat, leaving Trevor little choice but to shrug his shoulders and walk forlornly off.

As soon as he'd disappeared, I finished the written details fairly sharpish, put my feet up and fell asleep.

I woke up about an hour later to find Trevor banging on the window and gesturing to the now filled suitcase, mission accomplished:

When I rolled down the window, I was met by an almighty stink ...

"Close up the case, Trevor," I told him. "It's attracting the flies ..."

Visibly gagging, he shut the locks and handed it over.

Upon which, I held it out at a suitable length from my snorkel, took it round the back of the lorry and slung it amongst the Colonel's rubbish, coming away with two First World War gas masks ...

"Put this on," I told him. "We'll need these for the second part of the job..."

However, since I couldn't get mine on over my Nazi helmet, I left it on the floor for later, adjusted the Hawaiian beach towel round my middle and drove off.

"You know," I said, thinking of the nun who'd taken a pot shot at us, "I don't know if it's my imagination, but there seems to be a fuck of a lot of highly strange people roaming about London these days. I don't know what half of them are doing running around loose. They all ought to be under lock and key..."

Trevor did make some sort of reply, but I couldn't understand a word he was saying through his gas mask.

"Right," I continued. "Now for the delivery ..."

I drove into the courtyard of Rathaven Mansions, Old Street, and parked the truck next to the south wall.

"Now then, Trevor," I said. "This next part of the campaign has to be conducted with military precision ..."

Failing to detect any sort of affirmative response, I ordered him to lift his protective facial wear, temporarily.

"What I want you to do is nip up onto the roof of the truck and climb in through the first floor window directly above us. *Then*, being as discreet as possible, I want you to go through and ascertain whether there is any Filf stationed on guard in the corridor outside ..."

"How?"

"I thought you were an *Inquiry* Agent?"

"Missing *persons* is *my* speciality. Not *housebreaking* ..."

"Don't worry about that," I said. "This is *my* house ..."

"Why might the police be outside, then?"

"Oh," I said, "Inter-Emergency Service rivalry, that's all ..."

"I understand," he said. "*We* get all *that* as well ..."

"Right," I concluded. "Any questions? No? Right, fall out!"

Just as he was about to clamber up the side of the truck he stopped and poked his head back ...

"How do I get in the window?" he asked.

"No problem," I assured him. "The glass is broken. I put my fist through it yesterday ..."

I'd already made *two* important decisions.

First of all, I decided to postpone briefing him on the real nature of our mission to Germany.

Since it had no bearing on the job in hand, there was little sense in giving him an unnecessary burden of material to offload at the first opportunity of squealing to interrogators.

And this led to my *second* decision.

To keep the engine running and count to ten.

Primarily because he was liable to be arrested coming through my front door any moment, and if he didn't show his face pretty fast, then he wasn't going to find me *waiting* for him when he did.

So it was a bit of a surprise when his head reappeared at the window ...

"All clear!" he shouted.

Grabbing my gas mask, I went and collected the suitcase, climbed up onto the roof of the truck and joined him inside my erstwhile apartment.

The *first* thing that hit me was the stench of charred paint from the fire ...

Out in the hall, the skylight was still broken and the floor was still damp, but the door of the flat opposite had been temporarily repaired and boarded over with planks. *As to the identity of the occupant, I would have loved to have found out, but I didn't have time and my suspicions were that he'd probably scarpered anyway.*

On the way downstairs, I lowered my trout and bid Trevor do the same.

Then, when we reached the flat directly below mine, I knocked on the door ...

Following a lengthy pause, somebody opened the letter box and peered out:

"Yes?" squawked a voice from inside.

"Special delivery for Mr Bagpope-Brindisi," I announced.

"Hello ...?"

Since she appeared to have difficulty hearing me, I bent down to the level of the letter box.

"I said ..." I whispered (... *and then, raising my voice to the level of a fire klaxon* ...) "SPECIAL DELIVERY FOR MR BAGPOPE-BRINDISI!"

"Oooer..." she said, and backed off a bit.

I poked my snout right through the gap and repeated my statement.

"He's not in!" she called out.

That was a stroke of luck ...

"Open up!"

"Who wants him?" she called back in a worried tone.

"*Nobody* wants him!" I shouted. "We've got a *delivery* for him. Are you going to let us in or not?"

"What is it," she said. "Money?"

"Not exactly," I said. "It's more a *case* of *good luck*, really ..."

"Are you a loan shark?"

"*Madam*," I said, "I am from the *Council*. Do I *look* like a loan shark?"

"I don't know," she said. "I can't see you properly, can I?"

"Then open up, or your husband's good fortune may end up going elsewhere ..."

"*Alright* then," she said at length, and turned the latch ...

When the door was partially open, I barged in, with Trevor close behind ...

"Where do you want it?" I said.

"Better put it in the front room ..."

In response to this request, I marched into her lounge and emptied the contents of the suitcase in a pile on her carpet.

Mrs Bagpope-Brindisi, who'd followed me in, suddenly screeched ...

"EEEEEEEEEEEK ...!"

I turned round.

"What's the matter?" I said.

Although momentarily lost for words, she suddenly flapped into life and started squawking all kinds of nonsense and running round the room like a dog chasing its tail ...

"Is there some problem?" I asked.

"Problem? *Problem* ...?" she screamed. "There's *dogs mess* all over my *carpet*!!!"

"*Is* there?" I said, surprised. (*I peered down for a closer look*). "So there *is*. Though it's too early yet to confirm whether the source is canine. We'll have to wait till we get the lab reports. Isn't that *so* ...?"

I turned to my assistant for his opinion.

He did mumble *something*, but fortunately it was inaudible through his ventilation equipment.

"How long have you had this problem, Madam?" I went on.

"You just *put* it there!" she yelled.

"Indeed," I said, "Though technically, I'm sure you will agree, I was merely the postman. I may have *delivered* it, but I am not the source from which it originated ..."

"Are you suggesting that *I* am, then?" she shouted.

"Hard to say," I said. "The source *may* be human. You may have sent it all to yourself in a bid to avoid the Poll Tax laws – and *here*, Madam, I must don my *second* hat (*metaphorically* speaking, you understand) as Poll Tax Enforcement Officer. You may be in breach of Regulation 7B which states that, 'Failure to disclose information on your spouse's bowel returns (and *here*, Madam, we are referring to *Mr* Bagpope-Brindisi) may result in a criminal prosecution, especially where it can be shown that there has been either negligence or an attempt to defraud, and I must caution you accordingly ..."

She collapsed into a rocking chair, turning first white, then purple.

"Neither me *nor* Mr Bagpope has ever been in trouble ... ever ..."

She mumbled on in this fashion for some minutes while I got out the documentation for the case.

"That's as maybe, Madam," I said, "But whatever the rights and wrongs of it, you have certainly got *something* to answer for, and it's sitting right here on your carpet for all to see ..."

"I don't know what my Harry is going to say..." she droned on, covering her mouth and nose with a handkerchief to stifle the smell.

"*Shit* is *shit*," I said, "If you'll pardon me saying so, Madam – which brings me to my *third* hat: I'm afraid you'll be required to confine yourself here until further notice, or until an Inspector from the Hygiene and Fumigation Department has been round to disinfect the premises – whichever occurs sooner – and you are instructed not to touch the evidence for a period of three calendar months. Here is the warrant ...”

I handed her the prewritten paperwork.

“All other residents of the block will be notified in due course, and full sized photographs of you and your husband will appear on the front page of the local newspaper in the *Poll Tax Shirkers* section ...”

“How could they do this to us ... how *could* they?” she moaned. “We’ve always been honest, decent, hard-working, tax-paying citizens all our lives ...”

It was tragic to see yet another poor couple being shat on by the Tory Government.

“But don’t blame *me*,” I called out to her as we left. “*I* didn’t vote for ‘em...”

So saying, I closed her front door, drew a great big red cross on the outside of it with a magic marker and scrawled the word ‘UNCLEAN’ *underneath for everyone to see.*

Then I returned upstairs with my assistant, gave the Colonel’s case a quick scrub with *Dettol*, retrieved the tickets for the *Orient Express* and climbed back out the window.

CHAPTER 35
LAGER ON THE ORIENT EXPRESS

I'm not a vindictive person. Anybody who knows me will tell you that. Except that very few people do know me: in my occupation I have had to play my cards very close to my chest and it would have been unprofessional to have had many friends. But I think I can say that anybody who has had any dealings with Dexter Kitehawk over the years has been treated fair and square. And the reverse is also true: anybody who has messed with me has lived to regret it. Dexter Kitehawk always gets his revenge ...

I mused on these thoughts to while away the time in the West End traffic and, when we reached Victoria, I pulled in to a sidestreet and suggested to Trevor that we go round the back of the truck and get togged up in a manner as befits two passengers for the *Orient Express*.

I was counting on the Colonel's wardrobe to supply me with the necessaries, and the Colonel came up trumps. A 1940s evening suit offered the required touch of class, complimented by a deerstalker and a pair of wellington boots. In contrast, Trevor reluctantly donned a 1950s station-master outfit and bowler hat, with a paisley tie adding the final touch.

Next stop was the luggage shop, where I bought a set of cheap matching suitcases with the residue of Baz's money. These I filled with the best of the clobber, including the gas masks and one or two other items of heavy-duty industrial application. Of particular note amongst the remainder of the stock was a superb range of fancy dress accessories – false noses, plastic knives designed to look like you've been stabbed through the neck, etc – and for where we were going, they'd be positively priceless. For ease of access, I packed most of them separately in the Colonel's case.

A half dozen cans of *Allied Froth* completed our provisions, following the purchase of which we headed for the Information Desk in order to ascertain departure details of the *Express*.

Due to a discrepancy between the time on my Mickey Mouse watch and the real time, we only just managed to scramble through the ticket barrier as the whistle blew, and consequently had to run alongside the accelerating train for half its length, hurling our baggage through the open windows as we went ...

We only just managed to hurl *ourselves* onto the rear carriage right at the last moment:

Trevor was the first to make the leap, and he helped pull me on just before a signal stanchion careered past ...

It would have sliced me in two if I'd been any slower, no mistake.

But our problems were only just beginning ...

Although *we* were safely on board, our luggage was all spread out in different carriages, and it all had to be retrieved.

"You go and locate our cabin," I said, "And I'll hunt down the cases ..."

Before I did *that*, however, I felt in need of a livener, and so I lingered in the void between two lounge cars and pulled on the ring of one of the cans of *Froth*, unaware of how volatile it had become during the chase:

The spray shot out sixteen feet in front of me and soaked everybody in the first few rows of the adjacent communal seating section ...

I wandered in to inspect the damage:

"Seen any cases round here?" I enquired above the general murmurings of discontent.

"Only *you*, you bloody idiot! Look what you've done to my suit!"

These words were uttered by a nasty, middle-aged stockbroker type, who looked like he used the Orient Express to commute to work in.

"Guard! Guard!" somebody else was screaming. "There's a lager lout on this train!"

This time, my aggressor was an old dame dressed like an antique lampstand, whose cries momentarily stopped me in my tracks ...

So *surprised* by this onslaught was I, that I could think of very little else to do but to stand there, look at her benignly and take a sip from what was left in the can ... and *burp*.

Her response?

To *up* the overall volume a bit further.

She just *wouldn't* shut up.

In *fact*, it was getting a bit embarrassing ...

"Lager louts! Lager louts!" she was screaming, screwing her eyes up in agony and then opening them to draw breath and to check that I was still there...

She had so much white make-up on, she looked like a decaying birthday cake.

If the *guard* had any sense he'd keep *well* away.

Unless he wanted to catch something like *mortality*.

This woman was ill ...

"You must be on the wrong train," I told her. "This is the *Orient* Express. The train for *Lourdes* left Platform 12 three hours ago ..."

Whilst playing mere spectator to these extraordinary antics in which she contorted her face into a sequence of ever-more hideously squashed balls of pain, I realised with some concern that the Colonel's case must have crashed past her on its way in and spilled all its contents around where she was sitting, because she was up to her neck in a pile of joke shop novelties.

To my *horror*, it dawned on me I was going to have to collect them all up, one by one ...

I found the empty case in the row behind her, where it had landed upside down over some old boy's head and snapped shut round his windpipe.

Not that he'd noticed, mind you.

He *still* hadn't woken up by the time I'd retrieved it, and this left me free to debrief the cantankerous dowager as quickly and diplomatically as I could.

The crunch came when I tried to grab what I thought was a false moustache from round her moosh, and found it was actually growing out of her top lip ...

In the ensuing struggle she pulled the communication cord, the train screeched to a halt, bodies went flying everywhere ... *and I had the great misfortune to land right on top of her in the aisle doing the horizontal dance of death across the floor ...*

At *which* point, the driver and the guard burst into the carriage and understandably demanded to know what I was up to:

In a moment of inspiration I grabbed a fancy dress stethoscope, slung it round my neck and staggered back to my feet ...

"Back! Back! GET *BACK* ...!" I cried. "This woman is *contagious* ! I want her put ashore and sent to the nearest isolation hospital ...!"

Hesitantly, they began to retreat ...

"We'll have to wait till we get to the next station ..." offered the driver.

"No time for *that* !" I shouted, waving my bus pass at them. "*Dexter Kitehawk*, BMA. She has to be removed now – and I mean *now* !"

"But we're on a viaduct in the middle of nowhere ..." said the guard.

"Have you got a stretcher?" I demanded to know.

"Yes ..."

"And ropes?"

"*Yes ...*"

"Then this woman must be lowered out of the window. And I want this entire carriage evacuated immediately and fumigated from top to bottom as soon as we reach Dover. Is that understood?"

"Yes ..."

Fortunately, the old dear was rolling around on the floor and moaning and groaning and frothing at the mouth and nothing coming out of her voice box was remotely coherent.

As soon as they returned with the necessary equipment, I supervised the ensuing operation, making sure she was lowered safely down onto the Vauxhall Bridge Road, where, unfortunately, a passing ambulance got caught up in the ropes, dragged her round the corner, crashed straight through the wall of Battersea Dogs Home and came to rest in the office of the Chief Vet.

The last I saw, she was being revived by a pack of labradors all falling over themselves to give her the kiss of life ...

"Nice work, men," I said. "We'd better get off though – we must be behind schedule ..."

"What did she have wrong with her?" asked the guard.

"Just about the worst case of Athlete's Foot I've ever seen ..."

I tracked down the arrival point of the *rest* of my cases to a private suite in the first sleeping car, where the occupant, a Miss Blondie Duval – a striking young woman with mirror eyes and coal-scuttle jewellery on her fingers – claimed to have thrown it all back out of the window.

"Well," she said in her defence, "They weren't *my* cases ..."

I trudged off despondently and found Trevor in a double-berth affair midway between engine and guard's van, breaking into a can of *Froth*.

"What's that funny smell?" I said.

He shrugged his shoulders.

"There's a message for you," he said.

"Oh?"

"It came under the door a few minutes ago ..."

"But nobody knows I'm *on* this train ..."

"*Somebody* obviously does ..."

Dexter Kitehawk: *You* are a Dead Man
signed: *The Stepney Light Infantry*

"Oh *shit* ..."

"Bad news?"

"Who the fuck is *this* from?" I shouted in angst.

"You're asking *me*?"

"As if I haven't got *enough* problems!"

I did wonder whether this was a good moment to fill him in with a few details about AF International, but he distracted me by informing me he had some problems of his own.

His *rucksack* had gone missing.

"Oh," I said, "You can kiss goodbye to that. It's probably gone the same way as my cases – straight out the window. There's a madwoman down the corridor. She chucked them all back onto Victoria Station because she didn't like the *look* of them. You won't see *that* again ..."

"No," he said, "It was strapped to my back when I jumped on board. After the porter showed me down here, I took it off and went for a stroll. When I came back it was gone ..."

"There's something very fishy going on here," I said.

"*You're* telling *me* ..."

"And the conclusion I've *come* to, Trevor, is that there is a tea-leaf aboard this train, which – considering it's the *Orient Express* – is nothing short of an outrage. I expected a bit more for my money than to be banged up with a trainload of crooks ..."

"It must have something to do with your note there," he said. "Are you sure you don't know who it's from? Try to think ..."

"Oh I know who it's *from*," I said. "It's from the Stepney Light Infantry. It's a *death* threat ..."

"The *O.S.L.I.*? Are you *sure*? Let me look at that ..."

I handed it over.

"You mean you've actually *heard* of this lot?" I said. "What are they, some kind of neo-Nazi group?"

"Not exactly ..."

"What does the 'O' stand for?"

"It *doesn't*. Stepney Light Infantry is a nickname for their paramilitary wing. O.S.L.I. stands for *Order of the Salvation of the Lord's Innocents*, or something like that. They're *religious* fanatics ..."

"*What?*" I said. "All I did was pull a funny face at the Ayatollah ..."

"No, *Christians* ..."

"What?!!" I shouted. "What do you *mean*, *Christians*?"

"Who have you upset?"

"Nobody that I know of ..."

But *something* sounded familiar from somewhere ...

I sat down on the lower bunk, reached into my pocket and pulled out some bits and pieces of paper I'd accumulated on my world tour – scrawled phone numbers, a few investigation notes, mementoes etc – and sifted through them absent-mindedly while Trevor paced up and down drinking.

I actually missed it altogether the first time, but when I gathered everything up with the intention of trashing the lot, the old sepia-tint photograph fell out – the one delivered mysteriously to my office on that first day on the job.

"*O.S.L.I. 1909* ..." I mumbled, reading the legend on the reverse.

"What have you got there?"

"One of a *series*, obviously ..."

I slung him the print.

"Yeah, this is *them* alright," he said, scrutinising it in close detail. "They started in the East End donkeys years ago. We arrested most of the current bunch about eighteen months back ..."

"What do you mean '*we*' ...?"

"On the Force. I used to be a copper ..."

"I think you might have told me that before I went and chucked a suitcase full of dogshit on some poor old dear's carpet ..."

"Don't worry, I was only a rookie. They threw me out. In any case, you didn't ask ..."

"What did they throw you out for?"

"It's a long story. Suffice to say, I know a bit about the O.S.L.I., and you're in trouble ..."

"Why?"

"They're an illegal order of chivalry who claim inheritance of the Templars. A secret society of fundamentalist Christian missionaries dedicated to the obliteration of vice ..."

"*What* ...?"

"Don't you remember all those ritual killings a couple of years back –

disembowelled bodies soaked in effluent, hung up at choice London locations...? They murder first and ask questions later. Take it from me – I used to know a bloke in Vice Squad who was a member of this lot, and he was *certifiable*. You've been sent a picture of your assassin through the post – that's how they operate. That row of medals on his chest – each one represents an execution successfully carried out – and now he's warning *you* he's almost caught up with you. But you're wrong about it being a death threat ..."

"Oh ...?" I said, hopefully.

"It's a death *decree*. There's a subtle difference. I wouldn't fancy being in your shoes ..."

"*Just* a *minute*," I said. "The bloke in this photograph would be about a hundred and ninety by now. How could he be an assassin?"

"You've got it wrong. 1909 is the target serial number. You'll be the one thousand nine hundred and ninth victim of the O.S.L.I. if they're successful, and they *always* are, sooner or later. The photo's a fake. A tinted collage on dated paper stock. It was probably done to order by an antique camera shop, but anyone with the right modern equipment could produce this effect. Basically, it's a portrait of their founder with somebody else's head stuck on it. The ceremonial regalia is original, but the face and medals are contemporary, superimposed. Quite a good job, though. I'd say it was probably knocked out a couple of years ago ..."

I leapt to my feet ...

"Give me that photo...!" I yelled.

Snatching it out of his hand, I screwed my eyes up and gawked at the would-be murderer staring out at me:

"EEEEEEEEEEEEEK ...!"

"Do you *know* him ...?" said Trevor.

"*Know* him?!!!" I choked. "It's my Uncle Grolly! It *is* my Uncle Grolly ...!"

"He must have avoided arrest when they were all rounded up," he concluded. "I wonder *how* ...?"

A whole series of apocalyptic images suddenly sailed through my brain – the fire in Quito, the bomb at the Iroquois – and there, blazing a trail from vengeance to destruction, was the modern crusading knight, riding on horseback towards the Millenium with the flaming torch of righteousness held high ... and my Uncle Grolly's mugshot pasted onto his face.

"Oh, I *know* how," I said. "He's been out of the *country* for the last two years. Chasing *me* ..."

"Was he *always* a religious fanatic?" he asked.

"*Never*, that I know of," I said. "In fact, he went round and chinned the local vicar one Sunday for ringing his bells too loud ..."

"How do you think he got mixed up with the O.S.L.I.?"

"Christ knows, but if there was a cup of tea and a punch-up in it for him, he'd throw in his lot with anyone. I thought he died in Parkhurst. Before I left the country, they wrote and told me that he was cutting me out of his will, only I never got the letter till the other day. He must have escaped around that time. It all fits ..."

"What was he in Parkhurst for?"

"Arson. He torched a chain of fish shops in Bethnal Green in the late sixties..."

"So he converted while he was in prison?"

"Looks like it ..."

"But why are they after *you*? Are you a pornographer?"

"No I bleeding well *ain't*," I said. "But I *know* a man who *is* ..."

"Oh ...?"

"*Corkscrews*. I've been set up ..."

Sinking back onto the bed in a mood of doom and gloom, I furiously tried to work out what all this had to do with the *Allied Froth* conspiracy.

Nothing, probably.

"I can't believe I've had that bastard a few paces behind me all this time ..."

"But *why*, if he's your uncle?"

"He's a nutter. In any case, he wouldn't know me from Adam. I was barely more than a kid the last time I saw him ..."

"You've got your answer then ..."

"*This* Vice Squad bloke you mentioned," I said. "His name wasn't *Greaser*, was it ...?"

"You *know* him, do you ...?"

"*Knew* him. He's dead ..."

"That doesn't surprise me. Who killed him?"

"I don't know, really. I found his body in a filing cabinet in the offices of an American neo-Nazi organisation. I first met him about eighteen months ago when he mistook me for a man who'd stuffed his sister, and from that moment on he continued to wage a vendetta against me. This wasn't helped by the fact that we were both investigating two separate cases involving the same criminal, and consequently kept bumping into each other in the most unlikely places – at least, he *claimed* to be investigating a case, but I found it very hard to believe he was a policeman. He always struck me as a half-witted Desperate Dan permanently smouldering on a very short fuse ..."

"That sounds like Greaser," he said. "But you say *investigating a case*. Are *you* with the job too, then?"

"In a manner of *speaking*, Trevor, *yes*. But I'm afraid I can't reveal any more at the present time ..."

"Okay," he said. "The way I see it is *this*. The O.S.L.I. have got a contract out on you, and – *well*, ordinarily, I'd say there was nothing I could do to help – but, well, in stealing my rucksack, they've antagonised *me* into the bargain. So, up to a point, we can help *each* other ..."

"They must have thought it belonged to *me*. What was in it? Anything valuable?"

"Few personal valuables – clothes, mainly, but as I may have told you before, there was a very important casefile in there. It's one of the reasons I'm travelling abroad. It represents a lot of hard work and I could stand to gain a fair bit of cash ..."

"Really ...?"

"I'll tell you what," he said. "I'll tell you about *my* case if you tell me about yours. How's that?"

"Well ..." I said, acting cagey, but there was no harm in telling him the basics.

After all, everybody from the KGB to the Limehouse tramp fraternity knew about it ...

"So you're *looking* for somebody?" I said. "Is *that* it?"

I'd had to break off rather abruptly from my run-down of Adolf Flite's criminal agenda, because – despite his apparent capacity to be intrigued by it all – I'm not sure he was on the same wavelength.

"It started a couple of years ago," he began, "When a client in a missing persons case contacted me outside of office hours and offered me a private deal..."

"*She* ...?"

"What?"

"*She* ...?"

"I didn't say '*she*', did I?"

Well, technically, I thought, *no.*

Except that his *tongue* was hanging so far out of his head I thought he was about to loop-the-loop ...

"Fancy ..." I murmured.

"Anyway, *yes*, as it happens. *She.* A pretty little thing called Hetty. We're lovers *now*, of course ..."

"Of course ..." I said, thinking, *I'm definitely in the wrong business ...*

"Originally, she'd got onto the firm to trace her father, but my boss pulled out when he uncovered evidence to suggest the man was a major embezzler and the sole suspect in a multi-million pound tax fraud. His employers knew all about him, but they were reluctant to prosecute. He'd been clever, salting the money away into several offshore bank accounts, and they didn't want the bad publicity. The family had heard rumours that he'd died overseas, but they couldn't get their hands on his cash ..."

"How terribly unfortunate," I said. "Why?"

"Apparently, he'd made a will leaving it all to a bastard son they'd been unaware existed. Initial attempts to identify and locate the son ended in failure, so the money went into limbo. That was when Hetty came to see me *privately* ..."

"*Tell me more ...*" I said, intrigued.

"Well, she's a stunner, really – an actress, a model ..."

"No, *no*," I said. "Tell me more about the *case* ..."

Who is this cowboy? I thought.

"Oh," he said, "Well, she was quite convinced that her father was still alive. More to the point, she was convinced that her half-brother was a fiction – that he was a ploy designed to stop the family getting rich ..."

"What was the deal she offered, or shouldn't I ask?"

"Prove there's no long lost son, and I can have half the old man's money for my troubles ..."

"So you're looking for his *son*, then?"

"I don't need to. Nobody knows the first thing about him. I'm looking for the old man ..."

"Any leads yet?"

"Several sightings, all unreliable. It makes the Lord Lucan affair look like a game of *Cluedo* ..."

"'*Ere*, just a *minute*," I said, puzzled. "If you *find* him, and he's *not* dead, how does that benefit *you*?"

"Simple," he said. "I force him to change the will in Hetty's favour ..."

"Oh," I said.

"And then I *kill* him ..."

"Fancy a drink?" I said.

"I *fancy* a *meal* ..."

"Follow me ..."

So fascinated was I by my companion's apparent potential for murder, that I momentarily forgot all about the Stepney Light Infantry and strode straight back out into the corridor like a walking executioner's dummy ...

As soon as we'd located the dining car and grabbed a table, I immediately probed him some more ...

"Of course," I said, "Starting off in Germany may not necessarily be your *best* first move. Where did you say he was last sighted?"

"Well, his trail ran cold in the Far East about a year and a half back. Since then he's been seen in all sorts of places he couldn't possibly be. Apparently, he became head of the South African Secret Police six months ago; three days later he opened up a soda factory in Milwaukee. You can see the problem I've got ..."

"I know," I said. "I've had all the same sort of leads myself. What's his name?"

"Sir Archibald Darkbloode ..."

"*Oh*," I said. "He's *aristocracy*, then?"

"No, no. *Common as muck*. It's an affectation. But that's how he signs his cheques, so that's how he's known ..."

"Any clues on the alleged son?"

"Just one ..."

"Go on ..."

"He refers to him in the will as 'Heathcliff' ..."

"Fancy that ..."

Hetty and Heathcliff.

It didn't sound entirely right to me.

But there you have it.

"But," he continued, "Going back to your *original* point. Germany may well be the wrong place to start, but I don't aim to waste time. I shall begin my investigations right here on this train ..."

"Oh yes?" I said, thinking it might be interesting to watch how an amateur operated.

"I'll give you a demonstration as soon as I get a suitable opportunity ..."

At that moment the waiter arrived.

"I'll have," said Trevor, "Clam Chowder, followed by Squid Borgignon with a leek & pineapple side-dish and Lobster Tandoori sauce – no raspberries..."

"And Sir?"

"Yeah ... er *no*," I said. "I'm feeling a little queasy. Just a glass of lager ..."

I let my gaze wander to the view through the carriage window:

The Kent countryside was rolling by, lit green and gold in the spring sunshine.

We ought to be in Dover before long, I thought. *Ostend by late afternoon ...* and back in the clink by tea-time, probably, if *Trevor* had anything to do with it.

Why?

Because *there* I was, in the midst of this reverie, when I thought I heard him mumble something and looked up to find his stare fixed on somebody across the aisle:

If he'd *said* anything, he hadn't said it to *me* ...

To my total astonishment – and the astonishment of his victim – *he suddenly got to his feet, descended on the lone character eating by himself, grabbed him round the neck and started snarling at him:*

"I *said*, doughnut-head, *are you* or *are you not* Sir Archibald Darkbloode? Well...?"

The poor man was being gripped so tightly round the windpipe, that he couldn't have answered if he'd wanted to ...

What he *was* doing, was *wheezing* incoherently.

"Speak up!" Trevor was yelling. "I haven't got all day!"

With his victim's face turning a nasty shade of purple, Trevor let go at the last moment and wandered back to his seat, leaving him gasping for air.

"It was just a shot in the dark," he said to me. "But if I hadn't have had my rucksack pinched, I could have checked his ID with the photo of Sir Arch in my casefile. As it is, I can't for the life of me remember what he looks like and therefore – *quid pro quo* – everybody on this train is a suspect ..."

"You know ..." I said (... *here I grabbed the lager out of the returning waiter's hand and took a hasty gulp* ...) "... that's an interesting *technique* you've got there, but surely you can't adopt that approach universally? I mean, you can't quiz everybody on the planet *individually*, can you ...?"

"Oh no," he said. "I've got a few other tricks up my sleeve yet. I've got a particularly good technique for getting to the bottom of issues involving large *groups* of people. Stick around and you'll see how it's done ..."

For the first time since meeting Trevor, I realised I'd unwittingly taken up with a psycho...

This man was *dangerous.*

And it was going to take all my efforts to contain him.

On the *other* hand, pointed in the right *direction*, he could be like a windfall of gold dust ...

Completely unmoved by the coughing and wheezing which was still audible from across the way, he sat there stirring his soup in circles and intermittently blowing on it, and this went on for several minutes until he finally took a sip ...

His expression changed.

"Oi, *moosh* ...!" he called out.

"Yes, sir?" said the waiter, on arrival.

"This soup's cold," he declared.

"I'll have it changed for you, Sir ..."

Surprisingly decent of him, I thought.

But Trevor had *other* ideas ...

"Oh, *excuse me,*" he said. "I didn't *know* you was deaf ..."

Eh ...? I thought

"*Sir* ...?"

"I *said* ..." he shouted ... *and here he slammed the bowl back out of the waiter's hand* ... "THIS SOUP IS *STONE* COLD! I DIDN'T ORDER *ANOTHER* ONE ...!"

The waiter didn't bat an eyelid.

"Then how can I help, Sir ...?"

"I'll *tell* you how you can help," he said. "You can get down on the floor and lick my shoes ..."

At this outburst, I heard some tittering from a table down the aisle ...

I wanted to shout out, "*Don't laugh, this man is mad!*" but I couldn't seem to prise open my gob ... and it was *too* late.

Smashing the plate aside, Trevor leapt to his feet, drew a gun out of his inside pocket ... and fired a bullet through the ceiling:

KERBLAM!!!

There was a scream.

"Eeeeeeeeeeeeeeeeek ...!!!" ... and a load of *glasses* all went tumbling over ...

CRASH !!!

"RIGHT!" he announced. "IF THE PERSON WHO STOLE MY BAG DOESN'T HAND IT OVER IN THE NEXT FIVE MINUTES, I'LL START SHOOTING HOSTAGES ONE BY ONE. *IS THAT CLEAR* ...?"

The carriage fell into a shocked silence.

Me?

I just sat there with a silly *grin* on my face.

Sipping a litre glass of lager.

All of a sudden, two men in guards' uniforms burst through the door behind him ...

"*THERE* HE IS!" they yelled. "*GET* HIM ...!!!"

Trevor took one look over his shoulder and – to the relief of everybody in the carriage (including me) – fled through the connecting door to the next one, with the guards in hot pursuit...

Deary me, I thought.

I wonder what *he* got thrown out of the police for ...?

"Don't worry," I said, as I took my drink and moved opposite the man Trevor had tried to strangle information from. "It's just a stroke of luck they've got psychiatrists swarming all over the train today ..."

He hadn't got his breath back yet, and he was still wheezing as he tried to collect himself.

Well, he'd had a *shock*.

So I introduced myself:

"Doctor *Reginald Freud*, BMA. I'm here for the quacks' convention in Vienna. And *yourself* ...?"

"That *man* ..." he croaked.

"Oh," I said, "He's quite mad. And *very* dangerous ..."

"Is he a patient of yours?"

"*Patient?*" I said, surprised. "Good *God*, no. That's Dr Treblinka. Head of the Criminal Insanity Research Unit at Broadmoor ..."

"How far are you going?" I asked.

I'd been sitting there watching him painstakingly replace his spectacles on his nose – the rim had got bent in the fracas with Trevor and would not sit right.

He was a thin, nervous type of about fifty or so, with a receding toupee.

"Bonn," he replied.

"That's a coincidence," I said, not elaborating. "Holiday?"

"Business," he said.

Then he thought for a moment.

"Why do you say *coincidence?* I thought you said you were going to Vienna...?"

I rose to my feet and made ready to leave.

"Well," I said, "I'm afraid you've *got* me there ..."

But the important thing was, *he* was going where I was going, and it was a dead cert that he was another guest for the Castle Froth. I pencilled him in as a dentist, initially, but he may have been just another random name from the computer.

Time would tell.

I'd already found the stethoscope invaluable as a theatrical prop, and, leaving it swinging round my neck, I took out a notebook and pen and decided to do a little gentle probing of some of the other passengers on board the train.

I'm afraid Trevor didn't know the first thing about collecting information.

One thing I'd learned in my two years abroad was that you never got anywhere by marching all over people in a pair of size twenty-seven jackboots. The thing needed in order to coax a few details from the public was the *art of the subtle* – politeness, diplomacy, and a keen eye for the unusual.

And *that*, I suppose, was why Trevor was a failed copper and a mere inquiry agent, and I was one of Her Majesty's *creme-de-la-creme* at MI5 ...

"Evening, ladies ..."

The first thing I did was to approach a trio of cheery, dark haired girls and, after clearing my tubes a couple of times, sat down next to them and introduced myself.

"Dr Randolph Shirt, BMA. I'm conducting a survey on behalf of the Royal College of Midwives concerning chiropody services in England and Wales, and was wondering if I could ask you a few questions regarding the state of fallen-arch treatment now that the NHS has been sold off to *Sainsbury's* ...?"

"Who's footing the bill for this?" said the first.

"Very funny," I said. "I couldn't buy you a pint of lager, could I?"

"Perhaps," she said. "On the other hand, if you don't clear off in the next ten seconds, I'll give you a demonstration of the working order of my big toe ..."

I readjusted my deerstalker.

"The pleasure's all mine ..."

However, before I could make a dignified exit, somebody tapped me on the shoulder from behind ...

Turning round, I found myself confronted by a matronly looking woman in her mid-fifties:

"Excuse me, young man," she said. "But did I understand you to say that the National Health Service has been sold to *Sainsbury's*? If so, I consider it an outrage ..."

"Well," I said, "It's a good way of drumming up custom, isn't it?"

"Would you care to explain?" she demanded.

"Well," I said, "Poison everyone with your frozen chicken and then fleece 'em a second time when they come back for treatment ..."

At that moment a great giant of a man dressed in German lederhosen and wearing a trilby made of straw tried to barge past me ... so I held out my hand in greeting: "Ah, bitte," I said. "Wie geht es ihnen? Es geht mir gut. Gut. Ich bin Doktor Eintracht Krankenhaus von Frankfurt. Und Sie?"

He looked me up and down.

Mainly *down*.

"If I was you," he said, "I'd learn to speak the lingo before you talk to strangers. Where do you think you are? Tibet? Other than that, do you mind getting out of my way ...?" (*and then, turning his attention to somebody else along his eyeline*) "... Cor, it's worse than Deptford High Street along here ..."

Bleeding cheek ...!

I had half a mind to stick one *on* him as he strolled away down the aisle ...
Perhaps Trevor had the right idea after all, I thought.
Where *was* he, anyway?
Suddenly a voice piped up behind me ...
"Hey, you!" it said.
I swung round to find Blondie Duval sitting there in a booth on her own.
"What do *you* want?" I said.
"Let me buy you a drink," she said.
"I'd rather you bought me some new suitcases ..."
"Hey, lighten up," she said. "You don't want to go through your whole life looking like that, do you?"
"Like what?" I said.
"Like you just swallowed an umbrella spring ..."
"Madam," I said, "I have to caution you that I am on a case, and I cannot tolerate anybody wasting police time ..."
"*Police?*" she said. "That ain't what I heard. I heard you was on your way to a party ..."
"Well, you heard wrong. And if you'll kindly excuse me ..."
"Hey," she insisted. "Not so fast. If you ain't off to a party, how come you had a suitcase full of party hats?"
"If you *must* know," I said, "It is a completely *exclusive* party which I am attending in my capacity as a law enforcement agent. Beyond that, my lips are shtoom. And it certainly doesn't concern *you* ..."
"Oh no?" she said. "Got an *invite*, have you?"
"I *have*, yes ..." I said.
Once again I attempted to take my leave, but she suddenly chucked a spanner in my spokes by raising her voice.
And her *stake.*
"Well," she declared. "Get a load of *this*, Groucho ..."
"*What* ...?"
"I've got *twenty-six* of 'em ..."
So saying, she took out a handful of the exclusive invitation cards and spread them all over the table like a full house.
I took one look down at them and slumped into the seat opposite her.
"Any sign," I asked her, "Of that *drink* you were threatening me with ...?"

"*Now*," she said, "I want some answers and I want 'em quick. Fire away ..."
"What were the questions?" I asked innocently.
"Don't play dumb with me ..."
"Okay," I said. "Here's an answer – the *only* answer *I* know: *Adolf Flite*. It answers every question you could possibly ask – except, perhaps, for *who is he? what is he? what's he up to? who's up to it with him?* and *how do we stop them?* – stuff like that ..."
"You're full of baloney ..."

Baloney? Baloney?

I searched my internal listings for that one but I couldn't find it.

"How quaint ..." I said.

"Well *listen*, Buster ..." she started to say ... *when my attention wandered to a disturbing clanking noise approaching from the far end of the carriage and I almost burped half my lager back into the glass in surprise ...*

The *clanking* was coming from an outsize *surgical* shoe ...

I pulled the flaps of my deerstalker down and hid behind my litre glass of lager.

"Did you hear what I was saying?" she kept asking. "You look like you've just seen a ghost ..."

I got to my feet ...

"Not at all," I said confidently. "This stuff goes straight through your bladder, doesn't it ...?"

"Speak for yourself ..."

"I'm just off to the slash-house. Be right back ..."

"You *better* be," she said. "I want some straight talking from you ..."

Keeping my drink at face-height as I passed Bertolt in the aisle, I gathered only that he was asking the waiter to find him a table, though it was a depressing enough confirmation of his identity to convince me of the need to return to the cabin for some heavier facial disguise ...

As I hurried on my way, I was accosted by a sudden and extraordinary collection of aural delights seeping out of an end-of-corridor WC, something like a cross between "*psssst!*" and the sound of somebody blowing off ...

I only stopped and turned round because the draught nearly blew my deerstalker out the window.

"Yes?" I said. "Can I help you?"

The door was slightly ajar, and so I pushed it gingerly inwards ...

I say *gingerly,* because there was a fair old hum leaking through the crack.

It was *Trevor.*

Squatting on the pot.

"Nerves," he said, apologetically.

"What," I said, "A *big* bloke like *you?*"

He shrugged his shoulders.

"Have those fellers gone?" he asked.

"Which fellers was that?" I enquired.

"That mob chasing me ..."

"Haven't seen them ..."

"I guess I was a bit rough on that guy in the dining car ..."

"He'll live," I said. "*Actually,* you might have done me a good turn, there..."

"How comes?"

"Well," I said, "He may not be Sir Arch, but he's definitely involved in the *Allied Froth* conspiracy. No mistake ..."

I'd nearly come to the end of my pint.

"All the same," he droned on, "I think I was a bit hasty there ..."

"Depends which way you look at it," I said. "I've learned that you just can't win in this game. After all, if he'd turned out to be Mr Ten-Most-Wanted you'd probably be a national hero by now. *Instead*, just *look* where you are: on the run from a mob of little Hitlers and painting the pan brown. The transformation from hero to villain and vice versa in this business is often a very thin line to tread and completely inexplicable in its rapidity ..."

He sat there giving me a puzzled look.

So I took a moment to try and analyse my last statement for grammatical errors and basic sense, but the only thing I could think about with any clarity was that another glass of *Froth* would like as not go down as well as the previous one.

"I'm a bit exposed," he said. "Can you come in and shut the door?"

"*Well ...*"

I took one look at him squatting there with his trousers round his ankles, knee-deep in the stink of recycled argeebargee, and decided that the *one* closet in which *this* clerk wasn't going to be conducting any business for the Queen was this very *small* one right *here*.

With or *without* the door shut.

"As it happens," I said, "I've just spotted trouble and I'm going to have to take a rain check ..."

And so saying, I pegged my nose and legged it.

Bursting into the cabin, I made a determined assault on the salvaged suitcase of the Colonel's equipment and immediately selected a stick-on moustache and an eye-patch in order to cover up most of what the deerstalker didn't.

Following this, I got hold of a magic marker and blacked out my front teeth.

Handsome, but cor dear it did narf taste foul (the things one is expected to do for Queen and Country).

Penultimate of the delicate series of artistic operations I felt compelled to carry out in the cause of fake mutilation was to select an iron-on scar and stick it across my forehead ... with *sellotape*, of course. *I had no intention of running a hot iron over my ironing board.*

But I was going to have to be very careful it didn't fall off at some inopportune moment.

My final move as I plumbed the depths of ingenuity, was to stick a Union Jack transfer on the front of the deerstalker, after which I headed back to the dining car ...

The *first* thing I noticed as I staggered through the door was that Bertolt had been placed in the seat next to Ms Duval, placing *me* in somewhat of a quandary as a result:

I didn't think there was much chance of him recognising me after all this time, but there was every risk that *she* might blurt out my name in passing – always assuming that she knew what it was to begin with.

As luck would have it, our arrival in Dover harbour pre-empted the need to make any sort of choice on further seating arrangements, and I was able to lose myself in the ensuing melee preceding embarkation.

I just hoped the officials weren't going to spot a discrepancy between my current scarred and toothless face as compared with the photo of the handsome smiling chap in my passport ...

I needn't have worried.

Just before I became next-in-line for scrutiny, there was a sudden eruption of chaos from somewhere behind me, accompanied by a gunshot and screams – *most of them mine* – and a great *shove* concertinaed everybody to the floor ...

I looked up just in time to see Trevor barge past and leap straight over the counter with a mad-dog expression on his face, using some poor old dear's head as a springboard as he went.

A small group of railway staff were right behind him, and the fray was immediately joined by just about every uniformed official in sight.

They couldn't *catch* him, though.

I watched in astonishment as he scaled some furniture and disappeared through a window into Dover dockyard ...

Embarrassed, thus, of any further obstruction to my holiday intinerary, I took advantage of the migrating staff and breezed through the deserted checkpoint.

Not that our passport control officer was off chasing *Trevor*, though ...

He, in fact, shit a brick and ran off in the opposite direction.

And I must say that all seemed rather typical to me.

Along with a few other shifty-looking types from the queue, I got back on the train and waited for it to move off again.

To *where*, I had no idea.

Some crank told me it was going to drive onto the boat, and the boat was going to carry it to Ostend, where it was going to resume its journey.

I told him he was an *idiot* because, not only would the boat sink under the weight, but that Belgian railway tracks were three times wider than English ones.

Why?

Because Belgians liked a lot of space between them and the next passenger, especially after a meal ...

"In any case," I said, "Who ever heard of railway tracks on a boat? And how does the train negotiate the gap from the quay? What does it *do*, fly? Drive up the gangplank? And when it got to the other end it'd be the wrong way round to drive off again, wouldn't it? Don't be so fucking stupid ..."

"*You* sir," he said, "Are a moronic imbecile, and offensive with it. I am terminating this conversation forthwith ..."

"Listen," I yelled out after him, "This train's got more chance of steaming up my arse than sailing to Belgium! What, do you think I was born yesterday ...?"

He opened a cabin door and went inside.

"Fucking Oxford Dons ..." I cursed.

As the Orient Express filled up again, I ruminated on the fate of Trevor and assumed that it was the last we'd see of him for a long time.

The rest of his *natural*, probably.

And when the train did move off again, it moved onto a boat.

Funnily enough.

CHAPTER 36
AFFAIRS OF THE HEART

Like an over-keen divining rod, my ever reliable front-lobal radar screen picked up the signal of a bar opening the moment the ferry sailed, accompanied by an impatient blip from my last pocketful of change ...

Under Fire

The place was almost deserted when I wandered in, save for a couple of lovebirds at one end of the counter and a solitary gent at the other, and so I homed in on a position equidistant from each and ordered a drink. "*Froth* please, cock," I said to the barman, picking up a stray copy of *Le Monde*.

"*Froth?*" he queried (he was a Frenchman). "*Bier* ...?"

"Well," I said, "Not unless they've branched out into pizzas ..."

I turned round and laughed ... but, finding no audience to share my joke, I turned back to clarify myself.

I wonder what all this is about? I thought, as I rifled through page after page of incomprehensible newsprint.

Like non-English language newspapers the world over, not one word of English graced its pages.

Not *one* word, that is, except for a little advertisement in the classifieds featuring the same logo I'd seen in the funeral parlour in West London:

DARC
Corporate Removals

On an impulse, I tore it out.

This, however, turned out to be a bit hasty, because it was only after I'd stuffed it in my pocket that I noticed a pen on the counter (hitherto concealed by the paper) and a half-finished crossword on the back page, leading me to the conclusion that I'd inadvertently purloined the bartender's own reading matter...

The transmission of an appropriate glare while he busied himself pouring my drink only encouraged me to display a pair of uncomfortable shoes, the guilt inside them shifting uneasily from one foot to the other as I replaced the rag back where I'd found it and searched for a diversion ... a *diversion* which finally arrived from the most *spectacularly* unwanted direction when the solitary gent suddenly started yelling something along the lines of "Drink! *Drink!* Whisky! *Whisky* ...!"

Any *earlier* thoughts I may have had on introducing myself to this character and telling him how marvellous I considered these 'train-boats' to be were deterred by this outburst; and, since our host had *already* ignored him, it spelt nothing but trouble for *me* ...

"Don't worry about the barman!" I yelled, attempting to pre-emp a near-certain shift of attention. "He ain't got over Alsace-Lorraine yet ...!"

This had no effect at all on the gent, by the look on his face.

The *barman* looked none too pleased about it either, as he slammed the drink down and snatched his newspaper away ...

Me?

I felt obliged to reflect on the advisability of a course in confrontation avoidance, the upshot of which was still unclear moments later when a hand descended on my shoulder and voice whispered excitedly ...

"*Dexter* ...!"

A *tingle* went down my spine, and a whole flood tide of emotional breakers went crashing across a shore somewhere.

It was *Jane* ...

"Well ..." (*I picked up my lager as I spoke*) "... I'm afraid you've got me at a disadvantage ..."

(It was a *good* job I'd been momentarily lost for words, because by the time the moment had *passed*, another hand had assaulted my *other* shoulder and I'd swung round to find *Laurel* looming over me ...)

The lovebirds.

"Oh, *come* on," she said. "I'd know you anywhere ..."

"Long time no see ..." beamed Laurel.

"*Je ne comprend pas* ..." I hissed in my best text-book Belgian, giving him a flash of my darkened dentures for good measure ...

"You know," he said, "It's absolutely remarkable, really, but with your teeth blacked-out like that you look even *more* like your little friend – you *know*, that *funny* old chap – what was his name? *Kirk?* Something like that ..."

Dirk ...?

(Here I became aware of the bar filling up around us – with Belgians, mainly, if their accents were anything to go by)

What did he *mean*, that I looked *even* more like him?

Compared to *what?*

I bit my lip and kept shtoom.

But it was *difficult.*

"Now, Dexter," said my former sweetheart, "Here we are, not having seen you for all this time, and you pretend not to know us. Why?"

I was getting a right dose of jacknifed chin, swinging round between the pair of them, so I reversed a couple of paces in order to address both at the same time:

"Oh!" I said. "It's *you* two! Hello Jane. *And hello Laurel.* How are the tomatoes?"

"Tomatoes are fruits, old boy ..."

"Exactly, exactly ..."

There was an embarrassing silence.

"How's business, then?" I said at length.

"Business has been very bad ..." said Jane.

"Up till *now*," added Laurel.

"Go on ..."

"Well," said Jane (adopting a suitably *business*-like stance), "Let's get to the *point*, shall we? I think we all know why we're here. Have you got an invite to the Schloss Froth? Because *without* one it's going to be a lot more difficult getting inside than *with* one ..."

"Schloss Froth?" I said. "What's that?"

"Stop wasting time, Dexter," she went on. "I think you've got an invite, and I think you should hand it over to *us* ..."

"Yes," added Laurel. "After all, it was on account of your meddling that Jane and I were demoted to routine office work for two years while my brother was able to continue perpetrating his crimes unchecked ..."

Meddling?

Bloody cheek, I thought.

"I told you once before that there was great danger in all of this," said Jane. "It's time to stand aside. Be a good boy. Give it here ..."

She held out her hand.

"I don't know anything about nothing," I said. "Nothing at all. I'm on holiday ..."

"Now," said Laurel, "You don't expect us to believe *that*, old boy, do you...?"

He was starting to get right up my nose again ...

"I mean," added Jane, "It's a bit of a coincidence, isn't it, that you just happen to be travelling on the *Orient Express* in the direction of Cologne? It's bad enough Laurel and myself having to hitch-hike ..."

"Don't talk to me about hitch-hikers ..." I mumbled.

"Yes," added Laurel. "You *owe* us ..."

Oh, really?

I tapped him on the lapel.

"As I recall," I said, *"You* owe *me* ..."

"For what?" he asked, apparently surprised.

"For a *curry*, for a start ..."

"This is tiresome, Dexter," said Jane.

I would have liked to have helped her – for old times sake – but I didn't want to help Mr Organic-Gardening-Gloves, and the truth is, they were as thick as thieves.

In *any* case, I hadn't spent the last two years risking life and limb just so that somebody *else* could steal my glory ...

"Like I said," I said, "I'm not in security work anymore. I'm on holiday ..."

"Oh? Where are you going?"

"Shark fishing ..."

"*Where?*"

"Up the Belgian coast ..."

"There *aren't* any sharks up the Belgian coast," said clever-clogs.

"Well," I said, "I should have a quiet, peaceful holiday, then ..."

"If you're on holiday," he went on, "Why are you in disguise?"

"It's *not* disguise," I said. "It's natural wear and tear. Most of this damage came from trying to salvage your reputation in that bar in Sydney after you legged it ..."

"Then why does the scar on your forehead say 'Made in Hong Kong' ...?"

"Now *look* here, Laurel," I said. "I'm getting a bit tossed off with you. I can't seem to set *foot* outside the country without you popping up where you're not wanted. In any case, who *is* this Adolf Flite? I've never *heard* of him ..."

"I never mentioned Adolf Flite," said Jane. "Did *you*, Laurel?"

I softened my voice a little. "*Listen* Jane," I said, "I shall always have a fondness for you, but it's no good trying to get anything out of *me*. A lot's happened in the past two years – I'm not the same man you waved goodbye to from Madras harbour. I can't remember anything about the case I was on, but if I did, I'd tell you. You *know* that ..."

They gave each other a *maybe-he's-telling-the-truth* look, which, in turn, gave way to a look of disappointment.

I was disappointed as well.

I'd just run out of lager.

The trouble was, as I took the last few coins out of my pocket, the invitation popped right out with them and landed smack on the counter in front of me like the principal exhibit in a copper-nobbling trial ...

Laurel had already snatched it away and given it the once-over before I'd even realised what it was ...

"Oi!" I yelled. "Give that back!"

"What's *this*, old boy ...?" (*he retreated a couple of steps ...*) "Don't *know* anything? Can't *remember* anything? Just going on *holiday* ...? *I'd* say you were *fibbing* ..."

"That's what we needed," said Jane. "The invite we've been looking for ..."

"Well, you can't have it," I said. "It's *mine*. It's addressed to *me* ..."

"It doesn't have a *name* on it," said Laurel, waving it teasingly just out of my reach ...

"It doesn't *need* a name," I said. "It's genetically fingerprinted and completely useless to either of you ..."

"Sounds a bit unlikely to me," said Jane.

"It mentions two tickets for the *Orient Express* here," said Laurel. "Where are they?"

"I gave them away ..."

"Never mind. The *invite's* the important thing. *Mm*, I'm going to enjoy this party ..."

"I'm *warning* you ..."

"Now just a *minute*, Laurel," said Jane. "That invite's as much *mine* as yours. We still need to discuss which of us should use it ..."

"It's not necessary," he said. "I *have* to confiscate this on behalf of Interpol, and so it naturally becomes my *duty* to use it ..."

"'*Ere*," I said, "I've got a good mind to biff you on the beak ..."

He started backing away at this point, moving into an area of floorspace being donated ever more generously by the assembled crowd, and – when I made an untimely grab for the invitation and slipped sideways on the polished surface – they suddenly scattered in all directions...

"I'll *rip* it up ...!" he shouted, displaying all the logic of a banana-case as he rushed to give a demonstration of his intent above my sprawled form ...

He must be some sort of crackpot, I thought ... so I staggered to my feet and took another *lunge* at him ...

"Come *here*, tomato-head ...!" I yelled ...

... but his ability to anticipate my movement and evade it accordingly, caused me to crash into the bar counter, where I picked up my empty pint glass and swung it in a great 180-degree arc, just missing his snorter by a fraction ... and the barman's snorter by even less. The momentum caused me to gyrate a second time ... after which I had the good sense to let go of the glass ...

"Aaaaaaaa*aaaarrrgh* ...!"

It shot out of my hand like a discus ...

CRASH !!!

The optics exploded as though they'd been hit by a bazooka!

Up went the white flag from the French contingent ... or was it the back page of *Le Monde*? A surrender signal, left flapping amongst a mid-air spray of multi-coloured glass and liquid, while its owner went ducking out of the way of the shrapnel like a reckless war correspondent ...

Enter the invading army.

In *one* clumsy movement, the loose cannon who'd been propping up the other end of the bar suddenly broke free of his moorings, barged into our midst, snatched the invite out of Laurel's hand, lurched past me, jammed himself up against the counter and started waving it around and shouting for whisky as though he'd just found a drinking licence ...

"I'll give *you* whisky ..." I said ... and snatched it *back* from him.

Then I unzipped my flies ... *and posted it to the war office.*

Well, it was the safest place I could think of at the time.

Inside *Dirk's* flies would have been safer, if he'd been there.

I couldn't afford to lose that invite.

At *least*, not unless I wanted to call in the transatlantic carpetbaggers and ingratiate myself with Ms Blondie Loudmouthed-Yanke in order to procure another one ...

"*Now* let's see what kind of a man-of-action you are Laurel!" I taunted him.

Naturally enough, he stood there hesitating.

But I hadn't bargained for *Jane* ...

Out of the corner of my eye, I saw her cup her hand and get ready to grab me in one of the world's most highly disputed hot-spots ...

"Okay, *okay* ...!" I said. "*Calm* down. You can have it. I know when I'm beaten ..."

I realised we were putting on quite a floor show for the neutrals, who all seemed quite entertained by our antics, and so I retrieved the much-coveted battle trophy and pretended to be about to hand it over:

"Oh look ...!" I suddenly said. *I pointed beyond her head.* "What's *that* ...?"

Works every time, that one ...

As she swung round, I yelled, "So *long*, pen-pushers ...!" and scarpered out of the door with a massive round of applause ringing in my ears.

Well, you can't afford to be *sentimental* in wartime ...

Tickertape

I got lost in a crowded coffee bar on the deck below, and moved in on the end of a table of six hirsute-looking types playing cards.

"Kitehawk," I said, keeping my eyes fixed firmly on the gangway. "*Dexter.* Don't get up ..."

"Beans," said the one sitting next to me. "*Wilbur* Beans ..."

"Just a minute ..." (*I backed off a bit*). "There's no particular reason they *call* you that, is there ...?"

"Nope," he said. "It's just my name. Why?"

I wondered whether he had a faulty exhaust.

"Oh ..." I said.

I relaxed again.

"No reason ..."

He gave me a querulous look.

"No," I said, attempting to reassure him. "I've just had a bit of bad luck with wind direction over the years and I've lost my no claims bonus. No offence, but they don't classify it under *acts of god* any more – at least, not unless the explosion is more than ninety megatons ..."

"*No?*"

"No," I said. "They won't pay out for love nor money. I even produced the cause last time – a cabbie from New Orleans – but *he* wasn't insured either ..."

"What are you talking about?"

"Nobody knows," I said. "Mind if I sit down?"

"You *are* sitting down. If you want to get any lower you could always try

the deck below ...”
I moved back in a bit.
“Do you want *in?*” he asked.
“In?” I said. “*In* what?”
“*Poker*. We’re playing *poker* ...”
“No thanks,” I said. “I’m an habitual cheat ...”
“Suit yourself ...”
Somebody laughed.
“That was a funny joke,” I lied.
“Where are you headed?” he asked, after a pause for play.
“Cologne,” I said. “*Köln*, to the non-English-speaking members present
...”

“That’s a coincidence,” he said. “Join the club ...”
“Was that another joke?”
“I’m not sure whether it counts. There was no advance planning ...”
“What club’s that, then?” I enquired.
“Pan-Germanic Vampire Fellowship ...”
I got to my feet.
“Cheerio ...”

“I *should* say,” he added quickly, “The Pan-Germanic Vampire-*Hunters*
Fellowship ...”
“No,” I said. “It doesn’t really help. Life’s too complicated as it is ...”
“You ought to relax,” he said. “You look like a potential coronary victim
to me ...”
I sat down again.
“There’s nothing wrong with my ticker,” I said. “I’m a member of the
BMA...”
“What,” he said, “*The* BMA? The *Blood-Munchers* Association?”
“Not quite,” I said. “What’s it got to do with you, anyway?”
He looked round at his companions.
“Well,” he laughed, “You could say our group has a stake in all affairs of
the heart ...!”
“Yeah,” I said, “Do you find you have to set aside a certain number of
hours every day, or do you just wait for inspiration to write your scripts ...?”
*The two at the far end suddenly hooted so loud that the shock wave knocked me off the
end of the seat ...*
Seeing *Laurel* prowling around nearby, I crawled under the table.
“What are you doing down there?” asked Wilbur Beans.
I started sniffing.
“It’s alright,” I said. “I thought I could smell laughing gas ...”
“Here,” he said. “Take this ...”
“What is it?” I demanded to know. (It *looked* like a roll of wire-wool)
“It’s a false beard,” he said. “Each one is impregnated with nitrous oxide
pellets. You’ve got to *laugh*, haven’t you ...?”

As soon as I'd adjusted the position of my false moustache and scars to accommodate it, I stuck the beard on and resurfaced, rueing the fact that most of the MI5 agents I'd ever heard about had been issued with *cyanide* capsules to chew on ...

"Of course," Beans suddenly declared, "It's quite a privilege for a non-member of the Fellowship to be given a beard. It means that you are now an honorary member, and I think I can speak for all present when I say that, as you seem a funny enough character, you're quite welcome to join our outing in the capacity of an observer ..."

"Oh yes, and what does that entail?" I said, distractedly on the lookout for signs of Laurel, Jane or anyone else looking vaguely out-of-place in a room full of sober people. (Right at *that* moment the only person I did recognise was Ms Duval, down the aisle, talking to some bloke with a tidal-wave hairstyle ...)

"Well," he went on, "As an *observer*, you can't participate in any of the hand-to-hand activities such as digging up the corpses at midnight, impaling red-blooded foreigners on stakes or firing silver bullets at estate agents, but you will, obviously, travel with us to unfriendly inn houses, gothic castles and fogbound graveyards. And, depending on the specific occasion, you might be called upon to indulge in some of the fringe activities – waving crucifixes around, chucking holy water at stockbrokers, drinking heavily, laughing heartily and going to sleep each night with a crate-load of garlic round your neck ..."

"You've aroused my interest," I said. "What's the itinerary?"

"We start off with the Rhine Castles. First stop, the *Schloss Froth*. Deserted since the late 1400's when the local tyrant, 'Fröth the Inhaler', accidentally cut himself shaving and severed the bloodline. But he's still about and receiving guests, apparently. Especially on *Walpurgis Nacht* ..."

"Froth the Inhaler!" I laughed. "Who's *he?*"

"Used to boil the blood of his victims and inhale the fumes as a cold cure..."

"Listen," I said, "I know about the Castle Froth and you've got it all mixed up. I won't go into details now, except to say that it's far from deserted. As a matter of fact, there's a big bash going on there tomorrow night, but you won't get in because it's by invitation only ..."

"Oh?" he said. "Are you sure? How do you know?"

"Because I'm one of the lucky ones with an invite, inclusive of luxury travel on the *Orient Express*, gratis ..."

"Well, that beats our mode of transport ..."

"Hitch hiking?" I said.

"*Worse*. Pushbikes ..."

I thought for a moment.

"Just wait here," I said. "I might be able to help you out. Only, don't lose those false beards, whatever you do ..."

I breezed into Blondie's recess and sat down opposite her.

"Oh, *there* you are!" I said. "I've been looking all over ..."

"*Say,*" she said. "Where did *you* get to?"

"I was trying to avoid that bloke you were talking to ..."

"*Who?*" she said defensively. "*Dusty* ...?"

She put a protective arm round her companion.

"No, no," I said. "*Bertolt.* On the *train* ..."

"Oh," she said. "*Him. That* wimp ..."

"Yeah," I said. "*That's* him ..."

Back came the arm again.

"Why, do you *know* him?" she said.

"You *could* say that ..."

"Is he connected?"

"From his plates up ..."

She banged her fist down on the table and rattled a load of empty cups in their saucers ...

"You wait till I get my hands on him!" she shouted. "He told me he was in orthopaedics ..."

Dusty then mumbled something about the shoe "... being on the other foot ..." to which Blondie let out the most raucous, grating screech of a laugh it has ever been my mispleasure to hear from a human being ...

Just in case I'd *missed* something, I glanced behind me.

Only to find everyone staring in *my* direction ...

"Don't look at *me* !" I shouted. "It was the most uproariously *unfunny* joke I've ever heard ...!"

I swivelled back just in time to catch Blondie in the death throes of that last laugh, gurgling and hiccuping ...

"What's the *matter* with everybody today ...?" I said, checking for damage to the nitrous oxide capsules secreted about my beard.

Even Dusty was sitting there with a soppy smirk on his face, like a drugs courier who'd just had a laughing gas balloon burst a slow puncture up his rectum.

I *did* keep waiting for an introduction, but since Blondie wasn't forthcoming with one, I decided to force the issue myself. *After all, he could have been anybody, and I wasn't going to sit there gassing about the case until I'd checked his credentials – though, with a haircut like that, I guessed he wasn't involved in any mainstream seriousness.*

In *fact,* come to think of it, *she* could have been anybody as well.

All I knew about *her* was that she'd thrown all my luggage off the train.

So I interrogated *her* first ...

"Who are *you?*" I demanded to know.

"None of your *damn* business," she said. "I ask the questions round here..."

"Fair enough ..."

"Let's get *that* straight *before* we start ..."

"Right. Okay then," I said. (*I turned my attention to Dusty*). "Who are *you?*"

He offered his hand.

"Is there more?" I queried.

Apparently there was.

(A *business card*, to be specific):

DUSTY QUIFF

Hairdresser to the Stars

Dallas, Texas

UK Address: 3451 Ocean Boulevarde, Deptford

At first, his overhanging haystack didn't accompany him as he reclined in his seat with a smug look on his face, but then it suddenly sprang back into position and hung there quivering like a wall of crude ...

"Dallas?" I said, wondering whether he had a deal to pipe barrels of oil straight out of the ground and straight onto his head.

"I've done the hair of everybody on Southfork," he said.

"What are *you* looking at?" I said to Blondie.

She gave me a funny squint.

"Yeah," she said, "Dusty's done all the stars. I've seen him turn the most awful heads of hair into works of art, but I reckon there ain't a thing he could do for *you* ..."

"That's alright," I said. "I'd hate to have to check on the latest OPEC price rise every time I took a comb out ..."

"Dusty did *his* hair once ..."

"Whose?"

"Gregory O'Peck ..."

I ducked out of the way as Blondie let rip at her own joke ... and found myself cowering in the shadow of a cheap playing-card earring she had hanging from her right earlobe. It was swaying hypnotically in time to the ebb and flow of her convulsion, and it only *stopped* swaying when she reached the gurgling stage again...

"Is this a working holiday for you?" I enquired.

"Why?" she said.

"I noticed they had a vacancy on board earlier on ..."

"Oh?" she said. "For what?"

"Reserve foghorn ..."

She screwed up her face.

"Now *listen*, Buster ..." ... *but I cut her short by switching my attentions back to her hairdresser and scrutinising his business credentials in more detail:*

"Deptford," I said. "I've heard a lot about this place lately. Where is it, exactly?"

"*Deptford*, London ..."

"*London?*" I queried. "Are you sure? What *part* of London?"

"South ..."

"*South?*"

"Of the *river*," he clarified.

"*What* river?" I asked.

"The *Thames*, dummy," interrupted Blondie. "*South* of the *Thames* ..."

"I didn't know there *was* any London south of the Thames ..."

Then I paused for thought.

"Oh," I said. "You mean *France*?"

"Get to the point, asshole ..."

"Well," I said, "The thing is *this*. I haven't been wasting my time on this tub. I need some of your invitations for a few friends of mine I just bumped into. They've got a score to settle with the occupant of the Schloss Froth, and it'll be better for all of us if we hit that place in numbers ..."

"Sure," she said. "Be my guest. How many do you want?"

"Half a dozen – no, better make it a score. I could donate the others to any worthy causes I come across ..."

She took out her wad of invites and rail tickets.

"Here, take 'em ..."

"Thanks very much," I said.

As I got up to leave, she grabbed hold of my arm ...

"But just *remember*," she added, "I wanna *talk* with you later. *Before* we hit Cologne – not *after* ..."

"I'll see you on the train ..."

"You better ..."

When Dusty stood up to shake hands, his hair sprang to life on an apparent delay mechanism and smacked me right on the nose ...

"If I was *you*," I said, "I'd buy a hat before we reach Ostend ..."

"Oh?" he said. "Why?"

"Because you need a quiff licence before you can set foot on Belgian soil. They don't *like* it over there. Last bloke I knew who tried to enter the country with one of them was done under the health and safety regulations. They quarrantined his quiff for three months. The prospects don't look good ..."

En route back to the card school, I almost sunk into a swamp of people all getting to their feet in a premature free-for-all as we docked in Ostend.

"Here you are ..."

"What's this?" said Beans.

"Six invitations to the Castle Froth," I said. "And, whatsmore, six tickets for luxury travel on the *Orient Express*. Overnight berths included. You can ditch the pushbikes in the harbour now ..."

"D'you hear *this*, boys?" he said. "Looks like we've hit the jackpot, although I don't know about the bikes. We're all rather attached to them, and the pumps often come in handy for squirting holy water when we're dealing with a job-lot of the un-dead. Perhaps we can put them in the guard's van?"

"I'm sure," I said.

"Anyway, you can consider yourself a candidate for full membership now..."

"Does that mean I get my own stake?"

"Afraid not. That only comes after three years work in the field. No offence, though – it's club rules. If it was up to me ..."

"Don't worry," I said. "It's no reflection on you ..."

Once again, I detected that noxious whiff of laughing gas as all six were hit by a collective paroxysm of hysterics ...

"You must teach me how to do that one day," I said.

"Just bite into your beard," said one of Beans's companions.

"Yeah," I said, "But it's the element of spontaneity that's missing ..."

"It'll match your *teeth*, then ..."

As if to contradict him, I inadvertently bit into my tongue and injected a shot of magic marker poisoning straight into my bloodstream, setting me up as a potential victim of septicaemia of the cakehole.

It was *only* six in the evening and things were already getting dangerous ...

"You *do*, however, get your own pan-Germanic bicycle clips ..."

So saying, he handed over an official presentation set, complete with a carrying case shaped like a miniature coffin ...

Mm, I thought. *More disguise.*

"And," he continued, "You also get to meet all of the boys in person. We are very privileged to have three fully-qualified members of the medical profession amongst our ranks. In addition to myself, we have Doctors Van Shingle and Van English ..."

"That's a coincidence," I said. *I shook their hands.* "Dexter Kitehawk, BMA..."

All of a sudden, I received a sharp prod on the shoulder and swung round to find myself confronted by some lout in bright orange shorts and a string vest ...

"Did I hear you say you were Dexter Kitehawk?" he said.

"*Who* wants to know?" I demanded, outraged at being poked in such a manner.

"Well," he said, "You're the man they couldn't *gag*, aren't you ...?"

"I *might* be," I said. "*Who's* asking?"

"Couldn't *gag* ...?" heckled some loudly-dressed woman who happened to be strolling by. "*No*, not when he's got a bottle of *beer* stuck in his mouth ..."

(She I took to be his appendage)

"Only," he persisted, "I was just wondering ..."

"Well?" I said impatiently.

"Well," he said, "I was just *wondering*. If you're the man they couldn't *gag*, why don't you just shut up voluntarily ...?"

I stood looking at him as he wandered away to join the embarkation queue.

"Not to worry," I said to Beans and his friends. "He's just one of my mental patients ..."

"*Tragic* ..." commented Beans, in a general murmur of sympathy for the poor psychiatrist whose thankless lot it was treat such ungrateful customers.

"Unfortunately," I added, "His lobotomy is wearing off ..."

To support which diagnosis, I took note of the contra-indications ... and slung the bicycle clips at him.

DINK!

Direct hit!

And ... *whatsmore* ... a hatful of *bonus* points ...

Zizzle ... twang ...

DONK!

They bounced right off his head and catapulted straight into the mouth of his wife, who immediately started wailing like a fire klaxon nobody could switch off. The clips were stuck fast, and her gob was frozen agape in the pose of a blacksmith's anvil ...

"YODEL-ODEL-EH-*HEE*-DEEEEEEEEEE ...!!!"

Exit the front row en masse.

As for my *original* target – her *husband* – well ...

When he looked round, I *waved* at him.

His neck went an angry red ...

"Your wife *like* opera, does she?!!!" I yelled.

He started to march towards me ...

"Well," I added, "Next time I'll give her a clip round the *ear* as well. She's tone deaf ...!!!"

When he launched into a run, I tore off over the table tops and back out onto the staircase, looking behind me only once to find he'd been tripped up by Beans and his crew, and had slid headfirst into a wall ...

Custom and Tradition

What happened to him immediately after that, I'm not sure, because I had to hang around belowdecks for quite a while, hoping the storm would blow over.

Eventually, however, the need for a call of nature became so strong that I ventured back upstairs and knocked on the first cabin I saw.

The trouble was, it was the *Captain's* cabin, and he answered my knock in person ...

"What do you want?" he said in perfect English.

(Well, I think he *was* English)

So I barged straight past him ...

"Excuse me," I said, "I just want to use your pisshole ..."

"Now just a minute ..." he started to say, flabbergasted.

"No, no," I said, spotting the small room in the corner. "I've cleared it with the Purser ..."

Before he had time to react properly, I'd sauntered in and locked the door behind me.

The trouble was, I wasn't *in* his toilet.

I was in his laundry cupboard ...

Breezing out again, I headed for another door in the opposite wall ...

"Get out of here at once!" he was shouting. "I shall have you thrown off the boat and arrested. I'm the *Captain* of this vessel. You should have gone ashore by now. Who *are* you?"

I slammed the door shut on him again.

"You can't do this!" he was yelling through the keyhole.

"No," I called back, "Not in *Belgium*, but it's quite acceptable in England. It's recognised in law. I'm afraid that's just one of the things you lot in the Common Market will have to get used to. *After all*, we had to change all our money to decimals. You'll just have to get used to old English traditions like squatters rights. *Now*, where's your pot ...?"

I realised I'd made another mistake the moment I turned round and saw his hammock swinging from the ceiling ...

I was in his *bedroom*.

But he was too clever for me this time.

He locked *me* in.

From *outside*.

After which, I could hear him talking to somebody on a telephone and summoning reinforcements.

The only way out was a gigantic loophole.

Well ...

A gigantic *porthole*, which wasn't quite the same thing.

Especially as the drop to the quay was a big one, something I gathered only once I'd laboured to unscrew its gigantic *bolts*.

In *any* case, my priority was a *slash*.

I couldn't *think* straight till I got that out the way.

As luck would have it, my assailant in the orange shorts and string vest passed by on the dockside below just at that moment, and so I swung into action ... and pissed all over him!

He looked up.

"Why don't you splash out and buy an umbrella?" I yelled.

He went berserk, clawing at the air and roaring like a dinosaur ...

"WEEUUUUUAARRRRR ...!!!"

"Careful!" I cautioned. "You'll blow your top!"

"I'LL TEAR YOU LIMB FROM LIMB WHEN I GET HOLD OF YOU ...!!!" he screamed.

"Where did you get that vest?" I enquired. "I ain't seen one of them since *mangles* were big news ..."

All of a sudden his wife hobbled into view ...

"Can't you *do* something about him?!!!" she shrieked.

"*You've* changed your tune!" I laughed.

"Wait here!" he shouted at her.

Upon which, he dropped his carrier-bag of duty-free and went haring back towards the gangway, presumably in order to seek me out ...

I was in a fix, no mistake.

I estimated his time of arrival in the Captain's cabin somewhere in the region of two minutes.

The *Captain's* reinforcements would probably arrive even sooner.

I therefore tried to ascertain the likelihood of surviving a drop into the drink below ...

There *was* a narrow chink of water visible between quay and boat, certainly, and this held a reflection of the rising moon.

But it was a dead cert I'd miss it and land face-down on the quay, flattened like a cartoon pancake.

Mrs Orange-Shorts was standing guard as well, just in case I tried it and survived.

She had the sort of face you could iron coats with.

I needed to think *fast*, though, because – personal safety considerations aside – I was going to miss that *train* if I didn't hurry ...

"I couldn't have my bicycle clips back, could I?" I called out to her, but she just gave me a heartless stare.

So I paced up and down.

And up ... *and down* ...

And round in a circle ... *following all routes back to the porthole.*

And it was while I was *standing* there – leaning out and looking for inspiration – that something clattered me round the head and fell on *past* me to the quay below ...

It was a *rope* ladder!

When I craned my neck upwards, I almost got decapitated by somebody abseiling *down* it in a big hurry ...

"Sorry Kitehawk," he said. "Can't stop ..."

Customs and Excise

Open-mouthed in astonishment, I stood there watching Trevor making a bolt for freedom down the side of the ferry ... until I heard the arrival of several pairs of feet in the outer cabin, followed by excited talk, accompanying commotion ... *and culminating in the sound of the key turning in the lock.*

"I think I'll *join* you ...!" I called out after him.

"Be my guest," he called back. "I don't like this boat much ..."

Putting one foot on the ladder, I decided to cast aside all the best mountaineering text-book advice and chanced to look down from a great height:

I couldn't quite believe my luck!

Mrs Orange-Shorts had mistaken Trevor for Yours Truly in the dark, and had begun clattering him about the head with her husband's discarded carrier bag of duty-free just as he

reached the bottom rung ...
"Take that ...!" she was yelling at him.
He didn't know what had hit him ...

... and *so*, while he staggered around on the harbour below me, groggily trying to protect himself from the rain of blows, I clambered down nimbly and raced over towards passport control ...

Once inside, I joined the tail end of the queue and tried to relax, but I was sweating buckets, and it couldn't have helped my cause much to keep looking round behind me like a pursued convict for signs of Mr and Mrs Orange-Shorts and the Captain of the ferry ...

Fortunately, a few late stragglers arrived to cover my rear, and I tried to concentrate very hard on the oncoming inspection.

Right at the last moment, the scar on my forehead wilted under my intense body heat and peeled off halfway, hanging from my face like a strip of freshly-deposited birdshit ...

The official gave me a beady look before taking my documentation, and when he finally opened his mouth to pose a question, he might just as well have been speaking *Chinese* for all I took in what he said.

Basically, I corpsed.

Which was a bit *embarrassing*, really, because the only thing I could think to do was to give him a great big wide-open grin ...

"Cor," I said, flashing him a lovely shot of my blackened choppers. "I d' narf fancy a piss ..."

This made no impression at all that I could detect.

In *fact*, the ensuing silence might well have gone on forever, if the sound of a telephone ringing somewhere in the vicinity hadn't broken our collective trances ...

Not that the official made any attempt to *answer* it, mind you.

I turned round to the queue behind me:

"Anyone expecting a call?" I asked.

At last the Belgian burst into life, gesturing – it seemed – at my eyepatch ...

What he wanted me to *do* with it I couldn't quite decipher, but – being aware that my mugshot depicted me with two *good* eyes – I raised it up and *winked* at him.

He didn't seem to *like* that.

So I transferred it my *other* eye, but this didn't help *either*, apparently.

In the end, I grabbed a pen out of his top pocket and sketched in an eyepatch and beard onto my passport photo ...

"Look," I said. "It's *me*, see ...?"

I think he was just about to gesture for some assistance, when I heard a voice pipe up behind me and the pair of us were suddenly surrounded by members of the Pan-Germanic Vampire Fellowship ...

"What's going on here?" demanded Beans.

They must have travelled quite a lot through Ostend, because their leader appeared to be well-known to my uniformed tormentor.

"Ah, Monsieur – *Doctor* – Beans, I apologise for the delay. There is a discrepancy with this man's passport, but we shall carry out our investigation elsewhere and delay you no further ..."

"Who?" said Beans. "Dr Kitehawk?"

"*Doctor* Kitehawk?" he said with surprise. "Are you acquainted with him?"

"*Acquainted* with him? He took out my appendix last week. *Saved my life.* First-rate surgeon. Respected man in the field, as my colleagues will testify ..."

"But *here* – under 'occupation' – it says '*Spy.*' How do you explain this?"

I snatched it back ...

"Give me that here ...!" I cursed.

Bloody cow, I thought. Natasha's idea of a joke ...

"You understand my dilemma, Monsieur ..."

Well ...

Joke or not, dilemma or no dilemma, by the time Doctors Van Shingle and Van English had stepped forward to give glowing accounts of my missionary work amongst the natives of Canary Wharf and other related humanitarian activities, the crisis seemed all but averted.

Or so I thought.

I'd only just returned my passport for clearance, when that *telephone* rang again ...

"Excuse me ..." (*I put my hand in my pocket and pulled out a mobile phone*) "... Hello?"

"*Kitehawk?*" said the voice at the other end.

"Speaking," I said. "And who wants to know?"

"Is there anybody about in there?"

"You *could* say that ..."

"Right, listen ..."

"Who *is* this?" I demanded to know. "And how did you get my number?"

"This is Trevor, and I put that phone in your pocket on the train, just in case I ever need to get hold of you in an emergency. I've managed to shake off that madwoman ..."

"How did you do that?" I asked, breathing a sigh of relief.

"I topped her ..."

I gulped.

"Yeah," he went on, "*She* won't be seeing another bottle of suntan oil ..."

"What about her husband?"

"I never saw any husband," he said. "But he can expect exactly the same treatment if he comes near me ..."

There was quite a holdup by now, and the queue were getting visibly impatient.

Aware of official interest in my call, I turned my back on the desk in an attempt to prevent them overhearing this somewhat incriminating conversation...

"Listen," Trevor went on, "I'm coming through in about ten seconds and I want you to create a diversion ..."

"Any suggestions?"

"Yeah," he said. "*Shoot* somebody ..."

"You know, I am sorry," I said, "But I seem to have mislaid my firearms licence ..."

But it was too late.

Trevor had already hung up ...

There was no way I could organise a diversion at that kind of short notice, even if I'd wanted to – unless what was currently occurring could be classified as such.

"Listen," I said to the Belgian officials. "I ordered a kissogram about three hours ago – well, actually, more of a *crank*-o-gram – and I've got a funny feeling it's going to turn up in the next minute or so ..."

But then a diversion of sorts *did* occur ...

Somebody barged right past me and crashed straight into the official who'd been giving me the most trouble.

Only it *wasn't* Trevor.

It was the *drunk* from the ship's bar.

Object?

A *drink*, apparently, since he'd already snatched my passport and was waving it around like a madman and yelling for whisky ... which was a *shame*, really, because out of the corner of my eye I saw Trevor crawling on his belly past the adjacent desk, and he might well have made it through unseen if the drunk hadn't decided to lurch across and try to help him to his feet.

What was going on in the drunk's mind I couldn't imagine, but in a matter of seconds every official had deserted his post and descended on the pair with a right old bundle ensuing ...

At some point during this melee, my passport came sailing out into the air and I caught it with my left hand and deposited it back into my pocket.

Trevor was getting the worst of the fracas, with the drunk spark out in a catatonic trance on the floor.

He – *Trevor*, that is – had about three pairs of hands round his throat and it looked to me as though the game was finally up.

"I DON'T KNOW WHY THEY CAN'T LEAVE THAT *POOR* BLOKE ALONE!" I turned round and yelled at those behind me.

Discretion being the better part of valour, however, I took a hint from Beans and followed him quietly through towards the train ...

CHAPTER 37
DARK DESIGN

While the blood flows black,
Round the taxman's chest,
Comes a long grass net,
Like his old string vest.

Vanity Larans

"I've been a bit lucky with checkpoints on this trip," I told him. "But it was touch-and-go there till you turned up. I must buy you a drink ..."

"It's the least we could do," he said. "After all, if it wasn't for you, we'd all be pedalling off by bike right now, instead of travelling in luxury ..."

"Well," I said, "It's really a woman by the name of Blondie Duval you've got to thank. She had all the spare tickets ..."

"Blondie Duval?" he said. "Who's she?"

"Oh," I said, "You couldn't miss her ..."

"No?" he said, intrigued.

"No," I said. "She's got a cakehole the size of Trafalgar Square ..."

"She sounds like a lot of fun ..."

"I'll introduce you later. She particularly wants one of your beards ..."

"Oh?" he said. "Why?"

"To use as a cakehole-cover ..."

We boarded the train and lingered in the corridor.

"Talking of introductions," he said, "Let me acquaint you with the remaining members of our outing. First, meet our resident poet, Larans ..."

"Larans?" I queried. "Do you mean *Laurens*? As in Van der Post?"

"No, no," said the poet. "*Larans*. As in Van *Ity* ..."

"Or," cut in Beans, "As in 'Vanity Larans', an epithet I'm sure you'll recognise ...?"

"Yes ... no," I said. "Anyway, pleased to meet you, cock, I'm sure ..."

He took a small bow and surprised me by uttering the following couplet:

"When the Squabblers come to the Schloss to Fight
Beware the shadow of Adolphus Flite ..."

My hair stood on end.

"Doctors Van Shingle and Van English you've met, of course," Beans
went on, "But I don't think you've made the acquaintance of our blood
specialist, Ian Van Trasyl ..."

I shook his mitt.

"It's funny," I said, "There's a lot of *Vans* in this group, yet you all travel
round by bike ..."

"Next, meet our distinguished *agent provocateur*, Mr Narsty Vilaan ..."

Crunch!

*Before I had a chance to sidestep this dubious honour, he'd grabbed hold of my hand
and crushed my fingers in his ...*

"That's Narsty Vilaan by *name*," he explained. "And *nasty villain* by
nature..."

"*Indeed ...*" I wheezed.

"Last but not least," concluded Beans, "Our matinee idol, Sal ..."

*So announced, the matinee idol stepped forward, gave me a continental chin greeting and
proceeded to croon a few lines from 'Mack the Knife' ...*

"That's Sal *Tranyvani* ..." he said, by way of reprise.

He was the only one without a beard.

"Okay," I said. "I expect you'll all want to find your cabins and unpack.
I'll see you later in the bar ..."

"Done ..." said Beans.

"And watch out for thieves!" I called after them. "The train's crawling
alive with them ...!"

*No sooner had I seen the last of their backs disappear through the connecting door to
the next carriage, when my old friend Bertolt appeared in their place and came clanking down
the corridor towards me ...*

So I turned to walk the other way ... *and walked right into the path of Orange-
Shorts and two Belgian plods ...*

"Hayeuaargh ...!" I slurred, as I accidentally turned an evasive hand-to-
mouth cough into a half-curse, half-sneeze, half-successful 270-degree non-
transit goose-step swivel and smacked my nose on the wall. "... *aarghuey*ah!"

*Taking a deep breath, I completed my clumsy manouevre, gave my sore conk a
surreptitious rub and got ready to face the lesser threat ...* only to find that he'd
disappeared.

Into one of the *cabins*, presumably, unless he'd never been there to begin
with.

Perhaps he was some sort of spectre?

Either way, an escape route had opened up, allowing me to hurry on
ahead of the gathering storm, dive into the nearest WC and bolt the door

behind me.

Here, I sat out the lengthy delay in Ostend Harbour, passing the time making minor facial adjustments courtesy of my reflection in the bog mirror. There was no question that a return to my quarters for a complete change of disguise was called for, and as soon as the wheels ground into motion, I took a tentative peek outside:

Finding the coast clear, I made my getaway with atrocious timing, stepping out from my concealment just as Bertolt re-emerged from his cabin dressed to the nines in evening wear, though he still looked faintly ridiculous with his oversize surgical boot sticking out of his trousers like a sore thumb ...

The *trouble* was, as I went to do a sharpish U-bend back into the WC, some joker barged in ahead of me and locked me out!

Whoever he was, he must have been dying for a piss ...

Which was neither here nor there, since Bertolt had already descended on me from behind and tapped me on the back:

"There is a terrible stink coming from my sink," he said. "And I'd like it fixed right away. Here is my key ..."

"Why, *thankee*, sir ..." I said, astonished at his cheek.

He must have thought I was one of the maintenance crew.

Nevertheless, I was mildly pleased he'd fallen for my disguise.

And even *more* pleased he'd handed me the key to his cabin ...

"*Fucking half-wit* ..." I mumbled as he went on his way.

Cor, I thought, *I wonder whether he's got any of them miniatures with him ...?*

I wandered along to his cabin and let myself in ...

Well, the *first* thing I noticed was that he was dead right about the stink.

The only plus point was that, for once, it didn't smell like somebody's rancid backpuff.

Even so, I decided it might be pragmatic to avoid striking matches – *just in case* – and switched on his light instead:

At first glance, the room appeared to be devoid of possessions, and so I opened the closet and hauled his suitcase out.

Without its accident-prone owner there to obstruct me, it was easy enough to break into, but the result was a disappointment. There were no miniatures, no bottles of *Froth* – not even a radio transmitter or a gun.

In fact, there were no clothes even, or any other kind of travelling accessories.

The case wasn't *empty*, though.

It was filled with shredded *newspapers* ...

"Well," I mumbled, "That's a puzzler ..."

Somewhat disappointed, I slung it back where I found it and headed for the door, giving the room a final scan before turning off the light.

And it was only *then* that I spotted something familiar sitting on top of the closet ...

After climbing up onto his bunk to retrieve Trevor's rucksack, I stood there like a pair of human scales, trying to weigh the balance between returning an appallingly heavy item of luggage to a man who no longer required its services, to leaving it in the possession of a man whose requirement of it was a total mystery.

Was it *really* worth stealing it back?

On a matter of principle, I decided, on balance, that it was.

It might contain some money that I could spend in Trevor's absence.

I decided, also, on *balance*, that Bertolt could de-stink his *own* fucking sink, and left him an anonymous note to that effect ...

When I arrived back at my berth, I loosened the various zips and toggles on the rucksack and upended it over the lower bunk, getting ready to trawl through what I imagined would be the full load of clean socks, shoe repair kits, phrase books and lists of prepared questions that any self-respecting flatfoot might have been carting around the world on his travels with him.

And so, it was all a bit of a surprise when, other than a walletful of travellers cheques and assorted foreign currency which fell out from one of the side pockets, the only item to make any kind of dent in the duvet turned out to be the gigantic casefile its owner had earlier made reference to ...

The Darkbloode Case

Congratulating myself on an act of espionage successfully accomplished, I settled down to read the assembled paperwork with the cheerful thought that experience had taught me (as it should have taught Bertolt) that Bertolt and sinks don't mix and, whenever they did, there was invariably a stink.

What I barely noticed – having become so intrigued by the file – was that the smell was still in the air, rather as though it had followed me down the corridor ...

The reason for my preoccupation was to be found in a growing conviction that, now that Trevor was out of the way, there might just be some pecuniary profit for me if I carried on his investigation myself.

Okay.

I couldn't go out of my *way* to track Sir Archibald down.

But, if I *did* bump into him on my travels, it might be worth making a *private* deal.

Especially as my Whitehall pension was latterly in doubt, and my main reason for continuing the hunt for Adolf Flite was now a philanthropic one.

After all, I told myself, *I've got to eat.*

Detail on 'Sir Arch' was all a bit scarce in the opening pages.

For example, under 'date of birth', the entry read:

Not known but frequently lied about

I gathered his nom-de-plume was the relic of a failed early career as a music-hall entertainer, something he'd taken up after being dishonourably discharged as a naval flier. Apparently, during manoeuvres off the coast of Cumbria, he'd opened up the bomb hatch by mistake and sunk his own aircraft carrier.

Much of the rest of the paperwork was taken up with handwritten notes outlining Trevor's plans for the future with his daughter, the avaricious and delectable Hetty, and I skipped through these rather quickly looking for the photo of the villain that Trevor had mentioned.

This however, proved to be an elusive item, forcing me to tip up the file and give it a good shake until a loose envelope fell out:

Archie D.
(The only known extant photograph. *c.1985*)

Well, it was relatively recent, at least.
"Now," I mumbled, "What have we got here …?"
I tore it open so carelessly that the photo sailed out and landed face-down on the floor.
So I *picked* it up.
And then I screamed out loud and *dropped* it again …
"*EEEEEEEEEEEEEEEK* …!!!"
Then I started clawing at my beard – *having forgotten it was full of nitrous oxide pellets* – and laughing hysterically …
"*WAAAAAA … HAHAHAHAHAHA …!!! OOOOOH … HOOHOOHOO …!!! HAHAHA …!!! OHOHOHOHOHO … AHAHAHAHAHA …!!!*"
Finally, as I staggered around gasping for air, somebody coshed me over the head …
CLUNK!

When I came round, I wondered whether I'd dreamed what I saw, because the photo and rucksack had disappeared again.

I wondered whether I'd *dreamed* it, because the photo was a life-sized photographer's portrait of somebody I *knew* very well …

Call him what you like.
Sir Archibald Darkbloode.
… or *Archie D.*
Call him *trouble.*
Call him what you will.
Call him the great indoor space.
Call him a few quid short of a pound note.
Any guesses?
Still in the dark?
How about *Hopeless Harry* and *Dopey Dick*?
Got it yet?

Course you have.

But who *was* he, though?

I mean, *who* was he really?

We may never know, of course.

But he was *there* alright.

In that photo.

In all his smiling, leering, pre-gold dentured, toothless glory ...

Death by Photography 2

The irony of copping a headache the minute I'd caught sight of Dirk's ugly mug for the first time in months wasn't lost on me, nor was the fact that he *was* smiling – almost as if he'd coshed me himself, as though he'd returned to haunt me, to pay me back.

This notion sent me lurching to the sink, only to find more of that sickly stench coming from the taps in place of water ...

I just couldn't get the photo out of my mind.

But, as I sat there finishing off Trevor's half-drunk can of *Froth*, the more I *thought* about it, the *funnier* it seemed:

There he was, going round the world and trading on his position as an Inland Revenue inspector, when all the time he was on the run for embezzlement.

Embezzlement, that is, of the Inland Revenue!

It was a pity that Trevor had vanished from the proceedings, because I could have sold Dirk's whereabouts to him for a cut of the profits.

But *who'd* clobbered me?

One thing was sure.

I needed to get that *file* back ...

The first thing I spotted in the Colonel's suitcase was a bloodied bandage, and so I ditched the eyepatch to make way for it, wrapping it – appropriately enough – round my sore head.

So far, so good.

Next, I swapped the moustache for a false conk (whilst retaining the beard, of course), rearranged my facial scars (adding an impressive row of zip-style stitching up my neck), dusted my hair with flour (for that *distingué* look) and coated my face with custard powder (for a jaundiced tinge).

Some stick-on wrinkles completed the facial, and left me looking not a little indebted to Richard Chamberlain.

Finally, I went to work on the clothes and decked myself out like a penguin – with tails, complete with top hat.

I didn't even recognise *myself* in the mirror this time.

A spot of *rouge* wouldn't have been out of place, but this was one accessory the Colonel didn't appear to have amongst his collection.

Well, he was a *colonel*, after all ...

Such were the thoughts that occupied my mind as I stood there admiring my handiwork from all stationary angles, a subtle twenty degree sidestep away from spotting the blunt instrument that had been used to bludgeon me, lying on the floor by my bunk ...

"Well, well, well ..." I said out loud.

A stale salami.

Wrapped up in a copy of *The Dandy*.

Theoretically, this made the *chef* a suspect.

And, if the chef's name was *Bjorn Borg*, then I knew I'd found my man ...

Courtesy of Trevor's wallet, I filled my pocket with readies and decided to make my way to the bar, wondering, as I did so, why Bertolt had stolen Trevor's rucksack in the first place.

Unless he thought it was *mine* – the same one I'd had with me on the Great Lakes.

If so, he must have soon realised his mistake.

And I couldn't see him bothering to *re*-steal it again.

In fact, I found it unlikely – in view of his past experiences – that he would have gone anywhere *near* me if he'd known I was on the train.

Unless he wasn't working alone ...

I grabbed my plastic stethoscope and left.

En route to the bar, I came across the very person I wished to quiz – *viz.* the porter – engaged in conversation with the dentist whom Trevor had tried to strangle on the first leg of the journey to Dover.

(*Well*, he *looked* like a dentist, and that was good enough for me)

What he was *up* to with the porter, I had no long-distance insight, but – like any true member of his profession – he seemed to trying to climb down his patient's throat ...

Funnily enough, he was actually doing a Bertolt and complaining vociferously about a stench which was now beginning to permeate the corridors as well, and – although he may have had a point – my immediate and impatient requirement was the porter's undivided attention all to myself ...

"I don't know what you're *talking* about," I said, barging into their midst. "This is the *Orient* Express, not the kiddywinky train to perrier-land. Stick a sack round your moosh and stop complaining. If you stop wasting all this energy yapping, then you *might* just save some air for the rest of us. There's a long way to go yet, and if *you* knew the Orient like *I* know the Orient, then you'd know it was going to get a lot worse before it gets better ..."

"I *beg* your pardon?" said Mr Dentist, flabbergasted.

"Well," I said, "You've picked the wrong time of year for Venice if you wanted to lay on the beach without a gas mask round your trout. As for Istanbul, so-called 'Gateway to the East', the last time I was there the Turkish dustcarts were on an overtime ban and the High Street was knee-deep in camel shit. If you wanted an hotel for the night you had to grab a pair of waders and shovel your way out of the station on foot. It was every man for himself, mate ..."

Even the *porter* looked at me as though I was mad.

I wondered whether I'd overdone it?

And I might *well* have wondered, especially when I got a lively poke in the back and turned round to find the old matron trying to get by with a handkerchief tied round her nose ...

"Young man," she said to me, "There are *no* beaches in Venice, and there are *no* camels in Istanbul. I don't believe for one moment that you have ever set foot in either of those beautiful cities ..."

"What you *ought* to have done," I responded, improvising, "Was stuck a peg on your snout and used that handkerchief as a muffler ..."

"Muffler? *Muffler* ...?" she said. "What do you *mean*, muffler?"

"*You* know," I said, "*Muffler*. Roll it up into a wad and shove it down your throat. Plug up the voice box. Give us all a rest. I was just giving this *herbert* here the same advice ..."

"How *dare* you talk to me like that!" she exploded. "Why, if my father were here now, he'd give you a good thrashing!"

"Yeah," I laughed, "*Him*, you ... and *Joe* the Dustman ..."

"I'll have you know I come from good stock!" she raved, squinting her eyes up maliciously.

"Good *stock*?" I said. "Who are *you* then, the *Oxo* heiress?"

All of a sudden, she planted a right hook straight on my jaw with a fist carved out of solid concrete and I sailed about four feet into the air and landed in a different carriage altogether...

Even then, I didn't stop rolling till I came to rest in a trough full of potato peelings.

I must have been in the kitchen car.

The appearance of a man in a chef's hat seemed to confirm this theory ...

"Dexter Kitehawk," I said, offering up my hand. "Flying Salami Squad. I'm investigating the disappearance of a truncheon-sized stick of cervelat. Are you in charge round here?"

Completely ignoring me, he picked up the trough I was sitting in, carried it outside and unceremoniously dumped its contents – including me – into an oversized plastic dustbin, before disappearing again.

It took a good few minutes of trying to walk away from the scene, before I realised that I'd actually landed upside down and *was*, in fact, standing on my head.

The moment this dawned on me, I buckled violently, crashed through the adjacent compartmental door and landed in a heap on the lounge car floor ...

"Right ...!" I cursed.

Intending to launch a counter-attack on the matron, I stood up, marched outside, slipped in a puddle of spud juice, boomeranged back off the wall ... and straight back into the lounge car again.

All of which left me counting fingers and trying to remember the address of my local fire station, an exercise prematurely terminated when a passing waiter in a white jacket asked me if I was ready for coffee.

"Not for *him*," said some old gobber in a smoking-jacket (at whose feet I'd landed). "It won't do him any good where *he's* going ..."

"Who asked *you* ...?" I said.

"A chair perhaps?" added the waiter, as he marched back past in the opposite direction with a trayload of coffee (but again, not waiting for a reply).

"By all means get him a chair," the Gobber called out. "He's not fit to stand and he'll appreciate a chance to pass his last days with dignity. I can't bear to see anybody lose control of their self-respect and I daresay *he* can't either ..."

"Oi!" I yelled after the waiter. "Stick that *chair* up your arse! I came in here for a *lounge*! If I'd have wanted to *sit*, I'd have come here on horseback ...!"

"You're not alone," he droned on. "I know from experience that your faculties start going one after the other. First the eyes, then the ears, then the legs. It all starts when you find hairs growing out of your nose. It's all one-way traffic after twenty-three. Look at *me*. I reckon I've got about one change of shirt left and that's it ..."

"What are you *talking* about?" I said.

"Old age, old age ..."

"*OLD AGE*?!!!" I screamed. "*This* isn't old age!"

"No?" he said.

"*No*," I said. "I've just been dismantled by the NHS, that's all ..."

All of a sudden, the waiter lifted me bodily from behind and plonked me into a seat opposite him.

Clonk!

I didn't protest.

"Have you let one go ...?" I said, feeling absent-mindedly round my nostrils for sign of mutant hairs.

"No," he mumbled. "But it's an *ill wind* ..."

"'*Ere*," I cut-in, "Don't I *know* you from somewhere ...?"

"You *may* do ..." he said.

"'Ere, *just* a minute!" I yelled. "Is this a *hair* growing out of my nose ...?"

"Where?" he squinted.

"Right *here*," I said, pointing straight up my beak.

"It could be a rogue hair," he said authoritatively. "Or it could be the first signs of a diseased follicle. Either way, if you're as young as you say you are, you ought to see a doctor ..."

"I *am* a doctor," I added. "That's the trouble ..."

Before I could continue this riveting conversation, the door to the carriage suddenly slid open and a woman burst in and descended on me in a dreadful panic ...

"Did I hear you say you were a doctor?" she said. "You must come quick – somebody's just collapsed in the buffet car ..."

"No, no," I said, trying to pull back. "I'm a *tree* doctor. You need a specialist..."

"No, no," she persisted. "Come *now*, quickly ..."

Since she'd already dragged me from my seat, I felt I had little choice but to comply, adjusting my fancy-dress stethoscope as I went ...

I had a good view of the back of her neck as I followed her along the corridor, noticing only – for what it was worth at the time – that she was a redhead.

In fact, I became so mesmerised by the shock of scarlet bobbing around in front of me that, when she stopped to open the door of a private cabin, I charged straight on inside like a reckless bull past a red rag ...

"Quick – *in here* ..." she said.

There *was* a body sprawled unconscious on the floor, but it wasn't until I tripped over his oversized foot, that I realised it was Bertolt.

We were in *his* cabin ...

He was spark out, no mistake.

"I thought you said he collapsed in the buffet car?" I said, without turning round.

"I *did*, sweetheart ..."

As I went to say something, the lights all went out for a second time ...

When I came to, I found myself trussed up like a turkey, with a gag round my mouth.

Bertolt was trussed up across the other side of the cabin, still unconscious.

The woman who'd lured me there was reclining in a chair in front of me, with a gun in her hand, smiling.

Next to her, in another chair, was a male accomplice. Some kind of a greasy type in an expensive suit.

Who they *were* was a mystery, though I'd definitely seen the *woman* before.

In my *office*.

Two years earlier, when she'd come in looking for a job ...

And that put her up to her neck in one conspiracy or another as far as I was concerned.

It *didn't* explain *Bertolt's* incapacity, mind you.

Especially since the most likely scenario was that they were all working for AF International, but I had a funny feeling I was going to find out before long.

As for her *friend*, he looked like one of the Italian gangsters from Bolivia, and it occurred to me that I could be in a bit of trouble, whichever permutation of villains they transpired to be ...

"Take his gag off," she told him.

Following her order like an automaton, he did precisely that and moved back a step.

"*Now*," she began, "Doctor Kitehawk ... or should I call you *Mister*?"

"Go on," I said. "I'm listening ..."

"Where's the rucksack?"

"I haven't got it," I said. "So, if you'll kindly untie me, I'll be off ..."

"Rough him up a little, Mario ..."

Mario sprung forward ...

"Just a minute!" I pleaded. "You're barking up the wrong tree ...!"

"Yeah," she said. "And you oughta know, being a *tree* doctor ..."

"Look," I squealed, "There's nothing in that rucksack that could possibly interest *either* of us. All it contains is a file belonging to a private detective on a missing persons case. He just happened to be sharing my cabin, that's all. Go back to Ostend and contact the local nick. You'll find him there. He'll confirm what I'm saying ..."

She looked puzzled.

"*Who?*" she said.

"Trevor. The private dick. It's *his* rucksack ..."

"Oh," she said. "*That* bozo ..."

"That's him," I affirmed, desperately trying to work out whose side she was on – the Corporation or the Rest of the World. *I was praying she wasn't another Nazi torturer, but it might be just as bad if she turned out to be from a rival law enforcement agency...*

"Well," she went on, "That tells me SFA. What it *doesn't* tell me is where the rucksack is. I know where it *ain't*. It ain't in *my* possession. But you're going to change all that. *Kapiche?*"

"Yes ... *no*. Pardon ...?"

"Whatsa-madda?" suddenly piped up Mario in a threatening hiss. "Donna you understand English?"

"Yes, yes," I slobbered. "You want the rucksack. But, *one*. I haven't *got* it. *Two*. I don't *want* it. And *three* ... I assure you there is nothing *in* it. *Verstehen* ...?" (I threw that last one in as a tester to see whether either of them responded with a Nazi salute but, since neither of them batted an eyelid, I assumed they'd either been de-programmed so as to be able to undertake field-work, or they were on our side but working for some other mob. A clever little deduction that clarified absolutely nothing at all ...)

The redhead stood up and started to pace around in front of me.

"Look here," she said. "I know for a fact that you've got the sack, because I saw you take it from *him* over there. How do I *know* that? Because he took it from me and I was about to take it back again when you showed up in here earlier on – I watched you through a crack in the bathroom door. And how do I know *that*? Because I stole it from the Bozo in the first place and you were the last person I saw with it ..."

"What we've got here," I confirmed, "Is a *chain* situation. You took it from Trevor, Bertolt took it from you, I took it from Bertolt and ... now somebody else has taken it from me ..."

"I don't buy it," she said. "And if you don't start squealing in the next five seconds I'm gonna have Mario here give you some Sicilian upholstery ..."

I noticed that Bertolt was beginning to stir ...

"It's obvious, *he* must have nicked it back again. *HIM*," I shouted, "*HE'S GOT IT!*"

"Don't worry," she said. "He'll get *his* soon enough. When I'm finished with you I'm gonna find out what *his* role in this little mess is. But until then, you're the big fish as far as I'm concerned because you were the one travelling with the Bozo and its only him and me knows anything about the case ..."

"About the Allied Froth Corporation?" I laughed. "You must be joking. Every Tom, Dick and Harry from here to Timbuktu has heard of Adolf Flite by now ..."

"I think," she went on, "That he was trying to double-cross me. And I think *you* were trying to double-cross *him*. That tells me the old man is still alive. And the answer is in that sack ..."

"Old man ...?" I said, puzzled. "*What* old man?"

"*My* old man. That's who ..."

Suddenly, the penny dropped who she was.

She wasn't a Nazi agent.

Or a British agent.

Or *any* kind of agent.

Hetty Darkbloode.

That's who she was.

Dirk's scheming daughter ...

"Oh," I said, enlightened. "So you really *do* want the rucksack ..."

"Is he trying to be funny, Mario?"

"You want me to cut him?"

"From ear to ear ..." she said, demonstrating with her finger the type of incision required.

It wasn't pleasant.

"Okay," I said. "There's been a slight misunderstanding here ..." (thinking, *so much for her being Trevor's lover.* If there was any double-crossing going on, *she* was doing *all* of it ...) "Let me *explain*. The answer to your father's whereabouts isn't *in* the sack. Trevor doesn't *know* where he is. *But I do.* The reason I'm travelling with Trevor is pure chance. In conversation earlier, it transpired that I met your father once, but I didn't let on. I'm not trying to double-cross you or Trevor. I've got other business, and if you let me get back to it, I'll tell you where he is. I'm not interested in the money ..."

"I don't believe you. Why did you steal the sack back from laughing-boy over there if you're not interested in the old man's money?"

"I'm an agent investigating a case of conspiracy involving a German multinational. *Laughing-Boy* as you call him, is on the payroll of that multinational and a prime mover in that conspiracy. I found the sack here by chance. I was actually looking for something else. I just thought I'd do Trevor a favour and return it to him, but somebody coshed me and, when I woke up, it was gone again ..."

"If this is all true, why did *he* steal it from me?"

"I don't know. Why not ask him? Maybe he recognised me when I got on the train in London and saw you coming out of my cabin with it. Maybe he thought it was a sackful of evidence against him ..."

By a stroke of luck I found I'd managed to work the ropes loose behind me.

This pair must have been straight off Green Street ...

"Take laughing-boy's gag off," she said to Mario.

Bertolt had recovered enough by now to be exhibiting one of his 'Boat-Race of Fear' (cert x) expressions – aimed at Hetty and Mario, rather than at me (who, I assumed, he hadn't recognised yet).

"Did you *hear* any of that?" she asked him. "Is *he* telling the truth?"

"*Bitte ...?*" he said.

"Hey!" she shouted, kicking his good foot for emphasis. "Speak English...!"

Bertolt just cowered there.

So she kicked *my* foot instead ...

"*You,*" she said. "Is he playing dumb?"

I shrugged my shoulders.

"What's his name?"

I shrugged my shoulders again.

"Mario," she said, "Check his papers ..."

What, I thought, *all those shredded ones in his suitcase?*

"Anyway," she said, "Where is he?"

"Where's *who*?" I said.

"My father. The old man ..."

"New York ..."

"You got his address?"

I gave her the details while Mario frisked Bertolt and took out his passport.

"Bertolt Reemer ..."

"What's he doing there?" Hetty asked me.

"It's a long story," I said.

"Yeah, but we ain't got time to listen to it now. How do I know you're telling the truth?"

"You'll just have to trust me. I hate him as much as you do. What are you going to do to him when you catch up with him?"

"Mario is going to give him a Sicilian car wash, if you know what I mean..."

"Kill him?" I said.

"In *one*. Mario comes from a long line of hit-men ..."

"Good," I said.

"Not so good for *you*, though ..."

"Oh?" I said. "Why?"

"He's gonna kill *you* as well. Nothing personal. You know too much. *Sorry*, sweetheart ..."

Just at that moment there was a fortuitous knock on the door and Hetty opened it a fraction to find the porter standing there with a plunger in his hand.

"Yeah ...?" she said.

He'd come to unblock the sink ...

So, while their attention was distracted, I got shot of my ropes, got to my feet and wandered over to Bertolt, who had an eager look on his face as though he thought I was going to untie him.

But I neither had the time or the inclination.

I just lowered my false beard and gave him a big smile.

A look of horrified recognition darkened his boat ...

"Well," I whispered, "I can't *keep* baling you out. Why don't you take up a safer job ...?"

Swinging round in alarm, Hetty and Mario were powerless to stop me because of the porter.

"Cheerio," I said, as I breezed past them. "Give my regards to Jazzy Joe ..."

"Who's *Jazzy Joe?*" called out Hetty.

"Runs a shirt shop in Hoboken. I gave you his address by mistake. If you want your Dad's address it'll cost you a million quid. See you around ..."

One more brush with death like that, I thought, *and I'm quitting for a safer job myself.*

In *lion* taming ...

What a *charming* daughter Dirk had.

In fact, all round, they were a charming family.

So much so, that it caused me to wonder what kind of a monster he might have bred as a son.

The only thing you could put forward in Hetty's favour was that she hadn't – by some miracle of fate – inherited her dad's looks.

Or *lack* of them.

My first inclination was to hide in my cabin for the rest of the journey but, on reflection, I decided it might be safer to instal myself in the most public place on the train and stay there.

After all, I couldn't guarantee there wasn't somebody waiting to kill me behind my closet door, or somebody else's closet door etc, and a murder in broad daylight seemed less likely.

I therefore decided to brazen it out in the bar.

Partly because it was out in the open.

Partly because I needed to assure myself that my disguise was recognition-proof.

But *mainly* because I needed a drink ...

Since I found myself wandering directly up to the counter without being hailed, accosted, tripped up or coshed, I had cause for early optimism on the effectiveness of my new persona ...

"*Une* lager, *bitte,* cock," I said to the barman, hedging my bets on his origins.

(When he responded by addressing me as *senor*, I decided he was hedging *his* bets on *my* origins as well ...)

Nevertheless, it was a transaction concluded despite its multi-lingual stumbling-blocks, upon which I picked up my drink, turned round to face the carriage ... and nearly swallowed the glass!

Almost every seat was occupied – either by a sworn enemy, or by a complete stranger looking ready to knife me just to see what kind of a sound it would make.

And they were all staring straight at Yours Truly ...

The reason none of this assortment of evil launched itself at me became clear when two *gendarmes* stepped out of the shadows and took their place either side of me at the bar.

Seeing in them my best hope of survival in the short term, I turned back to face the optics and attempted to engage them in conversation ...

"Phew!" I said. "Am I glad to see *you* boys!"

Neither of them batted an eyelid.

So we stood there, the three of us, staring straight ahead and guzzling our drinks.

I *say* guzzling because, when I'm nervous, I have a tendency to spill most of it down my chin.

Not that either of the Belgian plods seemed fussy about drinking alongside such a display.

In fact, *one* of them appeared to be farting along in time to it.

He must have been a genuine diplomat ...

In the reflection in the bar mirror, I got a good look at the array of faces aligned against me, and it *didn't* make pleasant viewing:

First and foremost were Hetty and Mario, occupying the front seats to one side of the aisle, while Bertolt sat opposite them, on his own – *and on an invisible leash* – something the worse for wear.

Behind *him* was Orange-Shorts, looking like he was trying to make up his mind whether I *was* who he *thought* I was, sitting opposite the dentist, who was sharing a table with the matron.

Behind *that* lot were the three girls who didn't want to know anything about foot massage, and further back I could pinpoint the stockbroker I'd soaked when I first came on board and the Intellectual I'd rubbished about boat trains.

Going even further back was a whole assortment of low-life who could have been anybody from the Friends of Inspector Greaser to the Four Horseriders of the Apocalypse.

No sign of any *allies*, as yet.

"What's the word on the stink, you chaps?" I asked the gendarmes – partly for conversational purposes, partly out of a genuine interest in what, if anything, was being done about the ever worsening smell.

"In case you have not heard, *Monsieur,* a body has been found in the plumbing of the train and a murder investigation is being carried out at this present moment. You will be given your instructions as a suspect in due course..."

"*Suspect?*" I said. "Who, *me?*"

"Certainly, *you, Monsieur*. Everybody on this *train* is a suspect, and I trust you will not be disembarking for the time being?"

"Not at *this* speed ..." I mumbled.

"Pardon, *Monsieur* ...?"

The darkened landscape was rattling by outside the windows at about 110mph.

That's when I became aware that we were both shouting at each other above the racket of the wheels ...

"*Cologne,*" I said. "That's where *I'm* getting off ..."

"Good. *Bon.* You will be contacted in good time. Every passenger is being interviewed ..."

"Who was the stiff?"

"*Pardonnez?*"

"*Er* ... nothing," I said, noticing Mario give me one of those *I'll slit your throat* demonstrations in the bar mirror. "I said," I said, stretching my joints, "I'm feeling *a bit stiff* ..."

"Well, don't do nothin' I wouldn't do *for* ya!" piped up a voice from a long way back down the carriage ...

I clocked the culprit in the mirror, sitting there and leaning out into the aisle with a mischievous grin fixed to her face.

"'Ere!" I yelled back at her, "You're not an *American* are ya?"

"None of your goddamned business, Buster. And wouldn't *you* like to know...!"

"I've had dealings with *your* lot before!"

"Oh *yeah* ...?"

"*Yeah.* It's about time you gave America back to the Indians and all cleared off back where you came from ... wherever *that* was ..."

"Is that so?" she shouted, to which I responded confidently that it was. "I told ya," she snarled, "You're so full of shit, you leak when you talk ..."

"You took your time getting here tonight," I said, changing the subject. "If you're looking for World War Two, don't bother. You *missed* it. We won it *without* ya ..."

Bertolt, amongst others, twitched.

"I got hung up," she said. "What's *your* excuse ...?"

"I got *tied*-up. Tied-up and *strung*-out ..."

Hetty and Mario shifted uneasily in their seats.

Good.

I now had two plods for company and one foul-mouthed ally bringing up my rear.

One more hyena impersonation and she might bring up my lunch.

And I had something on just about everybody in the carriage.

Suddenly, I seemed to be the one holding all the advantage, and that made me feel decidedly better ...

"Are you gonna buy me a drink?" she called out.

"What's it worth to me?" I called back.

"How about you buy me a drink and I don't come and squash your hat down around your face?"

I examined the wicked twinkle in her eyes and thought about her proposition for a few moments.

"Sounds good to me," I said. "What'll it be?"

"Gimme a San Andreas Shake. *On the rocks.* Old Johnny Barman there knows how to fix it ..."

"*Johnny?*" I said. "He's a *Moroccan*, then ...?"

I watched him pour several measures of pernod, tequila and some other unidentified spirit into a shaker, and waited until he'd mixed up a drink which came out opaque Pacific blue ...

"And the *rocks* ...?" I queried.

By way of finale, he lobbed the glass from one hand to the other, threw a series of counter-top cocktail implements into the air, juggled the lot in a rotating sequence past my eyes and finished up by floating a couple of crushed roof-slabs of ice across the surface of the waves ...

"Cheers," I said.

"Don't mensh ..." he said, as he exchanged the finished masterpiece for a modest selection of the global currency cheques spread out in my hand.

"Don't worry," I said. "I *won't* ..."

And so, with this startling concoction in one hand and a pint of Froth in the other, I sauntered down the aisle, conscious all the time that I was running a malevolent gauntlet ...

"Where's Dusty?" I said, grabbing the spare seat next to her. "Had enough of life in the fast lane, did he?"

"Who knows?" she said. "Maybe he's taking a shower. Maybe he's coked up somewhere. Maybe he's got a client. *Maybe* he's blocking up the drains. What's the low-down on this guy they found in the pipes?"

"Ain't you heard?" I said. "All they found was a calling card and a severed quiff ..."

"Yeah," she said. "That's what I heard ..."

"You *did?*" I said, surprised.

"Yeah," she said. "That's right. I heard you was the biggest bullshitter since Goebbels ..."

"This is a popular place tonight," I said, as more and more people began to file into the carriage, occupying the vacant seats and tables and ordering drinks.

"This is where the investigation's being held," she said. "*That* much I *do* know. It's going to be a public enquiry ..."

"A public fry-up?" I yelled in angst. "What the hell's a public *fry*-up?"

"I said public *enquiry*, you asshole ..."

"A public *enquiry*. Shit! That's *all* I need ..."

"Why?" she said. "What are you hiding?"

"It may have escaped your notice," I said, "But I'm in disguise ..."

"Oh?"

"I can't get involved in a murder case. It'll blow my cover ..."

She laid a hand on my arm.

"Listen, honey," she said, "You blew your cover the first time you broke wind ..."

"Yeah," I said. "I need friends like *you* ..."

"I'm all you *got*, honey. I'm your *alibi*. I've been with you all night. And *you've* been with *me*. In my *cabin*, get it?"

"That won't help me if you spent all night stuffing dead limbs down the pipework, will it?"

"You gotta take a chance ..."

"Who *are* you, anyway?" I said to her.

"Didn't I tell you?" she said.

"I don't believe you *did*, no ..."

"I'm your fairy godmother," she said. "Lady Luck ..."

By the Short and Curlies

"Attention please! I am Detective-Inspector LeGras, of Ostend Police ..."

These words were uttered by a man standing up at the bar end of the carriage, dressed in plain-clothes, about 4ft 9ins tall – or short, whichever way you looked at it – and commanding absolutely no attention whatsoever.

He cut such a slight figure, and had such a weedy voice, that the general level of conversational hum did not noticeably drop.

Looking round for an escape route, I found no such route immediately obvious:

The rear exit was now blocked by the two gendarmes I'd been chewing the cud with earlier on at the bar, and there was a third one with LeGras, standing at his side and towering over him like a chimney pot.

"He'd never get a job with the City of London Police," I told Ms Duval, as he tried again for some attention, still without success. "*RAUS* ! *RAUS* ! *ACHTUNG* ! *ACHTUNG* !" I yelled, deciding to offer him some assistance but immediately zipping up my *innocent* mask so that those turning round wouldn't know who'd been shouting ...

This was particularly true of the Inspector himself, who was peering forward and squinting like a cat sniffing at a rubbish sack.

"Thank you. And I would like to introduce a colleague who has offered his services to the investigation I intend to conduct. Detective Chief Inspector Black, of Interpol ..."

I sprayed lager all over the couple sitting at the table in front of me as Laurel stepped out of the shadows and offered himself for view ...

The carriage finally went quiet.

"As I am sure you will now be aware," LeGras continued, "A dead body was found earlier this evening aboard this train – the *reason*, of course, for the rather unpleasant odour you have all had to endure – and, after a preliminary examination, I have decided to open an investigation for murder ..."

"What makes you think he was *murdered?*" suddenly piped up a voice from nearby.

With horror I realised it was Blondie mouthing off, and cringed as attention was focused on our table ...

"Who asked that?" said LeGras, squinting forward again. "Will the person who asked that question please step out to the front for identification?"

Blondie failed to comply with this request, but rather added a little more to her original question ...

"Hey! If you need glasses *that* bad, pal, how do you know he's *dead?*"

Le Gras decided to forego further interrogation of my table companion and dismissed her remarks with the following statement:

"The body was dead. There is no question of that. It was cut up into little pieces and placed inside the water tank situated at the rear of the train. I do not think it was suicide ..."

"So he *drowned*, then?" I shouted out, helpfully.

"No," he said, rejecting my assumption. "Neither do I think he was dying for a drink, ha ha ...!"

The trouble was, nobody laughed except LeGras.

I sat there wondering whether Laurel had recognised me, but he gave no sign that I could detect.

Even so, it had to be considered a mistake to have opened my mouth ...

"I think," LeGras went on, after attempting to recover his poise, "That I should perhaps offer a few words of explanation regarding my presence here on the train. I was originally alerted to a potentially explosive situation by the Harbourmaster's office in Ostend, regarding a man who had gone berserk between London and Dover ..." (*I assumed he was talking about Trevor*) "... Some of you may have been witness to an incident in which he brandished a gun in the dining car and threatened to kill hostages. Police at Dover were alerted, but somehow he managed to evade them and continue his journey on the ferry. Fortunately, we managed to detain him at this end and prevent him re-boarding the train. He is now being questioned about the incident at Ostend Police Headquarters. It has not yet been established whether he has links with any terrorist organisation ..."

Trevor a terrorist?

That was a puzzler.

"Nobody was seriously hurt in the incident ..." (*Try telling that to the Dentist*, I thought) "... but a passenger did go missing during the disembarkation period..." (*I assumed this was Mrs Orange-Shorts*) "... and as yet, is still unaccounted for ..."

I could save this plod a whole lot of time and trouble if I spoke up, I thought, *but how do I do it without incriminating myself or giving my identity away?*

"The woman in question," he went on, "Was last seen waiting for her husband on the quayside. She is the wife of a senior adviser to the British

Government, Sir Charles Malet ..." (*Orange Shorts? Government* adviser! About *what?* Gaudy beachwear? Throwing your weight around? Carving up the NHS ...?) "... Any information on her whereabouts will be treated in the strictest confidence. The primary investigation into her disappearance is taking place in Ostend but, as Sir Charles is unable to delay his journey to Germany, I have been assigned to accompany him and carry out further enquiries into any leads which may be provided by passengers aboard this train ..."

"So," said somebody sitting near the detective, "You think Lady Malet may be the unfortunate victim in the water tank?"

"No," said LeGras. "The body – or what was left of it – was already in a state of decomposition consistent with a time of death of three to four days ago. That unfortunate person was killed in London, probably ..."

"Do you think she's gone the same way?" asked some loutish type not far from my own table. "Perhaps her husband's a *wet* ...?"

CRASH!!!

Suddenly, Sir Orange-Shorts leapt up and went for the throat of his tormentor, knocking over a table complete with several rounds of drinks ...

"Cor dear," said the surprised victim just before being strangled. "I only meant to say she might have fell out of the Think Tank and into the *Drink* Tank..."

It took all of LeGras and his three gendarmes to drag the emotional government adviser off of him, by which time he was bellowing and weeping like a baby and repeating the name 'Sandra' over and over again ...

I must say that I breathed a sigh of relief to see him being led away out of the carriage, and if I'd had access to any *real* medical equipment I'd have offered to sedate him *myself.*

Hopefully, I'd never see him again.

He did appear to be on a very short fuse, and I was only glad that somebody else had managed to upset him as much as I had.

That *somebody else* was rubbing his throat where Sir Charles's hands had left fingerprints, and was looking a little sorry for himself ...

"Well," he offered to those passengers giving him accusatorial stares. "I didn't know he was sitting right *next* to me, did I? He don't *look* like a politician, does he? He looks more like the right-back for Leyton Orient ..."

"Please, please, calm yourselves down," LeGras was saying. "Foul play is not, as yet, suspected in the disappearance of Lady Malet, but, considering her vulnerable position as a potential political target, we cannot, at this stage, rule out the possibility of kidnap ..."

Getting rather intrigued by this cock-and-bull story, I accidentally picked up Blondie's San Andreas Shake and took a mouthful of it by mistake ...

Five seconds later, my stomach started rumbling and my eyes rolled right off the Richter scale as a great chasm opened up in the floor of the carriage, exposing the sleepers of the tracks beneath hurtling backwards at over a hundred miles an hour ...

Horrified, I lunged over to one side and accidentally flattened Blondie up against the window.

"Hey!" she yelled. "Don't you get *fresh*, Buster!"

I lunged back quickly enough, only to find with further horror that I'd been rendered inactive.

I could neither move my limbs nor my tongue.

All I could do was sit there like a vegetable and listen to the Inspector continue his speech...

"The *search*, as I say," he said (after coming out of a lengthy squint at nothing in particular), "Is continuing in Ostend, and during contact with headquarters from Aachen I can tell you that Lady Malet has not yet been found ..."

Aachen?

I didn't remember stopping there.

I must have been incapacitated in Bertolt's cabin at the time.

"Do you *mean, Monsieur*," piped up a Frenchman from the rear, "*Aix-la-Chappelle?*"

You could spot the Germans by the way they turned round and scanned for the culprit of that last statement ...

"*Oui. Bon. Aix-la-Chappelle. Aachen*," confirmed LeGras.

"Why didn't you get reinforcements?" asked somebody else.

"We had not, at that time, discovered the dead body. Like you, I was merely aware of a bad smell coming from the water taps. It could have been a rat ..."

"Eeeeeeeeeeeeeeeeeeeek!!!"

Some bloke screamed and fainted ...

CLUNK!

In the ensuing melee it looked, for a moment, as though LeGras was going to fall through the gap in the carriage floor but, instead, he stopped just short of it and balanced himself precariously on the edge ...

"The whole investigation will be strengthened by the West German police when we reach Cologne. I have radioed ahead with the details thus far ..."

"Is there any connection at all, do you think, between Lady Malet's disappearance, the dead body, and the man you have in custody in Ostend?" asked some half-bright from the cheap seats.

"*This*," said LeGras, "Is why I have widened the investigation because, at the present time, it is unclear what connection, if any, there is between these three people. And it is why I am taking the opportunity to address you all together and appeal to anybody who has any information to come forward and see me in my cabin and pass it on. Anything said will be treated in the strictest confidence ..."

"Could I just ask ..." (*this voice belonged to the stockbroker, who made a point of standing up and positioning himself in the already overcrowded aisle*) "... just what exactly it is you *do* know about anything?"

That would have made me laugh, could I have but moved my jaw muscles.

"*Monsieur ...?*"

"Let me phrase it another way, then, since you don't appear to understand the Queen's English ..." (*here I would have saluted, could I have but stood up*) "... There has been nothing but chaos on this train ever since it left Waterloo ..."

"Victoria," cut in somebody behind him.

"*Victoria*," he said, correcting himself contemptuously. "*Utter* and *complete* chaos, culminating in a murder, with a filthy and diseased body contaminating the water supply. And then to top it all, *you* come along – Mr *I-Don't-Know-Anything-About-Anything*-Le Gras – and spend half an hour of what should have been a pleasant holiday for me asking this carriage-load of crooks and cut-throats whether they would like to tell you anything about any of the crimes they've committed ..."

Murmurs of outrage greeted this particular statement and, once again, it took some time before LeGras was able to readdress the assembly.

"I can understand your displeasure, Monsieur, but I must beg you to have patience ..."

"Is there nothing you can tell us that might help us to remember something we may have seen, some link, some detail we dismissed as unimportant at the time?" asked an unidentified woman from the aisle.

"Well," he responded, "In connection with the man being held at police headquarters in Ostend, we are particularly interested to interview a second man. We believe his name to be Kitehawk – *Dexter* Kitehawk ..." (*I nearly shit a brick at this statement but, of course, I was still muscle-dead*) "... He was known to be travelling with the prisoner – they were, in fact, sharing a cabin – though we are unsure at this stage whether they were acting together or not. There are several suspicious circumstances surrounding his presence on the *Orient Express*, and he is known to have become involved in an argument with Sir Charles on board the ferry. He was last seen at passport control and is believed to have re-boarded the train – destination and present whereabouts unknown ..."

"Can you tell us anything *more* about him?" piped up the woman I couldn't see. "Such as what he looks like etc? What are the *suspicious circumstances* you mention?"

Can't you shut up? I yelled internally.

"That's *you*, pal," mumbled Blondie.

You can shut up and all, I went on ...

"He is posing as a doctor and is travelling under a false name. Disguises have been found in his cabin and a guard has been posted outside. My colleague would like to say a few words regarding this man, with whom he is acquainted..."

I sat there helpless to defend myself as Laurel stepped forward ...

"Kitehawk has been known to Interpol for two years now and, although I cannot specify the classification of his activities, I can tell you that he is very dangerous and any approach should be made with caution. I think it not unlikely that he is involved in both the disappearance of Lady Malet and the murdered man in the water tank. I shall also be available for conference in Monsieur LeGras's cabin ..."

The extent that bloke would go in trying to steal my ticket for the ball!

"And so," concluded LeGras, "I would appreciate it if you would come to my cabin with your passports. Please stagger your visits. Your names can be checked, questions asked, and hopefully you can be eliminated from the enquiry..."

Unless Laurel was playing a very complicated game, it didn't appear as though he recognised me.

Perhaps he intended blackmailing me into handing over the ticket?

The only passengers in the carriage who knew my identity for sure were Blondie (who wasn't letting on for some bizarre reason best known to herself) and Hetty and Mario (whose interests were in keeping me on the loose because they were after Dirk's address).

"Just one last question before you depart, Inspector," said the lout who'd upset Sir Orange-Shorts. "What was the identity of the body in the tank?"

"We may never know. It was so badly mutilated. But I can tell you that it was a youngish male, no older than thirty-five. He had no bodily markings that we can tell, except for a small birthmark above his collar bone – in the shape, well, something like that of a workman's boot ..."

At that moment, I became distracted by the appearance of somebody standing beyond the compartmental door behind LeGras – somebody with an enormous physique, and so tall that his head wasn't visible through the glass panel.

My concern wasn't *with* his head, however, but with something much closer to his heart ...

A large object glinting just inside his lapel was all the identification I needed to realise, with some surprise, that I'd actually *seen* the killer with the German Iron Cross before. I hadn't recognised it for what it was at the time, although my original assumption that it was a *weapon* was prophetic enough ...

There wasn't much chance of him pushing his way through the door until the plods had all departed, but the fact that I was sitting there near-paralysed left me feverishly trying to think of some desperate means to escape.

It did cross my mind, briefly, to dive through the gap in the floor, but I had a feeling that this might disappear the more the cocktail wore off.

In any event, an unexpected development was about to occur to render current options redundant ...

A rather well dressed woman suddenly appeared from behind me and marched all the way down the aisle to the front, calling Inspector LeGras back as she did so ...

"Monsieur LeGras! Monsieur LeGras! One moment! Before you leave, I have something to tell you concerning the identity of the murderer ..."

He turned round.

"Madame ...?"

I definitely saw at least half-a-dozen people shift uneasily in their seats (including me), and the entire carriage went silent with tension.

You could hear a *pin* drop.

"That man *there* is the murderer!" she suddenly declared. "He has a butcher's knife in his jacket pocket ...!'"

For a moment, nobody moved.

She was pointing straight at Mario – and, well, as far as the *knife* was concerned, she was *dead* right ...

"*I'm* not the murderer!" he shouted. "*He* is ...!"

He was *trying* to point at *me*, but his aim was way off target, and, in a moment of chaos, one of the gendarmes lunged at him, three other people stood up and pulled guns on each other, the stranger burst in at the far end of the carriage ...

SCREEEEEECH ..... !!!!

... LeGras pulled the communication cord, the train screeched to a halt, the entire lot of us fell arse over head onto the floor and ...

The lights all went out.

KERBLAM! KERBLAM! KER*BLAM BLAM BLAM BLAM* *BLAM...!!!*

Several guns blazed away like shutters on the dark, and I felt the snap of a handcuff on my wrist.

Click!

Something was coming.

Something shuddering the earth in the distance, but not thunder.

Pounding the sleepers, coming our way ...

In the pandemonium breaking out all around me, it would have been hard to say who was struggling most on the cuffs, or for what purpose.

I couldn't see who held me prisoner, but somebody was beginning to drag me along the floor, away from the trouble at the front of the carriage and back towards the nearest exit, rather as though I were the reluctant partner in a coercive marriage ... *and a halo of invisible icy fingertips settle on my scalp and tease the nerve-lines down my spine; for it is a wedding without a soundtrack, the cries and shouts and bumps and bangs displaced by the shiver and vibration of an approaching presence beyond the carriage walls, a livid and seething thing, like an animal of the night ...*

I've been hauled to my feet now, the bodies fumbling for stability around me are like the blind waves of an adverse tide, impelling me towards the source of attraction, a door shaped like a slab for the betrothal of sacrificial lambs ...

Here it comes.

The beast beyond – far down the carriage – the unsummoned guardian of the altar, its trinity of eyes looking in from outside, flaring up in chemical cloud at each window in turn like a malicious photographer's toy as it rumbles up from behind on the adjacent slow line, hunting for somebody or something ... and in the rush of opposite charges I'm about to be dragged through the gateway ...

"AAAAAAAAAA*AAAAAAAA*ARGH ...!!!"

And straight into the path of another train ... where we leapt by headlight ... north-north-west ... *elf* by *zwölf* at the collision of worlds ... *hands clutched in dangerous purpose* ... freeze-framed for the exact duration required to materialise in mid-air beyond the passing engine ... *and land, the pair of us, in one of its empty coal trucks.*

For just a moment, it looked as though the two base-metal projections might converge on parallel tracks as our new cart to damnation gathered momentum and accelerated beyond the troubled slowboat of the Orient ...

Postcards of the Dark

And so, this was how I was brought into Germany, carried south at a rate of change hitherto unmatched even by the *Express*, a face in open-air shadow rushing through the lit-up cities of Cologne and Bonn, all flickering slide-shows against the speeding night.

And all along the way, the black water of the Rhine was never very far from our view, eventually spilling in spectacular tributary far underneath the tracks as we crossed the Moselle bridge towards Koblenz ...

Koblenz was a dark place by night, a quarry of unlit mediaeval buildings carved out of the face of the surrounding cliffs, set between outposts of rusty iron sidings which went nowhere into the grass and weeds, last place of repose for more conventional travellers before the main line was swallowed up by the mouth of a lengthy tunnel.

Some way beyond the old town, we emerged in dense woodland lit through with shadows cast from a full moon.

Here, a honeycomb of trees were united in living movement by a biting cold wind whistling across the dark landscape, cloaking the approaches and domain of Castle Froth, whose tiny lights could be seen nestling high above us on a mountaintop like the eyes of carrion crow.

As if by design, the train slowed enough for us to leap off, and we tumbled down a grassy embankment and landed with a bump against a large, grizzled oak.

In the distance I could hear the howling of wolves ...

CONCLUSION

DENOUEMENT AT THE SCHLOSS FROTH

CHAPTER 38
CASTLE OF THE CLOUDS

"That was clever," I said. "Is there any *particular* reason you're trying to kill me?"

I would have spoken up sooner, but I'd only just that minute recovered the use of my jaw muscles. Bumping my head against the tree seemed to do the trick.

"Hey, Buster, you're *alive*, ain't ya?" she snapped. "Stop complainin' ..."

"Oh, it's *you*," I said. "I thought I'd been arrested by Interpol ..."

"Sorry to disappoint ya ..."

"Anyway," I said, "How do you *know* I'm alive? Where's your proof?"

All of a sudden she stabbed me with a hatpin ...

I squawked!

Then she lunged forward and started to tickle me violently below the ribs ...

"Does *this* answer your question?" she was demanding, "What's the progress report on your location? Dead or alive ...?"

I had a lot of difficulty answering this one, intermittently snort-laughing – as I was – and hooting and whooping like the laughing policeman. The *handcuffs* prevented escape ...

"Alright, *alright* !" I spluttered. "I'm alive ... I'M *ALIVE* ...!!!"

"Hey," she said, "Are you sure? First time, is it ...?" (*She'd let up temporarily, but was hovering over me just in case she needed to strike again ...*)

"Madam," I said. "Life is one thing. *Quality* another ..."

There was an unnerving pause at this point.

But, as soon as my words struck home ... so did *she.*

"Listen, asshole ..." (*she was now quite mercilessly torturing me while I writhed around in agony in the undergrowth*) "... you were goin' nowhere fast on that train. That was the *Slammer* Express as far as Mr Dexter Kitehawk was concerned. I did you a *favour* back there. *Get* it? This way you get to go to the Ball *after* all. And you got *me* for company ..."

Here she finally took pity on me, stopped tickling me ... and sat down next to me.

"You're *one* lucky guy," she concluded.

Not being quite sure yet what kind of a maniac I was dealing with, I decided not to provoke her any more.

Instead, I tried to concentrate on removing some of the pinecones embedded in my back, but with only one hand free it wasn't easy.

So I spat the grass out of my mouth instead ...

"Look, Blondie," I said (*thinking it might be pragmatic to adopt a more conciliatory tone – at least until such time as I got free of the cuffs*), "It's just that all my disguises were on the train, and now I'll never find that rucksack ..."

"Rucksack?" she said. "I never figured you for the rucksack type ..."

"No?" I said.

"No," she said. "I got you pencilled in as the carrier-bag-and-tweezers type..."

"Tweezers?" I shouted. "*Tweezers* ...!"

"*Say*," she cut in, "What did you *have* in this sack, anyway?"

"Nothing relevant to the Flite case ..."

"Now," she said, "Are we talking about *Adolf* Flite, or are we talking about more of your luggage?"

"Never mind about all *that*," I said. "What do you *mean* by tweezers? I *demand* to know. I'm absolutely outraged ..."

"Don't get so touchy, Buster. I'm working on the fancy dress problem. You *need* me ..."

"You still haven't told me who you are. Who *are* you?"

"I told you already. So, shut the fuck up ..."

"What's your interest in my affairs?"

"Fuck *you* !"

Charming language for fairy godmothers, I thought.

Utterly charming.

In *fact*, I was just sitting there thinking this might possibly be the most unladylike exhibition of verbal deportment I'd ever been subjected to, when ... *a civilising memory of Fiona chucking axes around suddenly materialised in my internal cinema via a faulty contrast control* ...

"You know," I said, "I knew a woman once who had an even *bigger* supply of foul language than *you* ..."

"Yeah," she said. "*That's* me. *Miss* Goody-Two-Shoes ..."

"But she was actually quite polite when she was sober ..."

"I guess that deals *me* out ..."

I rattled the cuffs.

"Are you going to *unlock* these or not?" I enquired.

"I thought *you* had the key," she said.

"*Me*?" I said. "Now, why would I have the key?"

"They're *your* handcuffs," she said.

"What do you mean, they're *my* handcuffs?"

"I took 'em from your case before I threw it off the train ..."

"You silly tart!" I yelled. "That means they're *magicians* handcuffs! We'll never get them off now ..."

"Stop griping. They'll have tools up at the Castle ..."

"Tools?"

"*Tools. Yeah.* They're *criminals. Safe-cracking* equipment. *Tools* ..."

"You're not coming near *me* with safe-cracking equipment ..."

"Suit yourself. Anyway, I like it this way. I can keep an eye on you ..."

"I don't suppose it's occurred to you that it might not be a good idea to turn up at an International Organised Criminals' Barndance flashing handcuffs around? At the very least they'll think we're taking the piss ..."

"Hey, it's fancy-dress, remember? Stick close to me and nobody'll notice..."

"Suppose we get attacked by wolves before we get there?"

"Wolves? This is *Germany*, asshole. Not Transylvania ..."

"I distinctly heard wolves earlier ..."

"*Dogs.* They were *dogs* ..."

"*Hounds,* maybe ..."

"So what? Hounds ..."

"You probably don't know what you're dealing with here," I said. "This may be Germany, but I'd say there's a distinct possibility that Adolf Flite is not human ..."

"You're crazy ..."

"Tomorrow is *Walpurgis* night. There could be anything roaming around these woods ..."

"You're giving me the creeps ..."

"Wolves, dogs, vampire bats. What am I going to do if one of these dark shadows suddenly leaps out and attacks me? I've only got one arm free ..."

"Well," she said, "We'll have to join forces ... and give it a *cuff* round the ear!"

At this, she suddenly had a fit of the shrieks that rocked her body so violently she almost tore my arm out of its socket ...

"Oh," I suggested, "So you're trying to wake the *dead* as well ...?"

"Hey, wait a minute," she suddenly declared. "I think I've solved your fancy-dress problem ..."

"Oh yes?"

She yanked me up off the ground ...

"Yeah," she said. "Turn your back and don't look round till I tell ya. This is gonna be a delicate operation ..."

I dreaded to think what she was up to.

In the background, I could hear her rustling her clothes, the significance of which went unchallenged as I stood there and shivered and looked up at the moon hanging like a bright, frozen stone in space.

All of a sudden, the nightscape vanished ...

I spluttered in shock!

She'd pulled one of her black tights over my head ...

So *surprised* was I, that for a minute I didn't know whether to faint, fart, fall in love or phone the police ...

"I'm not sure I don't prefer you like this," she said, ignoring my eventual, stifled protests. "Won't nobody recognise you now, and your volume's been adjusted to the right level at the same time. *Now*, if you behave yourself on the way up to the Castle, I might even cut you some eye-holes and a breathing socket later on ..."

"Thanks very much," I said, speaking muffled through the mesh.

"Don't mention it ..."

"I *won't*," I said. "But you could have taken my top-hat off first ..."

Despite the extra layer of clobber I'd acquired, my initial dramatic rise in temperature began to cool rapidly in the night air.

"Come on then, Buster," she said at length. "We're late for that party ..."

"Just a minute," I said. "Where's *your* disguise?"

"This is *it*," she said. "I'm really a brunette from Hawaii ..."

Aloha!

Tugging me along by the cuffs as she went, Blondie trudged off into the woods with zero concern for my minimal level of vision, and however carefully I tried to follow, I fell arse over tit on several occasions, lacerating my free hand and other exposed parts of my flesh in the process.

I *had* to assume we were going in the right direction, because of the way she kept dragging me up over one incline after another, but I could no longer see the Castle Froth looming over us in the distance. *Obscured by darkness, trees and a layer of black nylon, it had vanished from view along with almost everything else.* Just about the *only* sense impressions I had at this time were connected with the ninety denier of stocking material clinging to my air apertures and the mass of twigs being crunched underfoot. *And*, as the former began to tickle me somewhere in the vicinity of my false beard, I let out an almighty sneeze, inadvertently bit into one of Wilbur Beans' nitrous oxide capsules and paralysed myself with hysterics ...

She pulled up sharp.

"What are *you* laughing at, Buster?" she said.

It was *funny* really, but it was really no *laughing* matter:

I was starting to *suffocate* in there ...

Oh my God, I thought. *I'm going to be found handcuffed and gassed to death inside a pair of women's tights ...*

"Let me out!" I screamed in panic. "I can't *breathe* in here! I'm going to die *laughing* in a minute ...!"

Just as my ribs reached fracturing point, she condescended to show some concern ...

"A bit grim in there, is it?" she declared ... *when the cuffs suddenly sprung open...*

And ...

She disappeared.

Goodbye-a!

into *thin* air ...

"Blondie ...?" I called, tentatively.
No sound.
"Blondie ...?"
No *Blondie.*
No *nothing* ...
"BLONDIE ...!!!" I yelled.
Thinking that the strain of my giggling attack must have forced the lock and sent her crashing to the deck unconscious, I got down on all fours and scrambled around the immediate undergrowth looking for her.
I didn't *find* her, though.
I *did* find the loose cuffs, but Blondie wasn't attached to them.
And this left me pondering other possibilities:
Perhaps one of us had inadvertently said a magic word?
The magic word.
The word is uttered, the cuffs spring open, and ...

The Lady Vanishes

I couldn't remember saying anything *remotely* coherent myself, but what had *she* said?
All I could recall was her asking me if it was a bit 'grim' inside her tights, though if anybody knew the answer to that, *she* should have done.
Grim.
Was *that* the word?
Alone for the first time in that dark forest, I wondered whether the answer lay not with the cuffs but with Blondie herself.
Fairy godmother?
Or wicked witch ...

Almost as though I were being offered some evidence for this proposition, an eerie whine suddenly erupted around me, sounding at first like a distant cry for help, but rapidly developing into the kind of racket that might have emanated from a harpy circling on a broomstick ...
"*Aloha ... Aloha ...*" the voice moaned.
"Is that *you*, Blondie ...?"
"*Aloha ... Aloha ...*"
Remembering somewhat belatedly that I still had an impediment to my senses, I raised

Blondie's tights to the level of my hat-brim, drunk in several lungfuls of fresh air and ... as I did so, something touched me from above – something like a *cobweb*, or a ghostly hand brushing against my forehead.

Something like *hair ...*

I took off at about 100mph, yelling as I went.

"If that's *you*," I was shouting, "Don't hang about *too* long. I'll send help. *Over and out ...!*"

The Man In The Nylon Mask

Clattering along like a madman, I clawed my way over the exposed roots and branches of the hideously deformed trees disfiguring my path, until – on the verge of a seizure – I finally slammed on the brakes and doubled over, wheezing like a flying banshee.

My *god* it was *hot* in those tights!

In my rush to leave the area, they'd slipped back down over my face, impairing visibility to such an extent that the proximity of a clearing bathed in moonlight only became apparent after I'd taken the trouble to roll them up past my eyes again.

Pressing wearily on, I realised that I was approaching something like a mountain track, perhaps even a road.

As I carelessly stepped out beyond the trees, I almost got carved up by a gigantic speeding limousine that shot past me with its horn blaring like a Harry James solo ...

BLAAA*AAAAAAAAAARE* ...!!!

"GET *FUCKED* ...!!!" I yelled after it, but it was all gone in a flash, the dust settling around me the only evidence it had passed that way at all.

Since the road was on an incline, I decided to follow it in the direction the car had gone – ie. upwards – thinking that if the *direction* wasn't right, the *altitude* would be, and it was as I rounded the first bend that I once again set eyes on the Schloss Froth...

I could see it clearly now in all its evil majesty: towering over the surrounding woods and valleys – up ahead, maybe just an hour's walk away, rising on a bank of mist. It was a Briar Rose fairy castle and it held, somewhere within its dark walls and sinister turrets, the secret of Adolf Flite and the Allied Froth Corporation.

Here was the end of the case, one way or another: the conclusion to my battle against evil spanning two years.

The silence had returned, the speeding car an unreal memory as I stood there gazing at the castle, a truly fantastic sight, set against the clear night sky with the stars frozen behind it like lights in dark ice.

And I might have stood there bewitched all night, if the sound of something approaching from far down the hill hadn't forced me to dart back into the undergrowth ...

Wolf Whistle

It finally rumbled into view from around the bend, a travelling carriage drawn by four black coach horses ...

It was the kind of vehicle which might have been seen on those roads in the last century, and the driver, all stout and old and huddled up against the cold inside several layers of clothing, tugged on the reins and brought his team to a standstill right next to my clump of bushes.

His face was hidden by a long scarf wrapped several times around his neck, chin and mouth, and by an old cap pulled down to the level of his eyes; and, while he continued to sit motionless, it was almost as though he *knew* I was there, as though he were *waiting* for me ...

Eventually, he shifted in his seat and began fumbling around in his pockets, but it was only once he'd extracted a pipe and proceeded to light it that I began to breathe a little easier.

Whoever he is, I thought, *he's just pulled up for a smoke ...*

Long before he'd finished his sojourn, I was shivering with cold again – so much so, that when he took up the reins to leave, I had half a mind to call out and hitch a ride.

But something about this strange apparition troubled me ...

Before cracking his whip, he paused to listen to an animal baying in the distance:

A few moments later, I almost swallowed my choppers as another one howled so loud that its snout could have been buried halfway up my arse ...

Thinking I could hear Blondie's dismembered voice all mixed up with it, yelling "*ALOHA!*" or some similar rubbish, I got to my feet in shock.

It was all guilty conscience, of course.

She was coming back to haunt me, because I'd left her alone in the woods...

When the coach finally rolled off, I saw a sign hanging at the back, and this made up my mind for me:

Schloss Froth – Shuttle Service

"Oi!" I yelled, darting out from behind the bushes and chasing up the road after it, "Taxi! *TAXI* ...!"

Actually, the sign said nothing of the sort: rather, it was something in German that looked very much like something in English, but I was now prepared to take a gamble on the earthbound status of the driver, at least.

I'd never really quite worked out how best to approach the Castle Froth: through the front door with guns and invitation card blazing – so to speak – or surreptitiously, through a side window with a faulty lock, say.

Of the two options, the second had been my favoured choice, but the current decision to disclose myself had severely limited its application.

Even so, I considered it important not to give up on the possibility that there might yet be an opportunity to vacate the coach quietly just before its arrival at the castle ...

The coachman brought his horses to a halt and waited until I'd caught up, making no effort to look round as he leaned back and opened the door for me.

"Tip-top!" I said, climbing aboard with confidence. "To the Castle Froth if you please, my man, and step on the gas ..."

Once I'd taken my seat, I looked back anxiously out of the window for sign of pursuers – *canine* or otherwise – but it was *inside* the darkened carriage that I ought to have focused my attention, because when we finally trundled off, I had the fright of my life to discover a dark figure sitting across the far side ...

"Chilly tonight, isn't it?" I said, stating the obvious for conversational purposes, but the stranger did not respond.

He made no movement and no sound.

"Are you alright?" I offered.

Still he made no response, and no matter how much I adjusted my position to try to get a better look at his features, he was bathed in such a pool of shadow that it was as though the mustiness of the air itself had congealed around him like an invisible film.

His shape suggested that, like me, he was wearing top hat and tails, and he might well have had Blondie's other pair of tights stuffed over his head for all I could see of it.

To say he gave me the creeps wouldn't have been saying anything.

"Murder, aren't they," I said, "These Acid House parties. Just got back from a big one at Basingstoke Airport. Thirty-six hours straight through. Disused tent on Runway 3 ..."

A steep curve in the mountain road suddenly forced a realignment of vehicle to nature and, for a fleeting moment, he was dramatically illuminated by the moonlight flooding in through the open window ...

That *Face* ...!

It was white like death, the eyes fixed ahead and staring at nothing ...
"Excuse me," I said. (*I grabbed hold of the door handle*). "I think we're here ..."

But, just as I was about to step off that gothic hearse, something behind the trees closest to the roadside caught my attention:

Eyes.

Several pairs of them, glinting in the moonlight, following the coach ...

A long, baying moan echoing through the woods confirmed a live animal presence and left me frozen in mid-exit, hesitating to drop in as a dinner guest for a pack of hungry hounds ... yet reluctant to remain behind as a nightcap for the Living Dead.

I wonder if he's looking at me? I thought, aware that, having turned my back on him, I shouldn't have lingered.

Ultimately, I had little choice. *The sleek dark shapes materialising to give definition to the detached eyes left me in no doubt as to the number of slavering dogs waiting to pounce the moment I should jump ... one* of which had dramatically appeared running behind the rear wheels ...

"*My* mistake," I said, not looking over at the stiff. "I must be punch-drunk..."

Securing my credit cards, I got back in and slammed the door shut behind me.

Clonk!

"Can't you go any *faster?*!!!" I yelled out of the glassless window.

Following a flurry of unintelligible cursing, moaning and a crack of the coachman's whip, the horses gave the carriage a violent jolt and broke into a high-speed gallop ...

When I stuck my hooter outside, I was alarmed to see the rest of the pack coming out into the open and joining the chase on the road, trailing a carriage which was developing a tendency to rock violently from side to side as it hurtled on at an ever-increasing speed – so much so, that I soon began to imagine myself in a scene from an old western in which an arrow flying through the window and embedding itself in the upholstery would not have seemed entirely out of place...

As we rounded the next bend, the leader of the pack – having gained a lot of ground without me noticing – leapt up and almost snapped my nose off ...

"Oi!" I persisted. "Can't you *do* something ...?!!!"

This time, his response was to rummage around directly above the roof of the carriage, turfing overboard a stack of suitcases and boxes which came flying past the window so fast that if I hadn't managed to duck back inside rather sharpish, they might have taken my head with them ...

"What the hell are you *playing* at up there ...?!!!" I shouted, venturing too soon to stick my neck back out and feeling the benefit of a trunk the size of Piccadilly Circus as it crashed me across the nut and sent me reeling backwards across the floor like a B-movie monster in slow-motion ...

I doubt if it killed any dogs, though.

I should think they could have *seen* it coming a mile away ...

Ere, just a minute, I thought with alarm, *if the coachman's up there on the roof chucking luggage about, who's steering the coach? Who had hold of the reins ...?*

KER*BLAM* **...!!!**

I staggered to my feet just in time to witness a ferocious gunblast light up the night ... and glanced out to find the idiot had blown a section of the rear axle away!

The wheels wobbled like half-spun coins as we careered around a bend so fast that the carriage tilted up on its side ... teetered over the edge of a steep ravine ... "OH MY GAWD ...!!!" *...* crashed back down again, and ... "Eeeeeeeeeeeeeeeeek !" ... **Crunch!** *Splinter* ...!!! *... rocked so far over onto its opposite side that a passing tree ripped one of the doors off ...*

I went and positioned myself in the open void:
The dogs had vanished now, only to be replaced by an altogether *different* nightmare ...
We were hurtling along the most frightening stretch of road I'd ever seen – like a crumbling land-bridge with a steep drop to Hell falling away on either side through a bath of cloud ... and *there*, at the end of it, was the *Schloss:*
Rising up like a wicked mausoleum into the night ...

Pas de Deux

"Oi!" I yelled. "Can't you slow *down* ...?!!!"
Far from taking any notice of me, he proceeded to urge the horses on faster still, cracking his whip like a man gawn berserk, and I didn't think it was possible for anything worse to happen, when ... *one of the dodgy back wheels suddenly came flying off and disappeared into the dark ...*
As a result of which, the carriage reared up into a 70mph balancing act on the edge of infinity and the corpse came leaping out of its seat, clattered me from my position ... *and pinioned me to the floor.*

Trying to get out from under him was like doing the Dance of Death with a Dutch landscape painter and I instinctively screamed ...
"AAAAAAAAAAAA*AAAARGH* ...!!!"
The *worse* thing about it was that we were completely face-to-face, and his *breath* was revolting.
I can't tell you what he *died* of, but I know what he *ate* for his last meal ...

The final act in this performance came when the coach, still balancing on one wheel, broke free from the horses, rattled across the Castle drawbridge, knocked several large chunks out of the stonework of the gatehouse on its way in (which, in turn, caused the portcullis to fall behind us, slicing the back end of the coach away), careered across the inner yard and exploded in a shower of firewood as it came to rest in the stables.

CHAPTER 39
BLOOD AND IRON

I lay there in the ruins of the coach, wondering whether it was too late for a surreptitious entry.

I gathered it was.

And, if my dancing partner wasn't dead before the crash, he certainly was *now.* The impact had shot him straight up through the half-collapsed carriage roof, where he was dangling by his neck like a macabre mobile, grimly creaking in the wind.

As for the *driver,* well ...

When I finally managed to crawl out from under the wreckage, I accosted him staggering around the barn with his head impaled in a bale of hay.

"What the hell did you think you were playing at back there on the road?" I demanded to know. "You could have got me killed!"

He made no attempt to remove the haystack and, instead, stuck his arm out and pointed over to what I assumed to be the main door of the castle, grunting incoherently like a drunken mute.

I had half a mind to take a *swing* at him ...

"*Gertch*' you old bastard ..." I growled.

His only reaction was to keep pointing, more insistently than before.

"Right!" I yelled. "I'm going! And do something about that bloke up there. Don't keep him hanging about – he wants a second opinion ..."

So incensed was I, that I took a flying kick at the damaged stable door as I went, knocked it off its hinges, lacerated a foot to match my hand, swung the loose handcuffs in retaliation, missed altogether, and clanged myself round the teeth.

By the time I'd reached the minaret-shaped portal, lifted the ancient iron knocker and let its gothic gargoyle head clonk back against the wood, my gums were still twitching and my front tombstones were playing a tune all by themselves like a Hannah-Barbara pianola.

Reason enough, I suppose, why it didn't immediately occur to me that I'd arrived on Adolf Flite's threshold completely alone and unarmed, without any form of help or back-up firepower at all ...

I waited patiently for a response, and I waited some several minutes while I shivered in the cold courtyard, unable to detect any sound of life within.

"Hello? Is anybody home ...?" I called out, giving it another couple of hearty raps for good measure, but my voice reverberated across the flagstones and remained unanswered.

Stepping back a couple of paces, I tried to see whether there was any sign of an establishment all set up and waiting for a trainload of holiday revellers to check in.

Like, for example, visible lights in the windows above, but all I received for my pains was a stiff neck. It looked to me as though the whole block was in darkness, although I found it hard to believe that my entrance had been unnoticed. *I should think half of Europe must have heard me arrive ...*

In view of the enormous size of the castle, I considered the possibility that I might be at the wrong door, but after reminding myself how little the mute coachman's directions had been open to interpretation, I picked up a discarded shovel and crashed it against the oak panelling a few times ...

"WHAT *ARE* YOU, ALL *DEAF* IN THERE ...?!!!" I yelled out at the top of my voice.

Just as before, there was no answer at all.

No sound, no light, no movement anywhere.

Castled.

Queen's Pawn to King's Rook Twelve.

Skint old boot to Pentonville Road, with three hotels on it.

Snookered in pursuit of the trivial.

And.

Don't think the *irony* went unnoticed, either.

The *irony*, that is, of me waiting there with a *spade* in my hand.

Generations of POWs must have been tunnelling out of their graves as I weighed up the possibility of *shovelling* my way *into* Colditz for a knees-up with the Jerries ...

I leaned back against the door and stood there watching the wind sweeping leaves across the courtyard.

The surrounding buildings – possibly all part of the same building – were dark and dead, and the lights in the stable were out now, the coachman long gone, vanished to who knows where.

There is little I hate more than the feeling that everybody knows where the party is except me.

I supposed I was *in* the Castle Froth?

It wasn't quite like I'd imagined, I must admit, the most immediately visible oversight being the absence of a garrison of Corporation stormtroopers, although there seemed to be precious little of value on display for a garrison to defend. Indeed, I couldn't have been more surprised by the unprepossessing nature of the Corporation's registered address if the Schloss Froth had turned out to be a tiny unmanned office in one of the sterile glass blocks of Bonn's financial district.

It was a ghost castle.

Windswept, and apparently empty.

tick tock tick tock
Abandoned by everything but the dust.
Deserted by time.
tick tock tick tock
Or was it just that my watch had stopped?
I shook my wrist and held it up to the moon:
For the first time ever, I noticed that the happy face staring back at me wasn't Mickey Mouse at all, but his alter ego, *Minnie*. I could only assume that the diminutive hands on the clock face landed her with a moustache at most times of day, hence my error. Right at that moment she looked to be exhibiting a north-west to south-east tramline across her nose, and all the signs were that it was going to be a long wait till she developed a pencil neck.

That's if her *ticker* was still working.

Either way, it was going to be a struggle to pass the hours till sun-up, by which time I might well have frozen solid in a blaze of ironic greeting best reserved for the undertaker.

I hunched my shoulders against the night air and let my gaze wander from one unforgiving landmark to another.

The empty gatehouse was still empty.

Or so it seemed.

The one discernible feature in an otherwise featureless outside wall.

Not much change there.

Although ...

It had *some* aspect of fascination, and this stalled the progress of my random review, probably because the arched stonework straddled the only evident route in or out of the courtyard.

Notwithstanding the fallen gate.

And notwithstanding the lack of any *ground* level access to the guard and machinery rooms, though it was far from unique amongst the edifices on show which shared this peculiarity. The only entry point appeared to be through a tiny closed door high up on the battlements.

And *that*, I suppose, was that.

True, the adjacent quarters beneath those battlements were inset with broken windows on the ground floor, but whether or not an alternative route into the main complex was accessible through that desolate place was neither here nor there. I had no intention of stirring from my impromptu sentry box to investigate the dark pools of the enclosure lying beyond the jagged glass, and so I shifted the sweep of my survey:

Directly opposite, and running across to my left, a line of cloisters bordered two sides of the courtyard, the unlit buildings underneath which they were constructed shielding further apparently hollow areas of the castle from which clusters of dark and indistinct roofs were visible. Beyond those roofs was the outline of a massive tower at the extremity which stood out like a forlorn oasthouse against the night.

The remaining side of the yard, which included both the main doorway (my current place of languishment), a small tower (part-hidden in a corner recess), rows of unlit windows (first floor and upwards only), and an uninviting dungeon aperture (sunk into the brickwork just above the level of the flagstones half-way along the block), comprised a face of the central structure so high that it concealed from view the remainder of a castle which could, for all I knew, have contained several courtyards all the same.

In fact, I might well have been in the tradesman's entrance.

It was a potential maze – one of which I had no idea how to enter, let alone exit.

Looking across at the hundreds of tons of immoveable portcullis spiked into the ground, it dawned on me that I was in a trap.

And this left me with little choice but to sit down and prop myself up on the doorstep like a returning night owl who'd lost his keys, huddled and shivering, the old arms stretching and the muscles yawning, already resigned to the prospect of spending the night in the doorway, when ...

CREAK ... the great oak door dramatically gave way behind me and I fell in backwards with a shock!

Clonk!

"That's what I call service ..." I mumbled, as I landed sprawled inside.

Since I could see nobody responsible for letting me in, I got to my feet and looked ahead into the dark hallway.

"Anybody home ...?" I called out hesitantly.

It must have been open all the time, I thought.

But, as I went to take a few paces forward ...

CRASH ...!!!

... the door suddenly slammed shut behind me, extinguishing what dim light from the moon had followed me in ...

I swung round to find a sinister figure lurking there in the blackness ...

"Hrrnnnn!!!"

"*Eeeeeeek* ....!"

When it started to shuffle forward, I jumped back in fright!

What creature from the Pit was this ...?

"Hrrrnnn*nnnn* ...!!!"

A further involuntary squeal escaped from my lips before I was forced to adopt such an exaggerated boxing stance that my reinforced shoulders slipped halfway down my arms ...

"Gheu*rrt out* of it!!!" I bluffed.

"Hrrrrnnn*nnnmnn* ...!!!"

Edging away, terrified, I slipped on the polished stonework and crashed into a man-sized dinner gong ...

BONG!

The entire place went **Cuckoo!** as I hit the deck ... literally fucking apeshit!!! *Flocks of stuffed birds went bursting out of their clocks, barrel-organs and calliopes were farting and grinding either side of me in the dark, an invisible Punch and Judy were* *battering each other over the nut with glockenspiel clubs, and a fucking Great Tom tower chime was ringing out the changes for a nine bells storm warning ...*

Helpless, stunned, and vibrating like a tuning fork, I lay there completely at the mercy of my hellish pursuer, whose black shape came spreading towards me across the dark ...

All of a sudden the cacophany stalled, a match flared up, a lantern flickered to life, and I was able for the first time to see it in all its hideousness:
"ARE YOU *MAD* ...?!!!" I screamed.
It was the coachman!
The *mute* !
Scrambling to my feet, I tried to hurl at him as much bluster as I could in an effort to mask my discomfort ...
"I SHALL HAVE YOU *SHOT* FOR THIS!!!"
Once again, his only response was to start pointing and grunting – pointing beyond me into the hall, something I now understood to mean, '*Walk this way ...*'
I don't know, I thought, *but for the headquarters of a multinational criminal conspiracy like the Allied Froth Corporation, I would have thought they could have afforded better staff than this incompetent old gobber.*
The *sight* of him was enough to make you sick up your breakfast.
And I didn't like him walking *behind* me either, but we hadn't gone very far when all of the lights suddenly came on, revealing a spectacular winding staircase and an altogether more *human* figure walking down to greet me ...

He took some time though, there were so many steps.
As he approached, I noted his general appearance – about 45 years old, jet black hair, piercing eyes, not tall, and he was dressed in an immaculate tuxedo.
He held out his hand and smiled.
"I am sorry if you have been kept waiting, Mr ...?"
So mesmerised by his eyes was I, that I didn't at first appreciate that he was asking me a question.
And so I smiled back, shook his hand ... *and kept shtoom.*
"Permit me to introduce myself," he went on. "I am Simon Flite, Executive Director of AF International. I trust your stay at Schloss Froth will be an enjoyable and fruitful one ..."
"I am sure it will be an highly enjoyable and very fruity one, Mr Flite," I said, *thinking to myself, Simon* Flite? That's a puzzler. Does he mean *Adolf* Flite? There surely weren't *two* of them ...?
An uneasy pause followed, during which an expression crossed his face as though he were trying to cue me for a song.
"Dexter," I said at length. "Dexter ... erm ..." (*here I hesitated*) "... Dexter Haute-Cooke ..."
"Well, Mr ..."
"Of *Haute-Cooke Culinary Cuisine (Import) UK Ltd.* We shift quite a lot of

your stuff ..."

"You fascinate me," he said, as he led me round the side of the stairwell and into a well-lit hall. "Tell me more ..."

"Oh, you know," I said, "The usual sort of thing. We import the beer, and then we mug the punters with it ..."

"*Mm* ..." he murmured.

I began to notice that the coachman was following right behind me – so close as to be virtually breathing down my neck – and he appeared to be hanging on my every word.

"Of course," I said, attempting to do a little probing of my host, "Most of our dealings have been with your *father* ..."

He suddenly stopped and swung round ...

"*Father?*" he demanded.

"Er ... *yes*," I said. "That's ... *Adolf* Flite ...?"

He glared at me in a rather unnerving manner for some moments with those intense blue eyes before he spoke again.

"You must have been on the books for some time, Mr ... *Haute-Cooke*. My father is dead ..."

"Oh I am sorry," I said. "You must miss him ..."

"Not really. He died many years ago. I never knew him ..."

"All the same ..."

"All the same," he said, as he finally relaxed his optical vice-hold and turned to wander down a narrower corridor lined with suits of mediaeval armour. "I take it then, Mr Haute-Cooke, that you are here as a representative of your company, rather than one of the hundred guests selected at random by our central computer in Cologne?"

"Funnily enough, no," I said (*not quite sure what to say for the best*). "I *did* receive one of your random invites and I am, in fact, here in *that* capacity – ie at random. It was just a happy coincidence, really ..."

"But you surely received one of our special *corporate* invites?"

"I would have done," I said. "But, unfortunately, just after we took in your last shipment of lager, the unthinkable happened ..."

"Oh?" he said. "What was that?"

"We went into liquidation ..."

"Oh, I am sorry," he said. "You should have contacted us. We are always ready to help long-term clients who have been loyal to the Corporation ..."

"I didn't like to trouble you. I have, of course, received many of your courtesy packages over the years ..."

"Merely a token of our appreciation ..."

"I'm not sure my butler would see it like that ..."

"Oh?" he said.

"An unfortunate accident ..."

"Drunk one too quickly, did he?"

"Not at all," I said. "It was all the fault of a rather over-enthusiastic postman, really – and a very high letter-box ..."

"I *see*," he said.

"*Mm* ..." I mumbled.

"It *fell* on him, then?" he concluded.

"No, no," I said. "It fell on his *drinking* licence. Killed him stone dead just the same ..."

"Are you *completely* bankrupt?"

"Pretty much," I said. "Apart from a few liquid assets. But I drunk those before I left, I'm afraid ..."

"Extraordinary ..."

"Isn't it," I confirmed.

We turned a corner and entered another long corridor.

"How was your journey?" he asked.

"Randomly interesting ..." I murmured, absent-mindedly.

"Of course, you won't know this, but, with the exception of a few close friends and some officers of the Corporation here in Germany, you are, in fact, the only guest to arrive this evening. It is very unfortunate, but the festivities planned for tonight have had to be cancelled. The Grand Unveiling and Fancy Dress Ball scheduled for tomorrow evening will, of course, still take place. Perhaps you would like to join me for a nightcap before you retire?"

"Very decent," I said, beginning to feel decidedly uneasy at the increasing proximity of the mute. "Charming fellow, your coachman ..."

"Of course," he said, "I was forgetting that you two had met. Everybody here at Schloss Froth loves Tommy ..."

"Really ...?" I said.

I half-looked round at him.

His head was still wrapped inside the scarf.

"Yes," he went on. "I gather that Tommy picked you up on the road. I see now why *you* made it and the others didn't. Tommy was returning from Lahnstein railway station where I'd sent him to pick up some of the guests, but he has informed me that the train has been delayed due to an unfortunate incident involving the police. I understand that the passengers will be boarded at local hotels until the matter is cleared up, but that hopefully our guests will be allowed to continue on to Schloss Froth tomorrow ..."

"How tiresome," I responded.

"May I ask how you got here?"

"Oh," I declared, "On foot ..."

"On foot?" he said. "It must have taken you ages ..."

"About two hours, no more ..."

"*Two hours?*" he said. "Where on earth have you come from?"

"Oh," I said, backpedalling, "I was *on* the train, but unfortunately I fell off just outside Cologne. These things happen ..."

"Well, it's all worked out for the best. You have avoided police involvement. *Good.* You must tell me what kind of an incident would have prevented the *Orient Express* from continuing its journey. It must have been *big*..."

"Oh, it *was*," I said. "And quite shocking, really. But the police looked to have it all in hand as far as I could tell. But it shook me up, I can tell you. I mean, you don't expect this kind of thing on the *Orient Express*, do you?"

"I shall have everybody flown here next time ..."

"Safest form of transport," I affirmed ... *before I realised that he wanted me to tell him what had happened* ... "Perhaps over that drink you promised me. I'm still in a state of shock ..."

"Of course," he said. "And you must be hungry. I'll get Tommy to fix you a meal ..."

"No, no," I cut-in, appalled at the thought of him touching anything that might be going into my mouth. "I don't eat ..."

"Never?"

"Oh no ..."

"Very well," he said ... *and then, turning to the coachman:* "Tommy, take Mr ... erm ... Haute-Cooke's luggage upstairs ..."

"No," I said. "I haven't got any. I left it all on the train ..."

"I'll have Tommy collect it from the station first thing in the morning ..."

"*Has he always been a deaf mute?*" I whispered, trying to avoid him hearing me.

"Who, *Tommy*?!" he laughed. "*Tommy's* no mute. He can speak as well as you or I, but he has a natural reticence around strangers. He's been an absolute godsend, really. And *loyal?* In the few months that he's been here, he has endeared us all to him ..."

"Where did you get him from, may I ask? And why does he cover his face?"

"Oh, my father brought him back in January from one of his business trips abroad," he said, continuing his reverie. "His *face?* It's a sad story. Some kind of accident at birth, I believe. I think my father took pity on him. His loyalty to my father and to the Corporation is unquestioning. I was just telling our guest," (*here he addressed Tommy again*) "That you would *die* for my father ..."

Tommy began to move his arms around and start grunting, culminating in an attempt at speech which was designed, I think, to show who he was loyal to ...

"M – a – s – t- e – r ... M – a – s – t – e – r ..."

"'*Ere*, just a minute," I said. "If your father died several *years* ago, then how did he bring him back from a business trip in January?"

Flite suddenly swung round on me again with a look of accusatorial menace in his eyes, and I knew straight away that I'd made an error ...

"You are mistaken, Mr Haute-Cooke. I did not say my father brought him back. He was brought here by my brother, Martin ..."

Brother?

Martin Flite?

Him of the *Corporate Handbook* fame?

How many of them *were* there?

It was beginning to look like the makings of an entire dynasty ...

"But his *loyalty* ...?" I blundered.

"His loyalty is to the *spirit* and *memory* of my father, who befriended him after the poor soul had deserted the enemy trenches at Ypres. We had not known his whereabouts for many years until Martin found him, quite by chance, languishing in poverty ..."

"So, he's actually an *Englishman?*" I said.

"Of course," said Flite. "That is why we call him *Tommy*. My father saved him from certain death in 1917 when he persuaded General Spitzdorf of the German High Command to employ him as an advisor – a *spy* – and, in return, he was able to give Germany much valuable information on the intentions of the British ..."

"Not valuable *enough*," I said, trying (*and failing*) to lighten the atmosphere. "In view of the outcome of the war ..."

"None of us could bear to see him fallen on such hard times ..."

"I see ..."

"But I have said too much already ... Tommy," (*here he turned to his servant*) "Go upstairs and prepare the Blood and Iron Room in the East Wing for our guest ..."

"M-a-s-t-e-r ... *M-a-s-t-e-r* ..."

"That's right, Tommy, run along. You know what to do ..."

I didn't like the sound of *that*.

And I didn't like the sound of the *Blood and Iron Room* either.

"And now, Mr Haute-Cooke, time for that nightcap ..."

He opened a door and led me into a dimly-lit, smoke-filled room.

I was pleased to see a bar situated at the far end of the room, around which a small group of people were gathered, drinking and talking quietly, three males and two females.

The three males looked like businessmen, mainly (or *crooks*, whichever way you looked at it).

"Come and meet our intimate little group ..."

At the sound of his voice the hum of conversation subsided, and their faces turned round in curiosity.

"Charmed ..." I murmured.

"Martin," said my host, addressing the man I took to be his brother. "This is one of our guests who happened to slip through the net. Fix him a drink, would you please? He is going to tell us all about the incident on the train ..."

He was younger than Simon, and he offered his hand. "Pleased to meet you, Mr...?"

"Haute-Cooke," I said, giving it a shake. "With an '*e*', of *Haute-Cooke Culinary Cuisine (Import) UK Ltd.* I expect you've heard of me?"

"I expect so," he said. "And what can I get you?"

"Have you got any lager?" I said. "Or is that a silly question ...?"

I did add a laugh to the end of this, but nobody appeared to find it funny.

Instead, they all stood there giving me rather serious, puzzled looks, and I noticed for the first time that they were drinking spirits.

"Simon," he said at length. "Do we have any lager for Mr Haute-Cooke? The bar seems to have run out ..."

"I'll ring for some ..."

So saying, he reached up and pulled on a bright red sash cord, the subsequent lack of response to which caused him to leave the room himself in search of supplies.

"I must introduce you to everybody," said Martin. "First meet Otto. Otto Possenreiser, of the *Possenreiser Pils Brauerei*, of Essen. Otto's company are old rivals of the Corporation from the days when both were small, family businesses. *Possenreiser Pils* are still a small company, but they do a healthy business. Otto bears no grudges ..."

He was a rather plump, bald, middle-aged gent with a large mole on the end of his nose, and he gave me a hearty handshake.

"*Guten Abend,*" he declared. "*Herr* ...?"

"That's *Haute-Cooke*," I said, saving him the trouble. "As in *haute cuisine* ..."

He clicked his heels together.

"Possenreiser *Pils*?" I queried. "You're a *tablet* manufacturer, then? A pharmacist ...?"

"Ha-ha," laughed Martin. "Actually, we think Otto's firm is really just a front for a secret rearmament factory in the Ruhr ..."

"*That's* interesting," I mumbled. "*Very* interesting ..."

Martin then went on to introduce me to the second of the group, a tall man with a frostbitten complexion:

"This is Herr Schurke – *Heinrich* Schurke – Head of Eastern European operations. You could say he's been sent to the Russian Front ..."

"Do they drink much lager out there?" I quizzed him.

He looked puzzled.

"I am afraid Herr Schurke speaks no English," explained Martin.

"Not to worry," I said, trying to put him at his ease. "Neither do I when I'm pissed ..."

(I did follow this up with a friendly elbow in the chops ... but he didn't look none too *pleased* about it!)

"And this," continued Martin, "Is Sonny Reithoek ..."

I tell you, he was standing so far on top of me, that I virtually crashed into him as I turned round ...

"Sonny is with the South African Secret Police – an old friend of the family..."

I almost swallowed my tongue!

Instead of offering the hand of friendship, he began fingering a nasty-looking rhino-hide whip coiled round his gunbelt ...

"The only crime," he announced, "That we allow in *my* district ..."

"Go on," I said, intrigued.

"Is *suicide* ..."

Sentence pronounced, he collared me as I went to duck out of the way, and then he extracted his leather dick-extension and proceeded to tap me on the chest with its handle ...

I did go to interject – *but he hadn't finished.*

Rubbing it under my chin for emphasis, he drew an imaginary line upwards in the general direction of my moosh ...

"And only *then*," he went on, "When it takes place in a police cell ..."

"Any sign of that lager ...?" I said, trying to extract my nose from his attention.

"*Positive* Suicide, we call it," he said, once he'd finally let go. "And don't *forget* it ..."

Grateful for any diversion from current tensions, I swung round eagerly to take the hand of my next social victim ... and unhesitatingly plonked a *kiss* on it.

"My wife," said Martin. "*Candida* ..."

"How do you do ..." I said, face to face with the most strikingly attractive woman who, it occurred to me, must have been Simon's sister-in-law.

I state the apparent obvious since, despite being related only through marriage to the Flites, she seemed to have inherited Simon's eyes.

And by my latest count, that made her the fourth member of the family resident there – three of which I'd never accounted for before – two of *those* being directly in the bloodline.

"You look like an interesting man," she said. "Mr ... *erm* ...?"

"Haute-Cooke," I said, saving her embarrassment. "It's hyphenated, of course. We go in for a lot of that in England ..."

"Of course," she said. "Do tell us about your experiences on board the *Orient Express*. Simon specifically chose that means of transport to impress his guests, but it all seems to have gone horribly wrong. Tell us what happened, and how you managed to get here tonight despite the difficulties ..."

"Yes do, *do* !" suddenly piped up a voice behind me, forcing me to turn round and confront the remaining member of the group, an exquisitely pretty teenager with flaxen hair and buck teeth ...

"Give Mr Haute-Cooke a chance, Heidi," said Martin. (*And then to me*) "Heidi is my niece – very beautiful, I think you'll agree – but she is precocious for her age and very spoilt. You must not let her bully you ..."

"Well," I said, "I didn't realise the Flite family was so large ..." (That made five now – or, I suppose, *seven*, if she was a blood niece).

"Oh yes," said Martin. "We're very well established – have been for generations," (and, *addressing his wife*) "How many main branches of the family are there now, *liebchen*?"

"Sixteen in West Germany alone," replied Candida.

"Gawd help the free world!" I yelled for a joke ... *but for one awful moment I thought nobody was going to laugh* ...

"I've asked Tommy to bring up some lager from the cellars," said Simon, reappearing with rather fortuitous timing.

"Tip-top," I said.

"Do you believe in ghosts, Mr Haute-Cooke?" piped up Heidi.

"*Dexter*," I said. "Call me *Dexter*. Do I believe in ghosts?" (*that was a puzzler*) "Well, no," I said, "Only in *spirits* ... ha-ha!"

"Mr Haute-Cooke, you are making fun of me ..."

"No," I said. "I'm not ..."

"Uncle Martin thinks the Schloss is haunted," she went on. "Don't you, Martin?"

"They were only stories to tease you, Heidi ..."

"*Go on*, Martin, you *know* its true. You really should warn Mr Dexter about what he may be in for. I'm quite terrified of spending my first night here myself. Tell him about the *headless madman* who stalks the corridors on nights of the full moon ..."

"You have an overactive imagination," said Candida, trying to reassure me.

"Oh I don't know," I said, conjuring up the most appalling scenario imaginable ... *when a door I'd never noticed was there suddenly flew open behind the bar and a hideous apparition appeared, giving me my second fright of the evening ...*

When I'd calmed down, I was able to see that Tommy was laden with crates, rather than severed heads, and these he proceeded to slam down on the counter in front of me.

Having changed out of his outdoor wear of cap and coat, he was now adorned in barman's garb, complete with black bow-tie.

Something was amiss, though, and it took me quite a while before I realised that it was more than just a case of a scruffy old cretin dressing up for polite society.

It was to do with his *hat* ...

He was wearing a First World War English infantryman's helmet which, because it was several sizes too big, was sitting over his head like a basin and obscuring his eyes.

Not only *this*, but he was still wearing his scarf which, having been pushed up to make way for the bow-tie, was *now* on a level with his nose.

Standing there behind the bar with a bottle in his hand, he looked like a soldier about to go over the top, and he seemed reluctant to hand it to me ... so I leaned over and *snatched* it from him.

"Open the bottle for our guest, Tommy," said Simon.

"No, it's alright," I said, feeling desperate ...

To the surprise of those around me, I coshed it down on the counter, smashed the top off, allowed the foaming brew to erupt over my hand, tipped my head back and ... up-ended the lot straight down my neck.

Following this performance, I opened my eyes, smiled like a half-bright, and ...

Awhuuurp!

(*burped*)

"I can see you are a *coinnoisseur* of *Allied Froth*, Mr Haute-Cooke ..." said Martin.

"Oh yes," I affirmed. "Me and *it* go back a *long* way ..."

"Simon, don't we have something a little special for our guest?"

"Of course," said Simon (*and, turning to his servant*) "Give him a bottle of the *Anniversary* edition ..."

Although Tommy did get one out of the crate, he seemed even more reluctant to hand it over than before, standing there and grunting at me, withdrawing his hand a little bit further every time I went to take it from him, all the time retreating backwards towards the optics as he did so.

As a result of which, Simon was compelled to walk round behind the bar after him ...

"*Tommy,*" he said, raising his voice just a fraction. "Hand it to *me,* Tommy..."

When he'd finally persuaded his servant to let go, he opened it himself and poured the sparkling, champagne-coloured liquid into a tall glass.

"Here you are," he said. "See what you make of this ..."

"Ah," I murmured, grabbing the proffered lifesaver. "My *favourite* ..."

I sunk it in one.

(Well, *almost* ...)

Just before reaching the final mouthful, I burst into a coughing, retching and sneezing fit, and it took all of some moments for the attack to subside.

"Tip-top," I said at length. "Got any more ...?"

This time the mute was ready and waiting with a bottle in each hand.

By the time I'd drunk the *third* one, the effect of the *first* one was beginning to react with my blood ...

"Can anyone *tell* me," I said, "Why I'm the only one here drinking lager? This *is* the headquarters of the Allied Froth Corporation after *all,* isn't it?"

Their faces held tense and puzzled expressions as I looked round at them, one after the other, and it was several moments before Simon broke the silence.

"You were going to tell us about the train, Mr Haute-Cooke ..."

"Train?" I said (*trying to think*). "Oh yes, terrible business. They *got* him, though, in the end, I think ..."

"Who?" asked Candida, positively interested.

"The police," I said. "The *police* got him ..."

"No, no," she said. "*Who* did the police get?"

"Oh," I said, "The *chef.* He'd been at it for years, apparently ..."

"The *chef?*" she queried. "*At* what?"

"Oh," I said (*taking another gulp of lager*) "Poison. He'd been trying to murder the passengers ..."

"How frightening," said Heidi. "How did they catch him?"

"Well, this time he slipped up because there were officers from the Belgian Health and Safety Executive travelling incognito on the train ..."

"And they caught him red-handed lacing the food with poison ...?" asked Candida.

"Oh no," I said. "Nothing quite so simple. He was too clever to poison the food. He'd been putting live sardines in the water supply. Of course, I noticed it when I first came on board in London ..."

"Really?" said Martin.

"Oh yes," I said. "The smell was unbearable. You couldn't turn on a tap without getting gassed ..."

"And *so*," Candida hypothesized, "If anybody drank the water, then they immediately perished ...?"

"*Well* ..."

"That's funny," said Simon. "I didn't know sardines were poison ..."

"Oh no," I said, "They're *not*. The sardines weren't *poisoning* people. That was the *cleverness* of it. They'd grown to such a fantastic size in the water tank that they were jumping out of the taps and *eating* people ..."

"Oh my God ...!" said Candida. (*She threw her arms across her chest*)

"Extraordinary ..." mumbled Simon.

"*Extraordinary*?!!!" suddenly piped up the voice of the South African Secret Policeman (who'd worked his way round *behind* me again). "*Outrageous* is what I call it! This man is an *imbecile*. And *whatsmore*, he's a *liar*. I've never heard such a cock-and-bull story in my life!"

"No, no," I said. "It's all true ..."

"Give me half-an-hour alone in the dungeons with this man, Simon, and I'll get to the bottom of it ..."

(It was *Heidi* who came to my rescue ...) "Oh, Sonny!" she said. "Leave Mr Dexter alone. He's only pulling our legs ..."

"Yes, leave him be, Sonny," said Simon. "Mr Haute-Cooke is our guest – and our *only* guest so far. I'm sure we'll find out more details when the others arrive tomorrow ..."

"And I'm sure Mr Dexter will tell us himself when he's feeling up to it ..." she added.

"Well," I whined, "It was all just such a *shock*, you see ..."

"Of course it was," she continued. "And all the more reason why you won't want to meet the ghost of Schloss Froth tonight. I hope Simon's allocated you a safe room in the West Wing ..."

"Heidi!" exclaimed Candida. "Stop filling Mr Haute-Cooke's head with nonsense. It's way past your bedtime ..."

"*Aber Tante* ..." she pleaded.

"Simon, can't you stop her telling fairy stories ...?"

"It's alright," I said, grabbing another bottle and trying to suppress a hiccup fit (and being totally unable to remember *what* wing I was in), "I'm in the Blood and Iron Room. Sounds safe as houses to me ..."

Suddenly the place went quiet ...

I looked round.

"Did I say something ...?" I asked innocently.

"*Blut und Eisen?*" said Otto. "*Ist das gut, Simon ...?*"

"*Nein, nein, Simon,*" added Schurke, with a tone of similar concern in his voice.

"Oh," he said (*looking a little uncomfortable*), "It has already been prepared. As Mr Haute-Cooke is our first guest, I thought we ought to honour him by making the room with the best view available, that's all ..."

"*Aber Simon,*" emphasised Otto, "*Blut und Eisen ...*"

I was just on the point of asking for some clarification on this business, when the door suddenly burst open and a great big figure wearing a fur coat, a monocle, and drenched from head to foot staggered in ...

Whoever he was, he was in an absolutely *foul* temper ...

"Is it raining?" I asked innocently.

Glaring across the room and trying to straighten his monocle all at the same time, he looked for all the world as though he was going to come over and *murder* me ...

The only reason he *didn't*, was because he found himself distracted by Tommy, who'd scampered over to meet him and was busy trying to remove his coat.

"Get out of my way!" he yelled at the unfortunate servant, launching an almighty kick which sent Tommy scuttling off into the corner cowering and nursing his wound while Heidi ran over to comfort him.

(*It was just as well he'd been distracted because, with a start, I realised I'd met the stranger before ...*)

It was *Lord Heehaw.*

All the way from Madras ...

So as not to be recognised, I pulled Blondie's tights down over my face and watched Simon's shape go over to meet him:

"I am not in a good mood, Simon," he said. "There are police roadblocks all over the place. I don't know what the devil it's all about, unless they've finally got wind of you at last. My chauffeur had to shoot three of them just to get past the barrier at Lahnstein ..."

"Trouble on the *Orient Express*, apparently. Chef went mad and tried to poison everybody. Got it first-hand from one of the passengers. Come over and meet him – I think you'll find him interesting ..."

Oh my gawd, I thought ...

"I haven't got time, Simon. This business could ruin everything. I've not seen more police on the roads when there's been an escaped maniac on the loose. Can we talk ...?"

"Of course ..." (*and then, addressing the rest of us*): "I have to conduct a little business. It's getting late. I suggest you all retire soon – we've got a long day tomorrow. Tommy will show Mr Haute-Cooke to his quarters. I shall be in the *Goethe* Room if anybody needs me. Goodnight ..."

"To top it all," I heard Heehaw say as they both turned to leave the room, "I got lost on the roads round here. I've been driving around all night trying to find this place. It's not exactly well-lit, is it ...?"

It must have been him, I thought, *who drove past me in the limousine earlier on. Reckless git ...*

Just as the door was closing, I raised the tights in time to see Tommy run up behind him and give him a flying kick up the arse ...

Modesty required me to quickly lower my veil once again, after which I watched in astonished half-vision as Heehaw burst back into the room and chased Tommy towards the bar, the latter leaping over it like a two-year-old and the former only prevented from following by Heidi running in between them to protect him ...

"Leave him alone, you brute!" she was yelling at him.

"Come, come," Simon was saying as he caught up with Heehaw, "We haven't got time for this. I'll deal with him later ..."

Heehaw looked fit to blow a gasket.

He *was*, however, persuaded to vacate the scene, nevertheless.

I wonder what those two are up to? I thought.

"I think it's awful the way that man treats poor Tommy," said Heidi, as she wandered away from the bar.

"So do I," I said. "But that's the English Aristocracy for you ..."

"*Why,* Mr *Haute-Cooke,*" said Candida. "Are you *cold?*"

I raised the tights and smiled.

"No, no," I said. "Just trying out my fancy-dress for tomorrow ..."

"What are you going as?" Sonny Reithoek condescended to ask me.

"Can't you *tell?*" I said.

"*Would* I ask?"

"I'm going as a *black* man ..."

"Did I hear somebody say that a maniac had escaped?" asked Heidi. "It's not *you*, Mr Dexter, is it?"

"*Me?*" I said. "Oh no, the operation was a complete success. I've been quite alright for months now ..."

"You *are* a tease!" said Candida.

"Isn't it *exciting*, though ..." said Heidi.

"I think we've all had *enough* excitement for one night," said Martin. "I, for one, certainly have. Run along now, Heidi. Tommy, show Mr Haute-Cooke to his room ..."

Otto, Schurke and Sonny all mumbled their agreement and, in a matter of moments, I was left alone in the room with Sinister Sid ...

On the point of reluctantly requisitioning his services, I was surprised to see *Heidi* skipping back through the door ...

"*The Blood and Iron Room is the most haunted room in the Castle,*" she whispered in my ear. "Isn't it exciting ...!!!"

And on *that* note, she ran out again ...

So, with Tommy all ready to do his duty and take me upstairs, I grabbed a couple of bottles and, against my better judgement, followed him.

The first stage of the journey involved a forced march down a corridor as ill-lit as the previous ones had been well-lit, the objective in sight being a door leading out onto a second, much larger courtyard, where I emerged to find the rain whipping across the flagstones and fork lightning streaking a sky which only an hour or so earlier had been as clear as a bell ...

Halfway across this hostile arena, whose distant borders seemed nothing more than markers between one shade of dark and another shade of dark, an enormous crash of thunder caused my top hat to fall off ...

As I bent down to retrieve it, an electrical flash suddenly illuminated the East Wing ahead of us in all its imposing menace:

High above the ground structure was a series of dark turrets nesting around a huge central tower whose summit seemed lost in the clouds, the whole overhanging facade like a spreading tomb cut with blank, empty windows, decorated with monstrous chimneys and gravestones, a bastion of hollowed stone and delusive spires perched on the cliff like an arm of defiance flung out from the main body against wind and weather and the invading hordes.

Tommy had to unlock the entrance specially for me, with an old rusty iron key.

"I suppose *Bismarck* was the last guest in this quarter, was he?" I said, as we paused on the threshold.

"*Komm sie in!*" he ordered, speaking recogniseable words for the first time as he fiddled with his lantern.

"*Just* a minute," I said. "Isn't there any electric light in this dump ...?"

I flicked a switch on the wall, but nothing happened.

"Apparently *not* ..." I mumbled ... *before I realised he'd disappeared down the corridor* ... "'*Ere* !" I yelled. "*Wait* for *me* ...!"

And so began my first acquaintance with the valved chambers and off-centre passageways that threaded a decayed honeycomb into the cold heart of the notorious wing, an involuntary acquaintance, a blind and hurried tour dragged from anxiety as I sought to catch up with the spectral coachman who rattled along ahead of me like an insubstantial shadow through a dark doll's house.

On we went, along the rusty steps of an ornamental winding stairwell which creaked and shifted alarmingly under our combined weight, only to emerge on a mad circular landing which scattered curved shafts of lantern light into the dark like the spokes of a Catherine wheel.

Next it was off on a lengthy trek through a dusty passageway lined on either side by objects covered in sheets (and, since these latter all resembled ghostly figures ready to pounce at the least provocation, my assumption that they were probably statues or suits of armour was not one I wished to prove by investigation).

Then it was all up a draughty staircase carved in stone, and along a dark and hazardous corridor laid choc-a-bloc with ill-defined furnishings left in apparently random positions and occasionally placed in tottering stacks up to the level of the ceiling as though the whole arrangement had been deliberately designed to antagonise the local fire inspector ...

"Where *is* this fucking room," I said. "*China?*"

Then he was at it again, up one staircase after another until all staircases became one steep spiral staircase.

"Are you fucking *sure?*" I cursed after him, puffing and wheezing.

"*Nein* ! *Komm sie mit* ...!*" he was bellowing, head-down in grim determination as he ploughed onwards and upwards into the dark, unperturbed by the exertion, apparently.

"*Not* China, then?" I said. "Outer space ...?"

Finally, we arrived on a short landing, and Tommy stopped outside an evil-looking door about half-way along.

"Room ... *room* ..." he said, pointing at it.

"Alright," I said. "*Open* it then ..."

"No ... *you* open. Here – *key* ..."

So saying, he handed me one of the many from his ring.

Confidently thinking the full extent of his brief would be complete only once he'd seen me in, turned the bed down and made me a cup of cocoa, I twisted the key in the lock and marched into a room barely more visible than the corridor that had led to it, the moon obscured by rainclouds beyond the French windows.

When I turned round to get Tommy to bring in the lantern, I found he'd left it on the floor outside and vanished ...

"Bloody deserter!" I yelled down the corridor, but my voice echoing back out of the darkness told me I was on my own.

I brought it in myself and closed the door behind me.

Noting little more than the surprising fact that it was a large, dark, square room, I went and stood right in the centre of it – which, my terrified logic told me, was the best place to be.

Unless, that is, the chandelier came loose and they rushed me from all sides at once ...

Talking of chandeliers, the precious little light cast by the lantern was incapable of transforming those far corners of the room clinging stubbornly to their cloak of darkness *whatever* the angle of my wrist, but I was, nevertheless, able to survey the main points as follows:

Wall (left). Stone fireplace, with well-stocked ceiling-to-floor bookshelves either side of it, and a panoramic ornamental mirror hung above the mantelpiece. *Wall (right)*. Covered in oak panelling. Large four-poster bed with drapes drawn back and head set against the panelling. Large dresser on near side of the bed. *Wall (outer)*. Large French windows (leading to balcony?). Indeterminate furnishings in either corner. *Wall (behind me)*. Door into corridor (through which I'd entered). Two paintings, one each side of the door, both portraits. *Floor*. Covered in thick pile carpet. *Ceiling*. High, with (naturally) chandelier (unlit).

Right, I thought. *Which of these features do I give a closer inspection to first?*

The four-poster bed, of course ...

Sauntering over to the bedside dresser, I put the lantern down and paused long enough to be overtaken by a fit of the creeps, giving in to an overwhelming desire to jump under the sheets and cover my head, where I lay for some considerable time listening to the sound of my heart beating in my throat.

It wasn't long, however, before I began to imagine all kinds of horrors stalking the room and decided, with some trauma, that cutting off my vision in this manner was only disarming me even further.

So I lifted the sheets and peeked out:

The more my eyes grew accustomed to the poor quality of light, the more the features of the room became familiar, and eventually I was able to relax enough to abandon the bed ...

Holding the lantern aloft, I walked across to one of the paintings hanging near the door and discovered it to be a portrait of some bewigged eighteenth-century figure, but whether or not the face was that of an ancestor of Adolf Flite was impossible to tell because the description plate had been removed.

The other portrait was similarly anonymous.

So far so good.

Time for a beer.

The trouble was, as I got ready to cosh one open on the mantelpiece, I absent-mindedly glanced up to inspect my *own* portrait in the mirror, and ... *immediately had to duck out of the way ...*

Crunch!

"*That* was a startler ...!" I cursed, as I came out of a double-back-somersault flip across the carpet and crashed my head on the balcony doorstep.

I'd forgotten I still had a false beard on ...

Quite where my *beer* had ended up as a result of this encounter, I had no immediate insight; but, in view of the continued jumpiness of my nerves, I decided my first priority ought to be a consideration of security, the upshot of which was a laughable attempt to try and push the dresser across the door as a barricade and discovering myself to be one of those entirely resistable forces which meets an immoveable object and flakes out on the carpet. *Its dead weight made the whole proposition impractical.*

Next, I examined the French windows as a possible access point for murderers or ghosts, but this also proved to be a pointless exercise. *The balcony beyond remained uncharted territory as I tried and failed to turn the locked handle.*

As an afterthought, I picked up a large brass candlestick standing nearby and smashed one of the panes of glass out, causing a great gust of wind to surge in and extinguish the lantern ...

For a minute, I couldn't think why I'd done it, unless it was to try to turn the same handle from the outside, but *that* was locked as well.

Is that right? I thought.

In the event, I found a key sitting on a nearby chest of drawers and made my exit in a more conventional manner, walking through with the curtains flapping about wildly in the wind ... *and I decided straightaway that Simon Flite had at least been honest about the view ...*

In daylight, I imagined it would have been magnificent, with the spacious balcony jutting out high over the sloping forests, and the stately tides of the Rhine winding through a carved channel in the cliffs and away towards the distant north. At night the illuminations from the river bank reflected off the water like fairy lights.

An involuntary transference of the senses took place as I leaned out and looked directly down over the parapets, casting my breath to the raiding currents of spring night air in exchange for a view, far below the tower, of castle walls which sheered away to the stone face of the mountain on which they were built – a drop of hundreds of feet to the woodland beneath.

At this hour, it was impossible to tell where the castle ended and the mountain began, although my desire to stand there trying evaporated the more it occurred to me that by doing so I was gratuitously offering myself up as a sightseeing sacrifice to any assailants who might come rushing me from behind...

Stepping back from the edge, I lifted my face to the freshening wind and drank in some of the last of the rain in the air, thinking that while it may have been a picturesque scene beyond, and a dizzying view below, the immediate images were less enchanting ...

From the eastern end of the balcony was *no* view at all. The tower was built almost on the corner of the wing, obscuring any sight of the castle behind it in favour of a dead drop out into the windy black void.

From the western end I could see one or two dim lights still visible in the lower realms of the central section, an otherwise dark and sprawling complex linked to the East Wing by a high and lengthy connecting terrace lined with battlements. This fortified terrace, which surmounted the north wall of the castle, overlooked the forests on one side and the east courtyard on the other, adjoining (at this end) a verandah which, far below me at the base of the tower, formed a roof for the main body of the wing.

Given the height of the balcony, I suppose the verandah *may* have been accessible, if only in theory and at a stretch – *of the imagination, perhaps, or of a long pair of braces* – and only with the assistance of a fucking great fireman's trampoline and at least forty willing pairs of hands ...

In the distance, beyond the central section, lay the West Wing, its lower half equally dimly-lit, while its huge oasthouse tower looked partially derelict.

Shifting my gaze directly overhead, I found that, although the Blood and Iron Room may have been high up, it was in no way the penthouse ...

Above the balcony, the wall gave way to a turret roof containing one solitary window in which, just for a moment, I thought I saw a figure looking down at me ...

"Where's my beer?" I cursed, as I stumbled back into the darkened room to look for it.

By the time I'd retrieved the drink and stepped back outside to finish it off, the figure in the window was gone.

Suppressing a shiver, I hurled the bottle away into the night.

I didn't hear it break.

I *could* hear the storm returning in the distance, though, and after re-entering the room, re-lighting the lantern and closing the French windows, I shoved a great iron chair in front of the broken pane, determined, at all costs, to stay awake the rest of the night, convinced that if I lost consciousness, I'd be a dead man.

In connection with this anxiety, I decided to keep well clear of the bed and sat myself down in an armchair which I pulled from a corner and placed in the centre of the room.

Since, however, I found it impossible to face all directions at once, I decided that, every five minutes or so, I'd shift the position of the chair 45 degrees clockwise and so give myself both a constantly changing perspective and a means of keeping myself awake.

"You won't catch *me* napping!" I yelled out.

But my words had a hollow ring.

Ten seconds later I was yawning ...

Thinking that some light reading might help, I headed off in search of a pot-boiler ... *and came back with a gigantic tome on Prussian militarism.*

"This is no good!" I cursed.

Rueing my lack of the appropriate mountain-climbing equipment, I slung it to one side and returned to see what else I could find, hesitantly scaling the north face of the bookcase and chucking volume after volume to the floor until I judged I'd accumulated a large enough selection to keep me on my toes till daylight.

Then I jumped down to inspect my catch:

Voluminous Lives of Maria Theresa, Frederick the Great, Bismarck; massive works on the Holy Roman Empire etc.

Not a lot there.

Anything *else?*

Schleswig-Holstein: A Road Atlas (1880 edition) ... *Austrian Pipe Cleaners* (illustrated catalogue) ... *Irene Strudl: A Biography* (Beethoven's ninth chambermaid) ... *Cookery* (Westphalian Style) ... *Witticisms Attributed to the House of Hanover* (5 vols) ... *How to Repair Dresden China ... How to Assemble a Prussian Helmet ...* etc, etc.

"Nothing!" I cursed, rifling through them. "All the same!"

I went and chucked the lot over the parapets.

While I was standing there, I saw the lights of a car fast disappearing down the road, away from Castle Froth.

"I bet that's Heehaw, the old bastard," I mumbled to myself. "*He's* got the right idea ..."

Once back inside again, I opted to continue my sentry duty from the bed, assembling my provisions on the dresser – lager, lantern, and ...

In view of the unreliability of my Minnie Mouse watch (and the fact that I couldn't see it in the dark anyway), I took a clock from the mantelpiece and brought it over to the dresser, omitting to note the time.

I'll get into bed, I thought, *but I won't get undressed.*

And I *won't* pull the sheets over my head.

Good.

And now for something to occupy my thoughts:

Tomorrow night I shall arrest Adolf Flite, and half his friends, and possibly half his family as well.

But, I mused, *there are still several unanswered questions which need addressing, if the case is to be resolved properly and the evidence fully accumulated.*

Namely.

Why have the portraits in this room had their nameplates removed?

Do portraits *have* nameplates?

What is Heehaw up to?

What have they got planned for tomorrow night?

Why have I been given 'The Most Haunted Room in the Castle'?

Why is it called the 'Blood and Iron' room?

Where is Adolf Flite?

Why did Simon say he was dead?

Is he *dead?*

Is he *human?*

What is Simon trying to hide?

Who is the Headless Madman?

Is he pertinent to the case ...?

It was rubbish, really.

It didn't make any sense.

But ...

That was the way I liked it.

After all, I thought, a case could be *too* simple ...

As I coshed the last bottle open on the dresser, it occurred to me that I ought to *save* it. *One way or another, I had a feeling it was going to be a long night ...* and I was already very sleepy. *Who was in the water tank on the train? What's in the el-dust file? Where is it? How many Flite's are there? Do we only count those in the bloodline? Or do we count all of them? How many does that make ...?*

Bit by bit, I was falling asleep and beginning to dream ... *and in a matter of moments there were Belgian Health and Safety Officials flying around outside and tapping on the French windows, and a horrible headless sardine knocking on the door ...*

CHAPTER 40
SKETCHES OF A HAUNTED HOUSE

"Some houses are born bad"

Shirley Jackson
The Haunting of Hill House

"... 𝖅𝖅𝖅𝖅 ... ... 𝖅𝖅𝖅𝖅 ... 𝖅𝖅𝖅𝖅 ... ... 𝖅𝖅𝖅𝖅 ... ... 𝖅𝖅𝖅𝖅 ..."

SHRIEEEEEEEEEEEK!

"... 𝖅𝖅𝖅𝖅 ... ... 𝖅𝖅𝖅𝖅 ... ... 𝖅𝖅𝖅𝖅 ... ... 𝖅𝖅𝖅𝖅 ... ... 𝖅𝖅𝖅𝖅 ... ..."

Madmen and Murderers

An ear piercing scream split the night and I sat bolt upright in bed:
The lantern was out, the room cold and black.
I picked up the clock and lifted it close to my face:

3.03am

Had there been a scream, or had I dreamt it?
I broke out into a cold sweat ...
The storm was raging outside, shaking the floor and igniting the room in flarelight:
clank clank
[*coming down the corridor* ...]
clank clank clank
[*nearer now* ...]
Who else could it be but the Headless Madman?
Clank Clank Clank Clank Clank ...
[*then, silence as it pauses outside, until* ...]
CRASH!
CRASH!

CRASH!
CRASH!
CRASH!
[*on the door so powerful that the wood arcs inwards and begins to split ...*]
Right, *that's* it.
I'm off ...
But *not* out the door.
Straight over the balcony ...
I dragged the sheets off the bed and hauled them across to the French windows, knotting them together furiously as I went ...

CRASH!
CRASH!
CRASH!
CRASH!
CRASH!
CRASH ...

Unable to find the key in my panic, I grabbed the candlestick and went berserk, shattering the remaining glass panes and damaging enough of the wooden frame to be able to half-step, half-tumble through and half-charge, half-stumble onward to the parapet ... where I slung the home-made rope over the edge.

?

What my *intention* was, I've no idea.

The drop to the verandah would have required the services of a *parachute* to negotiate.

Never *mind* a rope.

As it *was*, I ought to have at least moored *one* end of it to something solid before I chucked it, if only to save me wasting the precious moments I proceeded to spend wondering what had *happened* to it ...

But it was a lucky *delay*, really.

Because, if I'd *survived*, I'd have dropped in on the roof verandah with exquisitely atrocious timing ...

I'd barely embarked on pondering the mystery of the vanished sheets when, to my horror, I spotted a figure far below on the castle face, climbing up towards the battlements with a *machete* between his teeth ...

So there *was* an escaped maniac, after all!

Chewing my fingers and giggling hysterically, I watched him ascend with stealth and haul himself over onto the terrace connecting the East Wing to the rest of the castle.

Now what?

He's looking *this* way and that:

From *east* to *west* ... and *back* again:

I sunk to the deck in relief as he crept off towards the central structure, drawn by its few visible lights.

The battering on the door:

I hadn't *notice* it stop, but *stop* it had.

So I poked my nose into the room and *listened:*

... clank clank clank clank clank

As soon as everything was still, I stepped back inside and barricaded the French windows up with any old bits of moveable furniture I could lay my hands on.

Then I did the same with the door.

Most of all, I would have liked to have jumped back into *bed* and barricaded *that* up from the inside, but I had to settle for hiding under the mattress instead.

The terrifying thing was that I *knew* who the maniac was searching for.

How?

Because I *knew* who the maniac *was* ...

In those moments when he'd looked from left to right, trying to assess the most promising direction, his face had been lit up by a flash of lightning, and I recognised in an instant those insane eyes I'd seen before.

They were the eyes of a madman.

And they were *looking* for *me* ...

There could be no other reason why Trevor was at the castle.

He had no interest in AF International.

I could only assume that he'd broken out of jail and been presented with damning evidence, courtesy of Hetty, that I was offering Sir Archibald Darkbloode's address to the highest bidder, and that I'd nicked his rucksack to boot.

Comforting myself with thoughts such as these, I began to drift off once more into a troubled and fitful sleep ...

Seance Fiction

When I next woke, it was quite obvious I'd been dreaming.

The lantern was still alight and the barricades were nowhere in evidence.

Not only *this*, but the bedroom door showed no signs of an assault, and – with the exception of the first pane of glass I'd broken early on – the French windows were still intact.

More importantly, the time was only 2.02am.

"My own worst enemy is my imagination!" I declared.

Then, whispered my imagination, *Get a load of this ...*

First the lantern went out.

Then I became aware of something oppressive building up in the darkness around me, as though the air were being charged with high voltage electricity ahead of a strike by lightning ...

SEEEEEEEEEEEER ...!!!

Suddenly my hair burst into flames ...!!!

"Christ Almighty ...!!!"

I leapt off the bed and went slapping myself round the carpet like a banana case ...

ZING!!!

"Eeeeeeeeeeeeeeeeeeek!" ... *only to hurl myself head-backwards against a bedpost as a brilliant white spotlight exploded across the ceiling and a column of crackling white light*

descended all the way to the floor ...

Flaring so *ferociously* was it, that I had to shield my eyes with my arms until it struck a white-out and atomised ... *and this left me staring spellbound at a translucent beam in which two figures were materialising like incandescent ghosts ...*

"*OH MY GAWD* ...!!!" I squealed, watching astonished as the apparitions began to dissolve into recogniseable human forms ... so that *there*, in the next few moments, standing just a few feet in front of me were ...

Sugar Ray and the Chief!

Frozen in a shaft of light ...

Am I dreaming again?

What's the time?

Have I been drinking too much?

"Am I going mad?!!!"

It was a diffuse light now, one which radiated around their core glow as they began to animate in jerky, staggered fashion like the images in a silent film, but when Ray's lips moved the result was an accompanying soundtrack which required no piano player or subtitles to indicate his words ...

"Don't worry, Boss. We ain't really here ..."

"Erm ..."

Not really here?

"Nah, you can't talk to *us*, but *we* can talk to *you*. Ain't that right, Chief?"

The Chief shrugged his shoulders, non-commitally.

He must be on my side, I thought ...

"Are you dead?" I said.

"Don't worry, Boss, we ain't *ghosts*, and you *ain't* goin' mad ..."

No, I thought, *but I can't exactly say things are all tip-top, either ...*

"We couldn't think of any quicker way to warn you. Chief suggested we write you a letter, but you'd probably be dead the time you got it. I would have loved to visit you in person, but, well ... you know how it is when you're a celebrity ..."

So what am I talking to?

"Now just sit back and listen, because these holograms is like telegrams. You pay by the word ..."

Holograms?

Pay by the word?

"We heard about this big party at the Castle. Chief got an invite – which upset *me* because I never got one – but we both figured you'd be able to take care of things on your own. *Until the other day*, that is. We heard something very interesting on the grapevine ..."

I stepped off the bed.

"Go on," I said.

"Well, we heard that somebody – somebody who goes back a long way with you and bears you a *particular* grudge – had got out and was fixin' to kill you. Ring any bells ...?"

Fascinated, I walked up and stood in front of the transmission and passed my hand through the images inside it.

He was right.

They weren't really there ...

"Only," he went on, "We figured you'd have your hands full with that mob over there and thought it was only fair to warn you. This way you can keep one eye in the back of your head as well ..."

Just to confirm it beyond doubt, I walked backwards and forwards through the beam like an usherette through a cinema projection.

"Now, the name of this guy ..." Ray went to say, *when his voice suddenly blurred...*

I jumped backwards to find the images beginning to shiver and break up ...

"*Go* on. His name *is* ..."

Oh no, I thought, *he's even repeating the name ...*

"Where's the volume control on this thing ...?" I cursed, desperately trying to lip-read.

Rourke?

O'Rourke?

Who the hell was O'Rourke?

"Is his name *O'Rourke* ...?!" I yelled.

(*his voice crackled back faintly*) "... and we thought you'd better know that he left New York by plane yesterday. He's on his way to see you now, and he *ain't* in a pretty mood. He's fixin' to get even ..."

"Is he an Irishman?"

"Anyway, I guess you heard the pips. That means we've run smack out of time, but just before we go, the Chief's got a message he'd like me to give you. He says he hopes you're enjoyin' the storm he's sent you and he promises it won't be as out of control as the last one. He says to use it wisely and he apologises if it interferes with reception as he understands this is sometimes the case. *Get lucky, Boss ...*"

I watched, disappointed, as the beam began to burn incandescent once again and furl round the edges at the base ...

Suddenly, it evaporated up to the ceiling, leaving just the original circular spotlight diminishing in size until all that was left was a tiny speck like the residual dot on a fading black-and-white TV screen.

Then all trace vanished.

I stood there staring up at its point of exit like a castaway at Cape Kennedy ...

The first thing I did was to fumble for my matches and get the lantern back in working order, and then I began to pace up and down the room, turning over in my mind what Ray had said.

Somebody coming to kill me.

Well, he'd just have to join the queue ...

I tried resurrecting my list of pursuers, but they were all either dead or they just didn't fit the bill.

Who did I know in New York?

Nobody.

That's who.

And who went *back* a long way?

Ray said he'd just got *out.*

From where?

Jail?

My Uncle Grolly went back a long way.

And he'd got out of jail.

But he hadn't *just* got out.

He'd already been on the loose for over two years.

As for *Trevor* – well, he'd probably come to kill me, but I'd only just met him the other day, and he'd come here from Ostend, not New York.

Holograms. Pay-by-the-word. One eye in the back of my head.

Mopping my forehead, I marched over to the mirror to see whether I was delirious ...

Hm.

False beard still in place but, unfortunately, I'd lost my top hat and tights to the elements earlier in the evening.

Did he say *O'Rourke?*

Or just Rourke?

O'Rourke, I mused.

O'Rourke ... *Rourke* ...

Warke ...

Murk ...

Dirk!

That was it!

Dirk!

He'd broken out of Bellevue and was coming looking for me!

Coming to *kill* me!

My old mate!

Looking for revenge!

It *must* have been Dirk, because he was the only one who matched the *modus operandi:*

He was in New York, he was *inside,* he went *back* a long way, and he was a twisted sod at the best of times ...

Anyway, after standing there petrified by this revelation for, possibly, four or five seconds, I decided to drop the subject into the 'out' tray.

He'd never get here.

He was a congenital idiot.

On the other hand, I thought, *supposing he'd hardened up in there?*

After all, it *was* a nuthouse for the *criminally* insane, wasn't it ...?

One eye in the back of my head ...

Suddenly, a *shadow* passed behind my reflection and I swung round in a panic ...

I must be imagining things again.

The room was empty.

But ...

When I returned my attention to the mirror, I found *two* faces staring back me from the glass ...

Heads, Hands and Feet

"Don't move, don't speak, and don't make a sound," said the extra head as it peered down at me on the carpet. "Or I'll cut your throat ..."

And then I really *must* have gone under, because the next time I regained consciousness I was flat out on the deck with the light out and the intruder gone.

Whether or not I'd been hallucinating or dreaming was a moot point but, for what it was worth, the face had belonged to one of the three dark-haired girls from the train ...

I crawled back onto the bed, wondering how much longer till dawn.

Now it was only 1.01am ...

Convinced I wasn't reading the clock properly, I leaned forward to reach for the lantern ... and it was a *lucky* thing I did, because a *horrible great detached hairy arm* suddenly loomed out of the dark and swiped at the space I'd just been reclining in ...

"**Aaaaaaa***aaaaaaaarrgh* ... **!!!**"

Shuddering and shivering, I edged backwards in terror as I watched the claw on the end of it probe the headboard, mattress and pillow, like the Prince of Tarantulas, crawling around, looking for me ... touching, feeling, *searching* everything – under the pillow, above the pillow – until it finally slithered on towards the dresser and came to rest on ... the *clock*.

But only for a moment.

After fingering the esoteric curves and angles of Swiss timing, it moved on ...

Keeping one eye well and truly on its movements, I grabbed the lantern out of its way, striking matches furiously like an underwater pyromaniac as I tried and failed, in my panic, to get it alight ...

All of a *sudden*, it snatched at the bottle of *lager* and vanished back into the dark with it ...!

"*Oi*!" I yelled. "**That's my *beer* ...!**"

Suitably outraged, I dived across the bed in the direction it had disappeared, but all I came up against were the oak panels beyond the headboard.

(Well, *that*, and ...)

"**Awhuu***uuuuuuuurpp* !!!!"

(... the sound of an almighty *burp*)

"Where's that lantern ...?" I cursed.

And then I heard that *other* noise coming back down the corridor again:

Clank Clank

"**My *God* !**" I yelled. "**It's like Piccadilly *Circus* in here tonight ...!**"

On top of all this, as I stood there fumbling with the matches, a ghostly voice suddenly

piped up behind me going,
  "**Wooooo ... Wooooo ...**"
  I turned round to find somebody standing there, covered in a sheet.
  I *knew* it was a sheet, and not a *ghost*, because I could see a pair of feet sticking out of the end of it.
  The *clanking* was getting louder as well:
  Clank Clank clank Clank ...
  I finally got the lantern going, and not a moment too soon ...
  CLANK ...
  CLANK
  CRASH!
  CRASH!
  CRASH!
  CRASH ...! on the door ...
  "**CAN'T YOU** *WAIT* **A MINUTE**?!!!" I screamed.
  "**Wooooo ... Wooooo ... !!!**"
  I turned to the sheet.
  "Just a minute," I said. "There's somebody at the door ..."
  Somewhat punch-drunk by now, I marched across the carpet, turfed the re-materialised barricades out of the way and opened up to find myself staring at the Headless Madman.
  Or rather, *he* was staring at *me.*
  I was staring at the vacant space on top of his neck.
  "Yes?" I said.
  When I looked down, I found him holding the head by its hair and realised he'd been using it as a door knocker.
  Whatsmore, I *recognised* the *head* ...

The Chinless Gourmet

  "Hello," I said. "I thought you were dead ..."
  When my former companion from the Schloss stagecoach went to walk into the room, I screamed out loud and slammed the door shut on him ...

  Then, as I turned round, I fell over the mobile sheet, stubbed my nose on the carpet and got up half-dazed a few moments later to find *Heidi* crawling out of it ...
  "What on *earth* are you doing?!" I yelled at her. "I've got a good mind to chuck you off the parapet! You could have scared me half to death ...!"
  "I'm sorry, Mr Dexter ..." she went to say.
  "*Dexter.* Not *Mr* Dexter. I'm *Mr* Kitehawk ..."
  "That's funny," she said. "I thought you had some sort of French-sounding name ... *Haute-Cuisine*, or something like that ..."
  "Oh, er ... that's right," I said, backpedalling. "Mr *Haute-Cuisine*. But you'd better just call me Dexter. I've had a trying evening ..."
  "Well, I'm sorry," she said. "I was bored. I just thought I'd come and give

you a fright, that's all ..."

"Yeah, well," I said, "You've got a lot of competition in *that* department tonight ..."

"Oh!" she suddenly shouted (she was pointing *behind* me) "I don't like the look of *that* ...!"

I swung round to find that hairy arm rummaging around the dresser again ... only this time, with the lantern alight, I could clearly see that it was attached to a body behind the oak panelling and was reaching through via a hatch in the wood, just above my pillow ...

"Don't you ever *knock* first ...?!!!" I yelled at it.

Charging over to the bookcase, I lifted out a fucking great volume on Bavarian Military Insignia and set about clattering the claw until it shot back into the wall ...

... **Zing!!!**

The hatch sprang shut behind it.

"*Next* time, use the *front* door like everybody else!!!" I screamed.

"Isn't it *exciting*," said Heidi. "Was that the Headless Madman?"

"No, no," I said. "The Headless Madman looks completely different altogether ..."

"How do you know?" she said. "Have you seen him tonight?"

"As a matter of fact," I said, "He's outside the door now. I've given him an appointment for 4.00am and told him to come back later. So you'd better be quick ..."

"*Is* he?" she squealed with delight. "Let me take a look ..."

"I was just *talking* to him. Didn't you see ...?"

"I had the sheet over my head ..."

"Well, no ... I don't think so ..."

"Oh, *go* on," she pleaded coquettishly.

"I'll tell you what," I said. "*You* open the door. How's that?"

"Alright ..."

So saying, she marched off to apprehend the suspect while I hid behind the bed ...

I heard her squeal, not in *terror* but *delight* ...

"Is he there?" I called out.

"*Oh yes ...*"

I peeked out to find her leaning round the doorway, looking down the corridor.

So, I went up and hid *behind* her and peered round myself, over her shoulder.

He'd obviously got tired of waiting and was clanking off into the darkness.

"And don't come back!" I yelled after him. "We don't want *your* sort round here any more ...!"

"He must be doing the rounds ..." she said.

All of a sudden he stopped in mid-clank ... and so I ducked down behind her.

"I wonder how he *does* that?" she said. "You *know* – with the *head* ...?"

"Oh," I said, "It's only an old conjurer's trick ..."

Conjurer or not, the Madman started walking back towards us ...

"Oh, I *don't know* ..." she said.

No.

And I can *tell* you.

Looking at his dead eyes, neither *did* I ...

I slammed the door on him again.

"How did you get in here, anyway?" I asked her.

"Through a secret passage. The castle's full of them. They're a bit creepy, though ..."

"You didn't pass a woman on your way, did you? You know – in the secret passage – dark hair, about twenty-five, carrying a knife ...?"

"Sorry, Dexter, no. Who is she? Another ghost?"

"No," I said. "I don't think so. She's probably got nothing to do with the case anyway ..."

"Case?" she said. "Are you on a case? Are you a detective?"

"Er ... no," I hesitated. *I could hardly tell her I was investigating her own family, even though she might have been useful, especially as she seemed to be able to find her way around the castle.* "No, I was just wondering whether it was *her* who stole my luggage ..."

"I thought you left it on the train ...?"

"She was *on* the train ..."

"So?"

"You ask too many questions," I concluded.

"Your *clock's* wrong," she suddenly declared.

"Why?" I said. "What time is it?"

"Must be at least 4.00am by now ..."

"And what time does my clock say?"

"Midnight ..."

"Are you sure?" I said, trying to think.

I went over and took it out of her hand.

"'Ere," I said, "This clock's going *backwards* ..."

The last time I'd looked at it, the time had been 1.01am, and I hadn't been asleep since...

"Where did you get it?" she asked.

"Over *here*, from the mantelpiece," I said, putting it back where I found it.

"How strange," she said.

I thought for a few moments, but it didn't make any sense.

Then again, *what* did?

"So," I said, "Tell me about this secret passage ..."

Her face lit up. "Well," she said, "There's a concealed entrance in almost every room. I got into it from *my* room via the bookcase. If you take out a copy of *Frederick, Prince of Hanover,* it swings round and you find yourself in a passage behind the wall. I presume an identical bookcase swings round from the other side to replace it. There are passages and tunnels all over the castle. I found you by chance, really. The concealed entrance in *this* room is the fireplace ..."

"Really?" I said, as I absent-mindedly leaned back on the mantelpiece. "The *fireplace*, you say ...?"

All of a sudden, it swung round 180 degrees and deposited me in complete darkness on the other side ...

"Let me out!" I yelled, banging on the mirror. "Let me out! There's *bats* in here ...!"

Actually, I couldn't *see* any bats because I couldn't see *anything.*

But there *might* have been ...

"Can you *hear* me, Heidi? Help! Let me out ...!"

Along with her muffled voice, I could hear her pushing and knocking behind the mirror, though it didn't occur to me at the time that leaning on it and trying to push it back from my side was probably neutralising her efforts ...

"It's stuck ...!" she seemed to be calling.

Whatever the reason, I couldn't shift it and neither could she, and communication through the glass was too muted to allow of the possibility of a concerted strategy.

To make matters worse, I began to get the strange sensation that Heidi was no longer *alone* in the room, and that she didn't yet know it ...

"Heidi?"

Suddenly, her voice went dead.

"Heidi ...?"

Seconds later, the scuffling stopped.

I stood there for a while, unsure of what had happened to her and not quite knowing what to do.

Surely not.

She was a *Flite*, after all.

It *had* to be another one of her tricks.

They must be putting her up to it ...

"Alright," I called at length. "*You* win. I'm terrified ..."

It was a half-hearted gesture, and one which received no response.

Somebody *else* was in there, no question.

Somebody, or *something.*

"Heidi ..." I mumbled, but I knew it was already too late.

As I stepped back from the mirror, a shiver rippled through me ...

Iron Maiden

Cursing the fact that I'd earlier left my matches scattered all over the carpet like a miniature logging accident, I searched my tails for the temperamental blunderbuss lighter and stood there pulling on the trigger and badmouthing the shop I'd bought it from, wondering – as I did so – whether, if something had happened to *her*, it was *meant* to happen to *me*. I was the occupant of the *Blood and Iron* room – Heidi would have been found there by mistake.

Eventually, this dubious novelty condescended to light itself, and I turned up the gas full blast to ensure its steadiness in the wake of an assault of draughts and crosscurrents coming from all directions, the illumination of my immediate vicinity being aided by the reflection of the flame in the mirror, although I hesitated to look directly at my *own* reflection. I'd had enough shocks of *that* kind for one night. Whatsmore, I didn't really want to know whether I had company on *my* side of the glass ...

It was a narrow, cobwebbed, stone corridor – each direction looking as uninviting as the other – and as I began to wander hesitantly towards what should have been the *real* corridor outside my room, I came up against a dead end and dropped the overheated lighter to the floor.

It puzzled me how all that lot had found their way round the place without any lights.

Heidi had even had a *sheet* over her head ...

Kneeling down, I discovered a very narrow opening in the wall to my left:

It barely came up to waist height, its dimensions matching the size of a small fireplace ... *or the doorway to an elves' grotto, perhaps – something which, the detection of a dim glow within seemed only to add to the uncanny suggestion of ...*

When I stuck my nose all the way inside, I found the space beyond opening up once more to full height.

So I got to my feet again.

Then, as I went to step forward, I stumbled on something and crashed arse over head into the corner ...

Although the thought crossed my mind that it might be a makeshift coffin to cart me away in during the night, the real purpose of the empty packing crate I'd gashed my shins on became clear the moment I took my finger off the trigger and stepped up level with the source of light ...

Two *spyholes* into my room.

The *eyes* of one of the portraits:

Somebody had *watched* me from here tonight ...

I saw no sign of a fresh struggle, but Heidi was gone, nevertheless.

The lantern was still burning on the bedside dresser, and there was something else:

Two great iron doors – like elevator doors – had closed across the French windows and, from the view in the mirror, I could see a third one blocking the bedroom door from the inside.

No sooner had I taken this in, when there was a tremendous mechanical grinding noise, as though a series of ropes and pulleys had suddenly lurched into action, and I watched horrified as the ceiling sprang a lattice of sharpened spikes and began to descend to the floor ...

In a matter of moments, it had crushed every bit of furniture in the room like a great garbage compressor, and I had to stick my fingers in my ears to escape the sound of splintering wood that could so easily have included my skull ...

Eventually, it came to a halt far beneath the level of the eye-slits, so that instead of a view into the room there was now a view onto the shaft above the ceiling, revealing two gigantic pile drivers and a cluster of Victorian machinery.

I had a good mind to scour the entire place room by room, arresting everybody I came across and telephoning the police to come up and cart the entire bunch of them away.

"Things have gone far enough!" I said to myself.

I'd already deduced that it must be about 4.30am, and this meant that I had at least another two hours before dawn.

What I *didn't* have was a weapon – though I still had the handcuffs in my pocket, which might come in handy, so long as nobody voiced a *grim* opinion on their lot.

To test my theory, I took them out, snapped them together and declared out loud:

"GRIM isn't the word for it ...!"

Click!

Presto.

They sprang *open* again.

And, as far as I could tell, I hadn't vanished into thin air along with Blondie...

Once I'd crawled back out through the pint-sized doorway, I retrieved the blunderbus and traced my way back down the passage as far as the mirror. There was only one direction to go – straight on towards the outside wall – and, as I continued on past the bookcase, a small stairwell loomed up ...

It was a good thing I'd seen it before the lighter had got too hot to hold, or I might have tumbled headfirst straight down it.

Winding below the level of my room, it brought me to a point where the lighter's services were no longer required ...

Requiem for a Dead Drunk

I stepped down into a cross passage bathed in moonlight.

In both directions, the rays shone in through arrow-slits, casting silvery pools on a stone floor curving all the way along as it followed the circumference of the tower.

A decision to turn right, rather than left, was prompted partly by the fact that it kept me in touch with the vicinity of my room, but mainly because I'd spotted, of all things ...

A drinks cabinet.

Just *sitting* there, on its own, opposite a large arrow-slit. (This latter I gave a cursory glance in order to confirm my location, duly noting the same view that I'd had from my balcony which, I surmised, was above the overhang outside.)

Good, I thought. *I'm continuing to skirt my quarters.*
Now for a drink ...

Well, it was like a large bookcase – several shelves – filled with bottles, not books. A coinnoisseur's selection of vintage *Froth*, apparently. The cabinet itself was dusty, though the bottles inside looked freshly stored and protected by two sliding glass doors.

The *trouble* was, it was *locked*.

I hesitated to break in for fear the racket might attract attention. *I dreaded to think who or what else might be in those passages with me.*

And besides, I told myself, *I might break the bottles in the process ...*

Any sign of a key anywhere?

Apparently not.

Wandering on a bit further, I came across the sister staircase to the first one, winding back up towards the opposite side of my room with a faint glow of firelight visible on the curve ...

Curiosity drew me up this second staircase only shyly, reluctant to stray too far from the drinks stash until I'd worked out a way to get my hands on it, and the foul smell which met me as I reached the landing made me wish I'd stayed where I was:

It stank like an animal's lair ...

Adjacent to the bedroom wall was a semi-circular stone chamber hung with lighted torches:

Fanning out from this chamber was a further series of passage entrances.

Well, I thought, *this here on the right is definitely the panelling behind my bed. I could even see the hatch where ...*

It took a moment before I noticed the empty bottle of lager stolen from me earlier lying off to one side on the floor, and a couple *more* moments before it registered that the floor itself was covered in *straw* ...

A pair of ruby red eyes was staring at me out of the darkness of one of the far passages:

Uh-oh.

But, as I turned round to hurry back where I'd come from, I took a single step forward and ...

Creak ... *the floor started to give way beneath me and ...*

Yawnnn ... with an explosion of dust and wood splinters, a trapdoor opened ...

CRASH!!! ... *and I fell feet-first into a dark pit, landing on a bed of damp, rank straw and hay.*

"**OH MY GAWD** ...!" I wailed, scrambling around and crunching up and down on what appeared to be the remains of a collection of human bones ...

Seeing something glinting beneath my feet, I reached down and picked a gold indentity bracelet from a decayed wrist-joint:

Daniel Baudivin

On the reverse was a simple message:

Be An Individual

I suppose I should have seen it coming, really.

If I'd had my *wits* about me.

Top up the tan?

If I hadn't been so keen to rip up the Professor's last book, I might have been able to sidestep the fate which was likely to see me join him on the missing list, bleaching in the moonlight.

I was already in a panic:

The trap was all of six by four, and the cold stone walls rose at least three feet above the reach of my outstretched arms ...

Mind *you*, if I'd had my *wits* about me, I wouldn't have been there in the first place.

Who goes to Rookery Nook for their holidays?

Attempts to wedge myself across and lever myself up over the smooth slimy surface proved useless, and only sent me sliding back to the straw with a bump.

"**Help!** *HELP* ...!" I called out, when ... *suddenly, the torchlight above me was eclipsed and I looked up in horror to find the hairy creature who'd stolen my beer peering down at me ...*

When it moved around to the side, its face was exposed to the light for the first time:

What on *earth* was it?

It looked like the result of some awful genetic experiment gone wrong ...

What *obscenities* had the Flites been up to here? What crimes against the natural order had given birth to the lurching brute which continued to stare down at me with those terrible red eyes, not moving?

Terrible, yes.

But with something like *puzzlement* in them ...

"**I'M AN ENGLISHMAN!**" I bellowed up at it. "**TOUGH AS OLD BOOTS! BAD FOR THE DIGESTION! STEER CLEAR! AND I HAVEN'T HAD A BATH SINCE I FELL OFF A FERRY SIX WEEKS AGO ...!**"

That should do it, I thought.

Any response?

Well ...

Its *response* – if you *don't* mind – was to reach down an arm to offer me a *lift* out!

"**WHOA ...!**" I yelled, backing up to the far corner. "**STAND CLEAR! I WASN'T BORN YESTERDAY ...!**"

HIIIIIIISSSSSSSSSSSSSSSSSSSS ...!!! ... and shooting *forward* just as quickly as a the straw underneath my feet came alive and *spat* at me ...

"**OH MY GAWD!**" I screamed. "**IT'S A *RATTLER* ...!!!**"

I was only half-aware of the Mutant vanishing as I stood frozen at the opposite end watching the disturbed reptile slither around in the straw, and I certainly couldn't have predicted the next intervention from above ... or the next sting in a tail which, as the rattles coiled and vibrated in anticipation of poisoning into paralysis a late-night snack, the Mutant reappeared and chucked the empty *beer* bottle at it ...!

A second offer of rescue was one which I felt I had little choice but to accept, and it must have been incredibly strong, because it hauled me out of that pit in one clean go and clambered on top of me to stare into my eyes ...

Follow that Mutant!

But it only wanted to lick my face.
Still, I fainted anyway ...

When I regained consciousness, my head was propped up on a pillow of straw, and the Mutant was sitting over the other side of the chamber with something equivalent to a mournful expression on its boat.

What I hadn't noticed before, was that it had a large iron ring around its neck, to which was attached a long chain.

The chain was connected to a second iron ring set in the wall, rendering it a prisoner that could wander no further than its leash would allow.

It looked a little like a cross between an orang-utan and a shaggy dog ...

Curious to know whether I was now *its* prisoner, I decided to get to my feet...

Well ...

The eyes looked up, but there was no attempt to stop me, and, as I went to leave, it started to whimper, tugging on the chain in a plea for release ...

I wandered over and patted him on the head.

"Sorry, old boy, but there's nothing I can do ..."

So saying, I grabbed one of the flaming torches from its holder on the wall, proceeded a few steps into the nearest passage and paused by a suit of mediaeval armour with the most fearsome-looking double-headed axe propped up in its mailed glove ...

The Mutant soon perked up when he saw me wrench it away from the metallic knight.

"Okay," I said. "Take cover ..."

Sticking his fingers in his ears as he went, he scuttled off round the corner ...

I didn't stop vibrating for about five minutes after I'd crashed the axehead down onto the chain, and it left me in such state of jarred paralysis that it was only when the Mutant leapt out and went up on its hind legs to lick my face all over again, that I gathered the operation had been successfully accomplished rather surprisingly at the first attempt ...

"Alright, *alright* ..."

If I'd had any thoughts of parting company at that moment, the Mutant apparently had a better idea, something he indicated by whistling at me.

I looked round to find him leaping the rattlesnake pit ...

I hesitated.

For *one* thing, I didn't fancy the jump.

For *another* thing, I didn't want to *encourage* him ... but when I saw him gallop down the winding staircase, it occurred to me that he was disappearing in the direction of the newly-discovered East Wing nightclub ...

So ...

"Hang on to your hats!" I yelled, as I took a lengthy run-up, leapt the void...

... and ran off after him ...

CHAPTER 41
COLD ZONE

When I'd got back down to the level of the cross-passage underneath my room, I found him trying to break into the drinks cabinet.

He was *clever*, though, I'll give him that.

Picking the lock with a piece of wire, the doors responded to his silken touch like a couple of slide trombones to a jailhouse jazz band.

And *my* mitts weren't far behind, either, as I reached for the top shelf and began pilfering its stock of green glass bottles glinting invitingly in the moonlight – *one for each pocket, two in each hand and half-a-dozen more lined up for places of sanctuary stuffed down my trousers* – all anniversary editions, all commemorating something different.

I was so spoilt for choice, in fact, that I couldn't think which monumental event in global history to celebrate first. The *Frankfurt World Dentistry Fest* of 1898, say, or the *Dettingen World Frankfurter Fest* of 1988.

Not that my acquaintance, uncluttered with the breeding of a gentleman of taste, had anything like the same level of measured reserve to his approach. He'd been tirelessly rummaging around all parts of the cabinet before settling on a row of unfamiliar slender-necked bottles occupying the second shelf, a clutch of which he'd swiped, two of which he'd already broken open ...

Curious fascination caused me to pause and ponder the funny face he was pulling as he stood there passing them to and fro underneath his nostrils.

Well ... *funny* it *might* have been *before* he took a sip, but deadly serious it became subsequently when he spat it all out again and hurled both bottles straight through the arrow slit!

And, as if this particular gesture of gratuitous nihilism towards his gaolers wasn't enough, he proceeded to gather as many of the remainder from the shelf as he could carry in his arms and went and chucked the lot.

I was so *alarmed* at his behaviour, that I grabbed a couple of those he'd been unable to collect at his first attempt and examined the labels:

ALLIED FROTH
Low Alcohol Pilsner 1988

I almost squeaked out loud!

The second one was even more astonishing ...

ALLIED FROTH
Alcohol-Free Lager

"My God!" I shouted. "What a tasteless joke!"
I walked over and sent them the same way as the others ...

When I'd got over the shock, I turned round to find the Mutant trying to reach up to the top shelf for a serious drink, but even on his hind legs he couldn't quite manage it.

So I lifted one down for him.

"Cheers," he said.

"Cheers," I said ... *before swinging round to check I'd heard what I thought I'd heard.*

"Did you say something?" I enquired.

Since his follow-up comment sounded more like the burp I might have expected, I echoed it accordingly, coshed the top off a souvenir from the secret wedding of Adolf and Eva, wished them health, wealth, a honeymoon with a bang, and got ready to toast the bodies ... *when the Mutant suddenly drew attention to a tiny light flashing in the back of the cabinet* – visible only now that some of the bottles had been removed. *He obviously regarded it with some concern ...*

"We've been rumbled ..." I said.

All at once, he grabbed hold of my arm, aimed his nose upwards in the air and stiffened his ears ...

By the time I heard it myself – *footsteps approaching at speed along the moonlit passage* – the Mutant had already fled, and from the sound of breaking glass in the direction of the staircase, I'd say he'd decided to carry off quite a lot of the booty *with* him ...

Following his trail of spilt beer, I scarpered up the stairs, back across the snakepit and down the nearest passage, where I lost him in the darkness.

I *say* lost him. Lost *myself* would be a more accurate assessment, since I was still blindly careering along without any light when a horrendous *Awhuurp!* suddenly blasted past my face and echoed away down the tunnel behind me like a tornado in a tin mine – confirmation of *his* general direction, maybe, but not of the distance between us, or of the location of either of us relative to anything else.

Eventually, I reached a multiple junction lit by one solitary torch and stopped to listen for sign of the possee:

To my surprise, they suddenly passed by right in front of me with their guns drawn – Simon and Sonny – *out of one passage and into another ...*

"He's escaped ..." I heard Simon curse, but ... as I edged backwards a couple of paces into the dark, I wondered whether they were referring to the Mutant, or to *me*.

Once their voices had grown faint and their footsteps distant, I stuck my head out to check the coast was clear:

Now, I thought. *Eeny, Meeny, Miny, Mo ...?*

Since each passage looked the same, I picked one out of the hat, grabbed the torch and stole along with the flames casting shadows on the brickwork left and right of me.

A few feet further on, the air suddenly turned to freezing as though I'd walked into a static draught ...

I knelt down and touched the stone floor.

And retracted it in shock ...

It was colder than the inside of an icebox.

Burning cold.

The torch was still alight, but I could feel no heat coming from the flames.

A couple of paces further on and the temperature was normal again.

So ...

I turned round and waved my free hand backwards and forwards through the space I'd been standing in, walking around the spot, probing, until I'd drawn an imaginary circle with a circumference of roughly two yards.

As far as I could tell, it went all the way up from floor to ceiling.

A *Cold* Zone.

I could even see tiny crystals of ice beginning to form around the fingertips of my lingering hand ...

Walking hurriedly on, I was met by a different kind of draught, the torch flickering in the crosscurrent between two arches, both of which encased narrow staircases — one winding upwards, the other a reverse mirror image.

This time the choice was a simple *four*-way one:

Up, down, straight on, or straight back.

Straight into trouble.

Or straight into more trouble.

Six choices.

By the time I'd finished rationalising the scenario thus, I'd already set off for the next level down as though merely paying lip service to the fact that I had *other* options obviated the necessity to *choose* one of them. My *feet* knew where to go, so why not follow them? My *feet* wanted to go *down*, because that's where the *way out* was.

So *that's* what I did.

Followed my feet.

To the passage below.

Which just happened to be identical to the one above, containing identical twin staircases, and an identical cold zone, in an identical spot ...

Down I went, past several more floors, confirming on every one the location of each antecedent stage of a multi-storey icy funnel, until, on one particular landing, I suddenly found my intention to probe further its source thwarted by a massive, wooden door blocking the entire passage in that direction, locked tight and impenetrable.

There was, however, a keyhole ...

The sight that greeted me turned my stomach a full wash-cycle on half-load.
Inside was a chapel, with a great stone altar bathed in moonlight.
And hanging above that altar was ... an animal carcass, *dripping blood.*

Since the downward march of the matching staircases had also come to an end, I had little choice but to wander the passage in the other direction, arriving eventually at the summit of a steeply winding stairwell looking not unlike a narrower version of the emergency escape route at the old Angel tube station.
Albeit minus the central column.

The oversight by the builders to include this latter detail meant that any stray movement in the wrong direction would be terminated by a draughty drop into a deep, dark void, and so I began the descent very carefully, hugging close to the wall as I went.

Five minutes later, the stairs were still spiralling away ahead of me with such hypnotic relentlessness that regular lapses in concentration had caused me to develop a tendency to do precisely *that* – ie, stray too close to the edge – *a phenomenon which, following my analogy, might best have been best avoided by the loud playing of a London Transport 'Mind the Gap' recording, something apparently lacking from the owners' budget ...*

It was, therefore, with some relief that I emerged, a tortuous time afterwards, in what could only have been part of the substructure of the castle. *I hadn't passed any doors on the way down* – internal *or* external – *and one or two fluted windows had been placed too high above the steps to offer a view of the world outside, but the sheer distance must have taken me out of the tower and straight down through the East Wing altogether.*

Met with more and more passages fanning off in every direction, I raised the torch and found one archway, in particular, to be larger than all of the others. This route I chose, hoping that as a possible central spine to the tunnel system, it might lead me somewhere significant – away from the eastern end of the castle and towards its centre.

Beneath its centre, probably.

It must have been getting close to 5.30am – just under an hour till first light.

And it didn't take long for something to happen ...

The Uninvited

It was *one* endless passage, and it was on a slight downhill incline:
The further I walked, the damper and slimier the stonework became.

I should think the whole castle must have taken several centuries and several thousand workmen to construct.

I could be wandering around here for years, I thought, *and never find my way out.*

I could die trying and nobody would ever know.

Whoever designed it must have been insane ....

And I *should know.*

If I ever found out his name, I was going to enter it as a footnote to my list of most wanted criminals connected with the *Allied Froth* case ...

Almost imperceptibly, the tunnel opened out into an enormous maze of arches and pillars – the foundations, surely, of the central block of the castle. No burning torches hanging anywhere, but a ghostly network of shadows cast all about me by the uprights and curves as I walked through them carrying my own light. Cold and draughty, damp and musty all at the same time, the rank air seeped from the stone and brickwork like a fetid miasma to cloak the columns and shroud the ceiling, drenching my clothes and layering my lungs with a cloying film of rotting sweetness as I stepped into the domain of decay ...

It began with a tingle in the back of my neck as I sensed something – a shadow – *not my own, moving with me, off to one side ...*

I stopped and hesitated in the path of a second shadow stirring in front of me:

tick tock tick tock

In one paralysing moment, the movement seemed to be all around me, as though the curves of the arches themselves were a jungle of tangled arms come to life ... *and the Raven swoops through the darkness, hooded reflection of a hand which rises from behind to slide the cold steel of a substantial blade in place across my throat.*

I immediately dropped the torch, understanding from less-than-subtle gestures that I was to walk on ahead into the centre of the maze, a spacious chamber amongst the receding arches, where I was brought to a halt and forced to stand silent in the dripping gloom, playing chicken with the serated knife-edge on my Adam's Apple, listening to my heartbeat as it counted down the seconds to eternity.

For, as I wondered at the identity of my captor, the approach of a second presence was announced in a voice as sharp as the tool on my throat:

"Long time, no see, Kitehawk ..."

When its owner, Hetty Darkbloode, stepped out moments later from behind a pillar, gun in hand, sporting one of the unfriendliest smiles I'd ever seen, it didn't take an Oxford Don to work out who was behind me wielding the cutlery ...

"Oh," I said, feigning relief. "It's *you* ..."

"Oh yeah?" she said. "Who was you expecting? Adolf Hitler?"

I glanced round at the decor. "Not really," I said. "For one awful minute, I thought it was the Architect ..."

"You're a funny man, Kitehawk," she said, not laughing.

"D'you think so?"

"Hoist him up, Mario," she ordered her accomplice in a kind of disinterested, throwaway, gangster-moll twang (*which, considering she was from some arse-upwards tip in the Yorkshire Dales, was quite impressive*).

Quick as a shiver, he'd removed the knife from my throat and slipped a pair of rusty iron manacles round my wrists.

These, as I soon found out, were attached to a weighty mediaeval chain, and the chain itself was strung through an iron ring driven into the arched ceiling, providing him with the means to haul me up until I was suspended, my toes barely touching the ground.

To secure me in this position, he locked the chain over a hook in a nearby pillar and wandered back to admire his handiwork with Hetty, the latter of whom had a flashlight that she began to take great pleasure in shining directly into my face ...

I didn't fancy this very much. The manacles were already beginning to bite into my hands, and my arms were stretched to the limit of their sockets.

"Look," I said, "I can't hang about here all night ..."

"Don't worry," she said. "This isn't going to take long ..."

"Your boyfriend's talkative ..."

"He won't be wasting any words on you. He's a man of action ..."

"Where?" I said. "Round the wrist?"

I think the only reason he didn't sock me one, was because he couldn't work out if it was a compliment or not.

"You must have thought you'd given us the slip back there," she went on.

"Something like that," I said. "I'm a bit surprised to see you again so soon, as a matter of fact ..."

"I *bet* you are ..."

"I heard you were all banged up in a hotel downtown, courtesy of the German police ..."

"Now, that's a funny *thing*," she said. "We *were* in a hotel, with a token police guard. And, since we ain't got nothing to hide, we thought we'd stay there till morning. But do you know something, I was just about to hit the sack when Mario says, 'Come over here, take a look a this, willya ...'"

Oh, I thought. He can speak English, then ...

"So I went over to the back window, and there were people climbing down the drainpipes, down the fire escape, down ladders, using sheets tied together – you name it – just to get away from the place ..."

"Yeah I know," I said. "I *stayed* there once. The food had *legs*. When I woke up in the morning the hotel was in a different street ..."

"Who's telling this story?"

"Carry on ..."

"Only it wasn't none of the *regular* guests – just the faces from the train. I figured either they all had something to hide, or they were all late for an appointment. The *same* appointment. So we decides to follow 'em. Mario here, he didn't think it'd look too good in the morning if we were the only ones who hadn't cleared off ..."

I tried to work out the logic of that one but it defeated me. "He's *clever* like that is he, your boyfriend ...?"

"Shut da fuck up!" he suddenly snarled ... *and slapped me round the face so hard that I went swinging backwards and forwards like a lightshade in a storm ...*

"We don't seem to have your full attention," said Hetty.

I didn't stop jangling for about five minutes.

"Now," she went on, "Are you listening?"

"Awub ... Awub ... Awub ... Awub ..."

"Shall I'll take that as a *yes* ...?"

"Awub ..."

"I thought they must be off somewhere real interesting, to be in such a hurry to get there," she concluded, ignoring the intermittent baby-burbling emanating from my static gob. "And besides, I had a feeling *you'd* be mixed up in it somehow ..."

"Awub?"

"Yeah, *you* ..."

Fucking Einsteins, I cursed internally, as Mario stood there straightening his hideous shirt.

What I really needed to do was turn the tables over and get some mileage out of *them,* for what it might be worth, but it all depended on getting my vocal muscles back in working order ...

"So," I eventually spat out, "Who was the stiff in the water tank?" (*My lower lip was still half-paralysed*)

"*You* oughta *know*. They got *you* pencilled in as the guy who put him there..."

"Eh ...?" I gasped. "Do I *look* like a murderer?"

"You look like a tic-tac man to me. But don't worry, you won't look like nothing so pretty when Mario gets through with you ..."

He started to rub his right fist in his left hand, to ram home the message ...

"I might have known he was a complete idiot, that bloke ..."

"Now, who's *that?*" she said.

"*Le Gras.* Fucking shortarse," I cursed. "Belgian detectives. It's enough to make you *spit.* Is that Interpol officer still in the frame?"

"Oh yeah," she confirmed. "Because it seems like they found out it was his *brother* in the tank ..."

I must have whistled out loud at that revelation ...

"Mark Black? Are you *sure* ...?"

"Yeah, that's him," she said. "Mark Black. That's the name ..."

It was like a shot of anaesthetic ...

Temporarily forgetting all about the pain, I tried frantically to assess the implications, particularly the tantalising question of who he'd *bought* it from ...

"And what about that government minister's wife? Did *she* ever reappear?"

"Oh *yeah,*" she said. "*She* showed up. Looking well and floating past

Ostend minus her head. So they say. Seems like you're the suspect on *that* count as well..."

"Me?!!" I shouted in outrage. "Trevor killed *her*, not me!"

"Yeah," she went on, "It's all down to the Bozo, apparently. He sung to the cops that you was his accomplice and they've got her husband to stitch up the gaps in his story. But it's worked out well for *us*, really. Bozo's safely under lock and key, and you're gonna cause *no* surprises when *you* turn up dead. Sir *what's-his-name* has already put it on record that he's going to avenge his wife, and so nobody's gonna suspect *us* ..."

"Yeah, well," I said, "There's only one thing wrong with all that ..."

"And what's that?" she asked, sceptically.

"Trevor isn't *under* lock and key ..."

"So, where is he then?"

"Right here in this castle. I saw him myself a few hours ago and he didn't look none too happy ..."

"You're lying ..."

"*Maybe he escaped?*" Mario whispered in her ear.

"Or maybe he did a deal with the police on *you* two?" I said, attempting to stir things up.

"*I still say he's lying*," she whispered back into Mario's ear.

I started whistling, innocently.

"How'd he get in here?" she suddenly asked me. "We had to break in a back window. Seems like everyone else from that train had invites. Some guy in a bow-tie was letting 'em in ..."

"Trevor *had* an invite. I gave it to him. But *you* know Trevor. He decided to climb over the walls anyway ..."

"I'm sick of talking. This place gives me the creeps. I want some information from you on two counts, and I want it quick. You're gonna die anyway so you might as well talk. Tell us what we want to know and I'll let Mario finish it quickly – just one clean incision, ear-to-ear. If not, well ... you wouldn't want to know about that. Right. *One*. What's my old man's address? *Two*. What's everybody doing at this place? If I know *you*, there must be money in it somewhere ..."

"My lips are shtoom ..."

"Mario," she said, "Get the tools ..."

"*No*, no ..." I wheezed, "No need for violence. He's in an insane asylum in New York. Or at least, he *was*. I've had intelligence on the grapevine that he's broken out. Apparently, he's on his way here now, and so he should arrive – if my calculations are correct – sometime tomorrow evening. Or perhaps I should say *this* evening. So stick around. I could give you a guided tour of the castle. And then, as soon as he arrives, we can all jump him from behind and clatter him over the head with spanners. He's coming here to settle an old score with me, after all. As to your second question, it couldn't possibly interest you. It's a political matter ..."

Sometime during this speech, Mario had reappeared with an oversized pair of blacksmith's tongs ...

"*Do you believe him?*" he whispered.

She looked up at me and went all thoughtful.

"No," she said at length. "Get to work ..."

"Shall I warm them up first?" he said, gesturing towards an old brazier filled with coal.

"Yeah," she encouraged him, "*Red*-hot ..."

"No need for the kid gloves," I said. "Give 'em to me *cold* ...!"

"Yeah," she said, "Give him some of each ..."

He then proceeded to fumble around in his pockets for a good minute and a half, while I watched him, incredulous.

"Have you got any matches?" he finally asked her.

She shrugged in the negative. "Ask laughing-boy up there ..."

"Have you got any matches?" he called up to me.

"You must be joking ..."

He *wasn't*, though.

He set about giving me a good frisking, during the course of which he pulled out my blunderbus lighter ...

"What's this?" he asked.

"Well, it ain't a box of matches ..." I said.

"What is it?"

"Whatever you do," I said, "Don't pull the trigger. You'll blow us all to bits..."

He got a light first time.

"I better gag him," he said. "In case he wake anyone up ..."

"Don't do that," she said. "We won't be able to understand a word he's saying when he starts to squeal ..."

What a pair of idiots, I thought.

Mario had already wandered across to the brazier, but intent and ability were clearly two different things for this animal, the means to get it alight apparently eluding him.

In fact, he was still standing there trying to figure out how it worked, when Hetty suddenly went over and snatched at his arm ...

"Hold it," she said with alarm. "What's that sound ...?"

Mario stopped to listen:

I must be going deaf, I thought. *I couldn't hear a thing.*

"*Quick, there's somebody coming ...*" she whispered. (*She put out the flashlight just as Mario dropped the hot lighter*). "Any sound out of *you*, Kitehawk, and you're dead meat ..."

She paused just long enough to aim the gun in my direction, before they both ducked away and left me to face alone whoever it was that approached from the far side of the maze ...

Charming, I thought, *leaving me dangling here in the dark like a butcher's exhibit.*

Sooner or later, I heard it too:

Footsteps.
Several *pairs* of them, at that.
Like a platoon of soldiers ...

An eruption of flashlight beams bouncing off the angles suggested they'd be all over me in a few seconds, *whoever* they were.

In a brief moment of optimism, I wondered whether it might be a rescue party, but the delayed arrival of accompanying voices with German accents and German words told me it was hardly likely to be a *friendly* encounter. "Oh, *excuse* me, Herr Flite," I imagined saying to my host, "I do hope I haven't caused you any inconvenience by letting your *Mutant* loose. And, being a trifle short on a *laugh* above-stairs, I just thought I'd come down and bolt myself into your basement ceiling ..."

While I indulged in this daydream, six very, very tall Aryan types strode dramatically past me, carrying all manner of heavy-duty equipment – picks, shovels etc ... and completely ignored me.

They then proceeded to deposit these items at strategic points around my immediate vicinity and marched off again, only to be replaced by a second mob bringing in a similar stack of construction tools.

Not quite what I expected, I'll admit.

I was in no doubt that they'd spotted me when they first came in, but they were obviously so engrossed in their work that they couldn't be bothered to acknowledge me, or stop for a chat.

What kind of people ignore a man hanging from the ceiling by his wrists?

I think it fair to say that their arrival caused me a certain level of justified fear, because it had been my experience that when the Nazis wanted to torture you, they always seemed able to adopt exactly this kind of blasé attitude, and it wouldn't have surprised me if the spikes and spades were intended for a little demolition work on sensitive parts of my body ... *an intuition apparently confirmed in a particularly shocking way when a relief detail marched in backwards unwinding a long reel of electrical flex ...*

"Who's in charge round here?" I demanded to know. "If you're looking for the International Dentist's Convention you've come to the wrong place. They're all over in the *West* Wing ..."

Their continued silence – save for the odd word to each other, such as "*Raus!*" and "*Hier!*" and "*Schnell!*" – was contempt enough, I suppose.

Anyway, I was just creaking around on the end of my chain and pondering, as I did so, which member – or members – of the villainry thus far assembled at the Schloss might be responsible for signing the warrant for this lot, when the last person I could possibly have wished to see in such a situation – *strung up, as I was, in a mediaeval torture chamber* – arrived ...

Fräulein Dorf breezed in like an efficient clerk-of-works, complete with a safety helmet on her head.

Oh no, I thought. *I'm in trouble now ...*

She'd had some bad fortune in her past dealings with me, but she wasn't an idiot like Mario. It was only pure luck that I'd escaped from her on two previous occasions. *Now she found me all neatly packaged courtesy of Tweedledum and Tweedledee, and one look at the equipment and the back-up crew told me she wasn't leaving anything to chance.* This would have to be third time lucky for her ...

So animated was she in directing the operations going on around us, that *she* too chose to ignore me for the moment, casting me only a cursory glance as she wafted by.

In fact, I went so dizzy watching her pass to and fro over and over again, that by the time she finally came to a halt with her back to me, I decided to accost her ...

"Don't mind *me*," I said, as casually as I could.

"Herr *Kitehawk* !" she said, swinging round suddenly with an exaggerated flourish of recognition. "How nice to *see* you! We *meet* yet again! I am so *sorry* we didn't have a chance to say goodbye *properly* last time. You are *looking* well, I must say. How *are* you? In *good* health, I hope ...?"

"Averagely tip-top, considering," I said. "You couldn't do me a favour and let me down, could you?"

She blanked my request – taking the opportunity, instead, to bellow some instructions at a couple of vacant-looking *jugendfuhrer* who'd just delivered a wheelbarrow and a ladder to the wrong sector (apparently).

"Isn't this just a little bit like taking a sledgehammer to crack a nut?" I enquired, watching with increasing horror at the arrival on the scene first, of a pneumatic drill, then of a box of explosives.

"Certainly not," she said.

"What exactly *is* it," I said, "That you've got planned for me this time – or shouldn't I ask ...?"

"For *you* ..." she mumbled, preoccupied with a growing mountain of scaffolding poles being stacked up precariously in front of us, "For *you* ... nothing! There is *nothing* planned!"

Once again she'd spun round and was beaming at me in an ethereal manner.

"You're just trying to *scare* me to death, aren't you?" I said.

Placing her hands on her hips, she temporarily transferred all of her undivided attention to me.

"No," she said, all matter-of-fact. "I am *not*. The Corporation and myself have parted *company*. Let us say we have had a difference of *opinion*. We no longer see *eye-to-eye*. I am now a free *agent*, so to speak. If there is still an order for your *execution* it will not be *I* who carries it out. *Verstehen*? I cannot *speak* for anybody *else* ..."

"Straight up?" I said.

"That is correct ..."

Well, it was a surprise and no mistake.

"So you're just going to torture me for old time's sake, then ...?"

"No," she said. "I am *not*. I take no *pleasure* from my work. I am a – what is the word? – a *professional* ..."

No *pleasure?*

She could have fooled *me* ...

"What are you doing here, then," I said, "If you're not on their payroll anymore?"

"I have come to collect what is *mine*," she declared. "In short, ten million *dollars*-worth of what is mine ..."

"Mark Black's Nazi treasure from the last war?" I said in astonishment.

"That is correct ..."

"But it's not *here*, is it?"

"Yes. Yes, it is *here* ..."

"Where?" I asked, dumbfounded.

She pointed at the floor.

"But how did you find out where it was?"

Distracted, at that moment, by the assembly of an indoor crane on the far side, she turned round to bark out more instructions – taking, as she did so, a piece of paper from her pocket which she absent-mindedly held up behind her for me to peruse, apparently forgetting that I didn't have a free hand.

I took it to be a map of some kind, but I was in no position to study it before she retracted it again and put it back in her pocket.

"So it's – *where?* Under the *floor*, is it?" I said.

"That is ... *correct*," she said. (*She'd swung round to face me again*). "*Buried* under it. *Cannot* you read *maps?*"

"Where?" I said. "Right here in this spot?"

"I do not know *where* under the floor," she said, "Or *how far* under the floor but, as you will have noticed, I have brought with me more than enough manpower and equipment to undertake a lengthy exploration ..."

As if to underline her statement, a great mass of arc lights all came on at once and bathed the cellar in floodlight, completely blinding me in the process ...

"Good," she mused, in a kind of reverie. "Now we have proper lighting ..."

Well, proper lighting we *might* have had, but my eyelids were still firmly closed to the glare when an enormous mechanical roar suddenly erupted behind me and I nearly jumped out of my skin as some idiot driving a motorcycle and sidecar careered past and almost decapitated both my heads ...

Legs! Legs, I mean *legs* ....

After zooming around in a great circle, he finally came to rest in a shower of dust, smoke, soot, grease and sparks, with the front headlamp embedded in one of the central uprights.

"Idiot ..." the Fräulein cursed as she watched the rider disembark from his seat and stagger helmet-first into a nearby refuse skip.

"Who *are* these blokes, then?" I said. "Your private army?"

"In a manner of speaking, yes. They have left the Corporation to join me. They are defects ..."

I think she probably meant to say *defectors*, but, looking at the upturned cavalryman trying to climb out of the trash-can, I let it stand.

"So how did you get hold of a map ... if you don't mind me asking?"

"From Mark Black ..."

"But I heard he was dead ..."

"He is *now*. A timely, deserved and fitting end to a *traitor* ..."

"But," I said, suddenly feeling responsible for his demise, "I made all that up about him fiddling and being a double-agent ..."

"No," she said, "Your information was corroborated and proved to be accurate. He'd been robbing the Corporation for a number of years. *Him* and the *Flite family*. So I have made a decision to confiscate the treasure for myself ..."

"But look," I said, "I thought the Flites *were* the Corporation?"

"Do you know anything about construction?" she cut-in. "I was wondering the best method of bringing a mechanical digger in here ..."

"'*Ere*!" I said. "Do they *know* you're planning to carve up their *floor*?"

"It is of no concern to me either way," she said. "I would have been able to keep the *disturbance* period to a *minimum*, had I a better-drawn *map*. I made the uncharacteristic error of removing one or two of his fingers *beforehand*. Consequently, he had some difficulty in holding the pen ..."

I cringed at that one.

"You've got an original line in killing," I said. "I'll give you that ..."

She suddenly swung round on me again ...

"Did I say *I* killed him?" she demanded to know.

I offered little response to this, becoming abstracted by the appalling pain in my shoulders, wrists and arms. *If I ever walk away from this situation,* I thought, *I don't think I'll have very many jumpers left that fit me.* And the last thing I wanted right at that moment was a *mining* operation taking place just a few feet from my lugholes. *Enough was enough ...*

"It's no good you digging *here*," I said, at length.

"*Bitte?*" she queried, half breaking away from her supervision of the delivery of a detonator.

"It's no good you digging *here*. And I should be careful not to let Fritz over there crash into too many more of these uprights ..."

"Why? What do you mean?"

"Well," I said, "For a *start*, they form the central foundation to this place. You only need to damage *one* of them and the whole castle collapses. And for *another* thing, *this* isn't the *ground* floor. You'll all fall through to the floor below as soon as you start digging ..." (not that *I* had any idea, mind you. I reckon I knew as much about mining as she did – *ie nothing* – and I certainly had no idea whether there was another floor below us).

"But this is the *basement*, is it not ...?"

"Oh yes," I said. "But there's a *sub*-basement under this one. There's even a cellar below that, I believe. There may even be a *sub*-cellar for all I know ..."

She began pacing up and down and mumbling to herself ...

"I must think on this a while. Is it possible I have made a mistake ...?"

Suddenly, she clapped her hands in the air and delivered an announcement in German, which, if the disappointed looks from all and sundry were anything to go by, meant she'd fallen for it – though, quite honestly, the fact that she hadn't checked any of this out beforehand made me glad I'd planted doubts in her head. *After all*, I thought, *I might be right ...*

Soon enough, her troops began dismantling the equipment and carting it all back out again.

"How is your father, by the way?" she said.

"My father?" I said. "Why? Do you know him?"

"Of course, you may remember ..."

"The last I heard," I said, "He was taking a bath in a lime pit at Dagenham Dock ..."

"A pity," she said. "I rather liked him. His teeth offered me a great challenge, being gold ..."

The penny dropped. "Oh!" I said. "You mean *Dirk*! He's not my dad – it's just a dialectical peculiarity of northern yokel hamlets to call everyone 'son', and so forth ... who my *real* dad is, I've no idea ..."

"Of course he is your *father*. Do you not think I check out all biographical details of the targets of my contracts before beginning the process of elimination? Come, you do him and yourself an injustice to be ashamed in such a manner ..."

"What *are* you talking about ...?" I said, as I watched the last of the tools being carried out.

Finally the arc lights were switched off and removed, leaving me alone with Fräulein Dorf and her flashlight.

She turned to go ...

"Goodbye, then, *Herr* Kitehawk," she said. "Or should I say, Herr *Darkbloode* ...?"

"Oi!" I screamed at her. "You're not just going to leave me *hanging* here, are you? Can't you let me down ...?"

She stopped and thought for a moment.

"No ... no, I don't believe that I can release you ..."

"Why not?!!!" I shouted.

"Because ..." she hesitated.

"Well ...?"

"*Because* it would be *unethical* ..."

And on *that* note, she walked off.

It was as though none of them had ever been there in the first place – Fräulein Dorf, her men and equipment – and once again I found myself alone in the darkness.

"Well, if it isn't Pinky and Perky," I said, as Hetty and Mario strolled back into the foreground.

"Shut da fuck up!" yelled Mario, stretching his vocabulary to the limits for the second time.

Hetty raised her gun to a level contiguous with my flies ...

"So, there *is* money in this place ..." she said.

"Of course there's money here," I said. "It's a mediaeval castle. What do you expect? I should think the market value alone is worth a mint ..."

"I'm talking about the ten million dollars in buried treasure. You were lying to us ..."

"If I'd have known you were eavesdropping, I'd have got everybody to speak a bit louder ..."

"In fact," she said, "I think you've done nothing *but* lie all evening ..."

"What's the view like in the other direction?" I asked.

"Give him a twirl, Mario ..."

Thus bidden, he grabbed hold of my legs and proceeded to spin me round and round in a circle till I was so dizzy I was on the verge of throwing up all over him.

Then he bent down to retrieve the tongs ...

"Leave it, Mario," she said. "We haven't got time for this now. I'm revising all plans in the light of new information that's come my way ..."

"Go on," I said. "Fill me in ..."

"That's the general idea," she continued. "I'm dispensing with formalities herewith. I don't know if the old man is on his way here or not, but it's just too bad you're gonna miss him. Say your prayers ..."

"But don't you want to know for sure ...?" I said, trying to stall them.

"With all that loot up for grabs in this place, *he* can wait a bit longer for judgement day. Besides, no-one knows exactly how much money he's put away over the years, but it's my guess that ten million is gonna make me a lot richer than rolling the old man ever will. *Kapiche?* Kiss goodbye to the planet, Kitehawk..."

"Wait a minute!" I yelled in angst. "What are you killing *me* for, then ...?"

"I thought you'd have guessed by now, *brother* ..."

"*What* ...?"

"And *all* along I thought you were just some fast-buck Eddie who'd taken up with the Bozo to double-cross me out of my inheritance. But you didn't need to kill the old man because he'd already left it all to *you*. It's funny, but when I was a kid I used to want a brother. I used to ask him to bring me one ..."

"Are you using the term *brother*," I said, "In the sense of global fraternal love ...?"

"That's right," she said, "In the sense of global, fraternal *flesh-and-blood*. You, me and the old man. *One big happy family that never was*. But he's *your* old man and he's *my* old man just the same, and that makes you *my brother* ..."

"Are you off your rocker?" I shouted at her.

Mario suddenly took another backhand swipe at me ...

"Hey!" he yelled. "Donna you speak to your *sister* like that!"

"Clear off ya git!" I cursed, trying to launch a kick at him.

"Let it alone, Mario ..."

"*Look*," I said, "*Dirk* – or whatever his name is – is not my *father*, and you're not my *sister*. I met him completely by chance in the jungle, from which point his affairs became entangled with mine because he insisted on latching himself on to me. You must be completely crazy if you think there's anything more to it. The whole idea is absurd. I wouldn't listen to that nonsense the *Fräulein* was coming out with – she's just got her wires crossed. She doesn't know what she's talking about, I can assure you ..."

"Oh, I don't know. The *Fräulein* seemed to me to know *exactly* what she was talking about – and besides, I can see the family resemblance now ..."

"Resemblance!" I yelled in outrage. "*Resemblance?* To *what?*"

"Yeah," she said, "The same front teeth missing, the same complexion ... did you know your old man was washed up on Morecambe beach when he was a baby? What a shame you missed out on hearing over and over again the family story. It's *all* true. *Our* grandmother found him *all* wrapped up in a cot of reeds and rushes, just lying there in the mud at low tide. People said he'd floated all the way from Africa. They said he was the outcast son of a Moroccan prince. They nicknamed him *Heathcliffe*. Now, isn't *that* romantic? Doesn't it just make you want to throw ...?"

She had a point.

And so I took the opportunity to stop repressing it, opened my mouth and chucked a stomachful of slimy bile all over Mario's expensive shirt.

He didn't look none too pleased about it!

Which was a shame, really, because just as he was getting over the shock, I felt a second wave coming on and launched a counter-offensive all over his quiff ...

"Don't worry," I said, as I hung there in front of him and watched it ooze past his eyes, slide down his cheeks, and dribble drip-drop onto his shoes. "It's all environmentally-friendly stuff – the *colour's* a giveaway ..."

"*Aaaaaaaargh* ...!" he yelled, trying to wipe his hair and his shirt, and trying to square-up to do me some damage all at the same time. "*Why,* you ..."

"Keep clear!" I yelled. "There may be *more* coming ...!"

"*Two minutes,* Mario," Hetty intervened. "Two more minutes and he's all yours ..."

With great difficulty of will, he stamped off out of range, huffing and puffing as he went, still trying to clear vomit from a face contorted in rage while Hetty proceeded to moan on like a deprived tinseltown starlet ...

"He never loved me *or* my mother. *Archibald, Richard, Heathcliff, Darkbloode...*" (she repeated each part of his name with venom) "... he was never there, never around. *Some* father. He'd go off on his travels and we'd never see him from one year to the next. *Heathcliff.* He must have hung you with the same handle because he thought you looked like him so much. You must have been the son he always wanted. The *favourite.* But that money's rightfully mine: for *all* those years he never spent a penny on me or my mother. And putting you out of the picture is the way to make sure I get it ..."

"No, look ..." I was trying to say, trying to pull on the chain with whatever energy I had left, but getting increasingly confused – *confused by her story, confused by the pain in my arms, confused because my arms were pulling on my neck and cutting the blood supply to my brain.* "Look," I said, "My *teeth* – they've just been blacked-out, that's all. My *skin* – it's all theatrical makeup ... and my *name* – it's Kitehawk, *Dexter* Kitehawk ..."

"Yeah," she was drivelling on, "It all figures. *He* was the original music-hall joker *himself*, in his time ..."

There had to be something wrong with her story, but I wasn't in much of a state to recognise what it was. "This is all a multiplied misunderstanding," I said. *"Honest.* A *chain* situation ..."

"What's your *real* name?" she taunted. "Come on, give us a song, sweetheart..."

"My name's Dexter Kitehawk," I intoned, like a captured private reeling off his name, rank and serial number, "Of Rathaven Mansions, Old Street, London. I was *born* in London. My mother was Mrs Dora Kitehawk, of 58B Clerkenwell Square, and she was far too well-bred to have consorted with the likes of *him* ..."

"How do you know? Did *she* tell you that?"

"As a matter of fact, no. She disappeared before my first birthday. I was brought up by a Mrs Winifred Troutpole, also of Clerkenwell Square. You ought to get a job with the Viet-Cong ..."

But as I turned it all over in my mind, it kept coming back to me that I'd never known my dad, never known who he was or whether he was dead or alive ...

"*Kitehawk*," she said. "That don't exactly sound like the handle of a *lady* to me ..."

"How dare you insult my mother!" I screamed. "What did she ever do to you?"

"She insulted *my* mother, that's what. She was my old man's mistress ..."

Rattling around on the chain, I was slowly going delirious ...

"And she *carried on* insulting her whether she was dead or alive. He cut my mother out of the will. And he cut *me* out of the will. Now it's *your* turn. How does it feel to know you're never going to be able to spend that money ...?"

"Look, Sis," I said, trying to plead for more time, "You can't send me on my way until I'm sure what you're saying is the truth. I've got questions I want to ask ..."

She looked at her watch. "Okay," she said. "I'll give you a dying man's request: one last question. But it better be worth answering ..."

I tried desperately to think of something crucial that would swing it one way or the other. *I just couldn't face the afterlife not knowing for sure whether I was really related to that boneheaded clonk or not.* There *had* to be *something* ...

"Okay," she suddenly declared. "Time's up ..."

"Alright, alright," I said anxiously, "I've got a question ..."

"Go on," she said. "Let's hear it ..."

"*Well* ... er ..." I floundered.

"Come on ..."

"Well ... er ... what I *really* want to know is ..."

"Well ...?"

"Where does your boyfriend buy his shirts?"

She stepped out of the way. "Okay, Mario," she said. "Let him have it ... "

"It's a pleasure ..."

"No, wait!" I yelled, as he came striding towards me. "*That* wasn't the question ...!"

But it was too late ...

I was half-aware of him taking an almighty swing on the tongs to smack me round the skull, when -

CRASH!!!

All at once — there was a sound of breaking glass behind me and I thought for a minute my head had exploded like a lightbulb ...

When I opened my eyes, I assumed I was still intact, because whatever had disturbed the murder scene had caused Mario to drop the tongs in fright ...

Unable, as I was, to see what was behind me, I watched instead a look of horror unfold on both their faces:

Suddenly, an enormous body lurched out of the dark, brushed past my left leg, careered straight into the would-be murderer and *grappled* him to the floor ... *as result of which, Hetty dropped the flashlight in shock and sent it clattering across the stonework, plunging the whole area into near-darkness ...*

An ensuing scream of Sicilian origin sparked off a train of confused activity around me, climaxing with a mad scramble for safety in which — on the crest of a mis-fire from Hetty's gun — the pair of them legged it like *Concorde* had just flown up their arse ...

Movement and scuffling followed, as the cause of the intrusion disappeared and then reappeared, bringing with it the flashlight.

It then proceeded to sit down on the floor and inspect the light by shining it into *its* face.

Then *it* discarded the light — seeing, presumably, nothing of interest there.

It was the Mutant.

For a minute, I wondered whether he'd come to return the compliment and release me from my chains, but it didn't take me long to realise that there'd been no advance planning to his actions.

Why?

Because the Mutant was pissed.

Completely and utterly *drunk.*

Arseholed.

Well alight.

Tanked up like a bumper car.

Five bags of confetti to a prial of Arabs.

A bit squiffy.

Out-to-lunch.

Raking in the winnings to an empty wind sock.

Damaged.

Stoned.
Hammered.
Zonked.

I looked down to find him flat out on his back with an upright bottle of *Froth* standing on his chest and several more – *some empty, some full* – all scattered around him on the floor.

When he'd crashed into Mario, it probably wasn't intentional.

Bit by bit, he began to stagger to his feet, simultaneously embarking upon a burping and farting spree of such alternate rapidity that he was repeating and backfiring like a box of percussion caps.

And *that* wasn't all ...

At some point during this exhibition, he grabbed hold of an adjacent chain to my own and started to swing around in great loops, continuing to fire and boom like an Ak-Ak gun...

"Look," I said (trying to address his form as he came and went), "I appreciate you saving my life tonight, but I'm not hanging around down here for *fun*. Can't you *do* something ..."

Like *he'd* done earlier, I rattled my chain to emphasise my request.

This brought him swinging to a halt just in front of me, and I saw that puzzled expression come into his ruby-red eyes again.

He *appeared* to be trying to *think* ...

Finally, he reached over, pulled my chain towards him and ... *tipped the remainder of his beer down my throat.*

Well, it was a timely livener, but not a long-term solution to my situation.

I began to fear that he didn't have the capacity to help me ... *until he confounded those fears by jumping down and galloping over towards the hook on the wall ...*

Craning my neck round to follow his progress, I thought he might just be on the verge of cracking the case when he stopped dead and looked round into the dark:

I swear I could see the hairs on the back of his neck stand on end ...

Suddenly, he tore off in the opposite direction, and no amount of yelling on my part brought him back.

I gathered *somebody* must be coming, because he'd already demonstrated his aural superiority in the vicinity of the drinks cabinet earlier on. *He'd sure known when Simon had been on his way, long before I'd ever heard him.*

So I waited, and waited, and ...

As I looked out across the indoor night, the temperature dropped.

...

I watched for signs, like footsteps or voices or torch-beams, but there was nothing.

The only change was the sudden cold – as though somebody had opened a door somewhere, and left it open.

I hung there shivering in the dark, looking down at the ray from Hetty's discarded flashlight as it lit up an arc of space in front of me like a dimmed spotlight illuminating the stage in a dark theatre.

Despite the icy temperature, I could feel beads of sweat forming on my face...

CHAPTER 42
ADVERSE WEATHER CONDITIONS
IN THE BASEMENT

Dark and still

Somewhere off in the recesses of the maze, the squall began.

The wind came first, harbinger of a storm:

The sound it makes gives the impression it is travelling in along the furthest edges and filling up every space like rushing water; then the process is repeated and repeated again along an ever-decreasing route until it seems to be circling the nearest walls, arches and columns to the centre.

Minute particles of frost form on my clothes and cling to my flesh as I watch the stage intently:

A handful of dirt kicked up from the floor is the first sign of movement, the first sign it has arrived ...

The iron chains stir and begin to rattle, and a storm of dust whips into the air as the gale hits the centre from all directions at once;

The smell:

Borne in on the wind, it is the same sickly-sweet odour from the back of Adolphus Flite's caravan; and it carries with it the same disease of foreboding that spreads just ahead of an encounter with his hounds ...

The whole cellar is now one huge cold zone, like the inside of a refrigerator or a cold store, but the atmosphere is far from placid: currents of icy air rip across the stone, howl around the uprights and cut through the arches;

The chains are now swinging so violently that the adjacent one crashes me across the face, and my own halter strains on its hook as my body is blown sideways on a carpet of air.

There is so much fast-flying dust I can barely keep my eyes open.

Next comes a whole cacophany of noise which explodes around me – first wolves and dogs and hunting horns – but nothing is there – then marching feet and train wheels echoing on the stone and cries of help and the sound of human wailing and moaning ...

In the midst of all this, the young dark-haired intruder from my room came into view, clutching at a pillar and trying to fight the gale ...

When she caught sight of me, she let go her grip, tumbled across and grabbed hold of my leg to stop herself being blown further backwards ...

"Oi!" I yelled out in pain. "Do you mind ...!"

"Who *are* you?!" she shouted above the roar. "And what's happening here...?!"

"I might ask *you* the same question ...!"

"Speak!"

"I've no idea what's going on! And I don't really want to hang around to find out! Can you get these *manacles* off ...?!"

"I'll try ..." she said, barely audible now above the increasing noise.

She tried to do it by clambering over me and, even though she was quite small, the added weight made me gasp out loud and almost caused me to black out ...

"Can't you lower me down first?!!!" I shouted. "It's all attached to a hook on the wall ...!"

"If I let go, I'll *lose* you ...!"

"Can't you *climb* over there ...?!"

As she attempted this feat, she kept talking:

"Who *put* you here?! Was it Flite?!"

"Flite?!" I shouted, trying to make myself heard above the increasingly fast windspeed, interspersed with the sounds of running engines, gunfire, more marching. "*Adolf* Flite?! No ! It was my *sister* ...!"

"Adolphus Flite ...!" she called back. "*Phoasdul Letif* ...!"

"*What*?!!!" I yelled. "*What* did you say ...?!"

Just then she slipped, and I felt the chain jerk on its hook ...

Craning my neck round, I found she'd fallen and was desperately trying to cling by her fingertips to the cracks between the flagstones. I could see she was shouting something, but I couldn't hear the words ...

She quickly lost the battle to hang on, half-stumbling to her feet in the face of an indoor hurricane which drove her remorselessly back into the mouth of the dark.

The spotlight is still empty, but something is surely coming ...

A piece of paper suddenly flew into my face from nowhere and stuck tight, cutting off my air supply for several dramatic seconds while it induced a delusion of smothering ... *before the whirlwind ripped it away again.*

The *shock* was enough to kill me ...

Gasping for breath, I watched it flapping about wildly in the crosscurrents, joined by thousands more pieces swooping and darting through the air, stalling in the light, dancing across the stage like a mad paper opera.

I looked on astonished at the demented shapes – white paper, coloured paper, pages from old magazines and newspapers, printed in all languages and none.

And then, just as quickly as they come, they vanish. The wind dies down slightly, as though to take a breath, and ...

Suddenly there was an enormous roar and explosion of force as though a Giant had spat out in fury ... *and the whole basement was full of tiny frogs falling from above* – all alive – *croaking and squealing, some of them landing on me for a few seconds before being blown away again on their mad flight to oblivion ...*

My body was now at an almost perpetual angle to the vertical, buffeted on the slipstream, and it was only the strength of my chain that kept me from being torn away;

More dust; clouds of ash and choking powdered bonemeal, followed in quick succession by mud and grime splashing erratically through the air, and blood, spattering the walls in fine spray showers ...

At the height of this deluge, came a long, agonised cry from somewhere off in the maze:

Almost in slow-motion, Trevor appeared in the spotlight, frozen in the act of trying to pull his gun from his coat, looking back with terror-filled eyes at some as-yet unseen pursuer ...

But the gusting wind became so strong that it billowed out his coat and lifted him bodily in the air, whipping him head-over-heels in an aerial somersault, after which he seemed to linger, suspended, before being gathered again and hurled through space at a phenomenal speed and away into the darkness.

He hadn't seen me.

I couldn't have *helped him* anyway ...

Moments later, the tongs leapt into the air as though they'd been snatched by an unseen hand, flying past my chin and almost accomplishing on their own what they'd failed to do with Mario directing them, and the flashlight shot up and danced around like a disco light made of candyfloss before crashing to bits on an upright. The beer bottles, too, rose up in a line and smashed into the ceiling, one after the other, and the brazier tumbled and scattered its coals across flagstones beginning to rupture at the edges as the pressure cooker earth beneath them began to spew out its secrets in fountains of filth – like a random guard of honour for *that* which finally, at last, came:

Sounds of wheels screeching, animals whining, whip cracking the air ... coming closer in the dark, but bringing its own light ...

It travelled across my vision like a half-formed moving negative film – a carriage drawn by a team of dappled horses – framed in the flickering light, travelling at incredible speed: *the vehicle is only half-materialised but the power is not just visual; it is Adolphus Flite, not driving or sitting in the coach, but sitting in my head, his hands – claws – hands – reaching out to touch the inside of my self ...*

His lips move and the words form carefully: Tomorrow Is Midnight. Tomorrow Is the End. Tomorrow We Come Full Circle. We Will Be No More Forever ...

But I can *also* feel something else ...

He is hurried now and beginning to recede, for I can sense *fear:*

Of what? Another presence? The approach of the day ...?

There is a definite waning of his power, however temporary ...

The image and the noises fade away, and somewhere close by there is a sound like that of a coffin-lid creaking shut.

Almost as an afterthought, there was a sudden explosion of thousands and thousands of nuts and bolts flying through the air and clattering at high velocity off of the stonework in all directions ...

I *flinch* violently – *one direct hit would kill me as sure as any bullet* – but, miraculously, I am untouched.

The wind dies quickly and I float back down to the vertical.

And then everything is still again.

And sunlight begins to flood into the furthest recesses of the cellar — through cracks and gaps and a far-off sunken dungeon window.

I close my eyes, exhausted, for just a few seconds, until I become aware that somebody is standing right in front of me ...

CHAPTER 43
A GAOL OF SUNLIGHT

"Well," she said, "Look who it ain't ..."

I raised an eyelid.

"Close the door," I said. "You're letting a draught in ..."

"You're in no position to get smart, wise guy ..."

"Hello, Blondie," I said. "You're a sight for sore eyes. Let us down, will you?"

"I ought to let you hang there till your shoes come back in fashion ..."

"What's wrong with my shoes?"

She sneered and looked fit to spit. "Give me one good reason why I should help *you* out, of *all* people?"

"Come on," I said. "Don't give me a hard time. I've had a trying night ..."

"Dexter Kitehawk. The *big* hero. I didn't notice you falling over yourself to help *me* out last night ..."

"I thought you'd vanished into thin air. I was *that* scared ..."

"You know," she said, "I must have been the only person to come here with twenty-six invites, who had to crawl in through the sewer entrance ten miles away ..."

"What happened?" I asked, intrigued.

"I got caught in a trap when them cuffs sprang a leak, and spent the next five minutes swinging upside-down from the trees on the end of a rope ..."

I couldn't help but be amused at the irony of Blondie being snared by a man-trap. It didn't sound entirely *likely* to me ...

"Then I got dropped into a hole in the ground, which just so happened to be a tunnel into this dump ..."

"I couldn't *see* anything, Blondie," I said. "*Honest.* I had your tights stuffed over my hooter, didn't I ...?"

She walked round behind me.

"Yeah," she said, "And what have you done with them? They were genuine *Delta Nylon* originals. Cost me a fortune ..."

That's interesting, I thought, as she unhooked me. *Very* interesting ...

I landed with a bump.

My arms reached the ground before I did ...

"Right," I bluffed, "What's next on the agenda?"

"What have you found out?" she demanded to know.

"Nothing I didn't already know," I said, expounding my knowledge. "The *usual* stuff. Adolf Flite is planning something big for tonight. Tonight is the night his *master* plan – whatever *that* is – comes to fruition. He's got a lot of family support here, but there's little evidence yet of the usual trappings of the Corporation – stormtroopers, neo-Nazi thugs etc – at least, not on *his* side ..."

She went to interject - *but I decided to carry on.* "... I *have*, however, discovered a few things I *didn't* know when you and I last spoke: *viz,* there's an archaeological dig about to begin in the sub-cellar, a chapel – *dedicated to Old Nick* – all set up for a service and waiting for the next live animal sacrifice, a hairy Mutant roaming around loose as drunk as a skunk, and a Headless Madman patrolling the upper corridors of the East Wing. *To top all this,* a woman claiming to be my long lost sister has turned up with a Sicilian bandit of no discernible intellect and questionable taste in shirts. The pair of them are short on temper, fuses, humour – and, *apparently,* cash. *Oh yes, and I nearly forgot –* there's also some kind of phantom ancestral Flite answering to the name *Adolphus,* who flies through the air on an invisible coach and horses accompanied by a recorded soundtrack of several centuries-worth of human misery and suffering. If the racket he makes was his only crime, I'd know a good place where he could get a residency every night of the week and the audiences wouldn't notice the difference, but as it is..."

"Have you *finished?*" she enquired.

"As a matter of fact ... *no.* I've *also* ascertained that an escaped lunatic from an asylum for the criminally insane – I nearly said *'inane'* there, by mistake – is on his way here now looking for a radical alternative treatment programme and could be arriving with the morning milk. And *that,* I think, is the state of play at the present moment ..."

"I ought to sock you on the jaw ..."

"It's *true,*" I said. "Didn't you see any of what was going on down here?"

"All I saw was you swinging from the rafters, Buster ..."

"Well," I said, "Ask *Trevor,* then. In the midst of all *that* lot, he came flying through the air backwards doing about a hundred-and-fifty in the fast lane ..."

"Trevor *who?*"

I was beginning to regain some feeling in my arms, and so I dusted myself down.

"Anyway," I said, "I'm just going to have a look round the back recesses before breakfast. I swear I heard a coffin door being closed from the *inside* just before you arrived, and I shall be very interested to get hold of a list of anybody who's died recently ..."

She shrugged her shoulders and followed me.

I thought for a minute she was taking the piss ...

The subtle intrusion of daylight did not penetrate very far in the direction I was going, and so I salvaged my blunderbus lighter on the way.

Not that I could get it to *light,* mind you.

"Where did you *find* all those invites, anyway?" I said. "Or shouldn't I ask...?"

"Where else?" she said. "On my doormat ..."

"Eh?"

"I answered a chain letter ..."

"Really ...?"

I was still furiously pulling on the trigger and fumbling my way round one of the damp arches when I came up against an obstruction ...

"You didn't get my shipment of Polish beer as well, did you?" I said. "You *know*, by *mistake* ...?"

Ignoring this compromising teaser, she handed me an unlit torch from a holder on the wall.

"Here ..." she said.

Before I had a chance to interrogate her further, the blunderbus suddenly struck gas, the torch flared up, and ... I marched round the front to inspect my catch:

"*Strewth ...!*" I wheezed.

There, straight in *front* of me was ...

Adolphus Flite.

Or at *least*, his skeletal *remains*, hung up inside a museum display case like an exhibit in the Palermo catacombs.

There was only one article of clothing adorning his frame, and it was this that I knew him by:

His *hat.*

Deprived of any hair or flesh to bouy it up, it had slipped down over his face, obscuring his eyes.

Oh, and the ruby ring, hanging on a curled talon ...

More on the hat.

It was a tall, black, Funeral Director's jolly topper.

I extinguished the torch ...

"Hey, what are you doing ...?"

"We don't need it, *look* ..."

There was a tiny shaft of daylight shining down from a vent somewhere near the ceiling behind me, and it fell dead centre through his ribs into the space where his heart should have been, illuminating instead the hollow void. His bones hung limp and discoloured, dusty – powdery – with age.

"I wonder what *he* died of ...?" she mumured.

"He's not dead," I went to say, "At *least* – "

Distracted by scuffling to my rear, I swung round to find somebody coming at me with a sharpened stake ...

"ROOOOOAAAAARRRRR ...!!!"

I instinctively ducked out of the way as he lunged past me ... only to watch him crash straight into the front of the tomb with his gruesome weapon, showering all three of us with exploding glass ...

CRASH!!!

"Hey!!! Jump *back* Jack ...!!!" shouted Blondie, as she twirled round to protect her face.

"Gotcha!" he growled.

Startled and shocked, Blondie stood there shaking her hair of glinting shards ...

"What the hell are you trying to do ...?" she was mumbling.

With some difficulty, the intruder finally stepped back out from the shattered cabinet and left the wooden stake embedded straight through Adolphus's heart.

"It's a little irregular," he said, attempting to recompose himself, "To have any non-full members present at the *denouement* of one of the *Un-Dead* but, under the circumstances, I think we can overlook it this time ..."

"*Un-Dead?*" queried Blondie. (She was looking at Adolphus when she said it, but she was looking at *me* when she answered herself). "I reckon you got the *wrong* guy ..."

Disregarding her thesis, Wilbur Beans removed a notebook from his top pocket and began flipping through the pages ...

"Now, it's a funny thing," he said at length, "But I can't find this creature on my checklist. This in *itself* is odd, since I compiled the list myself using every authoritative reference work on the subject. He does not appear in any conventional compendium of vampires ..."

"No?" I said, expecting Blondie to have something to say on the subject.

Apparently mistaken, I looked round to find her taking it all in with her mouth slightly *agape* ...

"What's the matter with *you?*" I demanded to know, but since it had little visible effect on her demeanour, I turned my attention back to a man suddenly preoccupied in performing a biopsy on his own beard ...

"Well," he said, as he finally extracted a rogue splinter, "Nice work, Dr Kitehawk ..." (*here, I think I detected a raising of Blondie's eyebrows at the designation 'Doctor'*) "... Without your valuable assistance in leading us to this place, we may never have stumbled upon this mystery. I expect by the time the weekend is over you will have helped contribute significantly to the body of known knowledge in this field and I shall be recommending your acceptance to full membership at the next AGM. In the meantime, I shall be off to hunt for a spot of breakfast. Hungry work at the best of times. Anybody care to join me ...?"

"Did you say he was a *vampire?*" Blondie suddenly interjected.

"Too early to tell, but we should know by sundown tonight. Unfortunately, I arrived a little too late this morning to make a clear diagnosis or a positive identification. This is work best done during the hours around midnight ..."

And on *that* note, he upped sticks and went.

Three seconds later, Blondie fainted, and I stood staring down at her slumped body like a half-wit in an encyclopaedia factory ...

She was out cold.

Which was a pity, really, because I knew absolutely sod-all about First Aid. I didn't know what to do for the best, really – kiss her, kick her, calm her down or call an ambulance. *A kiss of life on those lips could have been the kiss-of-death for Yours Truly.* I'd have probably fallen through to Calcutta, the gap was so wide ...

"Blondie, *Blondie* ...!" I started to yell into her lugholes, half-lifting her head up and intermittently slapping her round the chops.

She was *alive*, at least.

Well, she was *breathing* – if that's the same thing – and *mumbling*, incoherently, as she began to come round ...

In a surprising moment of lucidity, she suddenly sat bolt upright and said:

"Did you say somebody was planning to dig up the cellar?"

"I did," I affirmed. "But not in *recent* memory ..."

"Who are they?" she demanded to know. "What's their connection? What are they up to?"

"There's no need to shout," I said. "I'm not deaf. I heard they were building an extension of the M25 ..."

"Here?" she said, taking it all in again. "Where?"

"Straight down your throat, according to the site manager ..."

I don't know why I said it really, especially after the kind of night I'd had ...

She gave me that sock on the jaw she'd been threatening, and even from the reclining position she packed so much punch that I went kranging backwards into one of the stone arches and dropped into the dream zone she'd just vacated.

Deserted by my erstwhile companion, I woke up alone in the shadow of the great broken glass coffin and tried to get up off the floor, rubbing the bump on the back of my head (where I'd hit the wall) and the bump on the front of my head (where Blondie had clocked me one), feeling like an eggbox on legs.

In the hope of finding a quick way out of the dungeon, I searched for the source of light shining onto the corpse and discovered an opening to a shaft set into the stonework of a nearby corner recess. It began around shoulder height and tunnelled upwards at a slight diagonal angle into the wall, narrowing – funnel shaped – to a small vertical arch at its summit.

Making all the wrong assumptions, I climbed into the aperture and levered myself along the slimy surface until I reached the vent, which – to my disappointment – I found blocked by iron bars.

Beyond the vent – and beneath it – was the bed of the moat surrounding the castle, filled with early morning mist, rather than water. It was dry now, and dry for centuries, probably, but the cellars at one time would have been flooded by such an overflow point, and this may have served to explain the lingering damp everywhere.

Such were the inconsequential details preoccupying my thoughts when I heard the sound of an *engine* overhead ...

Pushing my face through the bars, I looked up through a break in the land-cloud to see a First World War *Storch* circling the towers above: *badly.*

In the ensuing seconds, when it disappeared from view, I lay there complacently listening out for it, unable to equate its position with the erratic stop-start pattern of its engine, until ... *it suddenly crash-landed into the moat right in front of me, sending a miniature atomic bomb of black burning smoke straight down the express route to my lungs while a two-hundred-ton flying pancake of heavyweight mud slapped me across the face and sealed up the exits.*

In *fact*, its wing almost cut off my outstretched head as it skidded on past and crashed into the lower ground floor of what looked like the derelict remains of the West Wing ...

Now I know why it's *derelict*, I thought ...

In a matter of moments, the pilot had staggered out of the cockpit with a hunting rifle in one hand, and hauling a live squealing *pig* behind him with the other.

This latter he dragged off through the mud with him and out of sight somewhere.

I recognised the pilot – *it was Tommy* – but I didn't immediately recognise what he was *up* to, until I remembered the carcass hanging in the chapel upstairs...

I soon began to feel inexplicably uneasy despite the daylight, and decided that finding a way out from the whole subterranean tomb of the *Schloss* cellars was an urgent priority.

Spitting out mud, moss and slime, and coughing up black balls of burnt petrol as I went, I slid back down the shaft and landed bang on my feet in front of the shattered cabinet, inches from the stake which was still poking out of Adolphus's chest at an angle diagonally above the horizontal.

He looked a little like he'd been speared and rendered immobile by a rogue javelin from the Munich Olympics.

Not only *this*, but the force of the impaling had caused his hat to tip even further forward:

If he really is a vampire, I thought, *he's going to wake up tonight with a chronic case of indigestion and more than a little difficulty in carrying out his threat to me ...*

It was only *then*, that it struck me the shaft of light aimed at his heart was no longer there. *Sensing it shining harmlessly onto my back, I realised with a start that I was obscuring it myself ...*

Suddenly, his hat tipped right over and fell to the floor, leaving me face-to-face with his cavernous eye-sockets:

I wanted to step aside, but I found it difficult to move – *fascinated by those eyes that seemed no longer black, empty, hollow.* They seemed to stir with life, with *intelligence* ...

Something was *moving* inside that skull – like worms slithering around ... like gums beginning to flesh out the teeth, and hair forming on the scalp. The mouth appeared to be framing a *smile,* and ...

The Cold Zone.

I realised *then* that it passed from floor to ceiling right through that very spot, the coffin standing dead *centre* inside it ...

Summoning the will from somewhere, I stepped aside and returned the imprisoning light to his heart, thankful as the moment passed.

CHAPTER 44
CHARADES

As soon as I stumbled across anything looking remotely like a meaningful junction in the basement tunnel system, I hoofed it up an adjacent staircase only to find myself back inside a web of narrow passages. I'd long since lost my sense of direction and had absolutely no idea *which* wing – if any – of the castle I was in, under or above.

Nestling in a recess of one such passage was an old gramophone with one of those *His Master's Voice* dogs curled up next to the cone ...

When I paused to light my blunderbus, I discovered a dusty 78 record sitting on the turntable, a vampish pre-war Benny Goodman classic of the kind designed to turn even the most respectable dancer into a fraught floor-tripper with paranoid cheekbones.

So I gave the handle a good cranking and lifted the needle onto the disc.

Then I started to *dance* ...

And it was in *this* fashion that I found my way back into an inhabited area of the Castle.

Unbeknown to me – driven temporarily oblivious to my surroundings by the music, as I was – *the floor began to gyrate 180 degrees, depositing me on the other side of the wall slap-bang in the middle of somebody's bedroom suite ...*

I only realised that the decor had changed, when a *voice* suddenly accosted me:

"That was quick!" she said. (*She* being the occupant of the room I'd just gatecrashed with my accompanying raucous soundtrack)

So embarrassed was I, that I instantaneously crash-landed out of a forward squirl and clattered the needle across the record ...

"Er ..." I squawked.

She was sitting in front of a dressing table on the opposite side of the room, and showed very little surprise as she observed my unorthodox arrival by means of the view in her dresser mirror. She was young to middle aged, had short auburn hair, and was sitting there combing it.

I needn't have got flustered.

She hadn't so much as bothered to *turn* her head.

"*Was* it?" I said. "I suppose it's all relative ..."

She swung round suddenly ...

"Oh, I'm sorry!" she said. "I thought you were Room Service ..."

"Afraid not ..." I said. (*I marched in to give the room the once-over*). "I'm one of the guests ..."

She looked vaguely familiar, from the train or somewhere (Hell, probably), but I couldn't place her.

"I expect you're here for the Reading of the Will," she said, betraying a momentary flash of excitement. *Not a word about who I was, or what I was doing dancing into her room at that time of the morning via the tradesman's entrance etc etc.*

The Reading of the Will?

I thought about that one for, possibly, a few seconds, before responding in the negative and marching on towards the door.

"No, I'm sorry," I said. "This case is far too complicated already. Got any idea where the Dining Room is?"

When she turned back to her mirror, I opened up a fraction and peeped out into the hallway:

Finding the coast clear, I was just about to bid good-day to my new acquaintance and go in search of the Breakfast Bar, when the approach of footsteps and loud voices gave me a fit of nerves and I dived back inside and slammed the door shut again ...

In my panic, I completely forgot about the secret passage and looked around feverishly for an escape route:

Madam continued to look highly unconcerned, as she busied herself at the dresser.

My *first* thought was to climb inside the Dumb Waiter, but, just as I stuck my right foot down the shaft, I had the great misfortune to meet Her Ladyship's breakfast coming up in the opposite direction and stumbled back out into the room crunching china plates and cutlery and trampling the food underfoot ...

By the time the expected knock came, I was hopping around the carpet on one leg and trying to free the other from a plateful of scrambled eggs stuck to my shoe.

"Why don't you hide in the wardrobe?" she said, as she got up to answer the knock.

Well, it was worth a try.

So I stumbled over and peered inside:

Finding it to be a *walk-in* wardrobe, I walked in and closed the door behind me.

Thereafter, I elected to stick peeper and jug to the keyhole in alternate fashion, by which device I made out two intruders, but only up to waist height. *Who wears snakeskin shoes this time of the morning?*

I did recognise *one* of the voices – that belonging to Simon Flite – but the other was unfamiliar, and the sounds were appalingly muffled. Something about a "train", something about a "will", and something about somebody called "Delores", the latter of which I took to be the handle of the room's occupant, but I would have needed a periscope and an ear trumpet to gather more.

This became particularly crucial when one of the intruders came and stood right on the other side of the keyhole, thus obscuring my view and blocking my audio reception.

As a result of which, I decided it was high time to back off, and attempted to lose myself amongst the maze of coats and clothes that seemed to stretch all the way back to Narnia.

I confiscated a Tommy Nutter bow-tie en route, thinking it might come in handy for the Breakfast Bar.

"This is no good!" I cursed. "Where's the elastic band ...?"

Eventually, I came up against a wall of wood panelling at the back end of the wardrobe and, feeling my way around in the dark, discovered an object standing in one corner, the shape of which appeared to suggest that it was some kind of gigantic circular hat-box.

Being rather partial to hats (*and*, being only too well aware that I was currently hatless, and therefore ill-dressed for breakfast), I lit the blunderbus, lifted up the lid and peered inside:

Empty, apparently.

Sticking my arms in to rummage about, I was rather intrigued to find that, not only was there nothing in it, but that it also appeared to have no base.

By some illusion, it seemed to be deeper than the level of the floor.

In an attempt to confirm this apparent geometric oddity, I probed its exterior surface and tried to shift it, but it was stuck fast.

So I leaned right back inside until I was almost waist-deep.

I don't know, I thought, *I'm sure I can hear voices in here ...*

All of a sudden, the wardrobe door sprung open behind me and a row of fur coats concertinaed into my back ... but it *wasn't* a *box*, and there was no bottom to it ...

"Oh my Gawd!" I yelled out, as I fell headfirst down a dark chute and went sliding away with my voice echoing and following after me ...

How much further could I fall, and where did it end up? A disposal bay ... *or Hell itself?*

With the sound of voices growing louder and the sudden appearance of light coming up fast beneath me, the chute suddenly curved violently and I shot straight out of the gaping wide-open mouth of a hollow tiger's head hunting trophy nailed to the Dining Room wall – *looking to those seated below, I presumed, as though the beast had just spewed up its last meal ...*

But it didn't end there. I was travelling at such velocity, and such a trajectory, that I skimmed aerodynamically along the surface of the dining table, scattering plates of this and that left and right as I went, covering the assembled diners in all kinds of muck and slosh from the best the Flite's kitchen had to offer, before finally sliding to a halt and coming to rest with my nose firmly planted in a great bowl of *sauerkraut*.

I *knew* it was *sauerkraut*, because I had no option but to taste it.

It wasn't *lager*, anyway.

Put it *that* way.

"Er ..." I said, as I rattled and crashed about in the broken crockery and tried to sit up or stand up or roll off the table as gracefully as possible, "I hope I'm not dressed too formally ..."

"What is the *meaning* of this!" demanded some old gent, whose face – *covered, as it was, in tomato juice* – just happened to be the first I saw when I chanced to look up.

I didn't immediately respond, though.

I looked the other way, instead.

Meeting as fierce a face on that side of the table (*albeit of the opposite gender*) I decided it was politic to get the hell off of there as fast as possible, and tried to do this by climbing down onto a vacant chair next to the drenched octogenarian.

There was a noticeable silence in the room since my arrival, which was a trifle disconcerting...

Unfortunately, I accidentally stuck a foot straight down into his lap, unleashing the most dreadful squeal into the air that I'd ever heard, and although he tried desperately to get out from under me, his efforts only made things worse and had the effect of *trapping* me there ...

"No, no," I said, feverishly trying to extricate myself, "Don't get up. No need to stand on ceremony ..."

All of a sudden, a gun went off in his pocket and blew a chunk straight out of his shoe...

I looked down to find his right brogue a pile of smoking leather.

"My God, I've been shot ...!" he yelled.

I decided to forego breakfast. "Stop complaining," I said. "It's only tomato juice..."

"I ... I've been shot. With a ... *tomato* !"

So saying, he hurled me off with superhuman strength and stood up to inspect the damage.

"Anyway," I said, addressing my next remarks to the shocked diners generally, "You shouldn't have any more trouble with the phone. I've rigged up an extension from the shower socket to the microwave, and a three-way coil loop from the lightning conductor to the gas mains in 'D' Wing. Who said the age of reliable repairmen was dead? I *would* leave a calling card but I had to chuck 'em all at one of Adolf's rottweilers on the way in or it would have had me for lunch. If anything else goes wrong, don't call me – *I'll* call *you* ..."

And, with a couple of butlers trying to examine the extent of the old boy's injury, I turned to leave.

However, I didn't get far towards the door before a voice from the table called out to me in the following manner:

"Why, it's Mr *Oatcake*, isn't it ...?"

When I paused to turn round and squint down the aisle, I discovered the cheery face of Candida Flite leaning out and smiling.

She *waved* at me as well.

"That's Haute-*Cooke*," I said, backpedalling. "Oat-*Cake* has an entirely different connotation in England ..."

"Really ...?" she said.

I wandered along and drew up a vacant pew next to her.

"Yes," I said. "Oat-*Cake* is what horses drop great piles of all over the roads..."

"You are a dreadful man, Mr Haute-Cooke," she said. "I shall have to do my best to keep my niece well away from you – we wouldn't want her to take you seriously ..."

With a bit of a start I realised I'd forgotten about Heidi and was at a loss momentarily to know how to respond.

"And where *is* she this morning," I asked innocently. "Not hungry ...?"

"We haven't seen her today," she said. "She often sleeps late ..."

That was no end of comfort. I feared the worst, but until I knew more, I decided it was best to keep shtoom. Heidi might well be sleeping *particularly* late that day...

"Join me for breakfast?" she asked, changing the subject herself.

"Why not," I said. "I hope I'm not too late. I did my best to get here as soon as I could ..."

"Not at all. Did you sleep well?"

"Like a log," I said, checking the state of my cranial bumps and bruises. "... *Actually*, no. The pillows were a trifle too soft for my taste and the conditions a bit cramped – being a veteran of the Great Outdoors – though I cannot fault the choice of *room*, from the point of view of the *view* ..."

"Poor man," she said. "I shall have a word with Simon when I see him. He's been up all night, working. It runs in the family ..."

"What's that?" I asked, curious.

"Being nocturnal ..."

"You surprise me," I lied.

"Glass of water?" she offered.

"Not when I'm on duty," I said. "Got any lager ...?"

"Tell me," she drivelled on, "What are your plans for the day?"

"Oi! Excuse me, cock!" I yelled at a passing waiter. "Sling us a plate of bacon and beans, will ya, when you've got a minute ...?"

"Why, Mr Oat-Cock ..." she went to say.

"That's *Cooke*," I emphasised again. "Haute-*Cooke*, as in ..."

"I know," she beamed. "It's hyphenated ..."

Distracting myself momentarily from this riveting conversation, I scanned up and down the breakfast table in order to ascertain who was present.

The old gent had been helped outside by the staff, and something like a semblance of normality had returned to the proceedings. I couldn't see anybody I recognised, and people were beginning to drift out.

"Where's that delightful character Tommy this morning?" I enquired, as a well-groomed waiter delivered my order. "Get tired of life in the fast lane, did he?"

"He's been such a godsend, that man. I don't know how our family coped before he arrived ..."

"Yes, yes," I said, cramming forkful after forkful of fried breakfast into my gob. "I can *see* that ..."

"So *useful* ..."

"Yes, yes ..."

"Butler, barman, general handyman ..."

"Go on ..." I said, thinking, *Butler, barman* ... and head *herdsman* to a mob of ritual funny-farmers ...

"And so *loyal* ..."

"Mm, yes ..." I mouthed, unable to actually make any sound come out there was so much nosh wedged into it.

"*But* – " (here, she suddenly grabbed hold of my eating arm) "One thing Tommy will not lower himself to do ..."

"What's that?" I mouthed. "Have a wash ...?"

"*Wait at table*. Understandable, really – a man of *his* breeding. Do you know, that every morning at the crack of dawn, that man *personally* catches and slaughters a live pig with his own *bare* hands ...?"

"It's no *secret*, then ...?" I said, after I'd finally managed to swallow some of the backlog.

"Oh no," she said. "And that's why you won't find *him* in the dining room *this* time of the morning ..."

"No?" I said. *I finally extracted my arm and got ready to poke it in the direction of my throat.* "Where *is* he, then?"

"In the kitchens ..."

"Eh?" I said. "*Why* ...?"

"Didn't I *tell* you?" she said. "He's the Head *Chef* ..."

After I'd crawled under the table and sicked up, I had this overwhelming desire to get some sleep, but the noise and clatter of the household staff clearing away the breakfast dishes prevented me from successfully grasping the opportunity of an impromptu slumber on the dining room floor and left me considering other options.

My *first* mistake – *after slithering out from under the table and, without noticing, straight underneath a used dishes trolley* – was to try and stand up without looking.

Being unable to fathom the nature of my obstruction, I ended up crawling on all fours for some distance with the trolley balanced on my back like a tortoise-shell.

Unfortunately, I ran out of steam before reaching my destination and belly-flopped back onto the deck, allowing the trolley to crash down a fraction later, shattering everything on it in one go.

By the time I'd worked out what had happened and crawled out from beneath, the wreckage of the plates was raining down on all sides onto the floor around me ...

Staggering to my feet, I found myself, for the third time that morning, crunching around in a sea of broken china.

Two waiters were standing to one side and observing me with apparent disinterest – *waiting, I supposed, for me to vacate the scene before moving in to clear up*. I couldn't tell from their inscrutable expressions what they thought of my performance, but I'd obviously interrupted their morning's work and set it back considerably ...

"Bomber Harris," I said, extending my hand. "False alarm. Thought I saw some Dresden ..."

"*Bitte?*" replied the chattier one, without accepting my proffered hand (I'd retracted it, anyway).

"Not really," I said. "We *won*, didn't we ...?"

"*Bitte* ...?" he repeated, while his colleague accompanied him with a suitably blank stare.

"Oh, I *see*," I said, thinking they must be offering me a drink. "No, I don't think so. I'll have a *lager*, though ..."

I left them to ponder that for a few minutes, while I took some time out to plan my itinerary for the day.

"What's everyone doing for laughs this morning?" I said at length.

They obviously didn't understand the Queen's, and so I decided take my leave.

"Don't worry about the mess," I said. "The *Yanks* are coming to tidy up later. After it's all *over*, that is ..."

I wandered out into the foyer and stood at the foot of a great palatial staircase carpeted in red, which led up to the first landing.

Once I'd decided that there wasn't much in the way of alternatives, I took my chances and began to ascend, taking great care to tread a path close to the banister and away from the edges of the pile, with my footsteps clacking on the bare stone margin as I went.

During my ascent, I pondered on just how much the Castle Froth resembled the Finsbury Park *Astoria*.

Except that, here, all the turrets were on the outside.

On reaching the summit, I veered to the left and put my jug to the first door I came to, which was ajar ...

Well, there was a single funereal voice droning on in there somewhere, certainly, though the only words I could make out were those that were repeated at intervals – *codicil, beneficiaries, estate* – and *Flite*, of course.

I pushed the door open a little further, and poked my hooter round the gap:

The scene that greeted me was of an array of stiff backs in upright chairs, all gathered in a semi-circle around a solicitor who was holding court and juggling a pile of documents as he went.

My intrusion caused him to pause and look up, cueing his audience to turn round and follow suit, as a result of which I was instantly assaulted by a host of raised eyebrows, raised and lowered spectacles, frowns, grimaces, half-smiles, sympathetic squints, looks of curiosity, expressions ranging anything from "Can I help you?" to "I'd like to help you to fuck off back where you came from as quickly as possible," and an unnerving deadpan glare from the woman I took to be Delores which said, in effect, "Do you know you've got half-a-ton of *sauerkraut* plastered all over your head ...?"

It was a sombre gathering, and I stood there in the silence, smiling like a half-bright.

"Somebody died?" I asked, in a tone of casual innocence.

All of a sudden, I received a tap on the shoulder from behind and edged back out of the door to find a butler standing there ...

"I'm looking for the Acid-House Rave-Up," I said.

"Refreshments are being served in the Morning Room," he said. "Coffee, tea, toast, buttered scones, *croissants*, *petits-fours* and Heidelberg fairy cakes are available ..."

"Yes," I said. "But is it a disco?"

"There is, I believe," he said, after some thought, "A little light music to be had after eleven am ..."

"Any flashing lights?"

He paused again. "The sun has a habit of reflecting off of the silverware in erratic patterns this time of day. Would you care to follow me ..."

"Very well," I said. "It's a start ..."

Keeping a few decent paces to the rear as I trailed him across the landing, I noticed that he very much resembled an English butler – especially in his walk.

"You're not a Kraut, are you?" I enquired.

He only half looked round, and he didn't bother to pause from his stride. "Sir ...?" he said.

"I say," I repeated (in case he had a *jug* defect), "You're not a *Kraut*, are you?"

"I am of ... *cosmopolitan* origins ..."

"Oh," I said, puzzled. "So you *are* a Kraut, then ...?"

He stopped *then*, and turned to give me his full-frontal:

"*Cosmopolitan* origins, Sir," he said again. "This does not *necessarily* mean I am *German* ..."

"Cosmopolitan?" I said, mystified. "You're from outer space, then?"

"No ..."

"A male model ...?"

"My mother," he affirmed at length, "Was a travelling ladies' maid of Welsh descent, originally. My father was a Latvian dentist ..."

We resumed our trek along the corridor.

"Do you know," I said, "I've got so much metal in my mouth that I once picked up the broadcast of a heavyweight title fight in Tokyo ..."

"Indeed?" he said, eyes to the front.

"Yes," I said.

"Who won?" he asked.

"I don't know," I said. "But it did narf hurt ..."

"Oh dear," he said.

"Yes," I went on, "Due to the high mercury content of the fillings, I was unfortunate enough to contract quicksilver messenger poisoning shortly after the final bell and it spread to my memory. I can't remember anything about it at all..."

I don't believe he commented on this revelation.

"In fact," I added, "I can't even remember where we're going. Can you throw any light on the subject?"

"Indeed I can ..."

A door loomed up in front of us, and he went to open it ...

"Hang on," I said, restraining him. "I just want to powder my nose ..."

(Having spotted an ornate full-length mirror in an adjacent alcove, I stuck my snout round in search of a badly needed *sauerkraut*-damage report, amongst other things ...)

"*Strewth* ..." I wheezed. *I'd never seen anything like it.*

The butler stood politely to one side, feigning indifference, while I waited some moments for the shock to subside.

"Handsome ..." I gagged. *I looked like somebody had dumped a stack of shit from the clouds and put hat-and-coat on it.* "Of course, it's a very strange coincidence, don't you think," I said, babbling away on automatic-pilot, "That the word *dental* is, in fact, the word *mental*, but for a single letter change ..."

"It's a point of view," he said. "Though I've always considered the reverse to be more appropriate ..."

I backed away from the mirror and gave him the benefit of a puzzled look. "Go on," I said.

"As in *non compus dentist*. Particularly appropriate in the case of my father ..."

"Did he ever have a surgery in Crowndale Road?"

"He got about a bit, certainly ..."

"He *had* to, I suppose ..."

"Quite so ..."

"I think I had a run-in with him once. Now *there's* a coincidence ..."

"He lost quite a bit of money over the years ..."

"I'm not surprised," I said. "I've still got half his mining equipment embedded in my neck somewhere. Did you know the electric chair was invented by a dentist ...?"

"Indeed I didn't ..."

"I haven't uncovered yet who invented America's other favourite execution prop, but in view of the fact that my childhood dentist tried to gas me three times, you can jump to your own conclusions ..."

"Speaking of *gas*," he said, "Perhaps you'd care for a little something before making your entrance?"

"What did you have in mind?"

He opened up the door of a grandfather clock standing close by and pulled out a couple of bottles of lager from behind the pendulum.

"I feel better already," I said. "What do they call you?"

"Leon," he replied, as he removed their tops and handed one over.

"Tell me," I said, "Just what exactly is going on in this place?"

"Something is not all it seems?" he said, replying in a disappointing manner by offering a question rather than an answer.

"Have you worked long for Herr Flite?" I probed.

He produced a business card before making his reply.

"Since this morning only. I am hired for the day ..."

ENGLISH BUTLERS IN EXILE
Reputable Agency
Bonn

"So you can't tell me what he's up to, then?"

"I'd say he's up to about three thousand marks in agency fees *so far*. We do not come *cheap*, I can assure you ..."

"No, no," I said. "What's your *remit* vis-a-vis the Grand Ball tonight?"

"Hat-taker ..."

I finished my lager, threw the empty bottle back where it had come from and caused the clock to chime twelve. "Dexter Kitehawk," I said, introducing myself formally and belching all at the same time. "And I'd be grateful if you could let me know if you see anything suspicious going on – *you know*, hats that don't quite fit, hatbands full of gelignite, trilby hats welded to their owners' skulls, reluctance to part with headware accompanied by death-threats to the domestic staff – *that* kind of thing ..."

"You're a policeman, then? A detective?"

"That's right," I said. "Scotland Yard SOD Squad – Special Operations in Deutschland ..."

"There are, of course, alternative activities available," he said, after some thought. "Herr Flite does have a rather well fitted-out gymnasium belowstairs – a facility he allows guests to partake of – and there is even an aerobics instructor on the staff, I believe ..."

I swiped the other bottle and opened the door of the Morning Room. "Not to worry," I said. "Keep in touch ..."

Homing in to a lounge chair close to my point of entry, I plonked my drink on a stand next to it, got down on all-fours and poked my head under the seat.

Considerations of who might be watching me were irrelevant at a time like this, though it was my impression that the room was only sparsely populated.

"Hello Haute-Cooke," came a voice from close by (sounding very much like Martin Flite's).

I banged my head as I stood up rather too quickly ...

"It's alright," I said. "Just checking for booby-traps ..."

"Oh?" he said, mildly puzzled (apparently).

"You can't be too careful ..."

"Afraid the chair might blow up?"

"Actually," I said, "I'm more afraid my *lager* might explode, but there you have it. It's a funny old life ..."

"Sleep well?"

"I've no idea," I said. "I was asleep at the time ..."

"Such wit ..." said Candida, who appeared on the scene with two cups of coffee – one for herself and one for Martin.

"*Wit* you call it ...?" (*This latest voice came from directly behind me, its owner having closed the Morning Room door and brought a hand down threateningly onto my shoulder ...*) "In *my* country we spell it with an *SH*, not a *W* ..."

I craned round to find the South African Secret Policeman bringing up my rear.

"Oh, *Sonny*," Candida intervened. "Leave him *alone*. I expect Mr Haute-Cooke belongs to the tradition of English Music-Hall comedians. It's the only reason I can think of why he's so perennially cheerful ..."

"I expect that's why they won the last war," offered Martin.

"*And* the one before *that* ..." I said.

"Quite ..."

"Mind if I join you?" I said, trying to sidestep the Boer's attentions. "Thought I'd just come and entertain the troops for half-an-hour ..."

"Be our guest," said Candida and Martin enthusiastically.

"Funny?" persisted my captor. "I'd like to take him down into the dungeons for half-an-hour instead. Then we'd see how *funny* he is ..."

"I don't know how you ever became an aerobics instructor," I said, as I finally squeezed out of his grip and pinched his chair. "You don't look anything like a chocolate ballpoint-pen ..."

He huffed and fumed a bit and then sat down in the chair I'd earmarked for myself when I'd first come in.

"'Ere, sling my drink over, will you? And I'll tell you a few jokes ..." I said.

"I don't think you were asleep at all last night," he declared, reluctantly passing my lager. "I think you were wandering around where you shouldn't be and up to no good ..."

"How do *you* know?"

"A few of the guests have arrived from the hotel in town this morning," said Martin. "But most will be coming on towards this evening. See anybody here you recognise from the train?"

I instinctively ducked behind my lager bottle. "I hope not ..."

"Why, Mr *Haute-Cooke* !" exclaimed Candida. "You're not on the *run*, are you?"

"No, no," I said, "But at the same time I'm not too popular with some of my former travelling companions ... friends of the Chef, mainly ..."

"He had *accomplices*, then?" she demanded to know.

"I should say he did," I affirmed. "Most of them are still at large, I hasten to add. It's one of the reasons I had to change horses in mid-stream, so to speak..."

"Do tell," she continued, conspiratorially.

I took a sip first. "Well," I said, "It's a thankless task, being a hero. I unfortunately forgot to put an *X* in the 'No Publicity' section of my ticket and, after single-handedly catching him in the act, I'm afraid my exploits were broadcast all over the train by a couple of incompetent Flemish flatfoots ..."

"How appalling," she sympathised.

"You said it was only *one* of the reasons you jumped trains ...?" said Martin.

"Yes, I upset quite a few other people as well. Seems there was an on-board Anglers Club going for the *Sardine of the Year* award. These things happen ..."

"What led you to suspect the Chef in the first place?" asked Candida.

"It was his nationality, of course ..."

"Oh?" said Martin, puzzled.

"Yes," I said. "He was Sardinian ..."

Candida suddenly leaned forward and lowered her voice ...

"That group over *there*," she whispered. "I think *they're* from the train. Are they friends of the Chef?"

I shifted my position to get a better look at where she was indicating, realigning my lager bottle in front of my face as I went ...

"No ... no," I said (*totally unable to see anybody at all, that alone anybody I knew*), "No, no ... I don't *think* so ..."

"Yes, yes," said Martin loudly. "Look, over *there* ..."

"Don't point," I insisted. "It's rude ..."

"By the *window*. Look ..."

"Oh no," I said in a muffled croak, "*Definitely* not ..." (I was hiding behind Sonny Reithoek's chair now ...)

(Why? I'd just recognised who they were *pointing* at, *that's* why ...)

Laurel, Jane and ...

Inspector Le Gras.

"Have you dropped something, Mr Haute-Cooke?" asked Candida in all innocence.

I sniffed the air ...

"Er ... no, I don't think so," I said. "I'm on lead-free anyway, these days. I'm not too sure about *Sonny-boy* here, though – there's a dreadful pong reeking through the back of this seat, now you mention it ..."

I knew I'd antagonised him by the way he suddenly started to shift about on his cushion...

"Mrs Flite," he said (*he was leaning round to the right-hand side of the seat in order to try to gain access to me*), "Must we put up with this intolerable nonsense any longer?"

But I was too quick for him ...

I'd already swerved out of his reach and was leaning round the *left*-hand side of the chair, where I found my view blocked by the horrible sight of his great fat arse bulging out of his drill shorts.

If he leaned any further the seams would split, no mistake.

"Can I give you a word of advice?" I said. (*I winked at Candida as I said it, before quickly ducking out of range as I anticipated his predictable swing back round to the left...)* "Get a filter attached to your exhaust. I know a good plastic surgeon – he might even throw in a silencer if you're lucky ..."

I then had to lay completely flat on the floor to evade his wandering arms, but, once I judged the danger to have passed, I popped my head up over the back of the chair and, using his scalp-stubble as cover, tried to get a better view of the trio of detectives over by the window.

Reithoek was just sitting there and cursing vehemently in *Afrikaans* by this time.

"I don't know how you can tolerate it ..." I said to him.

He ignored me.

"Drinking tea," I continued, "In the same room as somebody with questionable ethnic origins ..."

He turn round threateningly ...

"Oh?" he said. "And who might *that* be?"

"Don't look at *me*," I said.

"Who are you referring to, then?"

I could see his curiosity was aroused, and that there was an advantage to be had in winding him up ...

"I'm referring to that bloke over there," I said, pointing at LeGras. "The shortarse with curly hair. I met him on the train. He claims to be a Belgian, but he's actually a Black Supremacist from the Belgian Congo ..."

"He looks *white* to me ..."

"Appearances can be deceptive," I said. "Have you ever heard of the term *albino* ...?"

"What about the other two? *They're* not black ..."

"Worse," I said. "*Much* worse. The bloke with him is a Nazi hunter and, whatsmore, he's a *Jew* ..."

He began to finger his whip ...

"How do you know ...?" he said.

"Isn't it obvious?" I said. "His *conk's* the giveaway. I measured it myself on the train ..."

"Measured it? How?"

"With a pair of travelling calipers ..."

"Travelling calipers?"

"Yes, and when I confronted him with it, he claimed to be a victim of the notorious Curry-House Nose-Murderer of a year or two back. He said it was in all the papers. Have you ever heard anything *like* it ...?"

Having stitched LeGras and Laurel up nicely, it just left Jane.

"What about the woman? She isn't *black*, and neither does she look Jewish..."

"Haven't you ever heard of the Pied Piper of Hamelin?" I asked.

"What are you talking about?"

"Well," I said, "It was all based on her exploits with the clarinet ..."

"Do you take me for a fool?"

No, full marks.

"Actually," I said (realising my literary allusion was lost on him), "I was just pulling your leg there. But she's the worst of the lot, really ..."

"Oh? What *is* she, then?"

"Haven't you guessed?" I said.

"Would I ask?"

"She's a white SWAPO guerrilla ..."

"How do I know this isn't one of your cock-and-bull stories?"

"You don't," I said. "But it's the truth. I swear ..."

"The one in the middle *does* have a rather large nose, I'll grant you ..."

"Go on," I said. "Go and measure it ..."

"Give me your calipers ..."

"What?"

"Give me your calipers. You said you had some calipers ..."

"Not possible," I said. "I lost them ..."

"What do you mean, you *lost* them ...?"

"I couldn't get them back out of his nose, could I? They're still up there somewhere, as far as I know ..."

"Martin," he said, leaning forward in his seat, "Do we know those three over there?"

Martin glanced round. "Not really," he said. "I think they arrived this morning. One of the agency staff probably let them in. Simon would know ..."

Reithoek got to his feet and spent a moment or two eyeing up the trio and straightening his waistband.

"Wait there," he suddenly said to me. "I'll deal with *you* when I get back ..."

So saying, he marched off towards their table.

Having lost my cover, I sunk back down behind the chair and got ready to make do with a sound-only transmission of the expected encounter ...

The first thing I heard was Reithoek asking in a less-than-polite manner to see their invitations.

I couldn't tell from the muffled squabbling which followed whether they'd been able to get hold of any invites or not, but I presumed *not*; the next thing I heard was Reithoek's dulcet Afrikaaner twang demanding to see their ID's.

It was going better than expected. Rubbing my hands together with some anticipatory glee, I was forgetting momentarily that LeGras would only need to show his police badge and spill the beans that he was here to apprehend a double-murderer answering my description, before he'd come marching back to sort *me* out ... but then something happened to throw the place into a tizz of sorts: *a scream down the corridor, followed by the sound of several pairs of feet rushing towards its source...*

When Leon entered the room briskly and delivered a message to Martin, I risked peeking over the chair in order to try to ascertain the problem.

Fortunately, I could lip-read:

"Herr Flite," I saw him say. "There has been a death, in the Elector Palatine Room ..."

"Trouble, Martin ...?" Reithoek called out.

"Just a little upset over the will ..." (*and then, turning to his wife*), "Nothing for *you* to bother about, Candida. I'll take Sonny with me. You may as well wait here..."

The last I saw before I had to duck down again, was LeGras flashing some sort of police identification at Reithoek and insisting he be allowed to accompany them to the scene of the kerfuffle.

Despite being ignored, he took the opportunity to follow them out of the Morning Room, closely attended by Jane and Laurel skulking around his coat-tails, leaving Leon to depart last of all, closing the door behind him as he went.

When I peered up over the armchair, I found Candida flipping through a copy of *Vogue*.

"All quiet on the Western Front?" I asked.

"You really shouldn't antagonise Sonny so, Mr Haute-Cooke. He means well ..."

"Do forgive me," I said, as I plonked myself on a seat next to her. "I didn't realise he was one of life's sensitive fellows ..."

"Sonny has an artist's temperament. He cannot bear to think people are laughing at him ..."

I had a mental image of him attempting to pick up a delicate little paintbrush and then accidentally snapping it all into little pieces in his great, gnarled rhino-hide fists. "Yes," I said, "I may have been a little hard on him ..."

"Do you ever take *anything* seriously, Mr Haute-Cooke?"

"Oh yes ..." (*Here, I mentally wandered off as the sound of a piano starting up became audible somewhere in the far recesses of the room*) "... Music, for example ..."

My God, what a bleeding racket!

"Beautiful, isn't it ..." she said, as she wandered off in sympathy.

"No," I said.

"Wagner ..." she waffled on.

"Is it?" I said, surprised. *It sounded more like Stockhausen to me.* Top of the Pops in Timbuktu.

"It was many years before Simon ever allowed that piece to be heard inside these walls again ..."

He's not a bad judge, I thought.

"Yes," she droned on. "Too many painful memories. He forbade it to be played ... *until now*. Too many unfortunate associations ..."

I wondered what *they* were? *Memories of a meander in a madhouse ...?*

Craning my neck outwards, I tried to detect something recogniseable amongst what appeared to be a random selection of notes and chords. "What kind of associations?" I asked. "Your tone of voice suggests something romantic..."

"Oh yes," she answered, in full reverie.

"What was he," I said, "In love with a cubist's artist's model ...?"

And *then*, just to top everything, a singing voice erupted by way of accompaniment, and people began to leave their seats in curiosity to wander towards the source of the noise, the scene of the performance, which was obscured from my immediate vision by virtue of the fact that it was an L-shaped room.

"So tragic ..." she sighed.

"Yes," I said, as I listened to the eerie creak and croak of the vocalist. "I can *see* that ..."

She suddenly grabbed hold of my arm and leaned forward in that conspiratorial manner she had ...

"You musn't mention this to Simon directly, though. He still hasn't got over it yet ..."

"But he allows the music to be played?" I enquired. "Surely it's a constant reminder to him?"

"*Well ...*"

"Why did he permit it?"

"He didn't – at least, not *formally* ..."

"He obviously doesn't recognise it. *I* don't recognise it. Do *you?*"

"Oh yes," she said. "It's a wonderful rendition ..."

I couldn't believe we were listening to the same thing. The voice, a grotesquely-accented guttural German nosepipe chant, was like the musical equivalent of about 30 heavy infantry divisions moving through Kew Gardens, with the piano like an accompaniment of random shellfire over Richmond High Street in the distance. *And it was getting louder.*

Well, the *piece* may have been totally unrecogniseable to me, but I had the spooky feeling I'd come across the style of the *performer* before ...

It warranted closer investigation, so I left Candida to her daydream, picked up my bottle of lager and wandered over to the scene of the sensory assault, where a small appreciative crowd had collected. *I gathered player and vocalist were one and the same person.*

"Has there been an accident?" I said to nobody in particular, standing up on tip-toes in an effort to discover the source of the racket.

"Search me, chum," said some shorts-beclad holiday reveller who turned round to offer me the benefit of a shrug of his shoulders.

"This has got to stop," I said (*and then, by way of introduction*): "Haute-Cooke. Control Officer, Department of European Noise Polution, ECG. *Interpolute*, for short. And *you're* under arrest ..."

"You can't do that!" he shouted, by way of protest.

"Who's in charge here?" I demanded to know.

"In charge?" he said.

"That's right," I said.

"Is there any more where *that* came from?" he said, gesturing towards my drink.

"For a price," I said.

"How much?" he asked.

I looked him up and down.

"Out of *your* price range," I said. "What's the matter with Benidorm this year?"

"Full of Krauts ..."

"Keep in touch," I said, and wandered further round the circle to try to gain entry.

The song was reaching some sort of hideous climax now, and drastic measures were called for ...

"Let me through!" I yelled out at the top of my voice. "I'm a throat specialist ...!"

To my surprise, it had no effect at all. The sea didn't part, the performer didn't stop. *I obviously wasn't in the company of very many English-speaking music lovers ...*

I took out my Kraut phrase book:

"*Raus*! *Raus*!" I yelled, and waited for a response.

This time, some woman immediately in front of me turned round to give me a flash of her choppers ...

"Who are *you*, then?" she said. "Charlie Chaplin?"

"That's right," I affirmed. "And I've lost my pianist. Got any suggestions?"

"This man is absolutely brilliant," she drivelled on. "Don't you think?"

Before I could formulate a reply, I suddenly realised who she was ...

It was that *deaf* woman from the *King's Head.*

There was something ominous about all this, no mistake.

She must have been an international talent scout for the Barbican Theatre ...

"Have you asked him to play *Summertime* ...?" I said, but I didn't bother waiting for a reply. *Instead, I got down on all fours and crawled through her legs as far as the second tier, taking advantage of the expected heavenward rapture into which she'd aimed her moosh ...*

But that was as far as I could get before needing to revise my strategy and redirect myself towards the perpendicular.

After jumping up and down several times I made a determined assault on the southern face of an Eiger-shaped troll in Tyrolean national dress and managed to suspend myself in a position from which I was finally able to scrape a glimpse of the culprit of the contralto and the keys:

It was ...

Tommy.

Complete with tin helmet and face scarf.

Tinkling away nine-to-the-dozen, like a man concentrating on a spot-the-ball contest.

I'm not sure if this was who I'd *expected* to see, but I ought probably have been able to *guess* with all the data available to me hitherto.

Put it *this* way, it was no *surprise.*

Another thing that didn't surprise me was that he was actually trying to sing through the scarf. I don't know what the intention was, but the result came out sounding something like this: -

Wir alles sind in einem gelb U-Boat leben,

Ein gelb U-Boat leben, ein gelb U-Boat leben,

Wir alles sind in einem gelb U-Boat leben,
Ein gelb U-Boat leben, ein gelb U-Boat leben,
(etc ...)
Wagner?
Really?

The more ecstatic he got, the more the crowd around him became infected with the excitement. And the funny thing was, the more excited *he* got, the more his scarf began to slip, so that for the first time since I'd met him on the road the previous evening, I could actually make out more of his face than just his nose. And there was something *unnervingly* familiar about the pockmarks on his cheekbones ...

He seemed to be aware his mask was slipping, because he kept trying to pull up the scarf between each line of the song, though this didn't audibly contribute to any improvement or deterioration in performance quality either way.

In fact, I just seemed to be on the verge of some startling apocalyptic revelation concerning Tommy's identity, when the sound of a gun being fired erupted in the distant bowels of the castle and some idiot grabbed me round the ankles from behind and toppled me arse-over-tit onto the floor ...

Stunned, and in danger of being trampled underfoot, I looked up to find some yob with a horizontal tricorn haircut clambering around behind the front row ...

I immediately put two-and-two together, *viz* he was *not* attempting to escape from the gunfire but *was*, in fact, desperately trying to usurp the grandstand position formerly occupied by myself ...

"And just what the hell do you think *you're* playing at?" I yelled up at him, but my words were rendered inaudible as they disappeared in the general din and cacophany coming from the piano area.

I got to my feet and tapped him on the back.

"Sorry Jock," he said, rummaging around in his pocket for money. "I've heard this bloke's dynamite and I just wanted a look. It's not the Royal Opera House, is it? Here's a quid – if you go and slip it to the butler he might find you an old crate to stand on ..."

Jock?

Jock ...?

"Excuse me ..." I went to say, but he'd already returned his attention to the performance.

"Shoosh ...!" said somebody behind me. "I'm trying to concentrate ..."

I swivelled round to find the deaf woman glaring at me.

"Fair enough," I said to her, before turning back to my usurper, who was now in mid-lunge at the weakest point of the front-row chain.

I looked him up and down.

Then I crashed my lager bottle down on his shoulder so hard that he fell backwards, pulling three of the people he'd been leaning on with him onto the floor ...

In the general push and shove that followed, I found myself for the first time in a prime position not two feet away from the piano ...

Unfortunately, the performance came to an abrupt halt at that point and, as quickly as the sea had parted, it closed up again and I began to get carried backwards in the melee that followed.

The last glimpse I got of Tommy was as he got to his feet, readjusted his scarf and pulled his tin hat down over his eyes before disappearing quickly through a side exit.

After waiting for the crowd to disperse and making sure the injured parties were all carried out with them, I hurried back in search of the shy celebrity.

As I did so, I paused to look at the keyboard instrument itself, though the arousal of my curiosity had no obvious cause.

After all, it was just a *piano* ...

I reached down, snatched at an old torn ticket tied to one of the casters and found myself scrutinising a shipping label:

DRY DOCK
SYDNEY HARBOUR

It was *Dirk's* piano...

CHAPTER 45
RETURN OF THE PRODIGAL SOD

I went out through the side door I'd seen Tommy leave by.

In fact, I almost *fell* out of it in shock.

I was in such a state, that I didn't immediately notice that I'd walked into a broom cupboard.

Questions.

I had a lot of them, no mistake.

Like, for example, *how did Dirk's piano get here?*

That would do for a start.

I began to pace up and down in the confined space.

Who'd *want* it? Who'd *bring* it here? Who'd *know* about it, anyway?

Who was Tommy?

The more the questions reverberated around my head, the more furiously I began to pace, oblivious to my surroundings. *The whole puzzle, with all its ramifications, began to play such havoc with my internal radar system, that I started to career around like a maniac, crashing into brooms, brushes, shovels, shelves and walls, knocking everything over left, right and centre as an indoor avalanche rained down around me.* Bottles of cleaning fluid and floor polish crashed to the floor, while a blizzard of soap flakes began pelting me from fringe to footwear and eventually halted me in my tracks like a snowdrift ...

I stood there absent-mindedly licking it from my lips as it poured off the end of my nose.

About seven and a half tons of vintage non-automatic *Dreft*.

As a *result* of which, I started frothing at the mouth ...

Dangerously close to poisoning myself, I was suddenly knocked senseless by a can of *Brasso* which smacked me round the nut and clattered away across the lino ...

"Where am I ...?" I cursed.

Whoever Tommy was, I had to unmask him. The possibility that I might find *Dirk's* ugly mug lurking beneath Tommy's face blanket was a problem I seemed unable to address in any coherent fashion. *Instead, I dwelled on the equally horrible possibility that Tommy was some kind of blood-relative of my erstwhile tormentor. After all,* Dirk was en route here *now*, wasn't he? He'd just '*got* out'. Ray and the Chief had said so. *Either way, the ramifications were dreadful, the questions completely mystifying.* What kind of a nightmare factory was this?

261

One thing was for *sure*.

Whoever he was, he'd already been at the Castle Froth several months ...

When I finally calmed down long enough to glance up at the source of the steady, irritating trickle sifting down on me, my attention was diverted to an open trapdoor in the centre of the ceiling:

That's where he'd gone.

But the sod had retracted the ladder after him, making pursuit impossible.

Unless I could climb up there some *other* way, that is ...

Doing my best to scale the shelves, my first attempt only had the effect of knocking the rest of the detergent powder on top of me, closely followed by the empty box.

I did a little better with my second attempt, lunging across at the open trap and hanging by my hands until the pain in my shoulders sparked a dungeon flashback, forcing a general retreat.

On my *third* attempt I reached as far, going on to destroy the remainder of the fittings as I kicked out with my feet to try to gain some leverage from the walls. *Then*, in one last desperate manoeuvre, I grabbed the end of the ladder (whilst swinging by one arm) and dragged it down on top of me as I tumbled back to the deck.

The means of ascent thus retrieved, I climbed up into a dark and narrow space between floors containing drainage pipes.

Not that I fancied the *job* much.

Right from the start, I had to be careful not to scrape my head on the low ceiling as I followed the only route between the tangled ironwork, down on my knees part of the way, flat on my belly the rest, a change in the decor finally appearing as reward for my endeavours, lying just up ahead:

Here, the level of the ceiling rose abruptly, and I found myself crawling out into an area lit by one dim electric bulb, looking not unlike a warehouse ...

Hundreds of wooden crates, all stamped *AF International*, had been stacked from floor to ceiling in rows stretching as far as the eye could see, cumulatively forming an indoor maze.

I sensed *Tommy* was nearby from the moment I stood up, and I therefore restrained myself from an impromptu inspection of the packed merchandise. Instead, I crept along one of the artificial aisles until I reached the edge of a cleared space amongst the boxes having all the appearance of a makeshift bedroom. *A hammock was slung between two enormous vertical pipes, and there were odds and ends of personal possessions scattered around the floor.*

I could *hear* him somewhere, moving about and singing to himself, but ... *his sudden appearance in the arena was much sooner than I'd anticipated, forcing me to duck back behind the crates to avoid his field of vision ...*

As quietly as I could, I took up a position from which I could spy on him through a gap between the boxes:

That great lumbering gait, shuffling across the floor – it was uncanny ...!

Sooner or later he *stopped* shuffling across the floor and climbed onto the hammock, where he proceeded to spend several minutes just laying on his back and staring into space before taking the trouble to unravel the scarf from his face.

In *fact*, I could barely control my patience at the deliberate lethargy with which he was carrying out this operation, and it was almost the last straw when he stopped for a rest before reaching the final furl ...

Come on you old git, I cursed to myself internally.

The *purpose* of his pause, however, was to remove his *helmet*, which revealed a thinning thatch of spiky black hair plastered across his bonce ...

Finally, the last lap of the scarf was complete, and I knew at once that the face beneath it didn't belong to any *relative* of Dirk.

There was no possibility at all of there being *two* people roaming around that ugly.

None whatsoever.

This was the *real* thing.

The one and only ...

"'*Ere*," I said, as I stepped out from my concealment. "Don't I *know* you from somewhere ...?"

In a panic, he tried to wrap the scarf back round his face, his arms flailing about like an upturned beetle as he succeeded only in toppling off the hammock into an entangled heap on the floor ...

"Bonehead ...!" I cursed.

Before I could do anything about it, he sprang to his feet like a two-year-old, picked up a stray lump of wood and proceeded to assume a threatening self-defence posture as though he were holding a rifle and bayonet ...

"*Ach-tung* !" he yelled, squinting at me through the gloom. "*Halt* ! *Halt* ! *Ach-tung* ! *Kommen sie hier ...*!"

I gave him the benefit of a couple of paces forward into the light, so that he could see me more clearly.

"*Achtung?*" I said. "What do you think you're *playing* at, you tyke?"

He was *faking*, of course, but he gave away no hint of recognition as he gestured that I'd come far enough.

"I've got to hand it to you," I said. "This is *some* stunt you've managed to pull off with the Flites. How did you do it?"

He stared at me motionless – *emotionless*. He hadn't changed much at all, physically. Except that he was even a bit *uglier*, if anything.

"I suppose you thought you'd crack this case all by yourself and steal my glory? Well," I continued, "You might as well know that I haven't forgiven you yet, for leaving me alone on the streets of New York ..."

Still he didn't respond, and I wondered if I was laying it on a bit thick ...

"So," I carried on, "You'd better start sharing everything you've found out, or I might just put a spanner in your works. If it wasn't for the apparent blind loyalty and devotion they've got for you in this place, I'd go and tell Simon Flite who you are right now ..."

"*Mas-ter ...*" he suddenly said. "*He* saved me ..."

"Does he *know* you're a spy?"

"*Mas-ter ...*"

"Come on, Dirk," I said. "You can cut all this out. You've got a duty to your country to tell me everything. So start singing – but not *literally* – you devious sod ..."

"*Mas-ter ... Mas-ter ...*" he moaned again, like an automaton, staring past me into space.

By now, I wasn't even quite sure whether he could *see* me, and I was starting to feel decidedly uneasy.

"I work for *Mas-ter* now ..."

"Mind you," I said, "Despite being a pack of lies about you in the First World War trenches, they got that bit about you being a deserting coward just about spot-on ..."

He suddenly took a swing at me with his pole ...

"You traitorous bastard!" I yelled at him. (*I'd only just managed to duck out of the way in time ...*) "After all I've *done* for you ...!"

It was a wasted appeal for gratitude, however, as he continued to lunge forward like a recruit trying to spear a potato sack, jerking and slicing at the air in front of me while I backed off diplomatically. There wasn't much danger of him injuring me by intention, but every chance he might catch me by accident with the random luck of an hopeless case.

He seemed in no mood to drop his new persona and engage in any nostalgic reverie on our past association, and I think this was more disconcerting to me than a tirade of abusive Bonehead pomposity bemoaning my treatment of him might have been. After *all*, he did have grounds for complaint. The last time I'd seen him was when I left him on the doorstep of a madhouse with instructions for the proprietors to lock him up and throw away the key.

"Come on," I said. "It's your old mate Dexter Kitehawk. Why don't you just drop that lump of wood, and we'll go and have a few drinks and smash the place up ...?"

This didn't appear to be having the desired effect ...

"No hard feelings ...?" I said, extending the hand of friendship, when ... *with a determined grunt he hurled such a vicious swing at me that he almost chopped my arm off at the elbow, but for some fancy footwork on my part ...*

"Is that a *yes* or a *no* ...?"

What I *really* needed to do was to hit him with some piece of information which would shock him out of his trance.

Or hit him with a lump of concrete.

Perhaps my best course of action lay in trying to provoke him into a slip

...

"This has gone far enough," I said. "You may have beaten me to the Castle Froth – and all due credit for that – but you might as well know I haven't been exactly idle myself..."

He stopped in his tracks momentarily, grunting and wheezing.

"... It's time to drop the mask, because I *know* who you are. And I'm *not* talking about *Dirk* the fearless Inland Revenue Collector. I'm talking about *Archibald Heathcliffe Darkbloode*, the tax embezzler and fugitive from justice. I'm talking about *you*, Sir Arch ..."

With one hand at either end of the pole, he resumed his forward advance like a mediaeval woodsman trying to knock an adversary off a log ...

"And how did I find all this out?" I taunted him, ducking and weaving like a matador in the face of an enraged and confused bull. "I found it out from your *daughter*. Hetty told me ..."

This last revelation brought him to an abrupt halt once again ... which was just as *well*, really, because I'd backed myself up against an impenetrable row of crates:

While he stood there puffing and blowing, presumably trying to work out the implications of this new scenario, I kept quiet and decided to let him stew on it. *Even though he was still hunched in battle position, I was convinced he was on the verge of cracking.* In fact, I was just about to deliver a little lecture in order to tip him over the cliff, when he suddenly let out an almighty war cry and drove the pole straight at my head, impaling it in one of the crates directly behind me, just inches from my cheekbone ...

I must admit, I stood there quivering in shock.

In *fact*, I was so stunned, that I was unable to react when he freed the pole and went to swing it for the kill ... *until a voice close by stopped him.*

Simon Flite stepped out from the shadows, looking stern – if impassive – and gestured with his hand for the weapon.

More insistent now. "Tommy. *Put it down ...*"

When his servant reluctantly obeyed him, I was glad to watch it clatter harmlessly to the floor.

Thereafter, Tommy backed off a few feet and stood there looking disappointed, eyes fixed firmly downward.

"Run along. We have guests to cook for. We wouldn't want to disappoint, would we ...?"

As he retrieved his scarf and shuffled off in silence, I was left with the feeling that I hadn't handled that scene as well as I might ...

Simon put his hands in the pockets of his jacket and began to pace up and down and stare at the floor. *Up till then, he'd ignored me, and it was a while before he actually addressed me directly.* I'd been wondering how long he might have been there eavesdropping, and how much he'd heard of what I'd been saying.

"You must forgive him, Mr ... *Haute-Cooke*. He has the territorial sense of a guard dog. You shouldn't have strayed from the main corridors. The Castle Froth can be a hazardous place for those who do not know their way around.

It is fraught with dangers ..."

Well, he didn't reveal any sign that he'd been listening in, but he might just have been boxing clever.

He was a cool customer, no mistake.

"Quite so," I said, relaxing slightly. "And you mustn't blame Tommy for any of this. I'd been pestering him for some lessons in self-defence and ... well, I think we both got carried away ..."

"Self defence ...?" he said. *He suddenly stopped in mid-pace and cast me one of his suspicious glances sideways-on.* "Are you expecting trouble?"

"Trouble?" I said. "... Not *as* such, no ..."

"*Then* ...?"

"Except," I continued, "In the sense that one should *always* expect trouble. Don't you agree ...?"

"*Trouble* ..." he murmured, more to himself than to me, as if to say "*I've had a lifetime of trouble,*" or something on those lines. "Come," he said, looking at his watch, "I expect you could do with a drink, and I have a busy schedule. There is much to do in the way of preparations for this evening ..."

As I stepped away from the wall of boxes, I realised that my drenched back was due to more than just a bad case of the nervous sweats. When Tommy had impaled his stick into the crate-frontage, he'd smashed a load of bottles packed behind it, and their contents had been streaming out all over me ever since. *I was soaked with lager.*

"As well as *trouble,*" I said, finishing on a note of optimism, "That's the *other* thing you could always expect ..."

"What's that ...?" he replied distantly, as he switched off the gloomy lightbulb and led me out through a more conventional access point.

"You could always expect that I could do with a drink ..."

He took me down a flight of stairs and opened the door of the room we'd *soireed* in the previous evening – the one where I'd met Martin and Candida, Sonny, Otto, Frostbite (whose real name had temporarily escaped me), and, of course, Heidi.

It was dark and empty now, something he rectified by switching on the chandelier and wandering over to light the bar.

"Help yourself," he said. "Tommy will be tied up in the kitchen for the time being ..."

"That's a blessing," I said.

"Sorry to leave you alone ..."

"You're never alone with a bottle of *Froth* ..."

"What ...?" he said, absent-mindedly.

"Nothing," I said, as I drew up a bar stool and leaned over the counter to rummage amongst the glassware.

"I expect some of the other guests will be wanting a drink before lunch. I'll send them down to join you ..."

"Not necessary," I said. "All the more for me ..."

"I'll also try to find a barman. I have hired several for this evening but their current location is, as yet, a mystery ..."

"To misplace *one* barman," I spouted, "Could be considered careless. To lose your entire bar staff calls for a drink. What's your poison ...?"

I did hear him mumble something behind me but, when I surfaced with two bottles, I found he'd already left the room, and so I coshed one open and proceeded to drink it, sitting there and staring silently at my reflection in the bar mirror.

With the curtains still drawn and keeping the daylight at bay, it could easily have been the previous midnight.

Naturally enough, my thoughts returned to the encounter with my former comrade-in-arms ...

Having already discounted the possibility that 'Tommy' could be a twin, relative, lookalike, German counterpart, clone, double, besotted fan etc etc of Dirk, I tried to weigh up possible explanations for his failure – deliberate or otherwise – to recognise me.

The most likely of these was that he'd escaped from the asylum and managed, somehow, not only to have found out about the existence of the Castle Froth, but to have actually made his way to it, infiltrated the domestic department, ingratiated himself with his employers, and become determined not to let his cover be blown – *least* of all by *me*.

The problem with this scenario was that it pre-supposed a level of intelligence, determination, ingenuity and subtlety that he just did not possess. He just wasn't *that* clever. *Devious* – yes – but clever? Definitely not. And it was asking an awful lot to believe that the Flites could have fallen for it.

Unless they were all as daft as he was. *Surely somebody in the Corporation must have recognised him?*

Notwithstanding his face blanket.

I'm sure I had a false moustache on when I came into this place, I thought. *What's wrong with all the mirrors round here ...?*

A second explanation for his behaviour was that he really *had* joined the enemy. I *liked* this one, because it fitted in nicely with my own assessment of him as a cowardly yellow swine, and Simon's cock-and-bull story about him deserting the First World War trenches and joining the Germans to become a spy would, in this case, have had an element of metaphorical truth about it. *Spite* – or *fear*, perhaps – would then explain his refusal to know me. *Depending on whether or not he'd told the Flites who he was to begin with.* Perhaps he feared to spill the beans on *me* lest he incriminate *himself?*

As I finished the first bottle and started on the second, I examined my third theory, which was, quite plainly and simply, that he was mad. My suspicions, that he'd begun to go potty from head injuries sustained when we crashed into the lobby of the Empire State, were confirmed by this display of an insanity achieving fruition. So maybe he really *didn't* recognise me. Or maybe he *did*. Either way, his behaviour needed no further explanation other than that it was the product of a deranged mind.

But there were two nagging doubts about this ...

Firstly, if he *was* insane, why wasn't he still banged-up in Bellevue? Secondly, I remembered having the distinct impression he was switching his attacks off and on at will during our last days together in New York and Long Island.

There was one more line of enquiry I was reluctant to follow – the sinister possibility that Simon had been correct when he'd said his *father* had brought Tommy here. Did Adolf Flite collect him from the asylum? *Or was it Adolphus Flite – the skeletal ghost – opening his cell in the dead of night and beckoning him to follow?* And why? *Did they now have some kind of a hold over him?* Was he in a hypnotic trance?

A flicker of cold crept along my spine ...

Regardless of which of these explanations proved to be correct, there was a further serious question that needed an *immediate* answer. If Dirk had been here several months – *and all the indications were that he had* – then, who was the subject of the warning given to me by Ray and the Chief? Who had *'just got out'* and was *'on his way'* to see me *'right now'*?

I did toy around with a few other possibilities, *eg* he was after the treasure, he was just doing everything he could to infuriate me because he was that sort of bloke, he was a purpose-built robot etc etc, before dropping the subject altogether for lack of evidence.

Despite having had my resources stretched to the limit in the basement earlier on, I couldn't quite lay my hands on a third bottle, so I got off the stool and wandered round in person to inspect the collection.

And it was while I was kneeling down behind the bar, that I heard the door open and decided to stay hidden where I was in the hope that whoever it was would piss off out again.

The fact that it was a carpeted room meant that I couldn't hear any footsteps approach, and I therefore had no idea of the whereabouts of the intruder from one moment to the next ...

All of a sudden a face poked itself over the counter and caught me crouching there like a tea-leaf on the pot:

"I'd like a whisky-on-the-rocks," it said.

"Sorry," I said. "We're closed."

"Closed?" it said. *It* was the Dentist from the *Orient Express.*

"That's right," I said. *I stood up and spelt it out for him.* "S-H-U-T. *Closed.* So clear off ..."

I don't know whether he recognised me or not, but I was in no mood to reminisce.

"But I was told the bar was *open* ..." he ventured nervously.

"Don't you understand English?" I said. "Now, piss off out of it before I chin you ..."

At this invitation, he paused for thought and began to go visibly red in the face with frustrated anger ...

"I am a guest of Herr Flite," he declared. "And I demand a drink before lunch! Give me a whisky-on-the-rocks ...'"

"Right," I said. *I swiped a glass from the slops tray, shoved it under the Pernod optic, siphoned off a short measure and slammed it down under his nose.* "Here's your drink," I said. "You'll find some rocks outside. Go and sit on a sharp one ...'"

"This is scandalous!" he shouted.

Ignoring him, I knelt back down to resume my search for lager, only to be subjected to a barrage of uninvited chit-chat as he stood there leaning over the counter and haranguing me from a distance just short of a foot or so from my right jughole.

"I shall see Herr Flite at once!" he was yelling.

"Do what you like, mate," I said, not having much luck finding any lager, but becoming fascinated with the discovery of a foot pedal attached to an electrical junction box. "He's not *my* employer ...'"

I wondered whether it was a device for summoning more beer.

"Right!" I heard him say.

"Go on," I said, looking up to find he'd gone blue with rage. "Piss off then...'"

I pressed it for a laugh, expecting all the lights to go out or an alarm to start ringing or something, but nothing happened – at least, nothing *electrical* that I could detect – *except that the lingering voice of the Dentist cut rather abruptly to something sounding like a strangled scream followed by a distant cry for help ...*

I stood up to see what all the commotion was about, but the room was empty.

"Good riddance to bad rubbish!" I cursed.

But it was a funny thing ...

I could still hear his whining *voice* coming from somewhere:

When I looked over the counter, I was astonished to find that a sizeable square of floor had vanished – more or less in the very spot where the Dentist had been standing.

It merited a closer look, and so I wandered round the customer side to avail myself of one ...

It was quite *extraordinary*, really:

There he was, sitting in a dark, box-like compartment, about ten feet beneath the level of the floor, having fallen through a trapdoor operated – presumably – when I'd pressed the foot pedal.

He stared up at me like a frightened cat as I peered in from above, and he looked very sorry for himself, I must say.

"Help me out, will you?" he said.

"Are you still here?"

"Get me out!" he suddenly yelled.

"Don't you ever stop whingeing?" I said. "You'll shout the bleedin' house down ...'"

He attempted to stand up ...

"Please," he said, trying to come on all reasonable in his desperation and stretching out an arm for help. "Please, *assist* me ...'"

"What's the matter?" I said. "*Accommodation* not to your liking? What *will* Herr Flite say? Too *dark* down there? Or is it just you object to sharing your bedroom with a nest of rattlesnakes ...?"

"*Rattle*snakes ...?" he quivered, looking around him in panic.

"Well," I said, "I fell into an identical trap last night, and the place was crawling alive with them. I'm afraid Herr Flite is an incorrigible practical joker, but you've got to admit it's *funny*, isn't it ...?"

He placed his hands on his hips. "*Now* I know who you are," he suddenly declared. "I remember you. You are the man from the train. The *murderer*. The man the police are seeking. Well, you won't get *away* with it ...!"

"Hold on ..."

Whistling as I went, I meandered back round to the management side of the bar, put my foot back on the pedal and looked over the counter to confirm my expectation that the trapdoor would close, replacing the missing piece of carpeted floor as it did so.

It must have been some kind of holding tank for drunks.

His voice was inaudible now, and so I waited a few decent minutes and then sprung the trap open again ...

"Ah," he called up, "So you've thought better of it, then ...?"

"You *could* say that ..."

So saying, I picked his drink up and slung it in there with him, closely followed by the glass.

Then I shut him *in* again, removing all evidence of his having been there, like the murderer he claimed me to be.

"Bloody Dentists ..." I cursed.

I could get to like bar work, I thought, as I knelt back down behind the counter to continue my hunt for a drink ...

I finally managed to cop hold of a quartet of dusty blue-tinted lager bottles minted, it appeared, to celebrate the driving-in of the final rivet of some kind of trans-German railway in 1953, and after getting to my feet and holding one of them up to the light to observe the cloudy, sedimented slosh inside, I decided against coshing it open in the usual manner and very carefully levered off the top by means of a fitted bottle-opener on the counter top.

"*Phut!*" it went.

"Keep in touch ..." I said, as I poised myself ready to sink its contents ... *when my attention was distracted by the door opening once again to reveal a large figure obscured by shadow, framed therein.*

As it began to shamble into the room, I took note of its ruddy complexion and colonial demeanour.

"Oi!" I shouted at it. "Shut the door!"

He shambled back and shut the door.

Then he shambled back towards the bar ...

"Give me an *Old Fashioned*," he declared, like a man with a mouthful of gobstoppers.

"What?" I said.

"I'll take an *Old Fashioned*," he said again, leaning his neck back as if to shift some of these confectionary marbles into a more comfortable position underneath his tonsils.

"An old-fashioned *what?*" I enquired. "An old-fashioned girl? An old-fashioned punch on the nose?"

He seemed to pause, as if he had trouble digesting this enquiry, but it's a short life and I felt obliged to interrupt him. "I know what *you* want ..." I said.

I grabbed a glass and did a round of the optics, shoving in a short measure of every brand of gin, whisky, vodka and rum I found hanging there, before shoving the result into his proffered hand.

While he stood there looking at it, I grabbed hold of his shoulders and indicated that he move sideways a fraction. "You're obscuring my view," I said.

Satisfied with his new position, he reared his head back and raised the glass to his upended neck and gaping-wide mouth:

I sprung the trapdoor suddenly and watched him disappear like a man on a fast elevator to New Zealand ...

Then I shut it quickly and prevented the glass from following him, leaning over the counter to watch it bounce and roll over the red carpet, soaking a wide area as it did so.

"Fucking drunks ..." I cursed.

When I reached to retrieve my lager, I noticed that it appeared to be *smoking:* a thin wisp of gas or spray was emanating through the neck and out of the top of the bottle ...

Even so, I hesitated for only a couple of seconds before deciding that I ought to sample some before it all evaporated.

No sooner had I grabbed it, however, when a whole group of people wandered in, chatting noisily and puffing cigar smoke into the atmosphere ...

I observed this rumbling storm-cloud as it came forward, drumming the finger-tips of my free hand up and down impatiently on the counter-top while they paused in the middle of the room to indulge, as it appeared, in a riveting discussion (all in German) on castle architecture (with particular reference to some obscure portion of the east wall of the lounge).

I slammed the bottle down in irate anticipation.

They took their time, though, before descending on me, their leader – a man with black velvet dinner jacket, bow-tie, crooked nose and acne – presenting his person for service.

"Yes, guv?" I said.

He then proceeded to spout something at me which sounded like the inventory of an armaments factory.

I gave him a blank stare.

He said a few words more, all completely incomprehensible to an Englishman.

"The bog's upstairs," I said.

He suddenly lost his temper and started shouting at me ...

"Oh," I said. "You *don't* want the bog then ...?"

But *would* he shut up?

No.

"Well," I said, standing my ground, "You can't crap on the carpet. Where do you think you are, the Tate Gallery ...?"

He tried to swipe me round the throat, but I was too quick for him as I stepped out of range ...

"*What?*" I said. "You don't even want to take your *trousers* off first ...?"

His entourage all began to mobilise around him – *some in baffled curiosity, some to add to the threatening stance he'd adopted* – and I was just standing there *listening* to all this, tapping my trigger-foot edgily and trying to calculate how many of them I could drop into the hold in one go when – a *hand* suddenly reached out from behind me and swiped the still-smoking bottle of beer ...

Before I had a chance to react, the *beer* – along with the offending *hand* – vanished through the secret door in the panel behind the optics.

"Well," I said to the angry mob surrounding me, "*His* career as a bog attendant is over *as of now ...*"

And so saying, I disappeared after the thief.

I charged – almost *somersaulted* – up a dusty staircase piled high with crates of *Froth,* and emerged unexpectedly onto a carpeted corridor, looking not unlike an extension of one of the more salubrious residential sections of the castle.

And *there,* just a few yards down the hall, was Lightfingered Larry ...

He had his back to me, oblivious to my presence, a great lumbering hunched sight in his submarine-deckhand's donkey jacket.

Which was odd, really, because I always remembered Dirk as a lean, grizzled man ...

For *that's* who it was.

He'd put on weight in his incarnation as Tommy.

Too much of the Good Life for Mr Bonehead ...

Declining to stand on ceremony, I rushed up behind him and launched a flying rugby-tackle at his midriff, causing the pair of us to collide sideways through the door of a dingy bedroom suite ...

On the way in, he cracked his head on a suit of armour and fell spark out on the carpet.

I came to rest a few feet to one side of him, where I chose to lay for the next few seconds, looking on in astonishment at his outstretched form:

His mouth was agape, and a cloud of vapour from the swallowed antique lager was drifting up out of it and hanging in a pall a few feet above his body ...

He was still unconscious when he suddenly burped and sent a puff of gas up to the ceiling like an Indian smoke-signal, complete with sparks.

Gawd help me if he farts, I thought, hastily rising on my pins.

By the time I'd worked out how much runway space I needed to deliver a long-overdue, medically effective kick in the gut, he began to stir, grunting and groaning, and huffing out smoke like a dragon ...

"*Ooer ...*" he mumbled with eyes shut tight. "*Weer* am I ...?"

"So!" I screamed. "It *is* you!"

He tried to get to his feet ...

"'Ow's that ...?" he mumbled.

"*Ow's that?*" I mimicked. "*Ow's that?* Why, you fraudulent old sod! What happened to *Komm Sie Hier ...?*"

"It's a *room* doo, Ar'll *gi'it* theet ..." he said, swaying and staggering from side to side and grinning and chuckling like a three-year-old.

I found this sudden transformation back to one of his range of bang-on-the-head personality disorders so disarming, that I wasn't quite sure what to do next. He still hadn't opened his eyes, and was behaving like a paralytic half-bright cretin who was drunk on nothing more than the joy of existence and the expectation that anything he might bump into would hold out the hand of friendship, be it a stranger with a smile or a strangler with a garotte, a hatstand dressed in hats or a salad dressed in mayonnaise.

"*Excuse* me," I said firmly. "Can I have your *attention ...?*"

"'Ellor son," he said, attempting to embrace the suit of armour he'd collided with on the way in. "Ar deen't recogneese ye stunding theer ..."

There he was, talking to the metal man, raising and lowering the visor, much as he'd once done in Lord Heehaw's residence in Madras before the latter had thrown us both out into the street.

"Did we win ...?" he was saying.

Well, it was worth a try ...

I retrieved the now-empty bottle of antique lager from its resting place on the carpet, casually walked up behind the witless Bonehead and ... *coshed him so hard across the back of the neck with it that my wrist bounced backwards vibrating like a cartoon lollystick ...*

But the operation was a failure.

"*Theer* ye are ...!" he said, tottering round to give me a full-frontal reminder that his teeth were still on the Gold Standard.

Because the risk of 'Tommy' re-emerging as the dominant personality was too great, I decided against following up with a blow directly to his skull, feeling instead that I would just have to take a chance on getting what I wanted from Dopey Dick. It might be my *only* chance to discover what he knew and gain an upper hand before the evening's festivities began.

I grabbed him by the collar with both hands in order to make my intentions clear:

"Right," I demanded. "*Who* and *where* are Adolf Flite, and what's the plan for tonight?"

First of all he gave me a vacant look, and then he added a vacant smile.

Then he started dribbling.

In the *end*, he said this:

"'Ow mooch are we oop?"

The loss of my *English / Northern Halfwit Pocket Dictionary* was one of my bigger regrets. "It didn't do you *any* good at all, did it?" I said, "All that expensive treatment at one of America's finest Homes For the Aged ..."

I let go of his collar. *It was like trying to talk to a tin of soup.*

"But you better not be trying to pull a fast one ..." I added, as I turned away in disgust.

"'Ow mooch are we *oop?*" he said again.

"*What?*" I said, irritably. "How much are we up *what?*"

"'Ow *mooch* ..." (*he paused for effect before continuing*) "*Mooneh* are we *oop* ...?"

I turned round again.

"Oh, you *disgusting* bastard ...!" I screamed at him. *He was standing there and licking his lips – a sight made twice as bad because he was still dribbling in-between ...*

"'Ow mooch," he slobbered again, "'Ow mooch *mooneh* did we get ...?"

"How much *money* did we get?" I queried. "Compared to *what?*"

"Yow knorr," he said.

"Do I?"

"'Ow mooch weer theer ... *in't sehf?*"

Safe? What safe?

"Ar remember a 'owse be sea 'n' it weer all foggeh 'n' damp 'n' all t' feernitewer weer coovered wi' sheets 'n' theer weer a *sehf* in't wall ..."

Apart from wondering whether I might actually understand more of what he was saying if he went back to speaking pidgin German, I got the impression he was talking about our break-in to the President's holiday home on Long Island Sound.

"Tell me," I said, "Can you remember what happened next?"

"Like ar seh," he went on, "Ar remeember t' *sehf* in't wall 'n' ..." (*Here he paused and momentarily adopted the expression of a man who was trying to think of a way to describe what a laundry smelled like before they invented chlorine*) "... Now *theer's* a queer thing ..."

"Well?"

"Ar remeember *anoother* 'owse far aweh 'n' doctors 'n' nurses 'n' ar remeember one neeght th' fog reteerned owtside 'n' soombodeh tappin' on't winder – *tap tap tap* – 'n' ar says 'Coom in, coom in, 'owever ye are', 'n' ee kem in, 'n' tweer man in black from top t' tor ..."

"Go on," I said, becoming intrigued.

"Well," he said, "T'weer obvious 'ow it weer ..."

"Weer it – I mean, *were* it?" I said.

"O'course. T'weer *Mayster* ..."

"*Master?*" I said. "Adolf Flite? *Adolphus* Flite ...?"

"Aye," he said. "'Ee weer a *flee-be-neeght* ..."

"Eh?"

"Aye, aye," the dopey git went on, "A *flee-be-neeght* ..."

"A *fly-by-night* ...?"

"Aye, aye, a *flee-be* ..."

"Yes, yes, thank you very much, I think I've got that one. I'm not deaf. No need to keep repeating yourself, you hopeless case ..."

"Aye, aye," he continued to drool, "'Ee weer one o' them. Aye, 'Ee *weer* ..."

"You witless cur!" I shouted at him. "Can't you wind yourself *on* a bit? I want to know what you mean ..."

"Ar *mean* he ..."

All of a sudden, two figures came striding into the room so quickly that they were on top of me before I could blink ...

"Thank you, Tommy," said Simon Flite. "That will do ..."

There was no hint of a smile as he aimed his gun at my neck from close range.

"Such a pity you have forced my hand, Mr *Kitehawk* ..."

I gulped.

"I *was* hoping that any unpleasantness could have been avoided at this stage, but I am afraid that your continued high profile poses too much of a problem. I must put an end to your unrestricted freedom around Castle Froth ..." (*and then, turning to Dirk*) "... Tommy, search our guest for weapons ..."

"'Ere," I said, "I'm not having *him* rummaging around my person!"

"You have no choice," he said.

"As an officer and a gentleman," I protested, "I expect to be dealt with by somebody of my own class ..."

There wasn't much chance of Tommy obeying him, though ...

He was just standing there in the background, dribbling and smiling, and exhibiting a personality Simon didn't appear to have encountered before.

"I trust I don't need to quote the relevant passage from the Geneva Convention on this point?" I added, for mileage.

Simon half-glanced round at his former butler, with some uneasiness creeping into his demeanour ...

"Tommy ...!" he commanded again. *He was finding it a little difficult to give orders and concentrate on his gun-hand at the same time.*

"Now, *theer's* a queer thing ..." mumbled Dirk, evidently perplexed by something.

It didn't surprise me when Simon finally gave up on the brainless Bacon Bonce and swung round to address his brother instead:

"Alright," he said. "*You* do it, Martin ..."

As Martin strode over to frisk me, I began to detect some beads of sweat forming on Simon's impatient, troubled, forehead, and I tried to think very quickly about what advantage there might be had in this situation.

Martin didn't frisk me very thoroughly, and he didn't *find* much, either – just my blunderbus lighter (which he appeared to think was a miniature gun) and the pair of joke handcuffs, which he took from me and jangled under Simon's nose.

"Good," said Simon. "Chain him up over there ..."

"There must be some mistake," I said, as Martin went about his work cuffing me to a water pipe running down one of the walls.

Neither of them bothered to comment, and Martin continued to smile nonchalantly while I looked over his shoulder.

As soon as he'd finished the job, he too turned round to observe his brother, who'd relaxed his grip on the gun and was taking advantage of being able to devote his full attention to the puzzle of 'Tommy'.

"I'd say your situation was looking serious, Kitehawk," Martin finally said, still with his back to me.

It was worth a try. "Yes," I agreed, "And now you've got me prisoner, there can't be any harm you telling me the plans ..."

"*Sorry*," he said bluntly. "Not a chance ..."

That, of course, left only *one* other option ...

"*Serious*," I said. "But I've been in situations more *Grim* ..."

Click!

As expected, the cuffs immediately sprang open, and I caught them with my free hand to stop them jangling against the pipe. Good.

Then I stepped up silently behind him, snapped them shut around his left wrist and took the blunderbus out of his right:

He swung round in surprise ...

"Harry Houdini," I said, extending my free hand in mock gesture. "Colditz Escape Committee. *Sorry* and all that, but you've been nicked ..."

"Simon!" he called out in panic ...

Quick as a flash, I rammed the other end of the cuffs shut round the spinal bar of an adjacent oak chair, stepped to one side and aimed the lighter at Simon before he had a chance to react.

"Drop it," I said calmly. "First the *penny*, then the *gun* ..."

He took his finger off the trigger and let it clatter untidily to the carpet, his face greying by the second.

"Dirk," I said to the witless observer. "Fetch it here ..."

"Ooer ..." he mumbled, puzzled, but then – confounding my worst fears – picked up the weapon and fetched it to me like an obedient dachshund. "Ooer ... it's a room doo, ar'll gi'it theet ..."

"Now piss off over there," I said to him, "Take the bracelet off the back of the chair, run the chain *through* the back, and then slip it over our *friend's* wrist ..."

I was astonished to watch him carry out this operation like a veteran 'tec, chuckling to himself as he went.

Good, I thought. Now they were chained to each other through the chair which, although it wasn't rooted to the floor, rendered them incapable of sudden meaningful movements. *To all intents and purposes they were immobilised and, more importantly, disarmed.*

I slung Simon's gun away and watched it skid across the floor to the far side of the room – *deciding, rather stupidly, to continue my bluff with the lighter instead* – before moving a second chair over to the vicinity so that they could sit down side-by-side in their captivity. *Even better.*

All I needed was for Dirk to keep quiet and refrain from commenting on the weather, his surroundings etc. A "*room doo*" was a bit too close for comfort to a "*grim day*" and so I took him outside in order to explain the facts to him.

"*Grim*. Understand? *Verstehen?*" I said, taking great pains. "*Don't* say it. Don't *say* the word. If you do you'll be struck by lightning. Okay? Got it? Don't say anything. Don't say anything at all. Don't open your mouth, not even to breathe. Don't say '*a room doo*' or anything resembling it. Don't make any comment. Don't do anything. After we've gone back in there, just sit still in the corner and shut up. *You've been warned ...*"

Although he was just standing there, dribbling and smiling, I had to assume he'd got the message and went to open the door again ...

"Ar knor!" he suddenly declared. "I moosn't seh *grim*. Is tharrit?"

"*Aaaaaaaaargh ...!*" I yelled. *I slammed it shut in front of me.* "Don't *say* that word!"

"Can I seh *grime*, f'r instance ...?"

"If you so much as *open* that *gob* of yours *once more*, I shall personally ram an electric food-mixer up your arse and give you a good whisking. Message received? *Good.* Over and out ..."

"M'lips're zipped," he said, tracing his nicotine-stained forefinger across his cakehole to demonstrate.

"*See* that they *are* and all ..."

After dragging him back inside, I turned the key in the lock to make sure we wouldn't be disturbed, and then I propped him up next to the suit of armour as a guard.

"*Now*, gentlemen," I said to my captive audience, "Down to business ..."

Their eyes followed me every step of the way as I marched forward with a great flourish.

"It's time to come clean," I said, pacing up and down and waving my lighter around for effect. "I think you *know* what I want ..."

They proceeded to give each other a puzzled look.

"No," they said in near-perfect unison. "What would *that* be, then ...?"

"Look," I said, "You might as well start squealing, because the game's up. It might do you some good, you never know. After all, your *father* is the one I'm really after. Tonight's proceedings will be brought to an end long before they begin ..."

"Impossible," said Simon. "You don't realise. Things are too far advanced. There is nothing you can do to affect the plans now. You are too late ..."

"There are policemen swarming all over the Castle, gentlemen, even as we speak. The Belgian, LeGras, for one ..."

"But he's looking for *you* ..." said Martin.

"That's as maybe," I said, busily backpedalling. "But when I tell him what's going on here, he'll switch his attention to the *real* culprits of the hour ..."

"And what *is* going on here?" said Simon.

I tapped the side of my nose. "Never *you* mind," I said. "You seem to forget, gentlemen, that *I'm* asking the questions ..."

"In any case," Martin went on, "He's after you for *murder*. Not just *one* murder, but *two*. Why not *join* us instead? With Corporation protection you could remain a free man forever. New name, new face. New person. New *persona* ..."

I stopped pacing and scratched my stubble with the blunderbus.

"No, no," I said. "It won't work ..."

"Look," said Martin, interrupting my train of thought, "Can you point that gun somewhere else? It's making me nervous ..."

I put it down on a dresser behind me, well out of their reach.

"Why not?" said Simon, as he proceeded to echo his brother's suggestion. "*Why* won't it work? *Join* us – everybody *else* has ..."

"New *career,* new *friends,*" Martin droned on. "Free supply of lager. For *life...*"

"No ..." I mumbled, "No ... I ... *Certainly* not. What do you *take* me for? I am a member of Her Majesty's Security Forces and there is an *end* of it. The interrogation will proceed ..."

Anyway, I was just about to resume my questioning, when I became distracted by a metallic clanking noise coming from behind me, sounding not unlike what I imagined might happen if ever Bertolt met the Headless Madman for a game of shove ha'penny or an egg-and-spoon race:

When I turned round, I discovered Dirk playing with the visor of the metal man again ...

"You Boneheaded Cur!" I yelled at him. "Can't you find something *else* to do? As soon as I finish here at this Castle, you're going straight back to Bellevue!"

"'Ee weer a *flee-be-neeght,* he weer ..."

"*You're* a fucking fly-by-night," I cursed.

"Aye," he drivelled on, "'Ee weer *one o'them,* he weer, aye. He weer *one o'them...*"

"*You're* one of *them,*" I said. "Now just be quiet ..."

"*Arsk* 'em," he had the audacity to carry on, "*Arsk* 'em 'ow cooms ..."

"Well?"

"*Arsk* 'em ... abowt it. Gow on ..."

"Ask them about *what?*"

"Arsk 'em *anoother question ...*"

"Oi!" I yelled. "*I'm* asking the questions around here! What did I just tell you outside ...?"

"Y' tol' me not t' seh a weerd ..."

"That's right ..."

"Aye," he said. "Burrit weer a *particulaweer* weerd. It were *gr ...*"

"KEEP YOUR TRAP SHUT!" I screamed. "*THAT'S* WHAT I TOLD YOU ...!"

Having finally made myself understood – *and not a moment too soon, either –* I was just about to pick up the threads of my cross-examination, when the wardrobe door suddenly creaked open behind me and a human form fell out backwards and clattered me into a heap on the floor ...

I don't know what shocked me the most, the news that it was *alive,* or the realisation that it was *Blondie ...*

In fact, I just about had time to stagger to my feet, when she beat me to it and barged me back onto the deck. "Get outa my way!" she said, as she tried to unruffle herself. "What are you bums doing in my room ...?"

"Look ..." I said, but her attention had already wandered to the captive Flites sitting right in front of her:

She folded her arms and straightened her back. "Well, *whaddya* know," she said. "If it *ain't* the *Brothers Grimm* ..."

Click!

"Oh *no* ..." I said out loud.

Bang on cue, the cuffs sprang open, and I instinctively leapt to my feet and lunged for the dresser ...

(If it had been a game of *Snap!* I might just have slammed my hand down before Martin did, but all three of us would have been disappointed. *The blunderbus was gone ...*)

Hearing a familiar sound behind me, I swung round to find Bonehead peering down the wrong end of the barrel and pulling on the trigger.

It lit *first* time.

"Shit ...!" I cursed.

But it was all too late now ...

By the time I remembered Simon's pistol, its owner had already picked it up off the floor.

"*Excuse* me ..." I said.

Without more ado, I chinned Dirk with such force that he went crashing into the suit of armour and fell right on top of it in the corner like an over-eager damsel looking for her shining knight ...

"Good grief ..."

Duty to the Crown thus performed, he staggered off around the room with his hands to his head as though he'd been hit by a sonic boom.

"Don't *waste* it," I heard Martin hiss at his brother. "Let them have it while you've got the chance ..."

"*Say*," said Blondie, "Did I interrupt some kind of a *party* ...?"

"Are *you* still *here*?" I cursed.

In the proverbial nick of time, there was a knock on the door, and we all looked across to find somebody trying to turn the handle from outside:

"Who is it?" called out Simon, nervously.

My relief turned out to be less than total, however, since the caller was unable to enter.

Some *idiot* had locked the door ...

"Dr Kitehawk ...?" came the reply from a familiar source (namely Dr Beans). "Is that *you*, Dr Kitehawk? Are you *alright*? Do you need *assistance* ...?"

In an apparent quandary as to what to do, Simon swung his gun to and fro between me and the door ...

Part of his dilemma seemed to involve the potential effects of committing a murder within earshot of one of the guests.

"Simon ..." Martin went to say ... *but if he was concerned at his brother's indecision, then his brother was about to change his tack ...*

"Tommy!" Simon suddenly commanded.

I looked round to find Dirk had gone AWOL upstairs again. *A blank, glassy, expressionless stare had replaced that of the familiar dope.*

"I am an empty vessel waiting to be filled," he stated in a dead monotone. "What is it you would have me do ...?"

The thickness with which he layed this on was enough to cause me to drop my arms in sheer disbelief ...

"I will have you come to see the *Master*, Tommy," said Simon (not *looking* at him – not turning his back on *me*) "The Master will want to *see* you, Tommy..."

"*Master ... Master ... His* wish is my command ..."

So saying, he began to march towards Simon like a somnambulist walking the high wire.

"*Say*," interjected Blondie. "Haven't I seen that guy before someplace? Didn't he used to be in the movies ...?"

"That's right," I said, as he strode past in his hypnotic trance. "*Look* ..."

Sticking a foot out, I tripped him up and watched him flip over onto the carpet.

"Used to be Dirk Bogarde's stuntman – *you know*, in all the *Doctor* films ..."

Tommy, however, didn't see the *funny* side ...

Leaping to his feet, he picked up one of the chairs and smashed it to pieces across the table (*as though, following my analogy, he were smashing a papiermache saloon-bar stool*), extracted a club-sized lump of wood from the wreckage (which looked decidedly as though it *wasn't* made of papermache), and went to lunge forward to *brain* me with it ...

"Tommy!" commanded Simon again. "*Kommst du hier ...!*"

With obvious great difficulty of will, he dropped the cudgel and turned to follow his employer.

The knocking from Wilbur Beans on the outer door was becoming more insistent, while Martin was whispering furiously in German into Simon's ear ...

Simon grabbed hold of Dirk's arm. "Come, Tommy, it seems you have developed a problem. Perhaps the Master will be able to put it right ..."

Well, I didn't like the sound of *that*.

And, as all three of them exited via the wardrobe, I started to cry and wail out loud ...

Blondie went over to let Beans in, but paused with her hand on the door handle.

"Hey!" she said. "What's the matter with *you*? You're still *alive*, ain't ya ...?"

"No, no," I crooned, inconsolably. "You don't *understand* ..."

"Oh ...?"

"They've just walked off with my Dad," I said, beside myself with grief. "My *dear* old Dad..."

CHAPTER 46
COUNCIL OF WAR

"That was a timely arrival, pal," she said, as Beans marched in and examined me with his stethoscope.

"My *pappy*," I wailed, laying it on with a trowel, "My dear, *dear* old *pappy*..."

"I just happened to be passing," he said, "And became concerned when I heard Dr Kitehawk's voice. Is he alright ...?"

"Yeah, you said that before about him being a doctor. What's he a *doctor* of, if you don't mind me asking ...?"

"He's a consultant, I understand ..."

"Never, *never* in the field of human conflict ..." I moaned on ... *when I was suddenly brought down to earth by a knock on the door.*

Blondie took the precaution of grabbing the blunderbus lighter before opening up a fraction and aiming it at whoever was standing there:

A few seconds passed, during which I could make out nothing of what the caller was saying, and then she retracted her head ...

"Kitehawk," she said. "Get over here. I think it's for you ..."

I wandered to the door as she wandered away, and peered out to find a young executive standing there with a mobile phone in his hand.

"I've come for the body ..." he said.

I stuck my head out a bit further and scanned up and down the empty corridor.

"What body?" I said, giving him a blank stare.

"The *Shampoo* Division ...?" he ventured, half telling me, half asking me.

"Excuse me a minute ..." (*I pulled the door to and turned to my colleagues*) "... Anybody here call an hairdresser ...?"

They stared at me quizzically.

"Anybody want to make a phone call?" I said. "Only he's got a mobile phone ..."

When I opened up again, he was still standing there.

"This *is* Room 307, isn't it?" he said.

I stuck my head round to read the number on the outside.

It *said* 307, clear as day.

"It might be," I said. "Who wants to know?"

"Well," he said, "I've come for the body. The Disposable Asset. *You* know. Corporate Carpet Cleaners. The *Shampoo* Division ...?"

"Have you got a piece of paper and a pen handy?"

"I've got a notebook and pen somewhere ..." he said, rummaging around his jacket.

I snatched them from him ...

"Thanks," I said. "Can I take a note of your number?"

"*My* number?" he said.

"That's right," I said. "If you don't mind ..."

He proceeded to reel off a series of digits, which I duly noted. Then I took Trevor's mobile phone out of my pocket and *dialled* them.

Sure enough, the executive's phone started ringing and he stuck it to his ear ...

"Hello?" the idiot said.

"TESTING, TESTING, 1 – 2 – 3 – 4!" I yelled down it.

He dropped it on the floor in shock ...

"What did you do *that* for?" he said, retrieving it with one hand, and rubbing his ear with the other.

"Future reference," I said.

"Future reference?" he queried.

"That's right," I said. "Keep in touch ..."

And so saying, I slammed the door on him.

When I turned round, I found Blondie busy trying to light the blunderbus, while Beans was sitting on the bed and sharpening one of his stakes with a penknife.

"Anyway," I said to Blondie, "Take a note of all that, will you? It might be important ..."

She took time out from peering down the barrel to aim a scowl at me.

"Did I hear him say he was looking for a body?" asked Beans.

"I say he was looking for *you*, Buster ..." she chimed in, squinting at me through the miniature gunsight.

I pointed at my chest. "*Me ...?*" I mouthed silently.

"It could be a practical joke," said Beans.

"*I* say," added Blondie, "It's their way of telling you your card's marked. *Advance warning.* You won't leave the castle alive ..."

"It could be an error," said Beans. "He may have been sent to the wrong room for the body. He may have come for the suicide victim ..."

"Go on," I said. "What suicide victim?"

"It happened during the reading of a will this morning. Doctors Van Trasyl and Van English attended the scene, but I'm a little short on details at the moment ..."

"Who was it?" I asked. "Anybody I know ...?"

"I don't know," he said. "Who do you know?"

Blondie looked directly at Beans. "Take my word for it," she said to him, "This guy knows *jack shit* ..."

"Anyone know the number for *Dial-a-Disc* ...?" I said, pulling out Trevor's phone again.

Blondie sinisterly took aim ...

"Midnight," she said. "You won't live past midnight ..."

This time she pulled the trigger.

It didn't light.

"We won't none of us live past midnight if we don't get moving ..." I said.

Beans began collecting up his equipment. "What," he said, "Are we *dealing* with here, exactly ...?"

"It's complicated ..." I started to say.

"I heard the alphabet was complicated for *you*, Buster ..."

"Does it have anything to do with the vampire in the cellar?"

"Unknown," I said.

"*That* figures," said Blondie.

"I'm not even sure it *is* a vampire ..."

"Well," said Beans, "We'll find out tonight. But, in the meantime, I'd like to offer you any assistance you may require ..."

"Good," I said. "I suggest we call a Council of War, immediately ..."

"Right," he said. "But may I suggest we hold it elsewhere? Your whereabouts in this room will have been noted and, frankly, I think we will all be sitting ducks if we stay here much longer ..."

"Any suggestions?"

"We could set up operations in my room. It's not far, and it overlooks the main gate, which could be useful ..."

"Let's get the hell out of here, then," said Blondie, pocketing my lighter in the process.

"Hold it," I said. "Let me check the coast's clear ..."

As I went to step outside, Tricorn Haircut suddenly appeared, paused outside one of the rooms down the corridor and fumbled with his keys.

"Seen any Krauts about?" I yelled.

"There's a couple of coppers looking for you downstairs," he yelled back.

"Go on ..."

"I'd have turned you in," he added, "But the reward's only two-and-a-half Belgian francs. Can't stop. Got to get myself spruced up. Keep in touch ..."

And on that note, he disappeared inside his room.

Doubtful, but partly baffled by this response, I allowed Beans to wander ahead, while Blondie trailed behind me fiddling with the lighter. *I clocked his room number – 303 – on the way past, noting also, for what it was worth, that there was a vacant WC opposite ...*

"Is there just the *one* bathroom on this floor?" I asked Beans.

"There is nothing *en suite*, I believe ..."

"Oh *good*," I said. "If you'll just hang about while I avail myself ..."

So saying, I nipped inside, bolted the door, stuck the plug in the bath and pissed in it. Then I legged it ...

As soon as I reached Beans' room, I shot straight over to the internal phone and picked the receiver up ...

"Room Service?" said a voice at the other end.

"Ah," I said. "Could you give Mr Funny-Haircut in Room 303 a message for me?"

"Yes," said the voice.

"Could you tell him his *bath's* ready ...?"

"Certainly ..."

"And could you tell him to *hurry*, or it'll get *cold* ..."

"Oh," I added, "And can you send a crate of your finest lager up to Dr Beans's suite on the third floor? *Danke schön*, cock. Roger and out ..."

I slammed the phone down.

"That wasn't very bright, was it?" said Blondie.

"Oh?"

"You've told them where we are. You might just as well have stuck a little target on your chest and a label saying *Here I Am, Aim Here* ..."

"That's all *you* know," I said. "As a matter of fact, I happen to have contacts on the kitchen staff ..."

"Oh yeah?" she said, contemptuously.

"In particular," I said, giving one of my theatrical flourishes, "I have an agent planted in a *butlerial* capacity who doesn't let anything occur without giving me the nod about it in advance ..."

"Where was he just now, then," she said, "When they were carting *what's-his-name* away?"

"It's all part of the plan," I said, making it up as I went along, in order to retain my authority.

"I say you're full of shit ..."

"In any case, I didn't mention any names, except that of the legal occupant – Dr *Beans* here, who isn't known to them in an *enemorial* capacity – and my voice has a quality of natural disguise to it anyway ..."

"It ain't the quality of your voice we're *talking* about here. It's your *order*. As far as I can see, you're the only mug *drinking* that junk round here ..."

"How *dare* you call me a *mug*, madam! Are you *blind*? The only person drinking *Allied Froth*? This is the headquarters of *AF International* – the Allied Froth Corporation! *Allied Froth* is a multi-million pound poisoning charter of international repute. Have sense ..."

"Screw you!"

I was just about to launch a counter-attack, when there was knock at the door ...

"Ah," I said, "That'll be my beer ..."

"Stay there, Dr Kitehawk. Lay low. *I'll* answer it ..."

"I've come for the body ..." said a familiar voice.

"Ah," I said, popping my head round alongside the Good Doctor, "The *Shampoo* Division, isn't it ...?"

"That's right ..." he said, hesitantly.

"I'm glad you've turned up again. Can I borrow your phone a second ...?"

Without waiting for him to signify any agreement to this, I snatched it out of his hand.

"What do you want with my phone ...?" he asked, looking puzzled.

"Castle Security," I said, producing the note I'd taken of his number earlier on, and handing it to him in exchange. "It'll be ready for collection in three days. Here's my number – *one* of them, anyway – don't ring at any time on the twenty-four hour clock ..."

He scrutinised the note. "This is *my* number ..." he went to say, but I'd already shut the door before he had a chance to finish his train of thought.

He knocked again.

"Still here?" I said. *I looked up and down the corridor.* "I shouldn't hang around too long – there's some funny people about ..."

And so saying, I slammed the door on him again.

"Here you are ..." (*I chucked the caller's phone over to Beans*) "... We can keep in touch now ..."

"Obliged to you, Dr Kitehawk, obliged ..."

All of a sudden, there was *another* knock on the door ...

"WHO GOES THERE?!!!" I yelled, without opening it.

"*Sir* ...?" came the reply.

I ushered in Leon, looking up and down the corridor as I did so. *The Shampoo Division had disappeared.*

"One tray of lager ..."

I followed him across the room and waited until he'd put it down carefully on the bedside table before swiping a glass.

"Well," I said, "It's less than a crate, but better than a snifter ..."

"Sir ...?"

"Anything to report?"

"Afternoon tea is currently available in the Holy Roman Lounge, or I could get you into a game of Bridge ..."

"Anything else?"

"In the way of *hats*, you mean ...?"

"Exactly ..."

"No ... not as yet, but you shall be the first to hear ..."

"Leon," I said, "Could you do me another favour?"

"Sir ...?" he replied, with a rather dark look of suspicious conspiracy that was all his own.

"I've lost – *mislaid* – some luggage ..."

"*Luggage*, Sir ...?"

"Yes. A *rucksack*, namely. And a suitcase full of fancy-dress equipment, without which my disguise may not be all it ought tonight. I understand that they may have been sent on from the train with all the other luggage, or they may have been impounded in error by a man named LeGras, who is masquerading as a detective. Alternatively, they may be in the possession of any number of other shifty characters from the same train ..."

"Indeed, Sir?"

"Do you think you can locate them for me – *discreetly*, of course – and bring them up here to Dr Beans' room?"

"I shall do my best, Sir ..."

I tapped the side of my nose to indicate that I'd make it worth his while, and then I put an arm round his shoulder and ushered him back towards the door.

"And," I said, "As a token of my sincerity, here's a little something on account ..."

So saying, I picked up a glass of lager from the tray, stuffed it in his mit and shoved him outside.

In the interim, Blondie had started flicking the bunderbus again, while Beans was gingerly sticking his nose into one of the remaining glasses – *as a result of which, he'd got a layer of foam all over his beard.*

"Give me that lighter!" I cursed.

I snatched it out of her hand and started flicking it myself, while she sat there and scowled at me.

Still it wouldn't light.

"Perhaps we should take an inventory of our weapons ...?" said Beans.

Blondie suddenly produced her hatpin ...

"Go for that trouser-zip, pal, and you're in *big* trouble ..." she said. "... And that goes for *you too*, Kitehawk ..."

I gave her a blank stare.

"You must excuse my phraseology ..." said Beans.

"Here ..." (*I slung the lighter onto the deck*) "... Anyone *top* that ...?"

Beans started to rummage around his vampire-hunters kitbag, before upending the lot onto the floor.

I looked at Blondie. "Well ...?"

Finally, she relented, and chucked the hatpin into the ring.

"Does the phrase *Phoasdul Letif* mean anything to either of you?" I asked, as we inspected our catch.

"Jack shit," said Blondie.

"He was an Arab terrorist, I believe," said Beans.

"Who?" I said, "Jack Shit?"

"Phoasdul Letif ..."

"Straight up?"

He rose to his feet. "I think so, but it's also a name for the Egyptian God of Chaos ..."

I looked down at the assortment of bits and pieces on the floor. "*Hm*," I said, "It's not very much to take on the combined Forces of Evil with, is it? – one faulty lighter, a hatpin, and a bunch of oversized pencils ..."

By way of response, Beans got down on all fours ...

"Well," he said, "Let's take a closer look at our arsenal ..."

"Say, is *he* getting fresh again ...?"

"I don't know," I said. "Why don't you get down on the floor *with* him ... and *ask* him?"

Suddenly, a glass of lager came flying through the air and missed me by inches ...

"Come in *range*, why don't ya ...?" she said, beckoning me with her forefinger.

"Of course," said Beans, "It might help to know a few details, like what's going on, and why you're here, etc ..."

"Over to *you*, Blondie ..."

"Well," she began (*while I listened, intrigued*), "I can't speak for Joe Bananas here, but ..."

"Go on," I said, *thinking how I preferred it when I had employees who didn't talk back, and drifting off into a reverie about the good old times when Ray, The Chief and Fiona were all in there with me neck-deep in the shit and standing shoulder-to-shoulder in the face of enemy fire. Ray, The Chief, Fiona and ...*

All of a sudden, an image of Dirk gatecrashed my head and destroyed the daydream like a drunk at a wedding.

"I'm looking for my Prince ..."

I wasn't sure I'd heard that one correctly, and so I kept shtoom.

"You mean you're trying to track down photographs?" said Beans.

"I mean," she reiterated, "I'm looking for my *Prince* – you know, as in *Prince Charming* – the man I intend to marry ..."

"What *is* that?" I said. "Some sort of code ...?"

"The man *you* call Adolf Flite ..."

My ears pricked up ...

"Yes ...?"

"Turned him into a frog, and holds him captive within this castle..."

I leapt off the chair ...

"Are you taking the piss!?" I screamed at her.

"I'd also like my magic wand and seven-league boots back..."

However, any further enlightenment on this matter was suddenly interrupted when a Harry James solo blared out downstairs, prompting an immediate reconnoitre of the window ...

"Careful, Dr Kitehawk! Don't let anybody see you..."

"Just as I thought..." (*I had my head stuck right out*) "...It's that *bastard* Heehaw..."

"*Who* ...?" they said, as they hurried behind me and leaned over my shoulder.

His limousine was standing in the courtyard below, amongst some driftwood scattered by the wind from the collapsed coaching stable in the far corner.

In time, the fur-coat and monocle-beclad peer stepped out of the rear seat, helped – *not by Tommy* – but by a penguin-suited footman, who took his case and walked in ahead of him while he paused to relight his cigar.

"This *is* a fortuitous booking, as you say, Dr Beans ..." I murmured, fingering the empty lager glass in my hand ...

On an impulse, I lobbed it straight down at him, and watched it bounce off his nut and shatter on the cobblestones beyond.

He went down like a man doing a parachute roll ... *without a parachute.*

When the footman rushed back out to try to help him up, he staggered to his feet with considerable difficulty, crunching up and down on the broken glass as he pushed his would-be aide aside and pulled a gun from his inside pocket ...

"*Duck* ...!" I hissed.

I just managed to drag my accomplices below the level of the sill before a volley of shots rang out, after which I had the unmistakeable impression that he was peppering the outside wall and windows at random ... until five or six bullets zinged into the room and ricocheted off the ceiling.

"I'm not sure that was very wise, Dr Kitehawk ..."

No, I thought, *nor am I* ...

I'd been grazed on the finger by a stray bullet, and the blood was trickling down my wrist...

"Look, *you're* a doctor, aren't you?" I said. "A *scientist* ...?"

"So are *you*, Dr Kitehawk ..."

"*Er* ... yes," I said, "*Exactly*. But have you ever heard of *el dust*?"

"No, I ..." he hesitated, "... I don't *think* so ... *no*. What is it?"

A moment's silence followed, during which I thought Heehaw had finished ... until he started to let rip for a *second* time.

"He must have been reloading ..." mumbled Blondie.

"Some sort of poison," I said. "It's what they put in the drink. It was originally an ingredient in Adolf Flite's Arizona Desert rocket fuel ..."

"Really ...?" he said, while Blondie stared at me with something like a serious look on her face for the first time that *I'd* ever seen one ...

"What's the matter with *you*?" I said.

Declining to favour me with a reply, she looked away while we sat there listening to glass shattering and stonework disintegrating further along the section.

During the next lull in shooting, I heard somebody raise a window ...

Chancing to stick my hooter above the sill line, I saw Tricorn leaning out down the block and trying to find out what all the commotion was about.

All of a sudden, his eyes lit on Heehaw, who was busy fumbling with bullets ...

"What do you think you're *doing*, you *maniac*?!" he yelled down at him. "You could have *killed* somebody ...!"

Heehaw didn't bother looking up until he'd finished filling his empty chambers, after which he calmly walked away from the spot beneath *our* window and marched towards the source of the complaint ...

Like a reckless giraffe, Tricorn still had his neck stuck out waiting for an answer ... when Heehaw started *blasting* away at him.

I couldn't tell whether he'd been hit or not, but he sure disappeared fast from that window...

"That guy must be *crazy* ..." said Blondie.

Crazy or not, he emptied his gun in record time, after which he caught sight of the three of *us* down *our* end and started to wander back, reloading as he went...

"Uh-oh ..." said Blondie, as we all ducked back into the room.

We needn't have bothered, though.

He couldn't have *gone* more than a few paces, when there was an almighty *Splash!* followed by a cranging *Thud!* as Tricorn's bathwater came sailing out the window ... followed, a couple of seconds later, by the *bathtub* itself – wrenched free by hand, presumably, from the plumbing holding it to the wall.

Its *contents* made a direct hit, although the *tub* actually hit the windowsill of the room *below* and fell in on top of anybody who might have been *underneath* it.

Heehaw was a picture ...

Most of what was dripping down his face and clothes was *piss*. And he'd lost his monocle in the process ...

Not that Tricorn would have been aware of that detail when he rashly stuck his neck back out of the window. "What do you think of *that*?!" he yelled.

Heehaw did manage to fire off a couple of shots at a target he couldn't really see any more, when *another* gun suddenly went off in the vicinity ...

A puff of smoke told me it was coming from the room below Tricorn's – *the one in which the bathtub had made its surprise entrance ...*

"*Now*," I mumbled, "I wonder who *that* is ...?"

Heehaw *ought* to have been stranded at the mystery gunman's mercy, but the latter was clearly a very poor shot ...

While his bullets were bouncing harmlessly off the courtyard in an arc well-wide of the fraudulent aristocrat, Heehaw's limousine roared into life and screeched to a halt alongside him. The driver – *wearing a chauffeur's hat and shades* – leapt out and started firing back at the second-floor window ... *with a sub-machine gun.*

The less-than-crack sniper fire came to an immediate end as the curtains were ripped to smouldering tatters by the automatic, but as soon the Chauffeur stopped to bundle Heehaw into the rear seat, a solitary shot rang out and – *confounding earlier trends* – knocked his hat off his head ...

As a *result* of which, the chauffeur dived behind the car for cover and started up all over again, blazing away at the shredded curtain until I caught a clear glimpse of *Mario's* ugly shirt lurking behind it ...

"My God!" I said. "It's like Gunfight at the OK Corral here ..."

In the midst of all *this*, it occurred to me that I could hear *voices* close by and looked up to find two of the three dark-haired girls from the train leaning out of a fourth floor window directly above me, watching the entertainment:

Noticing, in particular, the one who'd threatened me *both* with a knife *and* with release from the cellar, I decided to *accost* her ...

"Oi! I want a *word* with you ...!" I yelled up ...

... but a bullet glanced off the wall not a foot from my nose as I said it, and I had to duck back inside again ...

And this left us with little choice but to lay there listening to the pattern of the gunfire – *first the handgun, then the answer from the machine-gun* – until it all finally went dead.

When I heard the limousine moving, I peered over the sill in time to watch its driver pull up directly below and guide Heehaw inside the main door to safety. *By this time, the girls had disappeared from the upstairs window.*

"So anyway," I said to Beans, "Forget all this gingerbread house stuff that Dopey Dora here was coming out with. Your brief for tonight is to locate some paperwork for me – the *el-dust* file ..."

Before either of them had a chance to comment on this, there was an almighty barrage of gunfire from deep inside the castle, followed by something akin to an explosion as a visiting committee broke into Mario's room ...

Moments later, the chauffeur and two uniformed guards appeared at his window amidst a cloud of thick smoke and threw the burned and battered bedroom door out into the courtyard.

No sign of Mario, though.

They all stood there for a few minutes, trying to figure out where he'd legged it to ...

In fact, I was just watching the buckled bath-tub go the same way, when Blondie suddenly let out an ear-piercing scream behind me and I almost toppled out myself ...

I swung round to find her pointing straight *at* me with an expression of *terror* plastered across her boat ...

"Blood ... *blood* ..." she murmured ... (*backing away*) ... "Kitehawk ... you've been *shot* ..."

I looked down to find that my injured finger had been leaking steadily along my sleeve, giving the impression that the entire limb had been mashed in a meat mincer ...

In order to demonstrate the facts and reassure her, I rolled my shirt up to the elbow.

"It's alright," I went to say -

... *when Beans suddenly came to life and lunged straight at the wound.* "Stand clear!" he yelled. "I'm a *Blood* Specialist ...!"

Only he didn't go for his medical kit ...

He went straight at it with his *teeth* and started to *suck* the blood up *wholesale...*

"What do you think you're doing?!!" I screamed at him, as I tried to disconnect his head from my arm ... *but I couldn't shift him.*

"The Blood Is The Life!" he yelled, rising for a moment ... only to plunge back and follow the vein down to my hand, *gorging* as he went ...

When he reached the *source* of the blood – *ie.* my damaged finger (*which caused me to scream out in pain*) – he finally let go.

I lurched away, wringing my hand in agony ...

"Why didn't you hit him on the head!" I yelled at Blondie, but she'd been rendered shitless and speechless by the sight of Beans's *face* ...

There he was, hovering over me with his beard stained red and blood leaking back out of the side of his mouth like a mosquito in a haematology lab ...

Three seconds after *she* fainted, I came out in sympathy.

"I'm sorry, Dr Kitehawk," he said, as I reluctantly rejoined the land of the living-dead. "I didn't mean to scare you ..."

"*Scare* me, you idiot ...?"

"I may have been a little too hasty, but you can't take any chances with open wounds. Best to suck out the poison straight away ..."

"*Poison?*" I said. "It was a *bullet*, not a rattlesnake ..."

"Quite so," he said. "Anyway, I've put a dressing on it, and I don't think you'll have any more trouble ..."

I looked down to find my trigger finger bandaged up like a miniature mummy.

"You've stitched me up good and proper, haven't you ...?"

"It was quite a severe cut, Dr Kitehawk ..."

"It *was* when *you* finished with it," I said. "And where's that raucous brain-cell, Blondie, gone?"

"For an afternoon nap, but she'll be back later ..."

"Tut-tut. Asleep on duty?" I cursed. "Where?"

He shrugged his shoulders.

"You haven't *eaten* her, have you?"

"Certainly not ..."

This all seemed highly *suspicious* to me, and so I decided to keep a watchful eye on him from that moment on.

A vampire-hunter who drinks blood.

Hm.

It all fitted the pattern.

That is, it made no sense whatsoever ...

The shadows lengthening across the room suggested to me that it was already late in the afternoon, itself an indicator that I hadn't had any lunch, and so I got onto Room Service again.

On this occasion, Leon didn't arrive by the door ...

There I was, just reclining on a pillow and twiddling my bandaged finger, when the bed began to spin round towards the wall ...

I only just managed to jump off in time to watch it disappear *inside* the wall.

As it did so, Leon rotated into view on an identical four-poster from beyond, armed to the teeth with lager bottles ...

"That was quick!" I said.

"We aim to please ..."

"Anything to report yet?"

"Indeed ..."

"Oh?"

"Lord Heehaw has arrived ..."

"Did we *miss* that ...?" I asked Beans, rhetorically.

"Ah," said Leon. "You already knew. The *commotion* ..."

"Anything else?"

"Then you may *also* know that there is a gunman at large in the castle, identity unknown ..."

"I know his identity," I said, matter-of-fact.

"Oh?" he said.

Only I didn't choose to tell him just yet.

"What about my luggage? Any sightings yet?"

"I have located *the* luggage, yes. I think you will need to accompany me in person to identify *your* items, as there is rather a lot of it ..."

"Good," I said, pocketing a bottle for future reference and marching towards the door. "*Lead* on ..."

"Excuse me," piped up Beans. "Do you think you could go back the way you came ...?"

I turned round to find him gesturing at the wall panel behind the four-poster.

"Sir ...?" said Leon.

"It's ... *well*," Beans mumbled, "I'd like my other *bed* back ..."

"What's wrong with this one?" I said to him.

"It's just ... *well* ..."

"Speak up, man," I commanded.

"It's just ... *well* ... the *other* one contains my teddy bear ..."

CHAPTER 47
KID TUT

Before leaving the scene, I gave Beans orders to stay where he was, guard the base camp, be there when Blondie returned from her sojourn, keep watch on who came and went through the main gate, be alert generally, and suggested he rouse the other members of his fraternity. I also told him to process the available information as he knew it and to come up with some answers by the time I returned.

In recollection of my experiences of the previous night, I accommodated a little involuntary shiver as I entered the passage behind his room, thankful that, on this occasion, I had company. There was maybe one hour's daylight left, and this would keep Adolphus Flite imprisoned in his glass tomb at least until I'd had a chance to search the luggage *and* get back again.

"Leon," I said, "Can I ask you something of a rather *delicate* nature ...?"

"*Sir* ...?" he rejoindered.

"The thing *is*," I said, placing an arm round his shoulder, "Can I *count* on you ...?"

The sideways glance he gave me was more akin to a man who'd just been asked to lay his trousers down for Queen and Country ...

"Can I count on you in a *crisis*, that is? Only, I shall need all the help I can get tonight. There won't be any room for neutrality pacts, and I shan't be carrying any passengers or taking any prisoners – and neither will *they* ..."

He paused to take down a flaming torch from the wall before proceeding.

"I think you can count on *me*, Sir ..." he said at length.

"Good," I said. "Only, it's important to know who you can trust in this business, and I'm currently a little thin on the ground in the allies department ..."

"Understood ..."

It struck me, as I followed him down the staircase and out into the damp vaults, that the effect of discovering an Englishman in such inhospitable surroundings – well, *loosely* an Englishman – was something of a bonus, an impression all-too quickly shattered when one of our less *upstanding* countrypersons suddenly assaulted my lughole ...

"*Psst* ...! Kitehawk! I need *help* ..."

I swung round to find Hetty staggering into the torchlight, a picture of terror and exhaustion as she collapsed against me, out cold ...

This didn't look like the same person who'd had me strung me up on a meathook during the early hours, and who'd been seconds from having me murdered in cold blood.

It *was* though, and after I'd laid her down on the flagstones, general dubiousness forced me to wander round the immediate vicinity on the look out for anything suspicious.

By the time I'd satisfied myself that her blown fuse of a boyfriend wasn't lurking nearby, Leon had produced some smelling salts and revived her, after a fashion.

"*Kitehawk* ..." she murmured, "*Kitehawk* ... you gotta *help* me ..."

That's rich, I thought. "Why?" I said. "Why should I help *you*?"

"I'm your *sister*, ain't I ...?"

"*Some* sister ..." I cursed. "Anyway, I've only got *your* word for that. Case not proven, as far as I'm concerned ..."

"*Listen* ..." she mumbled on, apparently half-delirious, "I'll *split* the money with you – *fifty-fifty* – how's that?"

"*Fifty-fifty*?" I said. "What about your half-bright business partner?"

"Forget him, Kitehawk ... he's a dead man. There's guys with guns all over the place. He ain't got a chance ..."

"He didn't *upset* somebody, did he? I find *that* hard to believe ..."

She grabbed my lapels ...

"Listen, cut the crap. I'll make it sixty-forty in *your* favour and we can settle-up another time – only, just get me *outa* here ..."

I went to nod my head ... *and then I changed my mind.*

"No," I said.

I gestured at Leon as if to say, "Lets leave ..."

"Hey! *Kitehawk* ...!"

She stumbled to her feet and came wandering after me ...

"You can *keep* the money," she was babbling, "Only ... get me *out*. I *want* out ...!"

"Give me *one* reason why I should ...?"

"This place is *evil* ..."

"Why *is* it," I said, "That you don't seem particularly out of place here precisely *because* of that fact ...?"

"No, no, it's true ..." she said. "*Listen* ... I've *seen* things ... *real* evil. There's a *gorilla* running around down here, and a guy with no head ... and *rats* ... and ..."

"*And* ...?" I queried.

"I saw the *Devil* this morning ..."

I stopped.

"Why can't you leave by the front door, like everyone else?"

"It's no good – that laughing-guy has got soldiers on it ..."

"Heehaw?"

"*Him the same*. Look, I don't know what's going on here, but I just wanna go home ..."

"I'll think about it ..."

"Hey, you won't regret this, Kitehawk, I promise you ..." she said, as she straggled haphazardly behind me through the maze of arches. "All debts are cancelled in my book ..."

I was just about to ask her *what* debts she was referring to, when we arrived at a patch of damp cellar passing for a luggage bay ...

Looking up at the high semi-circular window through which so many expensive bags and suitcases had been so unceremoniously dumped from the courtyard outside, I wondered whether survival past the first night for any of their owners could possibly be a consideration uppermost on the Flites' agenda ...

At the very least, this was *one* German hotel which would never make the travel guides on the basis of four-star customer care, and considering that the author of *The Corporate Handbook* was also *co*-author to his guests' destiny, it was all a bit of a laugh, really. *I had a good mind to send a letter of complaint through the internal mail ...*

But time was not on my side.

The light coming through that solitary window was beginning to fade, and the rate at which the shadows were lengthening was cause for alarm.

"You remember that rucksack ...?" I said to Hetty.

"The *Bozo's* rucksack?"

"That's right," I said. "I want you to look for it amongst this lot, and ..." *(turning to Leon)* "... If you could give me a hand to look for my suitcase ..."

"Just a minute!" she shouted. "I'm *finished* with all this! The rucksack's *history*. You said you'd get me *outa* here ...!"

"Well, you'll just have to wait!" I yelled back at her.

"What does the suitcase look like?" asked Leon.

"It's no good, Kitehawk. The rucksack ain't here ..."

"Oh?" I said. "Where is it, then?"

"The cops have got it. And if your suitcase has got anything to do with you, they've probably got that as well ..."

"*LeGras* ..." I cursed.

"Do you still wish me to look, Sir ...?"

"Sure," I said, "She might be lying ..."

"And the description ...?"

"Oh, it's an old, brown, battered effort – used to belong to a Colonel – got straps round the outside ... that sort of thing. You couldn't *miss* it – it reeks of *Dettol* ..."

Leon scaled the stack like a mountain-climber, tossing out all manner of bags and cases as he went, while I paced up and down and tried to work out my next move.

Eventually, I had to *stop* pacing, though, since it occurred to me that the shadows had spread into an overall pool of gloom which was beginning to encroach on our position beneath the window ...

"I haven't got *time* for this ..." I cursed to myself.

For want of something better to do, I took out my second bottle of lager and knelt down to cosh the top off on one of the suitcase locks.

As I *did* so, I noticed the identification label hanging from the handle:

Laurel Black

I kicked it round the floor a bit, before booting it off into the gloom.

And do you *know* something?

It felt quite *good* to do that.

So I started kicking a few *more* cases around ...

In *fact*, as fast as Leon could chuck them down, I was kicking them away with the same relish as if it had been their *owners* on the toe of my boot, rather than their suitcases ... which is *why*, when Leon lobbed down a stiff black valise plastered in deluxe *Orient Express* labels, I went to heft it into the ether with a mighty goal-kick ...

"*Careful* with that one ..." he said, as he clambered down the diminished hill of luggage.

"*Porquoi?*" I said, stalling in mid-heft.

"It contains a bomb ..."

"*Aaaaaaaaaaaaaaaargh ...!*"

I threw it up in the air ... and *caught* it again, like a man tossing a pancake.

"A *bomb* ...?" I squeaked. "How do you *know* ...?"

I was at such a complete loss as to what to do with it, that it crossed my mind, briefly, to chuck it in Hetty's direction ...

"Because, Sir ..." (*and here, he mercifully took it from my grasp*) "... It's *ticking* ..."

So saying, he shook it a few times and stuck it to his ear.

So I stuck *my* jug next to *his* and ... *sure* enough, it *was* ticking.

"It might be an alarm clock," I said.

"Only one way to find out ..."

"Oh ...?" I said, as I caught sight of Hetty disappearing behind one of the stone pillars ...

"*Open* it ..."

Tick-Tock, Tick-Tock, it was going.

"Are you *serious?*" I said, incredulous. "Let's get *rid* of it ..."

"Where ...?"

Well, he had a point.

"*You* open it, then ..." I said to him.

I watched his face, as one of those enigmatic frowns rippled over it.

Then, with mind made up, he carried it a few paces away, calmly placed it on the floor and ...

Click!

Click!

Snapped the locks open.

"It's not *locked*, then ...?" I said helpfully, hiding behind the same pillar as Hetty.

He lifted the lid gingerly and proceeded to crouch there, staring into the case with beads of sweat forming on his temples.

"*Well* ...?" I said. "*Is* it a bomb ...?"

"Unfortunately ... *yes* ..."

At great risk to myself, I crept up behind him.

"What do we do *now*, then ...?" I said, as we stared down at a mass of wires, a lump of jelly and a clock face.

Tick-Tock, Tick-Tock ...

"Timing device ... *red* wire, *black* wire ... explosive charge ..." he mumbled, tracing his finger round the case. "Yes, I think it's all here ..."

"Do you *know* about bombs, then ...?"

I could feel a slight draught up my back.

"No," he said at length.

"Kitehawk, I'm *cold* ..." I could hear Hetty moaning.

"Well, what do you propose to *do* about it, then?" I demanded.

Suddenly, he plunged his hand inside the case and pulled out ... a passport, which I hadn't seen.

"Careful ...!" I yelled at him.

He handed it over. "Here," he said, "It might give you a clue as to the owner's identity ..."

"Look," I said, "Can you tell when this thing's set to blow?"

"Not really ..."

"So, it *could* go off any minute ...?"

"Indeed ..."

"What do you suggest we do, then?"

He got to his feet.

"I suggest," he said, "That we ... RUN ...!!!"

And so saying, he kissed goodbye to the stowaways on the *Lusitania* and careered straight past me and away into the dark before I could stop him.

Tick-Tock ... Tick-Tock ... Tick-Tock ... Tick-Tock ... TICK-TOCK ...

I was still staring after the receding trail of his reputation when I realised that the pool of light beneath the window had vanished *with* him, and that the basement darkness was complete around me.

Whoosh ... a breath of wind and a scattering of dust ...

"Leg it ...!" I yelled, as I tore off at about a hundred miles an hour with Hetty wailing behind me as I went.

"*Kitehawk* ...!"

I had no time to worry whether she was keeping up or not, charging around through the dark caverns like a mental patient, with no idea of where I was or where I was going, and no intention to stop until I got there.

And it was in this fashion that I bolted round one particular corner and ran smack into a solid mass of iron and fell spark out backwards onto the deck ...

When Hetty finally caught up and slapped me awake, I opened my eyes to find myself staring straight up at what appeared to be a twice-than-man-size cartoon rocket, embedded in the stone floor.

"Who the hell put *that* there ...?" I cursed, as I got shakily to my feet and rubbed yet another bump on my eggbox bonce.

"What *is* it ...?" agonised Hetty.

When I touched it, my hand recoiled in shock ...

"Ow!" I yelled. "*This* thing's hot – and I mean *hot* ...!"

"Let's get out of here, come on ...!"

"It *can't* be a spaceship," I mumbled. "There aren't any windows in it ..."

"*Kitehawk* ..."

Looking up at the ceiling, I was surprised to find a circular wooden trapdoor above it.

Now, I thought, *is that how they got it in here, or is that where they plan to fire it through ...?*

"Kitehawk ... *come* on!"

"Do you know," I said, as we legged it into a nearby dumb waiter, "It would come as absolutely no surprise at all to learn that that thing there is a nuclear missile ..."

I pressed the button for the third floor, but nothing happened.

So I pressed umpteen *more* buttons, all with the same result.

All of a sudden, a frog hopped past my foot ...

"What the hell's the *matter* with this thing?!" I yelled.

As I stepped back off the platform and feverishly scanned the carriage from the outside, I swear I could hear Adolphus Flite cackling fiendishly in the dark ...

"What are you *looking* for?" said Hetty in a panic.

"What do you *think* I'm looking for?!!!" I screamed, hammering my fist on anything that might start the lift. "I'm looking for the *control* panel ...!"

"They're *screws*, you bloody case! This is a *dumb waiter* – get back in here and help me pull on the rope ...!"

"*You're* not a chip off the old block, *are* ya ...!" I said, as we started tugging away like a couple of bellringers working our way up to paradise on foot ...

Up past the kitchens we sailed, a mass of steam and smoke and people in funny white hats ... one of which, yelled out "Hey!", threw a breadknife at me and pinned my tails to the rear of the cab ... *and onward to sanctuary* (somewhere).

"That'll come in handy ..." I said.

Unfortunately, I pulled the knife out and spun round just as we passed through a sedate lounge on the first floor, causing a maid to scream out loud and drop a pile of teacups on top of the old boy who'd blown his shoe off at breakfast.

"The tails are finished, though ..." I cursed, as I ripped them off and slung them out on the second floor landing.

We more or less *fell* out onto the *third* floor, the pair of us puffing and blowing like a pair of trilby hats on Derby Day.

Bearing in mind that I was now half-undressed as well, it should have come as no surprise when the Matron from the train sailed by ...

"Disgusting!" she commented in passing. "In a public place as well ..."

"Hey!" yelled Hetty.

The Matron stopped dead and turned round. "Are you addressing *me*, you impudent trollop?" she said.

I couldn't *believe* what I saw next ...

Hetty marched straight up to her, punched her square on the jaw, caught her before she hit the deck, turned her over and started to squash her nose into the carpet ...

By the time I reached her, she was mouthing obscenities in Italian and it was all I could do to drag her off the old dear ...

"Come on," I said, "There's no call to *murder* her ..."

"Oh no?"

"*No.* It won't do either of us any good drawing attention to ourselves ..."

"Are you going to get me *out* of this dump or not?" she demanded to know, hands pressed firmly on hips.

"Yes, yes," I said, "But I don't even know where we *are*. This bit's more like an hotel than a castle ..."

Looking round, I noticed a full-length curtain flapping and thought I might be able to get my bearings if it transpired to conceal a verandah.

"Hold on," I said, "Wait here ..."

Well, it concealed a verandah *window* alright, but there was no *verandah* to go with it. *One step too many and I'd have toppled out into the clouds ...*

We seemed to be somewhere along the front face of the central structural complex.

This much I gathered by hanging onto the curtain and allowing the cool evening breeze to rush in past my face:

Close by were the beginnings of that long stretch of battlements leading to the East Wing, as dark and foreboding in the fading daylight as it had been in the dead of night.

In the other direction, the sun was fast sinking in the distance like a lit blood orange.

By the time I'd swung back to safety, I found Hetty sitting exhausted in an armchair and felt compelled to drag her awake ...

"Come on," I said, "This way ..."

Stepping over the still unconscious matron en route, I turned a corner and frogmarched Hetty down a branch corridor leading away from the outside of the castle.

At the *end* of which was a large fluted glass door ...

It must have taken me about three-and-a-half minutes to wrestle it open against the wind-trap beyond, a cloistered walkway skirting three of the four sides of a miniature, sunken courtyard complete with ornamental fountain and Romanesque statues.

All of which did precisely *nothing* for my worsening mood, notwithstanding the fact that it was almost pleasurable to watch Hetty traipsing along ahead of me with her hair being tossed around in the breeze, its colour tinted flame-scarlet in the reflected rays of a dying sun captured in the windows above.

The scent of familiar territory beyond the equivalent fluted glass door at the far end of the walkway quickened my pace, and I wandered in out of the artificial gale to march past Blondie's old room (307), and on until I reached the corner door (303).

"Okay," I said, "I've got a little business to conduct with the occupant of this room. What I want you to do, is to go down to Room 300 at the end of the corridor and ask for Dr Beans ..."

"Kitehawk ..."

"Don't worry," I said, "It's a *safe room*. Everybody in there is a completely trusted friend ..." (*here, I may have had a dubious wince pass across my face*) "... Dr Beans will be able to give you a mild sedative and order some food from Room Service. I shall be along shortly and we'll work on a plan to get you out of the Castle ..."

As soon as she started walking, I knocked on 303's door, waited for Tricorn Haircut to answer and barged past him ...

"Castle Security ..." I said, making a beeline for his internal phone.

"Hello, Kitehawk ..."

He took the trouble to close the door behind me.

"How did you know my name?" I said absent-mindedly.

"*Wanted* posters ... all over the castle ..."

I picked up the receiver.

"Hello ...?" I said. "Get me Room 300 ..."

Blondie answered.

"It's *me*," I said. "Put *Beans* on ..."

"It's Doctor Asshole, for *you* Doc ..." I heard her say.

"Hello ...?" he said.

"Listen *carefully*," I said. "Any second now there'll be a knock at the door. When you open it, you'll find a woman standing there looking a bit on the rough side and claiming to *know* me. What I want you to do is, jump her from all sides, give her a knockout elephant drop and tie her to a chair in the corner – *are you getting this ...*?"

"To the letter ..."

"Make sure you keep a watch on her at all times and never turn your back on her – she's a very dangerous criminal. I'll be in touch, over and out ..."

I put the receiver down.

"Who is she?" said Tricorn. "An enemy agent ...?"
"*Enemy agent* ...?" I said. "*No.* She's my *sister* ..."

"I thought you handled yourself very well this afternoon," I said, as I breezed back towards the door.

"You wouldn't happen to know anything about who pissed in my bath earlier on, would you ...?"

"*Sorry, old boy* ..." I said, just before I legged it.

Speaking of *baths*, it struck me that what I needed more than anything else at that moment was a quick forty winks, and the *bathroom* seemed like the ideal place.

Of *course*, when I got *in* there, I found there was no *bath* to speak of. And *that* meant there was nothing to curl up in. *Some idiot had ripped it from the wall.*

"Bloody vandals ..." I cursed, as I reclined on the floor and kissed goodbye to the land of the vibrantly alert for a couple of hours.

I woke up in complete darkness with a stiff neck and a damp back, and it wasn't until I'd switched on the light and shielded my eyes for a few seconds, that I realised why ...

After pulling the bath out, that *idiot* had stuffed one of his socks into the plumbing to staunch the leak – *the consequence of which was, that a steady stream of water had been trickling down the wall onto me for the entire time I'd been asleep.* My clothes – *what were left of them* – were soaking wet, and this left me little choice but to tear them off, swearing as I went.

Halfway through this practiced procedure, the passport from the bomb valise tumbled out onto the tiles ...

Picking it out of a puddle, I discovered it to be an Israeli passport, the photograph inside belonging to one of the trio of dark haired girls from the train, my room, the basement, the upstairs window etc ...

I slung it into the corner.

"Bloody terrorist ..." I cursed.

My first priority was to rescue the mobile phone from my damp trouser pocket, and, as soon as I'd accomplished this feat, I rang Beans's extension.

The voice at the other end sounded like it was coming from the bottom of the Atlantic ...

"What time is it?" I said.

"*Glug ... glug ... glug ...*"

I smashed it against the wall a few times and tried again:

"Beans, it's *me*," I said. "What *time* is it? Only, there seems to be a discrepancy between the *real* time and my Micky Mouse watch, which stopped two hours ago ..."

"What time does your watch say?" came a voice, barely less scrambled than before.

"Half-past six ..."

"Then it's half-past eight ..."

"Are you trying to be funny?" I said.

"Where *are* you?" it demanded.

"Who wants to know?"

"Look, the party begins in half-an-hour and we're starting to suffocate inside these outfits ..."

"*Outfits* ...?" I queried.

"Fancy dress ... *remember?*"

"You've got *costumes?*" I said, surprised at his initiative. "Have you got a spare one for me?"

"We've got *something* for you, but it ain't a *costume*, Buster ..."

"Who *is* that?" I said. "Is that *you*, Blondie? *Where's* Beans?"

"Yeah, he's tied up right now ..."

"What about *my* fancy dress?"

"Improvise ..."

"Alright," I said. "I'll be along in a minute ..."

As I stood there inspecting myself in the full-length mirror, I began rueing the fact that I was probably the only person in the place who'd had the foresight to set off with – *literally* – a van load of fancy dress equipment, who looked like having to go to the ball stark naked.

And I can *tell* you, it was *not* a pretty sight ...

Potential props were at a premium. All I could see were about four hundred rolls of bog paper and a box of *Rake-O* bath cleaner.

Effing and blinding as I did it, I picked up my soggy herringbones and tipped out the pockets:

"*Now*, what have we got *here* ...?" I mused. "... damp party invite, one-and-a-half Belgian francs – *I could turn myself in to LeGras for more than that* – one disintegrating *Players' No.6*, two dried peas, a handful of *Scrabble* letters, a dead man's dog tag, a City of London parking ticket and a sherrif's badge ..."

Not a lot there.

I looked back in the mirror.

Naked.

From kiss-curl to Khyber pass.

Naked ... *except for my bandaged finger.*

I looked from the bandage to the sherrif's badge, *and then* ... at the bog rolls.

I had an idea ...

"Now ..." I said, as I poked my nut out into the corridor to check the coast was clear, "The trick with *this* little number will be to avoid letting it dry in any one particular position, or I could be in trouble. Keep the muscles flexible ... keep moving ... don't sit down ... etc ..."

Being damp, it *reeked* a bit, and there was an unfortunate tendency to sound as though I were walking through slush and creaking like a man-o-war adrift o' Cape Horn, but it was the best I could do with the available materials.

The sherrif's badge had been the most difficult item to attach, and I'd speared myself in more than a few delicate places before I'd managed to pin it on properly.

The bog rolls had worked a treat. I'd wrapped them around every part of my body – *being careful, of course, to leave eye, nose and mouth slits* – and I'd been correct in assuming that the bath cleaning powder (when mixed with water and slapped on over the paper) would act every bit as good as flour-and-water paste. I'd had the foresight to check the ingredients of *Rake-O* beforehand, but there didn't appear to be anything that might cause problems – all it consisted of was bleach and caustic soda, and so I could have made a milk shake as easily.

Who was I?

King Tut.

The Curse of the Mummy's Tomb.

And, with a rather clever little touch, if I did say so myself, the badge turned me into 'Kid Tut'.

I wheezed at my ingenuity ...

Before leaving, I picked up the murdered professor's identity bracelet and looked at the messages written on obverse and reverse:

Daniel Baudivin

Be An Individual

Taking a few minutes to play around with the *Scrabble* letters, I came to the conclusion, for what it was worth, that one was an anagram of the other.

After awarding myself a fifty point bonus and an honoury degree from the LSE, I bent the bracelet backwards until *Be An Individual* was on the outside, snapped it shut round my wrist and vacated the bathroom.

I wasn't quite able to manouever my limbs in a supple enough manner to close the door behind me, but I emerged into the corridor confident that, covered from top-to-toe as I was, I'd made myself utterly unrecogniseable to anybody – *the In-divisible man* – the perfect disguise ...

"Hello, Kitehawk ..." said Tricorn, breezing past me as Horatio Hornblower.

This rendered me completely speechless until I realised he must have seen me going in there earlier on ...

I knocked on room 300.

At least, I *went* to knock, but somebody had stuck something on the door:

WANTED!
Dexter Kitehawk
Serial Killer
Have you seen this man?
All information to (and further information from): Inspector Benny
LeGras, Room 645, North Tower
REWARD: Negotiable

It was followed by a paragraph or two of small print in which the victims were named as Lady Alexandra Malet and Mark Black Esq – who, it alleged, were murdered on Ostend Dockside and the Gents Toilets at Victoria Station, London, respectively.

What was Lady Malet doing in the Gents Toilets at Victoria Station ...?

It then went on to suggest that I may have been responsible for the murders of about half a dozen other well-known celebrities and crooks and finished up by suggesting that I was extremely dangerous and not to be tackled when pissed...

I ripped it off the door, screwed it up and chucked it as far as I could throw it.

What did it mean, I wondered, 'Reward *Negotiable*' ...?

I knocked on the door in the manner a real Mummy might.

Then I waited and listened to the indistinct rustling noises which served as a prelude to the turning of the handle, and the opening of the door by a fraction...

Peeping out at me was Blondie.

"Yeah ...?" she said.

As I went to walk in, she slammed it shut in my face ...

I don't know why, but the only thing I could think to do was to roar at the top of my voice and start hammering on the door with both fists ...

Anyway, it was all to no avail, because she wouldn't open up again, and it was while I was carrying on in this manner, that one of the many penguin-suited Kraut domestic staff wandered by behind me, glancing at the stream of puddles leading back toward the bathroom and giving me a rather funny look.

"Do something about that *mess*, will you ...?" I yelled after him. "It's a bloody disgrace ...!"

Suddenly, the door opened again – a bit *wider* this time – *revealing Blondie with a puzzled expression on her face ...*

"Is that *you*, Kitehawk ...?" she said.

"At ease," I said, barging past her and expecting to find Hetty tied up in the corner.

There *was* somebody in the corner – trussed up like a turkey dinner – but it *wasn't* Hetty ...

She was standing behind the door – and, as I swung round to discover – was getting ready to *clobber* me one ...

"Whoa ...!" I said. "What's going on here ...?"

"What's the big idea – you telling *him* to tie *her* up ...?" demanded Blondie.

Noticing that Beans was rather fortuitously *gagged* as well as *bound*, I marched over and grabbed hold of the lapels of his Dracula suit ...

"You mean he tried to tie my *sister* up?" I said, outraged. "What do you think you're *playing* at ...?!!"

He looked a bit flabbergasted, to say the least!

"You *bastard*!" I continued, trying to wink at him reassuringly, but I don't think it was getting through the eye slits very clearly. "*Well*," I said, as I turned round to face my irate sister and her new friend, "I think you did the right thing, anyway ..."

First of all, I was hit by a right hook from Lucretia Borgia, *then* by a left hook from the Wicked Fairy, and as I staggered around in a twilight world of stars and lights, I heard *Blondie* tell me she was going to get my sister "on a train" and that she'd "see me later," and I heard *Hetty* tell me she was going to make me a "Sicilian watercress sandwich," and that she was going to be waiting for me back in England when I stepped off the boat, "to make sure I *ate* it ..."

And on *that* note, amid a bucketload of Anglo-Italian obscenities, the pair of them disappeared out the door.

When I *stopped* staggering around, I picked up a bottle of lager and sank it as quick as I could, momentarily forgetting about the doctor sitting there chairbound.

Eventually though, I did become aware of his muffled protests and untied him.

Sometime afterwards, he had the cheek to say this:

"*What*, if I may *ask*, Dr Kitehawk, are you going to the fancy dress party as, then ...?"

I looked at him in astonishment. "Can't you *tell* ...?"

"No," he said.

"I'm *going* ..." I said, picking up the remaining lager bottles and not waiting around for him to catch me up, "... ALL GET OUT!"

And on *that* note, I *went*.

CHAPTER 48
TWO GUESTS
FOR THE LAGER BARONS BALL

"Dr Kitehawk ... Dr Kitehawk ..." I could hear him calling, far down the corridor behind me.

Turning the corner, I made my way towards a staircase decked out in plush blue carpet, the walls adorned with portraits of notable German criminals from the past three-and-a-half centuries.

As I did so, I noticed that my slushing was beginning to decrease while my creaking was beginning to increase and, whatsmore, I was beginning to *itch*.

And so I started to *scratch* ...

Labouring my way down the stairs in this fashion, I passed a rather well-dressed Kraut couple going in the other direction, who seemed to think it was perfectly alright for them to turn up their noses at me and register the word *Aghast!* in neon lights all over their ironing boards:

I roared and growled at them in a ferocious manner and generally caused them to leg it up the stairs a bit faster than might otherwise have been the case ...

Another flight down, and I stumbled upon the penguin from earlier, on his way to the damp patches on the third floor. *He was lugging a foam vacuum carpet cleaner with him, and he didn't take much notice of me, preoccupied as he was by the job in hand.*

"Where's the party, cock ...?" I enquired, as I stopped to cosh a bottle open on the polished banister.

He started shouting and gesticulating at me in German ...

"Be quiet! *Shtoom!*" I yelled, becoming aware of more people ascending from below. "Or I shall have you shot ...! *Raus ! Raus ...!*"

He backed off a bit, but not entirely.

And so I demanded, in future, that he use the Domestic Service Staircase and proceeded on my way ...

The joy *was*, that I had complete immunity from recognition, and this was beginning to give me a sense of well-being and a feeling that I might accomplish quite a bit during the course of the evening.

The approaching group of Germans, all decked out in costumes from the Court of Frederick the Great, greeted me as they passed ...

"*Guten Abend* !" said one.

"*Guten Abend* !" I replied.

"*Guten Abend* !" said another.

"*Guten Abend* !" I rejoindered.

"*Guten Abend*," said a third. "*Wie geht es ihnen* ...?"

"*Guten Abend* !" I said with a flourish. "And the *rest* of it ...!" .

"Good evening, Mr Haute-Cooke," said Candida, dressed as Cleopatra ...

"You look like you've lost something," she said, as she paused on the staircase.

Yes, I thought. My *credibility* ...

"Yes," I said. "As a matter of fact, I *have*. A fancy dress party ..."

"Follow me ..."

I did a U-bend and went back up the stairs with her.

"Tell me," I said, "How did you recognise me, if you don't mind me asking...?"

"Call it *intuition* ..."

"And how is your charming niece, Heidi, this evening?" I asked, aware that I could be opening a can of beans.

"Haven't seen her, I'm afraid. She was meant to spend this afternoon with Sonny ... and so I suppose she did ..."

"How delightful for her ..."

So *that* was his game! He was a bleeding *child* molester ...

Talking of tins of *beans*, we picked up Count Dracula en route, charging down the stairs like his arse was already four yards in front of him, and so I grabbed him by the neck, swung him round in the opposite direction, and introduced him to Mrs Flite.

Thereafter, she led the way, wafting out of the central section and along the battlements, which were lit now by a line of pretty electric lamps.

Further ahead – and further behind – other small groups of guests were meandering, some in fancy-dress costumes, others in evening wear – towards the roof terrace of the East Wing...

It was, however, almost completely unrecogniseable as the place in which I'd spent my first night:

I daresay the ruins of my erstwhile domain, the Blood and Iron Room – somewhere up there in the main tower – were still bathed in darkness, without a candle or a lightbulb in sight, but somebody had been hard at work that day in the lower realms, preparing things for the party.

A quiver of anticipation rippled through my stomach as we wandered in off the verandah and approached the top landing of the Grand Staircase, the sound of hundreds of voices becoming apparent from below, along with the reassuring *chink chink* of hundreds of accompanying glasses ...

Once again, the stairs were lined with portraits, though it was difficult to tell who this *particular* collection represented, because every single one of them had a *Wanted* poster plastered over it.

In *consequence* of which, I felt obliged to tear each one down as we descended, as nonchalantly as I could, screwing them up and dropping them behind me as I went.

"That horrible little Belgian man, LeGras, has been asking for you all day," Candida suddenly declared.

"Yes," I said. "He owes me money ..."

"*Does* he indeed ..." (*She sounded quite disgusted*)

"Oh yes," I said, "I've been bankrolling him for years. He's into me for quite a bit, actually. In fact, he borrowed rather a large wedge from me on the train here – to pay off gambling debts, mainly, I think ..."

"Squalid little man ..."

"I believe *also*," I said, as I slung an empty beer bottle behind me, "That he's got a *drink* problem ..."

"Well, *really* ..." she said, apparently lost for words.

I paused by one of the posters.

"Of course," I said, "It's not for *you or I* to sit as judge and jury ..."

"Oh no, quite ..." she agreed.

Underneath *Wanted*, someone had written in magic marker: 'By Nobody'
I tore it down and wandered on.

"It's all rather sad, really," I said, "This business of him telling everyone he's a detective ..."

"He's *not* a detective, then ...?"

"Far from it," I said, as I paused by the next poster.

"What *is* he, then?"

"He's actually a snack bar attendant ..."

"Good God!"

"Do you have a pen on you?" I asked.

"No ... I'm afraid ..."

"I have one, Dr Kitehawk," piped-up Beans.

So saying, he offered me a gold-plated ballpoint.

Underneath *Wanted*, I wrote the words 'By Queen and Country', stuffed the pen somewhere it didn't hurt and carried on walking ...

"Oh no," I said at length, "If I was Simon, I'd have sent him packing long before now, but then I expect he decided it was best to humour him ..."

"Why?" she said. "Is he dangerous?"

By now, we were approaching the ground floor, and the entrance to a large hall was looming.

"Mm," I said. "He's the M2 Hat-Murderer ..."

"My *God* ...!" she said, reaching a hand to her chest. "And he's *here*, in our family home ...?"

"Mm ..."

At this juncture, we all paused underneath a great banner exhibiting a poignant legend:

LAGER BARONS' BALL

"What can we do ...?" she said.

"Well," I said, "I should bolt down the silver for a start. Other than that, boot him off the battlements. It's the only way ... though, you must bear in mind that this is the *war* hero in me speaking. Others may prefer a more cautious approach ..."

"I shall have a word with Simon ..."

"Mm," I said, "I think that's probably best ..."

"Yes," she said, mind made up. "But it doesn't alter the fact that you are a terrible, *terrible* man, Mr Haute-Cooke ..."

"Care for a dance?" I said.

"*Why* not ... "

The trouble *was*, as I breezed up with Candida on one arm and Beans hovering behind me, I found my way barred by a doorman armed with a guest checklist, and two Corporation stormtroopers armed to the teeth with a bit *more* than that ...

"Frau Flite," the man said.

He clicked his heels together and let her pass.

I thought for a minute he was going to let *me* pass as well ... *until he suddenly stopped me.*

"Name?" he demanded.

Well, I couldn't give my identity away, could I?

"Ah ..." I said, stumped. "*This* is ... er ... Dr Beans, the famous bloodsucking leech behind me ..." (at which I shoved him in *front* of me) "... And I am ..."

"And *you* are ...?" he said, crossing the latter off his list while the guards lost all pretence to subtlety as they loomed intimidatingly around my immediate floorspace ...

"And *this* is my *friend,*" said Candida. "From the United Nations. Isn't that *correct* ..."

"*Yes* ..." I said, taken aback.

"He is my *personal* guest," she went on, "And I am afraid I did not have time to add him to the list ..."

"That is no problem," he said. "But I do need to enter a name, Frau Flite – for *security* purposes, you understand ..."

"Yes," I said, "Quite ..."

"And your name *is* ...?" he said. "Mr ... Herr ... *Monsieur* ...?"

"*Senor,*" I said at length, as the guards backed off to resume their positions scrutinizing the party. "Senor *Percuellier* ... Senor *Perez* Percuellier, at your service..."

So saying, I clonked my ankles together and gave him a mildly elaborate theatrical bow.

"FRAU CANDIDA FLITE, HERR DOKTOR FILBUR BEANS UND..." he announced, "... SENOR PEREZ *PECULIAR* ..."

"No, no," I corrected him. "Not pe-*cu*-liar. That's Per-*quair-lee-air* ..."

He tried again. "SENOR PEREZ PER-*QUEER-LEER*, von dem United Nazions ..."

"How about *The Memphis Kid* ...?" I said.

"*Bitte* ...?"

"Never mind ..."

We wandered in and lingered at the top of a little flight of stairs leading down onto the revelry arena, a position from which I was able to note the large dimensions of the hall:

It was crammed full of people in all kinds of fancy-dress costumes – most of whom were standing around *chatting*, rather than *dancing* – *though there was a Viennese four-piece fiddling away in the distance. The air was heavy with smoke, and penguin-suited butlers were wandering around with trays of food and drink.*

Marvelling at the discreet entrance I'd managed to make – *with Candida's help, of course* – I went to take a step forward, and ... *in a split second of horror, my outfit suddenly seized up, and I fell headfirst onto the dance floor.*

"Who put that *staircase* there ...?" I cursed, as I rolled to halt.

In a matter of seconds, I'd been lifted back to my feet by a couple of penguins, and Dracula and Cleopatra were all over me, checking for breakages (in the latter's case) *and, presumably, blood* (in the case of the former).

Luckily, my impromptu acrobatics seemed to have aroused only minimal interest from the nearest groups of guests, and so I was able to resume a fairly discreet pose again rather quickly ...

"Are you sure you're *alright*, Mr Haute-Cooke ...?" Candida was saying. "Or should I call you Mr *Percuellier* from now on ...?"

"You can call me Dexter," I said, wondering why she'd adopted a protective interest in me. "Though, I think we may have to skip that dance for now, as I seem to be developing some temporary mobility problems ..."

The bog rolls were drying out fast, and a section covering my right wrist had vanished during the fall, revealing my Mickey Mouse watch to an unprepared public.

Thank Christ that's *all* it revealed ...

Even *so*, I could see that I might have to make twice as many visits to the nearest convenience than usual – half the time to have a piss, and the rest to slap more bog paper over me.

It was only *then*, with a start, that I realised something *dreadful* ...

I'd omitted to leave access flaps in certain delicate areas due south of my midriff, and this meant that I was going to have problems having any sort of a piss at all.

Gawd help me if I suddenly wanted a *crap* ...

Notwithstanding the *bog* paper.

Either way, it was certainly no prospectus with which to fight the powers of darkness and, since midnight was less than three hours away, it occurred to me that I was already in a bit of trouble ...

Scanning the hall for familiar faces, none could I see – friend or foe – *though many of the assembled throng were wearing masks.* What I *could* see of interest had more to do with the layout of the place:

Roughly in the centre of the hall was a raised circular podium, on top of which sat the quartet, and at the far end of the hall was a spacious theatre-type stage, flanked by curtains.

A huge banner had been hung from the overhead:

GRAND UNVEILING CEREMONY – MIDNIGHT TONIGHT

"Never mind about the dance, Dexter, *talk* to me ..." said Candida. "Tell me why you're here ..."

"Me?" I said. "Quality control. Just a random check, really ..."

"No, no," she insisted. "Tell me the *real* reason you're here. Go on, I won't breathe a word to anybody ..."

"Well," I said, rashly, "I've actually come to arrest a lot of criminals, *amongst* whom – I'm sorry to have to tell you – your *husband* numbers ..."

"*Martin?*"

"Yes, I'm afraid so ..."

"Good," she said, to my surprise.

"*Good* ...?"

"Yes," she said. "*Excellent* ..."

"I thought you'd be shocked ..."

"*Me* ...? No ..."

"But he's your *husband* ..."

"Mm ..." she said.

"Don't you want to know *why* I'm arresting him ...?"

"Oh, I *know* why," she said, to my further surprise.

"Oh?"

"He's a good-for-nothing crook ..."

Time for a drink, I thought ...

"And you ought to arrest that nutcase of a *brother* of his, as well – *Simon Flite* ..."

On *which* disarming note, she wandered off to play hostess ...

"What a stink!" came a voice. "Is that *you* in there, Kitehawk ...?"

I swung round to find Tricorn sailing by, doing the Viennese Waltz with Lady Hamilton.

They looked like two wrestlers trying to get out of a double-half-nelson Boston crab ...

"I think I preferred your *other* costume ..." I said.

"Oh ...?" he said, as they whirled away across the dance floor. "What was that ...?"

"*Mind your own fucking business* ..." I cursed, under my breath.

The more I thought about Candida's denunciation of her husband and his brother, the more it occurred to me that this was the first real confirmation I'd had of my suspicions concerning the Flites and, bearing in mind that it came from inside the family, it was a bit of an arrow in my hat.

That bloody bog roll was starting to unwind from my left foot ...

It was doubtful, however, whether anybody of any great importance would be announced on their way in – LeGras would hardly wish to advertise himself to me in this fashion, and the same could be said for just about everybody else connected with the case.

I looked up to check on the current batch of arrivals, but I was none the wiser:

"MR NORMAN LAMOT AND MRS LAMOT ..." (*I think this was the tubby English off-licence baron and his wife, dressed up as walking fruit machines, but I could have been wrong*)

Another thing I was none too clear about, was the current whereabouts of the Count, since he appeared to have wandered off without permission.

I therefore extracted the mobile phone from a place of secrecy about my person and dialled his number.

"Yes?" he said.

"Where *are* you?" I said.

"Mingling," he said. "And attempting to find my colleagues ..."

"Seen anybody you recognise?"

"Not really, though the fellow about to make an entrance is well-known in scientific circles ..."

"Oh ...?"

I glanced round.

"SIR EWAN SCINTAO ..." announced the Doorman.

I watched as a swarthy character dressed as a pirate entered.

He paused on the top step, looked left and right, and descended into the hall.

"Speciality?" I queried.

"Gravity research ..."

"Scintao ... *Scinto* ... Skint-o ..." I mumbled to myself, thinking it had a familiar ring. "No, sounds like he's on the earhole to me. *Over* and out ..."

"FRAULEIN DELORES BECKMANN ..."

"*Hello* ...?" I said out loud, swinging round just in time to watch Delores the legatee descend to the dance floor, dripping in diamonds, wearing a Gatsbyesque costume from the Jazz Age.

I took particular note of *her* for future reference.

(In *fact*, the way things were going, I was likely to be consigning a number of *other* matters into the same bin, because that *itching* was just getting worse and worse ...)

When I finally reached distraction point, I stretched down with some difficulty and managed to tear off part of the loose bog paper, and this I handed to a stray penguin in return for another drink.

It didn't do much *good*, though, because more and more of the cursed stuff just started to unravel itself, and since I didn't think there was very much chance of making it through till midnight with my costume still intact, I was left with yet one more problem to solve.

Perhaps not the *most* pressing, though, because I'd just seen the outline of Sonny Reithoek's charming frame appear in the entrance way and stroll to the top of the steps ...

I watched him pause by the railing to one side, a position he leaned on for several minutes while he scanned the guests menacingly:

Eventually, he snapped his fingers and summoned the two stormtroopers for clandestine instructions, at the issue of which they proceeded to march down into the arena, putting on Herman Goering masks as they went ...

Assuming that he'd ordered them to wander round and keep an eye open for enemy activity, it looked to me as though (with a walkie-talkie and a gun alongside his rhino-hide whip in what was becoming a rather overcrowded waistband) he was in charge of security for the night.

At *least*, he wasn't in fancy-dress.

Put it *that* way.

Unless those *drill shorts* of his could be described as such.

Either way, I was inclined to wonder whether I was really in the best place or whether, in fact, I shouldn't be somewhere else – *like*, say, belowdecks, or just about anywhere except at the party – trying to prevent what was going to happen from happening *before* it happened.

But what can you do without staff?

I got on the blower to Beans again, trying to whisper and shield it from view, in case either of those guards were prowling around nearby ...

"Can you give me a progress report?" I asked him.

"That's a negative," he said, and rang off.

What am I? I thought. *Alone in the world?*

I dialled again.

"Beans," I said, "Any sign of Leon yet, or of any of *your* mob?"

"That's a negative," he said ... *and rang off again.*

"How would you like me to set fire to your beard?" I enquired, after ringing a third time.

"I think you may have dialled the wrong number ..."

"Oh?" I said. "And who am I, then, the Speaking Clock?"

"Is that *you*, Dr Kitehawk ...?"

"How many *other* people have got your extension? Anyway, I'd just like you to interrupt your busy social schedule for a moment. There's something I want you to do for me ..."

"I'm all ears ..."

"Okay," I said, "*This is the plan*. I want you to find your way down to the basement and check up on that skeleton in the glass case. And be *discreet* about it..."

"*What?*" he protested. "On my *own* ...?"

"I'm afraid I can't spare the staff to give you any assistance, and I need to stay here to keep a watch on *this* lot ..."

"Alright ..." he said reluctantly.

"Keep in touch at all times ..."

"*Roger* ..."

"Who's *he*?" I said, but he'd already hung up.

Which was *just* as well ...

I had to conceal the phone pretty damn quick because I'd spotted one of the Goerings in my vicinity, and I seemed to have caught his attention ...

As luck would have it, he was distracted by something *above* him before he got to me, and, as I looked up to see what *he* was looking at, I got a faceful of dust ...

I took the opportunity to disappear into the crowd, but not before a small chunk of ceiling plaster had landed in my drink.

Two minutes later, I was still looking for somewhere to sling this dubious windfall when one of the refreshment penguins happened to wander by, and – declining to take any chances – I snatched the entire *tray* off him.

More dust – little handfuls of greyish powder – continued to fall at random intervals.

"SIR CHARLES MALET ..."

I craned my neck above the crowd to catch a glimpse of the vengeful politician, and nearly fell about laughing when he descended the steps dressed as...

... an orange.

It was now 10.00pm by the Hall clock.

Suddenly, there was the sound of a *commotion* going on behind me ... a glass dropping to the floor and breaking ... voices raised in protest – outrage – scuffling noises *etc* ... and I turned round to find *Trevor*, his hair sticking straight up as though it had been permed with bleach, trying to pull the mask off a highwaywoman ...

Her *companion*, who'd tried to come to her assistance, was now getting the same treatment, but his attempts to resist caused Trevor to let go suddenly, thus allowing the mask to catapult back against his face with a sickeningly audible elastic *Twang!*

Amid curses and shouts in German, Trevor ducked out of the way and went off to try and unmask somebody else – presumably looking for *me* – in the latest exhibition of tactful private investigation as conducted by a certifiable psychopath.

"*Shit* ..." I cursed.

I got ready to make a bolt for it should he look like approaching, but he disappeared in the opposite direction the moment one of the guards arrived on the scene ...

More commotion – this time over by the entrance, where some old boy, completely starkers from head to foot, was trying to gatecrash the party ...

After struggling with the doorman, he grabbed the microphone and staggered to the top of the stairs, intent on *announcing himself* ...

"ANEURIN BEVAN!" he yelled. "NAKED INTO THE CONFERENCE CHAMBER ...!"

All of a sudden, Sonny Reithoek burst through the door with about forty stormtroopers and bundled him away before he had a chance to bluff the delegates ...

I was so *distracted* by this interlude, that when my phone suddenly bleeped at full blast, I went for it in such a panic that it shot out of my hand like a slippery fish, and it was as much as I could do to grab it out from a fancy dress monk's hood before the increasing number of Goering masks – *standard stormtrooper issue for the evening, it appeared* – got wind of what the noise was ...

"*Who* wants to know?" I hissed.

"It's gone," said the voice.

"Pardon ...?"

"The *skeleton*. It's *gone* ..."

"*As I suspected* ..." I said. "Okay, you can come back up now ..."

"Wait, there's something else – something we missed last night ..."

"Oh ...?".

"Well, I think I've found the *el dust* file ..."

"*El-dust* file ...?" I queried, surprised. "Really? Are you *sure* ...?"

"I'll bring it up ..."

"HERR OTTO POSSENREISER ..."

It was the old lager manufacturer with the red conk, doubling as Hindenburg (the airship, that is, not the Baron von), and I suspected his pal wouldn't be far behind ...

"HERR HEINRICH SCHURKE ..."

"Alias *Frostbite* ..." I said to myself.

"The *Shampoo* Division?" came a voice from behind me.

I did a slow-swivel ...

"Have you come for the body ...?" I said.

"Room 307?"

I lifted one leg off the floor.

To my surprise, he lifted his *opposite* number ... *and rolled his trouser-leg up to the knee.*

It was a good job I couldn't *match* stage two of this esoteric ritual, or he might have got carried away.

Instead, I pointed at the bog roll unravelling itself from my calf and gave him a shrug of the shoulders.

He handed me a brown envelope and disappeared.

As soon as I was able to find a quiet corner, I took out a sheet of paper and read what was written on it.

"Waiter ..." I called to the nearest penguin. "I need to get some of my luggage. Can you direct me to the basement ...?"

He *could*, and he *did*, and when he opened a side *door* for me, I went clomping down one of those dark, stone staircases, only to meet Beans coming up, apparently empty-handed.

"Where's the file?" I demanded.

"Here, I found it amongst the broken glass ..."

So saying, he handed me a tiny card.

"What's this ...?"

"It's a histopathology tag – an identification label. You must have seen them. The sort of thing you get on the display cases in morbid anatomy museums..."

phial of el dust

"Oh," I said. "It was *that* sort of file. Not *paperwork* at all. No wonder Parker couldn't find it ..."

"What does it mean?"

"I'm not sure ..."

"But," he said (*with some concern in his voice*), "Surely the implication is that the *skeleton itself* is *el dust*. There was nothing *else* in the container – *the phial* – this morning, and ... well, if it's *in* the *drink*, then ... *what*? Are we all partaking of his *remains* ...?"

"Like some sort of *un*-holy communion, you mean ...?" I laughed. "I don't know ... probably not literally ..."

But *something* was beginning to fall into place ...

"*Nothing else in the phial* ..." I mumbled to myself. "*... Nothing* in the *file. I am the incubus. I am* ... oh yeah, I *get* it. I know what it means ..."

"Well?"

"Never mind," I said, with my heart in my mouth. "I'm off to do a little research. I'll meet you back at the ball. How far is the coffin, and in what direction ...?"

So this is it, I thought, as I stared at the remains of the empty glass container:

The Hell Dust file.

Or rather, a *phial of el-dust* ...

... a bottle of *Phiall Foduste*. A tube of *F L Delusiopath*. A glass of *Phoasdul Filet*. A case of *Phoasdul Letif* ...

... a coffin for *Adolphus Flite*.

i am the incubus . adolphus flite . nadhet ropatreorc pristi

The trouble was, as I was standing there and trying to work out the third (and last) part of the icon anagram by recalling crucial bits of both *Unholy Trinity* and Martin Flite's *Handbook*, I heard voices approaching and had to duck quickly behind the nearest pillar to avoid detection.

Imagine my surprise when, as the voices grew louder, who should pass by on their way to god-knows-where but a party of terrified schoolchildren ...

Forgetting, momentarily, that I was made up as a frighteningly realistic Mummy, I lurched out of the shadows and nearly killed them all stone dead with fright ...

"Calm down!" I said. "It's fancy dress ..."

All of a sudden, one of the little sods ran up and kicked me in the shins, while their irate teacher started to batter me round the head with her clipboard ...

"Madam!" I protested. "My intention was *not* to scare ..."

"How *dare* you!" she shouted. "Jumping *out* on us like that!"

I tried to back off out of her way ...

"What are you doing down here?" I said. "Don't you know the dangers ...?"

"From *you?*"

"Yes ... I mean, *no* ..."

She folded her arms. "We are lost," she said. "What do you make of that?"

"Lost?" I said.

"We are on a school visit to the Castle Froth and sometime earlier today we took a wrong turning from the public area and have been wandering around these godforsaken cellars ever since ..."

"*Public* area?" I said. "You've *got* to be *joking* ..."

"Do I *look* like I'm joking?"

"Look," I said, trying to gather my senses, "You have to get *out* of here. You are in great danger – there is a *bomb* in this basement ..."

"A *bomb* ...?" she said, shocked.

"Yes, amongst *other* things," I confirmed. "A *bomb* ..."

As if to underline my warning, a distant thud rocked the floor and another clutch of dust fell from above ...

"Was that *it?*" she demanded to know.

"No ..."

I *knew* it wasn't the *bomb*, because the sound came from *below* the basement.

"What *was* it, then?"

"It is a former Nazi executioner mining for treasure ..."

"I see," she said, sceptically. "And I suppose you think that this kind of nonsense is good for frightened children ...?"

They didn't look very fightened to *me*. At least three or four of them were starting to unwind the bog rolls round my ankles and seemed to think this was a great laugh.

"*Good* or *not*," I said, "It is *certainly* not good for the *bomb* ... or for the *castle*, for that matter, which may collapse about our ears at any moment ..."

"I shall report you to the police when we get out of here ..."

"Then let me prove it to you ..."

So saying, I proceeded to lead the way to where I thought I'd left the black valise.

However, when we arrived at the luggage bay ...

Surprise, surprise.

Along with the rest of the cases (which had also mysteriously vanished), it was nowhere to be seen.

"It's gone," I said.

"I *see* ..." (*here, she began advancing on me all over again and poking me in the chest*) "... I wish to know your *name* so that I can report you to the police ..."

"I *am* the police," I said. "As a matter of fact, I am *above* the police, and am currently investigating an international lager conspiracy ..."

Even some of the little horrors looked sceptical about *that* one.

"Show me the way out!" she demanded.

"As is your wish ..." I said, and went off to hunt a route back to the Ball.

"I still require to know your name," she said, as she continued to harangue me up the staircase, "For when I *report* you ..."

I can *tell* you, it did my credibility absolutely *no* good whatsoever, traipsing across the dance floor with *that* lot on my tail, but I seemed to have little choice.

Even so, I had absolutely no intention of telling her who I was and, instead, told her my name was *Trevor*.

"Could you show this lot the way out ...?" I said to the doorman, who was busy announcing some late guests.

"MISS RHODA LeFLIT ..."

A little pixie in a clown's mask ran by.

"Only, they're lost ..."

All of sudden, the enormous frame of Sonny Reithoek appeared in the doorway and barred their way ...

"What's going on here?" he demanded to know.

I knew I had to keep quiet, because he was sure to recognise my voice.

"Are you in authority?" the teacher piped up.

When she marched round me to meet him, he said nothing, but looked down at her in a menacing manner.

"Only," she said, "I want this man reported to the police for trying to scare the children ..."

"Trying to *scare* the *children* ...?" he said.

He was fingering his rhino-hide whip when he walked up to inspect me, cue for the Viennese quartet to stop playing and a hush of sorts to descend on the hall ...

"In any event," she said, as she attempted to gather her brood together to leave, "We must return to town ..."

Although he made no response to this, he'd taken his whip from his waistband and was gesturing behind him with it as if to say, 'Wait there'.

"Don't I *know* you from somewhere?" he said, tapping me with the butt end of it.

I kept completely shtoom.

"We must go," said the teacher. "Come along children ..."

"Stay right where you are!" he suddenly commanded. "Nobody leaves Castle Froth after nightfall!"

Quite why I chose this moment to rather stupidly open my mouth, I'm not sure to this day, unless it was to ram a size twenty-seven roller-skate down the entertainment rink masquerading as my throat ...

"I *told* you," I said, "You should have listened to *me* ..."

Well ... you could have heard my hair turn white in the silence, as about three-hundred-and-fifty hostile pairs of eyes launched their daggers at me ...

Raiders of the Lost Kiteark

"I *knew* I knew you!" he suddenly shouted.

"*Whoops* ..." I squeaked.

"Captain of the Guard!" he bellowed into his walkie talkie. "I have a man and a woman here – I want them chained up in the dungeon for questioning. There is also a party of schoolchildren – I want them all confined to my private quarters, where I shall interrogate them personally ... *on the double!*"

In an impulsive act of unparallelled heroism on my part, I pulled my mobile phone out, and ... smashed him right round the side of the head with it!

As he began to stumble, I coshed him a few more times till he hit the deck ...

"Run!" I yelled at the teacher. "Get out of here ...!"

"Quick, children ...!" she shouted, as she set about herding them through the door amid screaming (*from them*) and yelling and shouting (*from the dance floor*)...

When the doorman made a move towards me, I coshed him as well ...

Following which, I grabbed the gun from Reithoek's waistband with one hand, his rhino-hide whip with the other, lassoed a chandelier and launched myself out over the assembled revellers, sparking a general pandemonium in which somebody took a pot-shot at me ...

I'd only just managed to reach *mid*-swing when I went crashing down across one table after another like a bouncing bomb, hurling glasses, bottles, packets of crisps, opera sticks, chiffon scarves, strings of pearls, diamond necklaces, *pince nez*, periwigs, stoles, cufflinks and ruffles into the air, as any number of Prussian aristocrats and their wives scattered in all directions ...

Thereafter, I scrambled to my feet quickly enough, waving the gun about (*with which I kept everybody at bay*) and legged it back towards the basement exit ...

Faces and masks parting on either side of me as I stumble across the dance floor ... and one in particular, off to the side ... a figure in an Adolf Hitler mask ...

As soon as I'd hurled myself through the door, I slammed it shut behind me and turned a great big iron key in the lock ... *only to find myself confronted by another one of Reithoek's henchmen looming out of the shadows to block my escape ...*

So I clattered *him* one as well.

In *fact*, I hit him *so* hard, that the mobile phone exploded into little pieces ...

Not to waste the opportunity, I dragged him down a few steps and off into a dark corner, where I set about purloining his uniform and his Goering mask.

Unfortunately, as I started to peel off my *own* costume, I discovered it was taking the top layer of my skin with it ...

When I finally got shot of the last of the bog paper, I was covered from head-to-foot in great lobster-red blotches and in some considerable pain, though I did manage to complete the swap before the sentry began to stir, and I was only grateful I had a mask to put on.

Not because I thought anybody would recognise me now, but because my face must have resembled a peeled tomato ...

My first priority was to find another route back into the party and, after a cursory exploration, I located a kitchen entrance through which the penguins were coming and going with their trays of food and drink.

Commandeering one of these for personal use, I tipped a full glass of *Froth* over my head and another one down my throat, before jumping the queue back into the party ...

The chaos in the ballroom had subsided, and the quartet had resumed with a rendition of the *Blue Danube*, but there was an unmistakeable feeling of tension in the air ...

Sounds of more mining detonations deep down in the substructure of the castle:
I watched as a hairline fracture appeared in the ceiling of the ballroom.
It was now 11.20pm by the main clock.

As I pondered my choices, I saw it again ... *the Adolf Hitler mask, bobbing around in a sea of masks and faces, like a detached head;*
I stand there for a few seconds watching it, fascinated, tracing its path through the crowd, when suddenly somebody bellows in my ear ...
"WHAT IS THE MEANING OF THIS?"
I inadvertently gobbed a mouthful of beer all over the deck as I turned round slowly to find the Captain of the Guard standing there ...

With neither the repertoire to respond in German nor the comprehension to know what he'd said in the first place, I kept completely shtoom. *He could have been shouting about the weather, for all I knew.*
"WELL?" he demanded.
As I got ready to go for the Boer's gun secreted in my jacket, he suddenly knocked the glass of lager out of my hand, smashed the other glasses racked up on the tray and started gesticulating and pointing into the crowd ...
Relieved, I gathered he was castigating me for drinking on duty and ordering me to patrol the dance floor.
"JAWOHL, HERR KAPITAN! HEIL HITLER ...!" I yelled.

I almost knocked my front teeth through my neck with an over-enthusiastic Nazi salute...

Marching off into the throng, I accosted the first group of suspicious troublemakers I came upon – *just in case the Kapitan was still watching me* – and started to harangue them in a language something like a cross between music-hall kraut, pidgin english and double-dutch, and after looking round to see if he still had his beady eye on me – *which he did* – I confiscated all the drinks in the vicinity and started breaking them on the floor for good measure.

Unfortunately, it didn't appear to be having the desired effect, because this *particular* group started to push and shove me and generally create a scene I could have done without ...

Once again, the disintegrating plaster came to my rescue when a choice fistful of it fell plum on top of the Kapitan and stopped him dead in his tracks:

Forced to remove his cap, he spent some moments dusting it while he cast glances up at the cracking ceiling, the end result of his scrutiny being the summoning of a nearby couple of Goerings who – as I gathered from his gestures – he was ordering to go and investigate the cause.

Seizing the initiative, I ducked right out of sight and legged it over to the far side of the dance floor ...

But it *is* amazing what a Nazi stormtrooper's uniform will do to a person, and I began to find it far more enjoyable to *confiscate* drinks than to accept them legally ...

In this frame of mind, I snatched the glass out of the hand of a man dressed as a Greek God – *ie* sheet, sandals, and trousers at half-mast – and sunk about six mouthfuls before giving it back to him and adopting an innocent pose lest the Kapitan had followed me over ...

An *innocent* pose, that is, albeit for an unsummoned burp.

"IF YOU SEE A MAN WITH A BIG LONG KITE ..."

I swivelled round.

"Who said that ...?"

" ... BEWARE THE REACH OF ADOLF FLITE ..."

"Is that *you* ...?" I said to the sheet.

When he raised his false beard, I lifted my mask:

"Dr Kitehawk," he said. "*Larans Van Ity*. You remember ... the *poet* ... but, what on *earth* has happened to your *face* ...?"

"Oh," I said, letting my Goering persona fall back into place, "It's nothing. I had an accident with a box of *Rake-O* ..."

"You must let Doctors Van English, Van Trasyl and Beans take a look at that ..."

"No thanks," I said, remembering the latter's penchant for the gory. "But I *would* like to *speak* to Dr Beans, if you can find him for me ... and the rest of your mob. I did have telephone contact with him, and he may be waiting for my call but, unfortunately, my handpiece has gone the same way as the outer layer of my flesh ..."

"*Good God* ..." he said. "What *evil* is there here ...? WHEN THE PIPER PLAYS WITH A LOADED DICE, BEWARE TRUMPS BLOWN BY ADOLF FLITE ... There's *more*, would you like to hear it ...?"

"Not right now," I said. "It's 11.30. Half-hour till showtime. Can you rustle everybody up?"

"Leave it to me ..."

Again, the Hitler mask, circling in the dark spaces behind groups of guests, dipping in and out of my line of vision, appearing and disappearing ...

And somewhere ... behind, above, below – just out of reach – that cackling laughter, and the feeling that, as midnight approaches, his power is getting stronger and stronger ...

"Say," piped up a voice behind me, "Give me an old-fashioned ..."

All of a sudden, the old boy from the drunk tank lurched into me and knocked the mask clean off my face ...

Somebody must have let *that* lot out!

"You idiot!" I yelled at him.

I tried to retrieve it from the floor, but in a matter of seconds it had been trampled underfoot by passing dancers ...

"Place your hands above your head and don't move an inch ..." I heard somebody say.

It was accompanied by a poke in the back from a gun butt ... *and a snap round my wrist of handcuffs.*

"Ah ..." I said (... *trying to turn my neck* ...) "I didn't recognise you under that ten-gallon hat. Inspector *LeGras*, isn't it ...?"

"Hello, Dexter ..." said Jane, appearing as Britannia.

"Hello, old boy ..." said Laurel, covered from head to foot in face paint, much as he'd been when I first met him in the African jungle.

"You've got it all wrong," I said. "This isn't *really* me. It's a Kitehawk *mask...*"

"I am arresting you for the murder of Mark Black in the Gents' toilets at Victoria Station on the night of the third of May," said the Belgian detective, "And for the murder two days ago of Lady Malet on the quayside at Ostend Harbour. Anything you say may be taken down and used in evidence against you..."

"Jane ... *Laurel* ..." I squealed, "Tell him I'm *innocent* ... you've got what you wanted ... you're *here*, aren't you?"

"Take him away ..." he said to two Belgian plods who'd stepped up from nowhere.

I couldn't *believe* it ...

After all I'd been through, I was going to be carted away helpless just a few minutes from the end of the world ...

"*Look*," I pleaded. "I'll do a *deal* with you. You don't *know* who Adolf Flite *is*, and without *me*, you'll cock it all up! There isn't *time* to piss about ... you *need* me ..."

My former prison buddies looked sideways at each other.

"What is he talking about?" said LeGras.

"You fools!" I shouted at them. "You mean you haven't told him what's going *on* here ...? It's twenty to twelve and the world is on the edge of the precipice ...!"

"Take him away ..." said LeGras again.

"They're trying to frame me!" I yelled. "It was that idiot *Trevor* killed Lady Malet!"

"Your accomplice?" he said, halting his deputies while a crowd began to gather around us.

"No, no," I said, "He's not my *accomplice*. He was a hitch-hiker I gave a lift to. As for *Mark Black*, it was an *inside* job – nothing to do with me!"

"*Inside* job?"

"That's right," I said, gesturing at Laurel. "Mark Black is *his* brother, and ... *Trevor* is his *other brother* ...!"

"You're lying ..." said Laurel.

Well, creating a *chain* I *might* have been, but it was an inspirational move which succeeded in shifting the great Belgian detective's attention away from me – however briefly – and onto two people who were starting to hop from one foot to another, shifty as a pair of Scottish banknotes ...

"Look in my inside pocket," I said. "There's an envelope ... it's from a firm called DARC – *Disposable Assets & Removals Corporate.* The *Shampoo* Division. They get rid of bodies for multinational corporations. It's a collection order for a load of stiffs, including Mark Black, only it was delivered to *me* by mistake. Check the signature on the requisition – I think you'll find it belongs to the man standing next to you ..."

But Laurel had already legged it ...!

"This is absurd ..." Jane mumbled, blanching like a sheet. "He's an Interpol officer ..."

"He's an *Interpol* officer," I said, as one of the plods removed the envelope and gave it to LeGras, "... *in the pay of the Allied Froth Corporation* ..."

"Look ..." (*Jane was beginning to sweat as she took the detective by the arm and led him off to one side*) "... It seems there may be *some* truth in what this man says. Matters of national security have prevented me telling you more ..."

"*Indeed* ...?" I heard him say.

"It would also seem that we do not have much time. I suggest that we *do* make a deal with him and ..."

Here, she looked over her shoulder at me and took LeGras further out of earshot, from which point on all I could make out were phrases like "immunity from prosecution" and "*psss psss psss*" and "*wsh wsh wsh* ..."

Following their little conference, LeGras took out his notebook and pen and returned to confront me:

"As there appears to be evidence of a much larger conspiracy involved in the two murders in question than ... erm ... at first appeared," he began, "And, erm ... as the Flite family appear to be implicated in some manner, I am intending to give you the opportunity to point out Herr Adolf Flite to me in return for ... well, it may go well for you in court, is all I can say ..."

"I think I may be able to persuade him to release you from your handcuffs if you co-operate," added Jane.

"Well ..." I went to say ... *when the whole lot of us were suddenly encircled by a large group of uniformed henchmen, and Sonny Reithoek marched into view with what looked like half my discarded bog paper wrapped around his bloodied face ...*

"Hand him over to me!" he demanded.

Le Gras turned round ...

"To *you* ...?" said the diminutive Belgian plod, towering underneath him like a mouse underneath an elephant.

"Monsieur LeGras!" I shouted. "*Arrest* him! He's a *child* molester ...!"

"*Is* he, indeed ..." said LeGras.

"I want this man, and I intend to *have* him!" said Reithoek (*bending his knees, attempting to finger the now-absent whip in his waistband ...*)

"Ask him about Heidi Flite," I shouted. "He's *kidnapped* her ...!"

He seemed to visibly blush at this accusation, though it only served to heighten the impression of a man about to boil and whistle all at the same time ...

"*Go on*," I shouted, riding my luck, "Search his room!"

"Perhaps I *will* ..." said LeGras, having the nerve to poke him in the chest as he did so.

"You have no authority here," said Reithoek.

"Yes he *has*," I said. "This operation's got UN backing. Ask Frau Flite ..."

The lights were beginning to dim ...

"Quick," said Jane, under her breath, as she crept up next to me with LeGras's notebook and pen. "While they're arguing ... write his identity down here, or point him out to me ..."

"Get me released, and I'll tell you ..." I said, gesturing at the bracelets ... and noticing with surprise that they were the *magician's* handcuffs!

"Tell me *first* ..." she said.

I scanned the darkening faces beyond the ring of stormtroopers:

The mask, hovering there, mocking ...

"*There* he is," I said. "That one *there* ..."

"Who ...?" she said, craning her neck. "*Which* one ... *where* ...?"

"*Him* ... that one ..."

"Good ..." she said.

"Now, the cuffs ..."

All of a sudden, Laurel strolled back into the foreground ...

"Sorry, old boy," he said. "No *can* do ..."

At which cue, Sonny slapped Le Gras to the deck ...

"Lock all the doors and windows!" he ordered his troops, and then – *pointing straight at me* – "*Seize* him ...!"

"IF YOU SEE A MAN, AND HIS TROUSERS ARE FLIMSY ..." I yelled, taking a leaf out of the poet's book, "THEN GIVE ME A DRINK

AND A TICKET TO *GRIMS*-BY ...!'"

Click!

The cuffs sprang open at the precise moment that the hall lights eclipsed, and with a deafening thud from the substructure – causing a ground tremor and sending screams from the arena into the air – I hurled myself straight through Reithoek's legs and skidded horizontally along the polished dance floor until I came to rest in total darkness.

Quarter to twelve, and the hour of chaos approached ...

A spotlight hit the stage:

"*Mr Simon Flite,*" announced the detached voice of Lord Heehaw, speaking through a public address system. "*Executive Director of Allied Froth ...*"

As Simon walked onto the boards, I was aware of all kinds of people prowling around in the darkened hall, searching for me, searching the groups of guests, holding up flashlights to their faces ...

"I would like to take this opportunity," began the Executive Director, "To welcome everybody here tonight to the First Annual Lager Barons' Ball ..."

First *and last,* I thought.

"I am sure," he went on, "That you would all like to join me in taking a few moments to remember the founder of AF of Lahnstein – my late father, Adolf Flite. I am sure, also, that you will understand when I tell you that, although he may not be with us in person tonight, he is very much here in *spirit* ...

"A little later on – *at midnight,* to be precise – I shall be revealing the latest product of the Corporation, which will be submitted to you all for approval. Since this is the end result of decades of research conducted by my father – a result, unfortunately, that has come too late for him to enjoy – I have arranged for a spectacular accompaniment to its unveiling, during which I trust each and every one of you will witness something *very* special ...

"Until then, *in the few minutes we have left,* I ask you all to drink a toast to my late father ... Adolf Flite!"

"ADOLF FLITE!" came the reply from the enthused throng.

"HEIL HITLER!" I yelled, *before ducking out of sight behind a stationery penguin and lifting a bottle from his tray ...*

"And now," he said, "I leave you in the capable hands of our Far East Promotions Executive, Lord Heehaw ..."

The detached voice began again, singing the praises of the Corporation ... *Simon walking to the side of the stage, when ...*

Gunshots ring out *and he stumbles* ... hit from all sides by assassins' bullets!

Three Bears jump onto the stage:

Shocked screams erupt all around the hall as the voice drones on over the PA, its source unaware yet of what has happened ...

One of the killers checks Simon's pulse while the other two hold their guns on the crowd:

More shots – this time from the back of the hall, from the stormtroopers:

The Three Bears dash offstage and disappear ...

Heehaw now, rushing on to make an announcement through the microphone, people clamouring past me in all directions as they panic to get out of the hall ... but the doors are locked.

Yet more gunshots:

From a sniper concealed high up above the stage:

Heehaw collapses forwards ...

Stormtroopers rush the boards and fire into the gods ...

Mario falls out of his perch, hits the deck, stone dead.

Heehaw ... in his death throes ... crawls to the edge ... pulls on a gigantic lever and ...

The clock chimes MIDNIGHT.

CHAPTER 49
THE FALL OF THE HOUSE OF FROTH

The spotlight vanishes.
An uneasy calm has descended since our host's murder, the stillness breached only by the hushed murmurs of the crowd, the clock striking the hour ... and *me,* opening another bottle of *Froth* on the side of someone's neck.
At the twelfth chime, a series of unearthly sounds are suddenly let loose and riven together from all directions, so that a dissilient clash of scream and depth-charge and the spattering of an indoor dust shower pave the way for an eerie, mechanical grind as the dance floor begins to move in the dark ...

People were already rushing in all directions – falling over themselves to get away from the shifting boards, when ... *a ghostly lantern lights the arena, and the floor rolls back between the central podium and the stage, revealing a great bubbling cauldron beneath...*

"*Strewth ...*" I wheezed.
And *beyond* that cauldron ...
Dirk rising up on a mad Wurlitzer organ, dressed in satanic black, playing-in the arrival of The Master ...

That bloke was in big trouble!
And then, simply, there he is:
Adolphus Flite, sitting on stage, a skeleton in a top hat, with one spindly finger pointed straight into the gloom.
At me ...

Me? I said without speaking, pointing at my ribs.
THIS IS THE MASTER SPEAKING ...
I begin walking towards the cauldron like a zombie ...
"THE MASTER!" people were shouting, screaming, the attraction irresistible. "THE MASTER HAS RETURNED ...!"
A few more steps and I'll be face-first into the drink ...
THIS IS THE VOICE OF THE MASTER ...
"WHAT WOULD YOU HAVE US *DO,* MASTER ...?"

All of a sudden, one of the large windows shattered, and in leaped ... the *Mutant*!

Whatsmore, he had the black *valise* in his hand ...

TICK TOCK, *TICK TOCK* ...

Here, I become aware of the chaos breaking out all around me – screaming and yelling, people diving over tables and climbing up the curtains to get away from him – and the spell is broken ...

Scattering bodies in his wake, the Mutant raced across the dance floor, grabbed Reithoek's whip (which was still hanging where I'd left it – *ie*. from the chandelier) and started swinging across the hall from one end to the other and from one side to the other, farting like a firecracker and looking for somewhere to drop the bomb.

He didn't have to look for long ...

Just as he reached the mid-way point in his flight over the cauldron, there was a mining blast directly beneath our feet and one of Fräulein Dorf's jerry-helmeted demolition engineers rocketed straight up through the floor and embedded himself in the ceiling.

The ceiling cracked wide open, and the chandelier, Mutant and bomb, all fell into the drink with a mighty **SPLASH!**

Five seconds later, the Mutant surfaced, hiccupping and burping, minus the chandelier ... *and minus the bomb.*

About half the assembled guests were already trying to climb out of the broken window, when there was a frantic clattering on the locked door to the hall:

"POLIZEI!" blared a voice from outside.

That schoolteacher, I thought, she must have got away ...

No further encouragement was needed for the stormtroopers to join the guests in a mass breakout via the window, and *who* should I see at the *head* of the queue-jumpers but ... *Sonny Reithoek*, his fucking great arse bursting out of his drill-shorts as he attempted to clamber all over those in front of him.

And do you know what hurt me the most?

He didn't even bother to say goodbye.

So ...

I picked up somebody's discarded matches, nonchalantly strolled up behind him, set the entire box alight ... and stuffed it in his back pocket.

Then, as the police came at the door with a battering ram ...

The skeleton's arm curls and jolts, and he beckons me with his finger.

The voice of the Master speaks again, even though I seem to be the only person listening to it now ...

I begin the walk of the condemned, unaware of the police (and others) bursting into the hall and switching all the lights on.

Here I am, hypnotised, just a step from the cauldron, when ...

"Hold it, Buster ..."

A hand stops me and I snap round to find Blondie standing there.

"Now," she said, "Didn't I *tell* you I was your fairy godmother? One more step and it would have been Goodbye Mr Dexter Asshole ..."

Looking around the hall, I find that not everybody has managed to scarper, and dozens of uniformed German police are busy shutting cuffs on people.

"I," said Blondie (... *she's not talking to me now, she's making an announcement to the whole place* ...) "I confiscate this vat of rocket fuel on behalf of the US State Department ..."

So saying, she swivelled three hundred and fifty-nine degrees on her high heels, holding up what looked like my old bus pass for the benefit of anybody who might have been interested.

I *say* three hundred and fifty *nine*, because, before she was able to complete a full circle, a bullet suddenly zinged past her ear and I saw the man in the Hitler mask disappear behind one of the curtains to the side of the stage ...

"*Rocket* fuel ...?" I mumbled to myself.

I knelt down to taste it ... and just missed being clattered by her right tail-fin as she launched herself past me and blazed off round the gap in the dance floor to chase the *Fuhrer's* after-image ...

At some point during this missile launch programme, I became half-aware that she'd accidentally jettisoned her base security ID card somewhere within reach:

BLONDIE PARKER

Employee

Disney World

Florida

Well, her name *was* Blondie *after* all, but it wasn't *Duval*, and it *definitely* wasn't a vat of *rocket fuel* ...

I wonder how deep it is ...? I thought.

I leaned over the edge and peered down through the rising bubbles:

THE *VOICE* OF THE *MASTER* ... THE *VOICE* OF THE *MASTER* ... which is why I didn't see the reflection of the figure looming behind me with a mediaeval *axe* in his hand until it was too late ...

"Why don't you take a closer *look* ...?" came a voice.

I swung round in shock ...

Staring down at me, with the Iron Cross medal hanging inside his lapel, was the enormous figure of my Uncle Grolly – one of the biggest, meanest looking blokes I ever saw ...

SPLASH!

As I plummeted to the depths, I realised it was no *German* Iron Cross, but the badge of the Christian fundamentalist assassin – the cross of valour awarded to Knights of the Order of the Salvation of the Lord's Innocents – *gong of the Stepney Light Infantry ...*

I saw four things as I floated round the base of the tank. A cast-iron bill of lading bolted to the bottom was one of them. The second was a strange green object which looked like a Martian free-range egg, except it was soft and leathery, and this I put in my pocket. The third was the chandelier ... and the fourth was *the bomb*, still ticking, except that now it was going TICK *GLUG* TOCK *GLUG* TICK *GLUG* TOCK *GLUG* ...

Well, it was worth a try ...

When my head resurfaced above the lager line, I found Grolly standing there with the axe raised in the pose of Lord High Executioner:

"Hang on Uncle," I said, offering him the case. "It's *me* – your *nephew* – *Dexter*. And *look*, I've found some *smut* ..."

The merest hint of a puzzled frown flickered across the surface of his impenetrable face, before he hesitantly lowered his arm and went to take my gift...

Quick as a flash, I grabbed him round the ankle ... and tipped him off balance.

CRUUUNCH! went his face, as the austere expression cracked down the middle like a ming vase ... *CLAAANG!* went the axe, as he dropped it to the deck ... and *"WOOOAAA ...!"* went his cry, as the elephant wobbled on the high wire ... *and took an involuntary dive right over me into the centre of the vat.*

SPLASH!

Seizing the opportunity to climb out, I rather stupidly went on to allow myself to be distracted by his antics, sitting on the edge to watch his comical attempts to haul himself up on the far side.

Not that he was any laughing matter, really. If the row of medals in his photo was anything to go by, he'd already murdered half-a-dozen people ...

I say *stupidly*, though, because it didn't occur to me to relocate his weapon of execution until I'd finished watching a couple of policemen drag him out ... by *which* time, another hand had beaten me to it, and I found myself confronted by somebody in a hideous mask ...

"I've waited a *long* time for this ..."

At the sound of his voice, I realised it was no *mask*, but a face ...

SPLASH!

Round and round in my head it went, as I somersaulted my way to the bottom of the tank for the second time, *I thought he was dead ... I saw it with my own eyes in the bar in New York ... the hit-man, Joe Maraschino, blowing him away by mistake...*

So *that's* who'd got out.

Luke Shavers.

Out of hospital ...

Well, the old tricks are the best ones, I suppose, and as I lugged the black valise with me all over again, I could see his wavy outline long before I surfaced, standing there just like Grolly had been, waiting to decapitate me ...

I thought, *What the hell are all these policemen doing?* There's a man *here* trying to kill me with an *axe* ...!

"Hang on," I said. "Look – I've found the *treasure* ..."

But any similarity between *this* and the *last* operation ended *there*.

I don't know whether my Mickey Mouse watch was waterproof or *not*.

But I *do* know its *owner* wasn't *lager*-proof, and his sense of timing must have gone the same way as his watchsprings.

Because ... when it came to timing my grab for his ankle, waiting for that same split-second of hesitation which *Grolly* had shown, I *hesitated* too long myself; and, when he snatched the case, he inadvertently stepped *back* a pace and left me lunging at a fistful of scotch mist ...

But ... so preoccupied with his *windfall* was he, that he failed to notice I'd revealed my *hand* – so to speak – and this left me with no option but to try and trade it in for the *hand of friendship* ...

"Help me *out*, then ..." I said.

"What ...?"

"That's a fine tomahawk ..." said a Red Indian Chief ... *who came up behind Shavers and, mercifully, took the axe from his grasp* ... while the worthy inheritor of a famous middleweight tradition shuffled up from the opposite side and relieved him of his luggage.

"You just *don't* give up, do you ..."

"*You* took your time!" I said.

As Ray helped me out, the Chief pushed Shavers into the spot I'd just vacated ...

SPLASH!

"We might have got here sooner, Boss, but we got mobbed by fans at the airport. You know how it is ..."

"Yeah," I said, "*Tell* me about it ..."

"Where is the Headbone?" asked the Chief.

"He's behind *that* thing *there*," I said, pointing at the Wurlitzer.

Ray screwed up his face. "He ain't *improved* much, has he, Boss ..."

"You're not a bad judge ..."

"You all about cleared up here now?"

"No ..." I said, as Shavers surfaced in the tank, coughing and spluttering. "I've got one more thing to do, but I think I'd better do it alone ..."

"Okay," said Ray. "We'll keep an eye on *him* ..."

On the way up to the stage I passed *two* people – *Grolly*, who was struggling with a group of coppers – and *Dirk*, who was still lurching over the keys in a mad mesmerised concert for all the inhabitants of the twilight world ...

I swung round.

"Ray!" I yelled. "The *case* – get *rid* of it. It's a *bomb* ...!"

He threw it to the Chief.

The Chief handed it back to Shavers ...

KRAAAAAAAANG!

The cauldron blew apart as though it had been hit by a torpedo, and all its liquid gushed away under the floor ... *taking Shavers with it.*

Phew ...

THIS IS THE VOICE OF THE MASTER ...

But ...

The skeleton's forearm suddenly jolted once again and I froze, hypnotised for a *third* time in the stare from those blackened eye sockets:

Here I am, marching onto the stage to meet my date with destiny, when ... a lump of plaster the size of an ironing board dropped square on Bonehead's nut, knocked him face-down on the keys and brought forward an impromptu intermission in the recital ...

I walked right up to Adolphus Flite and stared at him face-to-face, man-to-man.

"How's your luck?" I enquired.

THIS IS THE VOICE OF THE MASTER ...

We obviously didn't see eye-to-eye.

So I plunged my hand straight into his left one ... and pulled out a *wire*.

That's funny, I thought.

When I traced it underneath the backdrop, I came across a door with a little red broadcasting lamp lit outside:

Since the door was marginally *ajar*, I poked my nose therein ...

The suspect, Adolf Hitler, was sitting hunched over an enormous computer bank, fiddling with the controls – light controls, movement controls, sound controls and speech controls ...

THIS IS THE VOICE OF ...

"DEXTER KITEHAWK!" I yelled. "AND *YOU* MATE, ARE NICKED...!!!"

But he was too quick for me ...

As I went to restrain him with the cuffs, he swung round, leapt up and pushed me into a stack of collapsible boxes in the far corner of the room ...

My response time?

Well, approximately four-and-a-half seconds to repel the assault of a cardboard *Mafia*, a further thirty-seven seconds to ascertain *my* whereabouts, *his* whereabouts (*he'd already darted through the door*) and the whereabouts of a bottle of aspirin; and an added split-second of stupidity in which I used the computer dashboard to pull myself up off the floor and (*in so doing*) accidentally shoved my hand down on a key marked:

RED ALERT

A bank of sirens were suddenly let loose ...

Back in the ballroom, I found myself surrounded by an airborne flotilla of cocktail glasses, sausages, menus etc, all hanging motionless against a backdrop of exploding colour and sound in which half the customers had *literally* floated up to the ceiling and the other half were hanging upside down by their hands as they clung to any permanent fixture bolted to the floor ...

To top *this*, the hands of the hall clock were spinning round backwards, day and night were flickering off and on outside the window like a faulty electric bulb, and the seasons were all spreading across the sky in reverse order ...

What the hell have I done now, I thought ...?

All of a *sudden*, an Arctic gale blasted in through the doors, one of the tables came loose and crashed up under my chin and, along with everybody else who hadn't hitherto succumbed to the in-house moonwalk training programme, I began to levitate towards the land of mid-Prussian entablatures and crystal chandeliers ...

As I reached out a hand to protect my head, Dirk came rolling and somersaulting past me, bouncing around off the plaster like an upside-down space-hopper, gleefully gurgling like a new-born baby ... and back to his incarnation as Dopey Dick.

I tried to launch a kick at him, but all movement was in slow motion ...

Bertolt wasn't far behind him, clanking about inside a suit of armour, having chosen a form of disguise to match his foot. *His raised visor was the giveaway, but just as I went to shut the cuffs on one of his chainmail gloves, something thudded into my back...*

Doing a sideways flip, I found I'd collided with a wooden packing crate of *Anniversary* bottles.

So I cuffed the *crate* instead.

But it wasn't my lucky *night*.

Just as I was just trying to work out the best way to unwrench the lid, the Deaf Girl from the King's Head wafted past, apparently chasing her passport ...

She was still in the throes of her last rapture, and she had my fancy-dress stethoscope slung round her neck.

"Sing!" she suddenly declared ... *and stuck the probe-end onto my throat.*

"Why ...?" I asked, but her momentum was already carrying her away.

I grabbed the errant passport and flipped through the pages.

One entry was a puzzler, to say the least:

Occupation: In search of excellence

"Did you find it ..?" I called out, as I slung the passport in her general direction.

"Not yet!" she called back. "But, oh what joy to be a pil*grim* ..."

Click!

The cuffs sprang free of the crate and I lost all my beer in one go ...

In the midst of rueing this calamity, I bumped into Adolf Hitler and tried nicking him a second time, but no sooner had I grabbed his arm when there was another detonation below the floor, and all kinds of machinery came shooting up through the gap where the cauldron had been, causing the pair of us to somersault away in opposite directions ...

Two pieces of this mechanical shower that particularly caught my eye were embedded in the ceiling just within reach:

One was a gigantic drum-shaped object that had the following manufacturing plate on it:

Cold Zones Ltd.
Directional Cellar-to-Roof Refrigeration Units
Ideal for Cold Drinks, Mortuary and Deep Freeze Purposes

The *other* piece, which looked like a prop from *Star Wars*, was still operational and had green lights flickering all over it:

Lager Beer Specific Gravity Research Prototype
Patent Pending. All enquiries to Sir Ewan Scintao ...

Just *then* I caught sight Laurel walking upside-down across the ceiling.

Gravity research? I thought. *What about air traffic control ...?* (Count von Zeppelin looked like he was about to burst into flames above the orchestral podium and there were at least fifteen Herman Goerings stacked up over the stage ...)

Sir Ewan Scintao.

Yeah, I thought. I *knew* he was con-man. The Flites were *done* ...

I found the master switch and shut it off.

About three hundred bodies all crashed back down to the floor with a bump ...

Stopping the *rest* of the show, though, was *another* matter ...

I'd barely reclaimed *terra firma*, when I was pelted by a miniature *Luftwaffe* of ice cubes and barged back onto the deck by Adolf Hitler as he made a mad dash for the window ...

Three seconds later, after I'd almost yanked myself up into a vertical line, I was re-deposited back where I'd come from like a man doing diving practice ...

"*There* he is! *Get* him ...!"

I looked up just in time to see *Jane* rush past me with about forty policemen in tow.

And talking of *Yanks*, where was Blondie?

All of a sudden, she stepped out from behind a curtain:

"Leave him to *me!*" she yelled. "He's *mine* ...!" .

This, in turn, was followed by just about every dick, agent, plod and flatfoot in the place all converging on the window to try to leg it out after him – and all set against a continuing background of sirens and lights like the *Keystone Cops Go Disco*.

I made sure the last of this mob had gone *past* or *over* me – and I *mean* made sure – before struggling, against the odds, to get to my feet again.

THIS IS THE VOICE OF THE MASTER ... THIS IS THE VOICE OF THE MASTER ... THIS IS THE VOICE ...

(There was that *voice* again ...)

THIS IS THE VOICE OF THE MASTER COMPUTER! ATTENTION ALL UNITS! THIS VEHICLE IS UNDER ATTACK! TELEPHONE THE POLICE IMMEDIATELY! THE CASTLE FROTH WILL SELF-DESTRUCT IN T-MINUS TEN MINUTES. YOU HAVE EXACTLY TEN MINUTES TO ABANDON SCHLOSS. THE OPTION TO OVERRIDE EXPIRED LAST WEEK ...

Before I had a chance to think either about this message or about joining the chase for a quarry that, by rights, should have been mine, a jet of steam from a lately-fractured central heating pipe shot straight up my trouser-leg and knocked me back off-balance ...

But it was a lucky *break*, really.

Because, in that moment, when I began toppling past the angles, I realised it wasn't worth chasing the man in the Hitler mask.

Why?

Because it *wasn't* Adolf Flite.

It was *Martin* Flite.

The organ-grinder's monkey ...

Before I'd hit the floor, I'd caught sight of Adolf Flite hiding in his perch above the stage:

The pixie in the clown's mask.

Rhoda LeFlit.

THIS IS THE VOICE OF THE MASTER COMPUTER. THE CASTLE FROTH WILL SELF-DESTRUCT IN T-MINUS 9 MINUTES ...

How did I know?

It was all in the *name*, really ... *and by the ruby ring, which gleamed in the dark like a third eye as the pixie threw its head back, cackled out loud and vanished behind some stage lights.*

I had to find some way to climb up there, and I had less than *nine* minutes to do it ...

"Ooer ..."

I swung round to find Dirk staggering around on top of the Wurlitzer, teetering on the edge of the abyss ...

"Ray! Chief!" I yelled. "Get that *idiot* down from there, and then the three of you get the hell out. Looks like this place is set to blow ..."

"What about *you*, Boss ...?"

"Unfinished business ..."

So saying, I bolted through the stage door and down to the end of a dark passage, where a wooden ladder was lying in wait for me ...

I took it carefully, one rung at a time, until I reached the high-level wall-hatch by which it was resting:

Tick tick, *Tock tock*, Tick tick, *Tock tock* ...

(This is my temperamental watch again, rather than another bomb, echoing the countdown of a parallel clock. Not the computer clock; a different clock altogether)

I popped my head inside:

Here I found a small room containing theatre props, cogs and ratchets, wheels, levers, lights and other bits of machinery, and an opening onto the scaffolding above the stage.

At *least*, I *say* room, and I *say* opening, but it was a dangerous and deceptive place, one in which the former imperceptibly became the latter, the floor being only half layered with boards which vanished altogether the further the structure projected out into the dark ... and I was already past the point of no return when I caught just a momentary glimpse of the clown's mask – somewhere *out* there, *in* that darkness – elusive, seductive, like a wicked decoy which lured me crawling out onto the precarious planks and poles, committed to the chase ...

Tick tick, *Tock tock*, Tick tick, *Tock tock* ...

THE CASTLE FROTH WILL SELF-DESTRUCT IN T-MINUS 8 MINUTES ...

All the way across the rickety bridge, I could see a large crowd of people gathered outside the computer room below, and by the looks of concern on their faces, I assumed they were all trying to figure out a way to override a more-than-likely un-overrideable computer programme ... a chase which, when I reached the far side, found me balking at the prospect of another ascent, offered courtesy of a second, very high, ladder which had been left propped in dubious fashion by the wall, balancing with no obvious anchor on a grid of diseased girders, themselves already suspended high above the theatre.

I took a moment to crane my neck up at the void above me, where the spacious darkness hung like funeral fog below an open loft door from which it all seemed to have come.

I doubted there was a loft above it, but something was up there.

And it was the only way on ...

Tick tick, *Tock tock*, Tick tick, *Tock tock* ...

I must have given birth to a dozen litters of kittens on the way up, all the time expecting a pair of hands to appear in the ceiling hatch and push the ladder away from the wall, but the closer I got, the less intimidating it began to look.

Whether or not this was because, conversely, the higher I got, the darker the void *below* me became, I'm not sure; but a *cupboard* is what it actually turned out to be; or a small distorted *room* tumbled sideways, filled with discarded dolls and books; and my relief was, nevertheless, audible, as I hoisted myself up through the hatch and shut the trapdoor safely behind me.

There *was* an alternative way out of this chamber – a door in the wall – and this had been left open to the draught beyond, a lengthy corridor which passed by on its way to a spectacular oval observation window at one end, and an idle dumb waiter at the other.

The rooms were all open – full of furniture covered in sheets ... empty, deserted ...

I hurried along to the *window* first, a sealed convex of reinforced glass, unopenable, spanning a rotting frame which looked once to have boasted arcane characters in calligraphic gold, now flaking and peeling and unreadable.

Here, I paused to catch my breath, looking out onto a sheer drop to nothing far below, while the first waves of a troubled dawn struggled to break across the far shores of the night.

The slight tightening of a distant cable and the merest of whispers along the corridor suddenly made me jump:

And it was only *then*, with something of a start, that I realised that the *waiter* standing idle at the far end of the corridor was far from *dumb*. This was the real thing – a genuine *lift* carriage ...

I swung round just in time to see a shadow disappear behind the closing doors ...

The dial was already rising as I broke into a run ...

More rooms on the way ... all open, empty, deserted ... except the *last* one, next to the lift:

SONNY REITHOEK
HEAD OF SECURITY

Muffled noises inside:
I barge the door down with remarkable ease and burst in ...

THE CASTLE WILL SELF-DESTRUCT IN T-MINUS 7 MINUTES ...
Heidi, sitting there on the floor, bound and gagged ...

"Dexter ..." she said (*I'm starting to unravel her now, to free her from captivity*) "Thank God it's *you* ... I thought for a minute it was Sonny coming back when I heard footsteps ..."

"No," I said. "You've seen the last of *him* for a while ..."

She jumped to her feet. "What will they do to him ...?"

"Well," I said, "I should think they'll confiscate those *drill* shorts of his at the *very* least ..."

"What now ...?"

"You've got to get *out* of here – and *fast* ..."

"What about *you* ...?"

"Me ...?" I said ... *becoming distracted by something laying just under the four-poster, not concealed properly in the time available ...*

"Yes, *you* ...!"

YOU!

All of a sudden she struck a blow to the back of my head ... and rushed on past me as I stumbled, half-conscious, to pick up the clown's mask:

"What's under the *Heidi* mask ...?!!!" I yelled.

I was still groggy from the assault when I clattered out after her, only to find the corridor deserted.

In *both* directions.

I stood there swaying on my feet, confused, thinking she must have gone up in the lift ... until I realised it was still stuck on the floor above – where *she'd* earlier sent it:

Tick tick, *Tock tock*, Tick tick, *Tock tock* ...

THE CASTLE WILL SELF-DESTRUCT IN T-MINUS 6 MINUTES ...

Suddenly, the window shattered at the far end, and I saw her tiny figure climb up onto the sill, outlined by the morning sun flooding in ...

She turned to glance *back* at me then.

And just for a *moment*, framed in the lit oval, she looked like the figure in the *Allied Froth* icon.

But *only* for a moment, before she vanished ...

As I hurried back along the corridor, I wondered whether she'd leaped or whether she'd fallen, but either way it was to a certain death on the rocks. I didn't think there was very much chance of spotting her body so far below on the mountainside, and when I pushed my face past the broken glass, the whipping wind moistened my eyes until I could see nothing clearly at all.

Then, as I went to retract my head, something bounced off the end of my nose and away into the morning ...

How many precious seconds I wasted puzzling over this would be hard to say, but it eventually dawned on me that it was her *ring*.

Craning my neck up, I saw Heidi scaling a drainpipe, attempting to climb to the battlements overhead ...

Tick tick, *Tock tock*, Tick tick, *Tock tock* ...

Beyond and *above* those battlements was the East Wing tower, rising up into an island of layered cloud like a corrupt ship of state, adrift and burning in the intensifying sunlight.

Well, I thought, as I got up onto the ledge and put a foot out onto the rickety old pipe, *this is the moment of truth, Kitehawk* ...

THE CASTLE WILL DESTRUCT IN T-MINUS 5 MINUTES ...

Then I thought, *bollocks*.

I got back inside the window, charged down the other end of the corridor and rang for the lift.

When I arrived at the roof verandah, the doors opened to a rush of fresh air and I stepped outside just as Heidi climbed over the battlements twenty yards away ...

THE CASTLE WILL DESTRUCT IN T-MINUS FOUR MINUTES ...

When she saw me, she craned her head back to cackle ... but as she did so, the fickle wind caught her mask and lifted it into the air and away over the edge ...

Quickly, she raised her hands to hide her face.

She appeared to be blind without the mask – *couldn't or wouldn't drop her hands* – and it was in this way, covering her face, that she began to run ... and *tripped* on something lying there on the stone.

And *stumbled*, one step beyond ...

Tick tick, *Tock tock*, Tick tick, *Tock tock* ... and began to *topple* towards the edge ...

One *moment* beyond ... *arms outstretched at true north* ... reaching for an assistance that was no longer mine to offer as I instinctively raced to save her.

Because time had already run out.

And *my* hand passed through *her* hand like light through water, and I watched helplessly as she tumbled over the parapet and hurtled down towards the rocks and forests hundreds of feet below, disappearing, before she reached them, into the early morning mists.

I stood and listened to the wind blustering across the deserted battlements, staring after her lost body, feeling hollow and empty.

tick tock, tick tock, tick tock, tick tock ...

Then, as I turned to go, I almost tripped over it *myself* – an object weighing a ton:

An Atlas of the World.

One of the books I'd thrown off the balcony of the Blood and Iron Room the previous night.

THE CASTLE WILL DESTRUCT IN T-MINUS 3 MINUTES ...

In view of the impending destruction of the Castle Froth, I decided not to chance my luck descending by lift and instead, found the entrance to one of those spiral staircases.

Choosing this route did, of course, increase the possibility that I would not make it out of there in time ...

Halfway down, I passed a coat rack from which hung a solitary shaggy fur coat, complete with zipper.

It was no time to linger – *and so I could not say for sure* – but, as I hurried on my way, I mused how it looked a dead ringer for a Mutant's outfit, *minus a Mutant...*

THE CASTLE WILL DESTRUCT IN T-MINUS 2 MINUTES ...

And here, with time rushing past me, and the ancient stone steps rushing up to meet me from infinity in a world gone mad, I step aside for a moment to ponder the possible:

I never did see Blondie again.

Here she is, a clockwork figure in a mantelpiece clock, coming out to test for sun or rain, in the offices of the Delta Nylon Company.

And here she is, leaning over the shoulders of her father's killers, poised to strike with her magic wand umbrella ...

And I never did see Beans again – but once, in a bar in Bruges, three years later.

Here he is, sitting by his mobile phone, claiming to be awaiting further instructions.

He asks me whether Blondie ever found her prince?

I tell him that she did, and that it turned out to be the Mutant; I tell him that a kiss from herself restored the Mutant to his human form and released him forever from the evil spell placed on him by the wicked warlock, Adolf Flite.

"So, it had a happy ending?" he asks.

Since he's already swallowed this load of old cobblers lock, stock and barrel, I tell him, "Unfortunately, no, for at the precise moment that she kissed him, she herself turned back into an alsatian dog and ran off to rejoin the rest of the pack in the Harz Mountains ..."

Here are Otto (back in charge of the family brewery, after spending a nominal spell in a German clink, denying to anybody who will listen that he ever had any involvement with the Allied Froth Corporation), Heinrich Frostbite (after a similar spell in clink, seconded to the Pentagon's computer research unit), and Sonny Reithoek, still serving a long sentence in prison – yes, but with absolute power over all of the weak and unprotected by the system ...

Here is Trevor, named by the schoolteacher as the courageous hero who saved her life and the lives of her schoolchildren – an act he is surprisingly self-effacing about ...

And LeGras, bestriding the corridors of the Brussels Police Headquarters, decorated and feted for his part in solving the mystery double-murder on the Orient Express: Who killed Mrs Orange-Shorts? A cursory glance at the body, when it was finally recovered from the water, clearly implicated her husband, Sir Charles Malet, as the driver of the dockside crane which deposited her there; and what of Mark Black ...?

As Inspector LeGras will tell you, he was murdered by his half-brother, Laurel Black – major shareholder in AF International. Here he is, sacked by Interpol, and clearly banged to rights ...

Ah, and who is this walking down the gloomy corridors of the restored Castle Froth, dusting the stuffed dummies with a feather duster as she goes ...? It is Candida Flite, and she has found a way to spoil the experiments of her husband, Martin, released from clink on health grounds. Here he is, feeding sodium pentathol to dolls dressed in masks of the famous, but none will tell him what he wants to hear. Benito Mussolini insists on reciting the train timetable for obscure areas on the Adriatic coast, while Josef Goebbels will only indicate that his lips are sealed (but then he is, of course, clearly lying ...)

And here sits Jane, underneath the scales of justice, weighing her clarinet against an uncertain future.

And finally, Adolf Flite ...

I cannot picture him, but he is there, somewhere.

I cannot picture him because, when Heidi lost her mask, there was no face behind it at all – just the blind, blank no-face of the Corporate Spirit.

Nadhet Ropatriorc Pristi.

But what about Dexter Kitehawk ...?

He has tarried a little long in this recess of the stairwell.

Must his manuscript lay unpublished until an invention of the twenty-fifth century uncovers his body from the ruins of the Castle and reads the contents of his memory ...?

THE CASTLE WILL DESTRUCT IN T-MINUS 1 MINUTE ...

"Wait for me ...!" I yelled ... *and legged it down the rest of that staircase like a sidewinder missile had just homed in on my arse.*

THE CASTLE WILL DESTRUCT IN T-MINUS 30 SECONDS. YOU ARE WARNED TO LEAVE THE AREA IMMEDIATELY ...

Straight into the ballroom and on towards the exit ... but there's a group of anxious people all standing around outside the computer room, including the *Chief* ...

THE CASTLE WILL DESTRUCT IN T-MINUS 10 SECONDS ...

I've got to warn him ...

Slam on the brakes.

Back up, reverse.

Engines on fast forward ...

THE CASTLE WILL DESTRUCT IN T-MINUS 5 SECONDS ...

"Chief!" I yelled, as I accidentally tripped and knocked *him*, me and half-a-dozen *other* people straight through the door ... *where I found Ray fiddling with the dashboard.*

FOUR ...

"Have you cracked the code yet ...?" said a panic-stricken voice.

"Nah, I thought I *had* it there for a minute ..."

THREE ...

"Ray ...?" I said.

TWO ...

He suddenly got down on the floor and put his arm round the back of the computer bank.

ONE ...

"*Ray* ...?"

CLICK!

"*That's* it ..." he said, as it all went dead. "*Got* it. Saved the world again ..."

"How did you *do* that?"

"Just pulled the plug out ..."

So saying, he got to his feet, dusted off his hat, and replaced it on his head.

There were sighs of relief all round as people began to disperse, and when we wandered back out across the dance floor, the Chief grabbed a table.

"Where's Bonehead?" I said.

"Hey," said Ray. "Ain't he with *you* ...?"

"It's a mercy," I said, "But no ..."

"Well," he said, "Last we see of him was when he suddenly zanged off, sayin' he was goin' lookin' for you and was about to solve the case all at the same time ..."

I glanced round the hall. It was empty now except for one or two small groups of people at either end, still being interviewed by the police.

"That bloke couldn't solve his shoe size ..." I mumbled.

"Hey!" Ray suddenly shouted. "What's this we hear about him bein' your long lost daddy an' you findin' you got a *sister* ...?"

"No," I said, "It was all a mistake ..."

"You mean he *ain't* your dad?"

"No," I said. "I had him radio carbon-dated last week and he's over three-hundred years old ..."

"*Him? Headbones?*"

"It's true," said the Chief, "That he is very old. Legend tells of a Headbone in the Crow tribe in every generation since the white man first came to America. I think this is the same *man* ..."

"What about your sister?" said Ray. "*Ain't* she your sister ...?"

"Hetty ...? No. There's no family resemblance. I was thinking of looking her up, though, when I get back ..."

"Oh?"

"Yeah," I said. "I think she *likes* me ..."

"Go on ..."

"Yeah, she's invited me round to *her* place for a watercress sandwich ..."

"I heard *that* ..." he said.

Just then, the Chief got down onto the floor and stuck his ear to it, as though he were listening for distant riders or an approaching train:

"Chief ...?"

"Is this earthquake country?" he said.

"I don't think so ..."

He raised his head for a moment.

"Buffalo ...?"

"*No ...*"

Once again, little handfuls of dust were falling at random ... followed by little chunks of *plaster* ...

And, as I looked up at a ceiling cracking apart from corner to corner, *I could hear it as well:*

Rumbling, like *thunder ... followed by a series of sudden, deafening, thudding explosions underneath the floor, deep in the substructure ...*

We all three of us got to our feet and, with Ray grabbing his hat and none of us saying a word, we started to walk towards the exit, our pace quickening all the time ...

"Hey, did you ever find out who was the first President of the United States...?" he suddenly asked me.

"No," I said. "Did you ...?"

"Nope," he said. "How about *you*, Chief ...?"

"No ..."

"What are we waitin' for, then ...?"

"*LEG* IT...!!!"

CHAPTER 50
AFTERS

We never stopped running until we got out of the main gate and across the drawbridge where, from a safe distance, we witnessed the spectacular collapse of the Castle Froth ...

It began with a slow-motion ballet for steeplejacks, as the spires danced in delicate formation around roofs which shivered and turrets which pivoted beneath them, but then the hand of an invisible conductor seemed to brush past and cataclysm struck the foundations. The walls keeled and the wings buckled, and the windows burst and the bowels spewed, and the four corner towers fell prostrate before its crumbling heart like the minions of a dark god.

With a great inhuman roaring that seemed to last for ever, and which sounded as though two subterranean beasts were locked in a ferocious combat to the death, the whole site became a grey bubbling crucible of stone and wood and glass until, finally, all that was left was a slumbering hill of volcanic rubble.

In those moments, when we stood gagging and choking and half-shielding our eyes, its shape could just be seen lingering in the contours of the forming tomb, its subsidiary mounds grouped guardian around it like desolate markers to the four winds.

And everything living and not living was covered in a fine layer of white dust, so that when the smoke finally cleared, it looked as though a giant had blown all of the icing from a stale wedding cake onto the surrounding woods and trees.

I suppose the whole thing never lasted more than a few minutes, though for some time afterwards there would be a further eruption of noise, intermittently, as though the fight was not yet over, the monster not quite dead.

And there, sitting in a reflective pose right on the summit of this mountain of debris, was the intact skeleton of Adolphus Flite, bleached white with dust, sinister symbol of a corporate nightmare.

We sat down on a nearby log and paused quietly to survey the scene.

"Shame about old Headbones ..." said Ray.

"Well," I said, "He had a good innings, and he was a bit overdue for a spell of unpaid leave..."

"It is true that he was very old ..." echoed the Chief, drawing circles in the dust with a twig.

"You gonna miss him?" asked Ray.

"Erm ..."

Before I had a chance to respond with integrity to this conundrum, there was a sound of marching feet and a voice bellowing orders, and we looked up to find a troop of dusty and dejected soldiers in jerry helmets surfacing one by one from the moat, marshalled on their way by the irate figure of Clara Dorf in a demolition hat ...

"Fools! Fools! *Idiots* ...!" she was shouting at them, megaphone in one hand and a set of construction blueprints in the other.

She either wasn't aware of us sitting there, or she chose not to notice us, as she marched her men away into the woods.

"Ain't we seen her before, somewhere ...?" said Ray.

"Maybe," I said. "They all look alike to me, these dentists ..."

He laughed. "Hey, did I ever tell you about the time me and the Chief crashed through the ground floor of the Empire State on a steam train?"

"I was *there* ..."

"Oh yeah," he said. "*So* you was ..."

He kicked at some dust.

"What the hell *did* happen to you back there?"

"I fell off," I said.

"Yeah, them brakes was a bit rusty ..."

It was a day not unlike the one on which I'd first met Ray and the Chief, bright but hazy.

"So how did they do it?" he said at length. "*Computers* ...?"

"A whole load of things, really," I said. "Sophisticated market analysis techniques, slick public relations, psycho-profile customer-prioritising, subliminal advertising, statistical massaging, high-frequency auto-suggestion, air-wave monopolisation, unscrupulous jargon-transmission, mass hypnosis, total telepathy, trans-national terrorism, high-tech reverse-polarity directional osmosis, turbo-drive matter/anti-matter manipulation – stroll-on you *name* it they *did* it ..."

"*Come again*, Boss ...?"

"All *aided*, of course, by a state-of-the-art megablaster *computer* system and a lethal hallucinogenic poison ..."

After looking at each other for about forty seconds like we were contestants in an inscrutability contest, we both laughed.

"Yeah," he said. "I *heard* that ..."

"Well, that's *my* story, anyway ..."

"So what *was* in that *cauldron* back there – the strongest beer yet ...?"

"*Er* ... no ..." I said.

"What then, Boss?"

"What's the *worse* thing you can think of?"

He sat and thought for a minute.

"Low-alcohol lager ...?"

"Close ..." I said.

He suddenly jumped to his feet ...

"Hey!" he shouted. "You don't mean he was brewing *alcohol-free* lager in there, was he ...?"

I stood up. "Again, *close*," I said. "But it was even *worse* than *that* ..."

"What the hell's worse than lager with no *alcohol* in it?"

"Simple," I said. "It was alcohol ..."

"*Alcohol* ...?"

"... with no *lager* in it. *Clever*, wasn't it ...?"

"*Lager*-free alcohol? *Shit* ..." he said, "I had no idea ..."

"And whatsmore," I said, taking out the green object I'd retrieved from the bottom of the vat. "I found *this* in there ..."

"What the hell's *that* ...?"

"It's a *lime*," I said. "Cut and sliced and ready to go in the neck of every bottle of *Speziell* ..."

"Now, what the hell would anybody want to put *that* in there for ...?"

"*Exactly*," I said. (*I chucked it at the skeleton*). "Seems like he was an even *bigger* criminal than we *thought* he was ..."

"What are your plans now, Boss?"

"Well," I said, "I've still got my salary cheque to collect, and one more arrest to make back in England ... that's if the *OSLI* haven't got him first. What about you ...?"

Just as he went to reply to this, something bounced off the back of my head and knocked me forward a pace ...

"*Hey* ..." he said. (*He reached down and picked it up*). "It's that *lime* ..."

I turned round and looked back at the skeleton grinning on its perch.

"Nah ..." said Ray. "*Couldn't* be ..."

"No ... of *course* it couldn't ..." I said, rubbing the back of my head.

I looked up to see if we were standing under a lime tree.

Just then, the Chief started hooting and slapping his knees, laughing like a crazy man at something neither me nor Ray could *see* yet ...

Suddenly, the skeleton flipped over backwards, toppled by the movement of the large flagstone on which it sat ... and out from under that flagstone crawled Dirk, black as soot from head to foot and lugging an enormous suitcase with him ...

He was *coughing* and *spluttering*, and *cursing* and *swearing*, and trying to get to his feet and trying to keep his balance when he got there ... *but he'd left a trouser-leg caught up with one of Adolphus's spindly feet, so that when he went to step away, he tripped bum-over-buttonhole down the hill of dust and rubble, taking suitcase and cadaver into the dried-up moat with him ...*

When we wandered over to observe this strange apparition and saw him wrestling with a jumble of bones and trying to get out from underneath a minor landslide, we had a good old laugh at his expense.

"Gerr*off* me y' booger ...!" he was shouting.

"Hey, *Headbones* !" yelled Ray. "You wanna hand with that *suitcase* ...?"

"Don't bother," I said. "He can't hear you. Ain't you *realised* by now? He's tone *deaf* ..."

Eventually, he managed to extract himself from Adolphus's grip and got up and booted it one for good measure. "Bloody skellingtons ...!" he cursed.

We then spent a couple of well-deserved minutes marvelling at his hopeless efforts to climb up the bank, before the Chief finally took pity on him and pulled him out.

"*Wait* for *me*," he pleaded, "'Y' *boogers* ...!"

Just before we left, I thought I saw traces of a foamy liquid beginning to swirl into the moat from under the ruins ...

"What the hell were you *doin'* under there, Headbones?"

"Well," he said, "I couldn't leave t' *treasure* there, now *could* I ...?"

That stopped us all in our tracks.

"You mean there really *was* money in there ...?" I asked him.

"*Course* there were ..."

"Well?" I said. "Where *is* it?"

"Well," he said, "What d' y' think ar've gorrin this *suitcase*, then? *Bottles o' beer* ...?"

"Actually," I said, "I thought it might be a change of underwear for the ferry ..."

"*Piss* off, y' *sod* ..."

"*Phew-ee* ..." said Ray. *He took off his hat.* "Mark Black's ten million dollar Nazi fortune ..."

"Well, *come* on then," I said to him. "Let's *see* it ..."

He suddenly dropped the case ...

"Now look!" he said. "Let's get one thing *streht*. Ar'm *confiscehtin'* this lot on berralf o' the *Inland Revenoo*, and that's theet ..."

"Pardon?"

"Ar *said*," he said, "Ar'm ... *joost piss off* !"

"*Well*," I said, adopting a Kitehawk flourish, "What a way to treat your mates ...!"

"Mehts? Mehts ...?!!" he yelled. "Ar marght giv' *Cheefy* here a share, an' *Sugar Ray*, but you can joost piss off if y' think ar'm givin' *you* enneh ..."

"After all we've *been* through together ...?"

"Joost *booger* off ..."

"Is it because I left you in the nuthouse in New York?"

"*Noothouse*? Noothouse!" he shouted. "Ar were never in no *noothouse* ...!"

"Yes you were," I said. "*Bellevue*. Asylum for the Criminally Insane. I left you on the doormat and rang the bell ..."

"*Well*," he said, as he placed his hands on his hips and got ready to deliver a Bonehead Pomposity Special ...

... "That's *joost* weer you're *wrong*, Mr *Clever* Clogs ..."

"Oh?"

"Ar were awake all the time – ar were joost *pretendin'* t' be asleep. An' ar saw y' pressin't bell. *Ornleh*, it weren't no bell. You joost *thought* y' were pressin't bell. *Actualleh* ... you were pressin't *screw* orldin' *bell t't wall* ..."

I glanced at him sideways, incredulous.

"If that's the *case*," I said, "Where the fucking hell have you *been* all this time?"

"Florida," he had the nerve to say.

"*Florida*?!" I screamed at him. "Doing *what* ...?"

"Gamblin', mehnleh ... 'n' drinkin' 'n' soonbehthin'. I 'ad a reet good teem so ar did ..."

"*You bastard* ..."

"It were a rich German widderwoman called Vera Nuba torl me all abowt Adolf Flite's Castle an' all this treasure 'n' weer it were ..."

"Well," I said, "It doesn't make any difference. As your rightful *heir*, I naturally *inherit* all this money ... should anything ever *happen* to you, that is ..."

"What d' y' mean '*heir*' ... an' what d' y' mean ''*appen t' meh*' ...?"

I tapped the side of my nose and gave him a sinister glint. "Never you *mind* ..." I said.

"*Course*," he said, "Ar could *recoonsider* ..."

"Good," I said. "And *don't* forget – I know all about you and the Inland Revenue. One word from me and they'll be waiting for you when you step off the ferry ..."

"Ar'm not going back *theer* ..."

"No?" I said, surprised. "Where, then?"

"Ostrehlia ..." he said.

"*Australia*?" said Ray. "What the hell's *that*?"

"Why?"

"Ar've got famileh there. Ar'm goin' t' see m' daughter ..."

"Hetty?" I said.

He stood the case down ...

"'*Etteh*?" he said. "Ow the 'ell's *she* when she's 'orm ...?"

"Never mind ..."

I walked on.

"Oi!" he yelled. "Can yow three giv me a hand wi' this *loogage*? It ain't 'arf *evveh* ..."

"What do you think, Boss?" said Ray.

"*Fair* shares all *round*, is it?" I called back to him.

"*Alreet* ..."

"That's handy ..." I said.

We'd just stumbled across a fully-operational chairlift ...

"*Sesselbahn*," said Ray, as he grabbed a cradle and climbed on board. "Me and the Chief caught it up here last night. Cuts out the middle loops in the road and takes about an hour off the journey. Built for the tourists ..."

I got into the adjacent seat, which had a choice view out over a field of sharpened stakes ...

"Tourists ...?"

"Yeah, me and the Chief's been brushing up on the guide books. We're planning to visit the *Lorelei* before we leave ..."

"What's that?"

"Old legend. She sits up above the river and lures boats onto the rocks ..."

For no apparent reason, a picture of Blondie suddenly came cruising along my stream of consciousness ...

"You fancy it?" he said.

"What?"

"The *Lorelei?*"

"No," I said. "I've already *met* her. I saw a fleet a destroyers sail down her *throat* the other night and it gives me indigestion just thinking about it ..."

The Chief had commandeered the cradle behind us all to himself, and Bonehead was following a long way back, his upright suitcase occupying the spare seat next to him like a representation of his form on Planet Abstract.

When we reached the other end, we were still facing a lengthy stretch of road down the mountain, and so I suggested we cut through the woods.

I ought to have known better by then.

Two hours later, we were still trying to get Dirk down from the trees after he'd snared himself in one of the same man-traps Blondie had fallen foul of, and it was only the fact that he wouldn't let go of the treasure that prevented me doing the decent thing and suggesting we leave him there as a warning to any other passing fly-by-nights not to tangle with the Inland Revenoo.

We *did* get him down, though, eventually, and it wasn't long before our Indian guide had stuck his ear to the ground and sorted out some transport ...

I felt like *La Longue Canabeans* as I tracked the Chief through the woods, farting from the exertion as I went, with my faithful blood-brother *Ray-cuss* cursing alongside me and the dastardly *Mag-Dirk* chasing our trail with his trunk of settlers' spoils ...

A steep embankment represented the last obstacle of the wilderness, beneath which lay the road, and the overland stage ... *which we'd just missed.*

But them old *Indian* tricks is the best, as Ray always said ...

Him and me scavenged our way down the slope and trotted round the bend, where we found ourselves staring after that carriage with the 'CASTLE FROTH – SHUTTLE SERVICE' banner tied to its back, apparently patched-up and repaired and rumbling along on all its four wheels, as good as new.

"Oi!" I yelled out. "Are you the *shuttle*, cock ...?"

Just as it looked like we weren't going to catch it, the Chief suddenly leapt out from an overhanging tree and brought the horses to a halt.

By the time Ray and me had caught up, he'd finished chatting to the driver and negotiated taking us into town.

Of course, we almost *forgot* about him, didn't we ...

Dirk, that is.

But he had an even *better* trick up his sleeve ...

Just as we'd begun to roll off down the road, his suitcase suddenly came flying through the open window, pioneering the way for its owner, who dived in headfirst after it like the Comanche had just set fire to his socks ...

The afternoon sun was beginning to sink in the distance, and, as I looked back out of the carriage window, an explosion suddenly rang out high on the mountain above us and that rocket-shaped missile I'd seen in the basement came hurtling out of the ruins of the castle amid a cloud of flame and smoke and gases, streaking straight up into the sky ...

Although the Chief sat in the far corner, apparently unconcerned by this occurrence, Ray and Dirk were leaning out and peering up at it like two blokes with telescopic neck-extensions ...

"What the *hell* is *that* ...?"

"More like," said Dirk, "Who's *in* it ...?"

"Unknown," I said.

"Oonless ... *oonless* ..." the dopey git was saying, "*Oonless* it's the 'Eadless Madman ...!"

"Oh shut up, you *soppy* sod," I said. "*Bertolt* was the Headless Madman. It was all in the clanking foot ... *CLANK* ... *CLANK* ... *CLANK* ...!"

(I was *lying* really, but how long can you go on supplying information to somebody who keeps his brain in his turn-ups?)

Once I'd finished watching the rocket tracing its course up into space, I sat back thinking how *thirsty* I was.

"No," I said, "There's only *one* outstanding thing that puzzles me about this case ..."

"What's that, Boss?"

"Well," I said, "Now that Adolf Flite has been vanquished ..."

"Go on ..."

"And now that all the executives of the Allied Froth Corporation are either dead or behind bars ..."

"*Yeah* ...?"

"And the corporation itself has been wound up, and all the outlets worldwide have been plugged, and all the assets frozen, and all the millions of bottles in the castle have been crushed in the ruins, and all the other supplies confiscated ..."

"What are you *getting* at, Boss ...?"

"Well," I said. "Where are we going to get a decent *drink* ...?"

The carriage went silent at that thought.

"Oonless ...!" suddenly piped up Dirk again. "*Oonless* ..."

"*Well* ...?" I said impatiently. *I couldn't imagine what he was going to say.*

"*Oonless* ..."

Here he reached into his coat and produced – one after the other – four perfectly preserved bottles of *Allied Froth 1954 V2 Rocketblaster Anniversary Editions.*

"*Oonless* you're a *clever* sod, *joost like me* ..."

"YOU SIR," I yelled at the top of my voice, "ARE A FUCKING GENT AND NO MISTAKE ...!" ... *at which public information announcement, I swiped one of the bottles and forced Dirk to hand the others round.*

So ...

There we were, just quietly savouring the brew, when the Chief suddenly broke the silence:

"This *Headless* Madman," he said. "What does he *look* like ...?"

"Well, Chief," I said, "He's got no head where his head should be, and another one under his arm ..."

"I've seen this man ..."

A hush suddenly descended as all eyes lit on the bloke in the plug hat.

"Oh ...?" I ventured hesitantly. "Where ...?"

"He's driving this coach ..."

Well ...

If a *pin* dropped, I didn't *hear* it.

We looked at each other.

And we looked at the Chief.

And then we all burst out laughing and said, "*Cheers* ...!"

THE END

ABOUT THE AUTHOR

Steve Empson manned the Church of England Enquiry Centre in Westminster single-handedly for twenty one years.

Despite the iniquities inherent in such a position, he was also lead guitarist in Islington band 'The Antelopes' in the early eighties. Their single *Prisoners* would be a collector's item if anybody ever heard it.

Steve was also a Braille transcriber at the RNIB.

But most of all, being friends with Dexter Kitehawk has not been good for his liver.